SEASON

— OF —

RESTORATIONS

A Novel

THOMAS DeCONNA

Black Rose Writing | Texas

This is a work of fiction. Names, characters, businesses, places, events, and incidents are either the products of the author's imagination or used in a fictitious manner. Any resemblance to actual persons, living or dead, or actual events is purely coincidental.

ISBN: 978-1-68433-873-3 (Paperback); 978-1-68433-918-1 (Hardcover)
PUBLISHED BY BLACK ROSE WRITING
www.blackrosewriting.com

Printed in the United States of America
Suggested Retail Price (SRP) $21.95 (Paperback); $26.95 (Hardcover)

Season of Restorations is printed in Book Antiqua

*As a planet-friendly publisher, Black Rose Writing does its best to eliminate unnecessary waste to reduce paper usage and energy costs, while never compromising the reading experience. As a result, the final word count vs. page count may not meet common expectations.

To Sheryl

Acknowledgements

Thanks to Jeff Blair, Clark Davis, Rachel Weaver, and the Denver Lighthouse Writers Group for help along the way.

SEASON

— OF —

RESTORATIONS

Where are the songs of Spring? Aye, where are they?
Think not of them, thou hast thy music too —
–John Keats

September 5, 2010

There is always more to do. He didn't know where to put everything; they must be concealed but not hidden; they must be discovered after his death, which he knew would be soon. Then again, much depended upon George.

Franklin Bowman, ninety-four years old and living alone in New Jersey, hunched over a shoebox that had been tucked away in his closet for years. Inside the box was a birthday card and a photograph that he wanted. His thick, mottled hands pushed aside other items that didn't matter anymore and pulled out the card and photo.

With the two things in hand Frank left his bedroom and started downstairs. Of course he felt fortunate, being self-sufficient enough to live in his own house and not being stuck in some nursing home. Then again, he thought, companionship and conversation wouldn't be bad. He descended the stairs as a younger man would, without pausing at each step, but pain shot through his knees and after reaching the bottom, he stopped.

Yes, he told himself, the pocketknife is on the kitchen counter...and what else do I need? The papers.

1

At the foot of the stairs Frank took stock of his family room, old-fashioned and crude, with its wide plank floors and braided area rug. It had an early-American feel because of its enormous fieldstone fireplace, a pillowed sofa, two wing-chairs, a rustic coffee table and two end tables made of pine but stained a walnut shade. Everything needed a thorough cleaning; for that matter, the outside of the house needed restoring, too.

It bothered him that he couldn't manage the simplest repairs. In his younger days before age bowed him down, Frank stood six feet two inches tall with a bodybuilder's physique; however, he never went to a gym or lifted weights. His sandy hair had turned stark white; his eyebrows grew thick and bushy. But his blue-grey eyes remained remarkably keen, and his face barely showed a wrinkle. Beginning in adolescence his teeth needed an orthodontist's care, but his mother said the cost was out of the question, so now dentures filled his mouth. Although the false teeth never fit right, he managed without complaint. Yet it hurt to compare himself to the man he once was. A man who had maintained his house and property with little help. A man who had become a corporal during World War II. A man who, penniless, had signed on with the Civilian Conservation Corps during the late 1930s and harnessed a chunk of the Adirondacks. A man who had been born into the farmlands and mining towns of Pennsylvania and cobbled together a life after his father died when Frank was six years old. A man who made a good living and had a long marriage.

Maybe I've done enough, he thought.

Frank stepped toward the kitchen when, without warning, his heart shuddered as if a wood vise were squeezing it. The photograph and card slipped from his hand as he gripped his chest. "Goddamn it," he muttered and stumbled toward the sofa where he grabbed its wooden arm and dropped onto the cushions. Although the pain was intense, he clenched his teeth defiantly. Through closed eyes he managed the torment and through closed eyes he saw a strange vision. During the last week he had seen it several times. Deborah, his dead wife, stood before him. She was young and vibrant; her hair was dark and long and loose. She stood erect and expectant the way she stood decades before Parkinson's devastated her. In Frank's waking vision,

2

Deborah wore her favorite chambray dress—the one she wore while gardening—and her arms stretched toward him as if she were holding a large, invisible ball. Now again, he reached to her, but she vanished.

Frank opened his eyes as the chest pain subsided, but his brain sank into a muddled state. Pictures popped into his brain. There he was, a boy riding a battered bicycle over dirt roads among green hills, and then the image changed to primal mountains with him standing naked to the waist, his muscles contracting, pumping, and glistening. He and another man worked a fierce, two-handled saw across the base of a broad tree, felling it with a shattering crash. And then a coffin. A silver tea set. Spinning slot machines. A men's clothing shop. A pair of work shoes that he never wore. A newspaper office with red-orange brick, elongated windows, and a roll-top desk. Then a woman's face in shadows but her visage glowing crimson from a match flame. Black hair. A young man with black hair and stained teeth. Frank swatted that vision away.

He breathed normally now. The moment had passed and he was all right. His calloused hands wiped sweat from his face as he gathered himself and noticed that the house was so still he could hear the mantel clock ticking. Around him, he saw again all that needed to be repaired or removed. He needed to restore things—things that had gotten away from him—and not just tangible things. Most of all, he must square himself with George. He nodded in agreement: tell him about Erica, at least. Frank hoped it wasn't too late.

He squinted toward the picture window that looked out onto the porch and front yard, wanting to see Deborah, but she wasn't there. He shouldn't die alone. Didn't he deserve to have his son by his side? But he knew the problem. For years, he had dammed up rivers inside of him, and he wondered if he could finally unlock the floodgates. He didn't know. But Frank knew he couldn't wait any longer.

———————   ——————

George Bowman drove into a new housing development that he'd read about in the *Denver Post*. Denver's suburbs had spread to places where people had no business trying to live, due to water scarcity and clay soils, and this housing site was one of those places. But, as he pulled up to the development, open for just six months, he had to admit it looked attractive with wide streets, smooth sidewalks, and uniform lawns dotted with miniature trees and shrubs. He stepped out of his Honda Civic and surveyed the model home. Recently, many housing developments offered the same features: a Craftsmen-style house with stacked stone and earth-tone color siding. All that was fine, but something was definitely wrong.

Before walking to the sales office, George leaned against his car. He was tired, not only physically but mentally, too. The feeling, as if he were walking under water, had persisted for months. Too often his movements and thoughts were sluggish. After a moment's rest, he peeled himself away from his car and made sure the back of his polo shirt was tucked into his jeans, and then he fingered hair from his forehead. His hair, more gray than brown now, had thinned dramatically during the past year. He had inherited his mother's fine hair and now he took on the crowfeet lines that had edged her eyes. He blinked a few times, the way men always blink against the strong Western sun, but while his eyes' natural reflex tried to make things sharp, his sight stayed unclear.

Inside the sales office a man in his thirties, wearing a gray suit, white shirt, and lavender tie, greeted him. The salesman, looking healthy and ambitious, said, "Welcome to Terra Sola!" He offered a firm handshake along with a genial smile and introduced himself: Alex Hamils, and then he launched a well-rehearsed pitch. "Most adult communities begin with folks at age fifty-five, but we're the only sixty-and-over development on the Front Range."

"Right. I read that in your ad." George wanted to get to the point that struck him the minute he saw the model. "But the ad said you sell patio homes."

"That's what we have."

"But I looked at the model from the street. It's a duplex."

"Not technically." The salesman's smile turned even more genial. "You see, two homes form a partnered unit, and the unit is a detached patio home."

4

"If they're attached, how can they be detached? Isn't that physically impossible?"

"Well, if you inspect where the homes meet, at the garages—actually, inside the garages—you'll see a twenty-four inch inter-zone between the units."

"What's an inter-zone?"

Alex gave an all-knowing nod and said, "Let's step into my office."

They moved to the back of the sales center, past framed sketches hanging on the wall of each model unit and past a glass-encased replica of the housing development—it reminded George of a Revolutionary War battlefield—to a rectangular space closed on three sides but open on the fourth.

"George," the salesman stated in a tone that a civics teacher might use to define a paragraph from the Federalist Papers, "an inter-zone is a dedicated space between the housing units that offers an air exchange and a specialized division." Alex pressed his tie against his shirt as he sat in an expensive office chair and motioned for George to take a seat. "The practice is not unique to our properties, and if you visit other communities of a similar nature, I'm sure you're bound to become more acquainted with the concept." To this, George could think of nothing to say. After a pause, Alex, beneath his prominent nose, formed a firm smile. "Tell me, are you looking for a retirement community? You are retired, right?"

George felt as if he were being appraised. He edged forward and backward in his seat, telling himself that he looked all right wearing a hunter-green shirt in good condition, but maybe his navy jeans had faded too much. "I retired from teaching in June."

"Ah, you were a teacher. A college professor?"

"No, I taught high school math."

"Oh." The salesman's interest diminished but he regained traction. "How many years did you teach?"

"Thirty-eight." George, half-lucid, he had dragged himself through his final teaching year when nothing made sense to him after Claire's death. Each day was a faulty equation that produced nothing but wrong answers. He had moved on from those dark days. Yes, he would always miss Claire, but now a different void existed within him and he wasn't sure how to fill it.

"Long time," Alex said, gathered sales brochures, tapped them against his desk into a neat packet, set his business card in front, stapled everything together, and handed it to George. "Take these as you tour the models." He picked up an elegant fountain pen. "So, after teaching all those years, you must have a substantial pension."

"I guess. But I started my career in New Jersey," he explained, "so those years don't count in Colorado."

The man of business tapped his pen on a legal pad and took a long, hard look at George. He laid the pen down and folded his hands together. "Most of our homebuyers are downsizing and focusing on a leisurely lifestyle. Our HOA fees cover trash pick-up, lawn care, common-space upkeep, snow removal, the community pool, and our rec-center. We include all of those amenities for three hundred dollars."

"Per year?"

"Per month."

"Oh."

"With purchasing the home," Alex continued, "paying a lot premium, and adding upgrades, our move-in price has been averaging in the low sixes."

George did a quick calculation. If he sold his house and used some of his retirement savings, he could swing it, but a barren feeling filled his stomach. "I see."

"We have an excellent community here. Social groups. Neighborhood activities. Indeed, some folks — men and women — have formed a jogging club. It's fun to watch the group jog by my office. I look forward to seeing them every morning."

George imagined that most of the people in this development were roughly the same age — his age, sixty-five. He pictured them jogging along. Then he pictured, after a number of years, the joggers changing over to a walking club and eventually to a dying club. "So much to look forward to."

"Yes, we have it all." The businessman tilted his head. "So, is Terra Sola the kind of place for you?"

"Maybe." His pulse quickened.

"Tell me, is it just you or is there a spouse involved? I noticed your wedding ring."

"Oh, no. Just me. My wife died sixteen months ago."

"Ah, a widower."

"Right."

"Well, you wouldn't be alone here. We have a number of single occupants of both genders."

George glanced at the packet of papers, reluctant to touch it, as a wave of nausea churned in his stomach. "To tell you the truth, Alex, I'm not sure about a lot of things right now, and retirement seems like a problem I just can't solve."

A look of eureka came to the man's face. "I have exactly what you need." He bolted from his desk and opened a vertical file drawer. After picking through plastic tabs and finding what he wanted, he handed over a pamphlet.

George read the banner's bold lettering aloud. "The Top Twenty-five Activities for Retirees."

"Folks have found this information a godsend."

He skimmed the list: *Enjoy Needlepoint, Join a Bowling League, Learn Woodworking, Begin Scrapbooking, Lead by Volunteering.* He wondered if being a public school teacher counted as volunteer work, and as the thought came to him, so did a fresh, dull pain that spread across his brow. The list continued: *Writing Your Memoir, Time to Travel, Read for Pleasure, Stay Fit, Beginners Scuba Diving.* As the pain sharpened and spread, George imagined himself scuba diving and saw air bubbles bursting as he tried to reach the water's surface. *Digital Photography, Hop on that Bike.* Not a bad idea about the bike, he told himself, but then his mouth went dry. *Spend Time with Family, Babysit Grandchildren.* His son Jack lived in California and had never married. His father lived in New Jersey, only a few hours' distance by plane; however, George knew a different kind of distance existed among the three generations. Then he read the list's last item: *Prepare Your Final Farewell: Organize Important Information.*

"Hey," Alex said, alarmed, "are you all right? You look pale."

George set the pamphlet on the desk. "Do you have any water?"

From a stainless steel mini-fridge the salesman snatched a plastic bottle. "Here you go."

George sipped the cold water and it flowed through his body like an elixir. His light-headedness dissipated. "Alex, thanks for your time, but I need to think this over."

"Do you?" The man laid his fingertips on the desk. "George, I had a rough start in life: orphaned, immigrated from the Caribbean Islands, no college or fancy degrees. But I have a knack for finance and I'm good at this job. And more than that, I know people. And I know you're not ready for this."

"Well…I."

"It's all right." The man leaned toward him in a confidential way. "You see, you're looking for something else. You should explore the possibilities that still exist." Alex Hamils smiled warmly and then waved a hand in a dismissive but inoffensive way. "But if you need me, I'll be here. You can bank on it." Abruptly, the salesman stood and offered a farewell handshake. George accepted it.

He left the sales brochures and retirement pamphlet on Hamils' desk and, stepping outside, felt grateful for the fresh air. While taking a last look at the community's model duplex—the patio home—he wondered how thick those walls between the dwellings actually were but told himself they would never be thick enough. Relieved, George started his car and left the retirement community behind.

On the way home he stopped at a Taco Bell. The drive-through lane was backed up and it would take awhile. It would be faster to go inside and order, but he told himself he'd have to stand in line and then deal with an attendant who, five minutes later, wouldn't be able to pick him out of a police lineup.

After his Civic crawled to the ordering spot, George spoke into the perforated metal speaker and ordered four soft tacos and a medium Pepsi, knowing three tacos would do but ordered four anyway, and he preferred Coke but Taco Bell served Pepsi. For the past twelve months he'd eaten more fast-food than he'd eaten in the previous twelve years combined, which added extra pounds to his six foot frame. He used to be a decent athlete and up until a year ago worked out at a local gym, but he let his membership slide. Sometimes, embarrassed when stepping from the shower, he'd noticed his altered body in the mirror: flab in place of muscle. And sometimes he thought of being younger when everything was fresh and alive and waiting, but he forced himself not to dwell on the past because it was the future that bewildered him.

Three miles from home, he glimpsed the plastic sack of tacos sitting on the passenger's seat and smelled the spicy scent filling the car. While stopped at a traffic light, he snatched the bag, opened it, and grabbed a paper-swaddled taco. He should have waited until he was home seated at his kitchen table, but he told himself it just didn't matter. After unwrapping a taco, he bit into its crunchy shell, cheese, tomato, sour cream, and greasy beef. Shreds of food fell to his lap and onto the car seat. Before the traffic light changed, he brushed most of the mess to the floorboard, but a few pieces stuck to the seat. When the light turned, his left hand held the wheel as his right hand held the taco. Often he had seen people drive and eat, and he had labeled them lazy slobs. He took another bite and this time, along with cheese and tomato bits falling to the seat, a dab of sour cream squirted onto the gear shifter. He tried to wipe and sweep everything to the carpet where other, older food particles had dried.

Hours later, as the sun set and an uneaten taco remained on his kitchen counter, George shut off the TV in the family room after watching part of a black-and-white Western on a cable station. Westerns, with their expansive views, arid land, and craggy formations appealed to him, as did the stoic protagonist who never said much and accepted his set of miserable circumstances as a matter of fate. The hero never looked for trouble, but trouble found him; however, the reticent man never complained. He did what must be done. Although it was a good movie, George had seen it before and even if he hadn't, he could predict the ending. Besides, he felt anxious, a feeling that troubled him most nights and lapped against him like stormy waves.

From the refrigerator he snatched a bottle of Coors beer and twisted off the cap. He'd never been a drinker, but on restive evenings like this one, a bottle of beer calmed him. He walked to the back porch, which a handyman had closed in about ten years ago. Here, George and Claire used to watch baseball games, but now, even though September was a great time for pennant races, he had no desire for the game.

Being a cool evening, he kept the windows closed but soon realized that his one-pocket T-shirt wouldn't ward off a chill. Draping a flannel shirt over his shoulders would be smart. He liked L.L. Bean flannel shirts with their traditional tartan plaids and kept two in his closet, but it seemed a burden to get one. So, he shivered and sat on a wicker chair with its yellow, green, and blue floral-patterned cushion, and he faced the backyard. The lot was perfectly square and bordered by pine trees that had grown so tall and thick, they cut off any view.

George sipped the cold beer, checked his arms, and noticed goosebumps. They reminded him of a time and place not so long ago. A condominium's outdoor deck, three stories up. Golden sunshine, mountain breezes, autumn aspens. Now, although he hadn't used it in years, he thought of the fireplace inside his house. It was odd how, after so long a time, a smoky smell still lingered in the hearth. An earthy, primal smell. Somewhere, perhaps in a novel, he'd read that the first hearth fire in autumn isn't necessary, as it is in December. A September fire drives out the season's first chill, so, more than anything, it's merely comfort. But, he wondered, what comfort would he feel?

He drank the last drops of beer and felt as empty as the bottle. Without much interest, he looked at the amber-colored glass and the attached label with its sketch of a cascading, mythical stream. He didn't need an oracle to tell him that his future held nothing but darker days and colder nights.

But that was it.

The feeling struck him like a sharp slap. He needed to fill his days in order to pass his nights. He needed to do something worthwhile. He needed to *be* something. To be *someone*. Since retiring from teaching, not only had he lost an occupation, he'd lost an identity. And what he needed wasn't in the retirement brochure that Alex Hamils had offered. Then what?

So, George sat within his sealed shelter — his closed-in porch with the windows shut and the television off — and drifted toward a blank and black suspension. He hoped that the silence, the beer, and the solitude would transport him to a site of solutions. And in this strange stupor, after some unmeasured time, he gazed at the pine trees and saw them—imagined them—uprooting and moving like pieces on a chessboard until they aligned in rows and columns. The finite, geometric pattern pleased him, and just when he felt completely calm and receptive, the phone rang and jolted him.

"Hello."

"George?"

It was a distant, familiar voice. "Dad?"

"Yes. It's been awhile. How are you?"

"All right." He set the empty beer bottle on a side table. "How are you?"

"Not so good." His father coughed, the guttural cough of a lifelong smoker. "That's why I called."

"What's wrong?" George's thumbnail started to skin the bottle's damp label.

"Well, it's more than a sore throat."

He was surprised to hear his father's voice, always strong and certain, sound weak and doubtful.

"Look," his father continued, "I know we've let things slip, but can you come home?"

"I," George stumbled, taken off-guard by the request. Thoughts scattered like dust through a fan: Why should I go to New Jersey? Don't I have enough to deal with? And what if I said no? How would that sit?

"What's going on, Dad?"

A harsh cough sounded in his ear. "You remember your uncle James?"

"Of course."

"You see, before my brother died, he told me that he had visions of his dead wife. She'd ask him to join her. It's happening to me now. I see your mother and she wants me to be with her."

His father was a proud man. A man who disliked weakness in others and loathed it in himself, so George realized this phone call wasn't easy to make. "How long has this been happening?"

"About a week."

"And how are you feeling, physically?"

"I don't want to talk about that over the phone."

No, his father didn't want to talk about many things nor did he ever have much time for others, forging a path for himself and shutting secrets inside of him as if he were a sealed box. When George was younger, his father's silence provoked him, pricked him into wanting to know the man better, but stone walls seldom break. After George married, he stopped searching for ways to bridge things with his father because George began building his own walls. So, father and son were never close; however, they were not irretrievably distant. They were simply men.

Through the receiver George heard a deep breath and pictured his father bracing himself. Then words sliced through the phone: "I need you, George."

George realized that his father's time no longer lay on a table; it was slipping off the edge; the man was past ninety. So he asked himself, Would it really be easier not to go? The answer flashed in his brain: Guilt would eat you alive.

He glanced at the beer bottle with its label now in shreds. "All right, Dad." He released the bottle. "All right. Give me a day to organize things and to book a flight."

The two men said goodbye.

No, he didn't want to leave his shelter, but George knew his father's situation was grim. He had to go.

He'd need a suitcase—that green one with the leather handles stored in the basement? And what about getting to the airport? A taxi, a friend—or he could drive there himself and park in the long-term lot. George looked toward the closed windows and thick pines, but it was too dark to see anything now. He felt the silence. He felt the evening ticking away. He heard his father's urgent voice. No, he didn't want to leave his sense of safety.

And then he sighed, knowing that a sigh never solves anything.

September 6

Awake early after not sleeping well, George forced himself out of bed. Naked and tired, he stood for a few minutes and reviewed last night's phone call. In a dream, had he decided not to go to New Jersey? He couldn't be sure.

He rubbed his face and then from an armoire took out a pair of white briefs, stepped into them, and brought them to his waist. Over his head he tugged on a gray T-shirt, and then stepped into a pair of jeans. He thought to find his green suitcase in the basement, but when he reached for the bedroom door handle, above it he saw Claire's sweater hanging on a hook. It was her favorite: a cardigan made from blue cotton yarn so pale that the sweater looked nearly gray. With a laugh, she had dubbed it her "schoolmarm cloak." Its two front pockets held everything from loose coins to broken pencils to safety pins. She kept the sweater on the hook year-round, finding chances to wear it even during some summer days, and George knew that by now he should hang it in the closet. Over the years its fibers had absorbed Claire's sweat and soap and skin, so once in awhile, like this morning, he held a sleeve of the blue-gray fabric, pressed his nose against the soft cotton, and breathed deeply. He smelled Claire. But he knew the scent was waning.

In the basement the suitcase was tucked away toward the back of storage shelves—pine boards set on two-by-fours—that he built when they first moved in. The shelves were extensive, and, although it was a simple project and although he rarely did projects like that, George had done a good job. The shelves held a number of common household things: an ice cooler, sleeping bags, Christmas decorations, placemats, Tonka trucks, board games, high school yearbooks. Things of little value but things that fill a home; things that fall from fashion but never from the heart. After finding the suitcase, George blew dust from its top, wiped its sides, and set it down.

On the cement floor next to the shelves were white cardboard boxes stuffed with teaching materials that he had packed and lugged home after his final classroom days. George hadn't looked at them since stashing them here. Squatting down, he removed the lid from one box. Inside, filed within manilla folders were tests, quizzes, background notes, study sheets, practice sheets, and tip sheets. Before leaving his classroom for good, he had winnowed the papers down to three copies per sheet just in case, someday, he'd need them; still, after all his sifting, the material filled four boxes.

"Amazing what you accumulate over the years," he said, knowing no one was there but needing to say it aloud. And yet, did four boxes equal thirty-eight years of teaching? Even if they did, four trips to the curb on garbage day would delete a lifetime's labor. He thought: And who would want this stuff? Again, he answered himself aloud: "No one."

After pulling out a folder, he opened it and found handwritten notes—detailed and clear—for his calculus class. From a different folder George took a sheet of paper and saw bell-ringer problems. He used these to start class and while students worked the problems, he'd mosey along each row and touch base with every student. Although he was tight-lipped and sometimes awkward with adults, he was a natural with kids. He'd ask them how they were doing, how many hours they had worked at part-time jobs that week, how the school's theater practice was going for the upcoming play, how did the varsity baseball team look for the spring, how was the editorial for the school paper coming, how keen will the pom competition be this year, or a

14

dozen other questions. If he had to pick one quality that made him proud, it would be his ability to connect with students on a personal level. He believed that anyone could learn material, but not everyone could empathize. He knew that good teaching was never limited to facts; it was always about the kids.

A sudden wave of anxiety crested inside of him. Impulsively, George clutched a handful of papers—too many. They slipped from his fingers and dropped to the floor. Painful thoughts stabbed him again: Instead of falling apart, you should handle Claire's death. That time in the garage was pitiful, and now you're failing at retirement. You're walking in the dark, clueless. Men are supposed to deal with troubles.

The moment passed, perhaps faster than usual, and then he gathered his school papers, reorganized them, and set them back in the folder. Teaching had ordered his life, had regimented his days, had defined much of his existence. Tenderly, he fixed the folder in place and tucked it among the others. When he knew that the boxes were neat and orderly, George grabbed his suitcase and headed upstairs.

Two hours later, after a breakfast of toast and coffee, and after waiting for an appropriate hour, George knocked on his neighbor's door. Since it was Saturday, Sam was home and answered. Although it was nine o'clock, his neighbor looked as if he had walked straight from bed with sweatpants cut off at the knees, a soiled T-shirt, and a baseball cap parked backwards on his head. George wondered if Samantha, Sam's wife, was awake. He had never known a couple with basically the same first name. To help—or to confuse—they called her Sammie.

"Looks like I woke you. Sorry."

"No problem." Sam waved him in. "What's up?"

"I need a favor." Sam was close to Jack's age, and George wondered if people of that generation ever acted as if they had moved past dorm life. "I might be going to New Jersey."

"Why?"

"My father called last night."

Ever since that incident, that day with the garage and the car fumes, George felt embarrassed talking with his young neighbor. It was a suicide attempt, and even now he had a hard time attaching that term to his actions. He remembered coming-to, sitting on his front lawn, coughing, and Sam hunched over his shoulders, asking him questions.

"He's not doing well."

"Sorry to hear that."

"He wants me...to get things in order."

Sammie, looking half asleep, walked downstairs to the landing behind them. She didn't wear a ball-cap over her sun-blonde hair, only a sleeveless T-shirt covering her bare breasts and an old pair of Sam's boxer underwear cut very high. The scanty clothes showed off her tanned arms and legs. "Hi, George," she said as if he were a daily visitor. She turned to Sam. "I'll make coffee." She looked at George. "Want some?"

He had tasted her coffee. "Oh no, thanks."

"I'll make a Starbuck's run," Sam said a little too quickly and gave Sammie a look. "Anyway, I want a blueberry muffin."

"I'll have the usual," she said and sauntered to the kitchen.

Sam said, "You want anything, George?"

"No, I had breakfast. Thanks."

His neighbor refocused. "Get things in order?"

George didn't want to explain and, honestly, couldn't explain. "Finances maybe. He's getting on in years. Doesn't have much time, but then again he's always been so strong. He may live longer than he thinks. Maybe he wants something else?"

"What?"

"I don't know," George said and his face flushed. "I haven't seen him for a long time." He blew out a breath, releasing some tension. "To tell you the truth, I'd rather not go."

"Do you have brothers or sisters?"

"No."

"That makes it tough."

"Right."

"And that means you *have* to go. No way around it."

George weighed Sam's words and knew that he himself was the only person his father could count on. Yes, the man had done some remarkable things in his life, but to George those accomplishments amounted to a paper list. He wanted to go deeper, as he had wanted to go years before. So, all right, it was his duty to go, but now he thought that maybe—just maybe—the situation gave him a chance—the final chance—to know his father.

"Do you have your plane ticket?"

"No. I need to go on-line to buy it, but I'm not too sharp with that sort of thing."

"I'll walk you through it on my laptop. No problem."

"Thanks." George took a breath and realized that indeed he was going. Sam was right: No way around it. "Anyway, could you watch my place? I'll stop the mail and newspaper. Just keep an eye on things?"

"No problem." Sam lifted his ball-cap and ran fingers through his short hair. "Want me to cut the grass?"

"I shouldn't be gone too long." George looked away, pretending to appraise his lawn. Truthfully, he didn't know how long he would be gone or how much he had to do or what part of him would return. "Tell you what, if I'm not back in ten days, would you cut it?"

"No problem."

"Thanks," George said, but he felt stuck inside of another insolvable problem.

September 7

The flight out of Denver International Airport was smooth and steady, and when George stepped outside of Newark Airport he immediately sensed the Eastern climate compared to the West's. Plenty of trees tricked the sun closer while gauzy clouds paled the blue sky, and the air, in some indescribable way, smelled of the past.

He would take a taxi, as he had done in Colorado, and now scanned the transportation area for cabs and found a fleet of them parked and waiting. To his surprise, among the yellow taxis, was an orange and red cab belonging to a company he recognized. A middle-aged man and woman, probably a married couple, had just left the vehicle. Wearing a tattersall shirt and khaki pants, George gripped his suitcase and hurried over. Sure enough, it was a Stallion Cab. Painted across the front and rear doors was a colorful image of a man wearing old-fashioned clothing and riding a galloping horse along a dirt road of a colonial town. With the driver's window rolled partway down, George approached and leaned toward it.

"Excuse me."

The driver, a black man who had been looking out the opposite window, jumped.

"Sorry," George said, "Didn't mean to startle you."

The driver looked at him and must have realized that George posed no harm, but the cabbie seemed anxious to state his situation. "Sorry, fella, I'm leaving. Dropped off some folks, and I'm heading out." He tossed a worn leather satchel with shoulder straps onto the passenger's seat. It could have been a messenger's sack. "Not looking for fares."

"Wait."

The man shifted the car from Park to Drive. "If you want to go somewhere around here," he nodded toward the yellow cabs, "go ask one of them to take you."

"Hold on a minute." George pointed to the picture decorating the car's side. "You're a Stallion Cab from Providence, New Jersey, right?"

The driver looked surprised. "That's right."

"Are you headed back there?"

"Yes, sir."

"Great, because that's where I'm going."

"No kidding?"

"No kidding. May I get in?"

The driver reset his meter and said, "Hop in."

George sat in the back and watched the cabbie skillfully navigate the airport's jumbled roads, through intersections and traffic, and after fifteen minutes of stop-and-go driving, he found the open interstate. From the console's cupholder the driver lifted a copper mug and drank a swig of water. The mug looked centuries old. The man wore a button-down herringbone vest over a blue work shirt and an Irish-style tweed cap that, like the cab and its driver, had seen many miles. "Yeah," the man began talking as if he had been following his own thoughts, "I usually don't go to the airport, but some folks from Providence needed a ride here. That happens a few times a year. Most of them yellow cabbies don't go to Providence. Hey, you're lucky I was there."

"That's one thing I'm always short on: luck."

"Not me. I got plenty of luck," the man said with a laugh. "But it's all bad luck."

"A lot of that to go around."

"Uh huh. Say, most people fly into Newark go on to New York City. Why you going to Providence? You know someone there?"

"My father."

The driver took a purposeful look in the rearview mirror and with a sly smile said, "I guess he's not a spring chicken." Then he doffed his cap, rubbed his gray hair, and laughed huskily. "You and me got the same pedigree."

George smiled and ran fingers through his own peppered hair. "I see what you mean."

Along the highway they made good time and after miles of silence the cabbie spoke again. "You say you're visiting?"

"Right. I live in Colorado."

"Way out west, huh?"

"Right."

"But you know Stallion Cab?"

"I grew up in Providence."

"Don't say." The driver with brown, yellow-streaked eyes took a closer look at George through the rearview mirror. "Hey, I know just about everybody in Providence."

"Oh?"

"Yes, sir. Born and raised. And I've been a cabbie there forty-five years. Traveled all over and met me a whole bunch of folks."

George leaned toward the front seat. "What did you say your name was?"

"Paul Vere." The man's weariness reflected in the rearview. "You?"

"George Bowman."

"That so?" The driver swallowed hard as if digesting the name. "Hey, your father wouldn't be Frank Bowman, the newspaper man, would he?"

"You know him?"

"Can't say I *know* him, but he ran the *Courant* for years and he wrote a hell of a lot of editorials."

"He did," George agreed. "Yup, that's my father."

"How do you like that? You know, when I was a kid, I had a newspaper route. Delivered the *Courant*. Yes, sir, my first job."

"A bicycle route?"

"Damn right. But what I wanted to say about your father was this, I liked what he wrote. He took a stand on things. Always looked out for the little guy, you know?"

"Right," George said and glanced out the window. "He has a strong public record."

"Yes, sir, a *strong* public record." Paul drove silently for awhile and then said, "As a matter of fact, I didn't know he was still living. How is he?"

George paused before choosing the easy answer. "For someone his age, he's doing all right." If the driver had asked, *Who* is he, it would have been harder to answer. He leaned back in his seat.

"Well, I say, God bless him." The cabbie nodded firmly. "Hell of a man, your father."

And then silence except for the meter clicking off the miles. After a spell, Paul said, "So, you traveling alone?"

"Yes."

Naturally, George thought of Claire. After staying home five years to raise Jack, she returned to the classroom, teaching fifth grade for thirty years, and he pictured her standing by a slate chalkboard in a denim jumper with a smile more constant than the sun. She had given so much of her life to other lives. Then he pictured her battered body being pulled from her wrecked car. A middle-aged man, who had not been drinking or had been distracted, who was not speeding or in a hurry, simply missed a Stop sign and hit the side of Claire's car, causing her death. Because George's life changed in one dreadful moment, he had no time to prepare for the strangeness of the days that followed.

"How long do you figure on staying?"

"Not sure. Actually, my father's not doing well."

"Sorry to hear that."

"Thanks. But, you know, he's lived a long life. Pretty much on his own terms, too."

"Yeah, I hear that." The cabbie nodded in agreement. "My old man died a few years ago. He was the same generation as your father. Tough old bastards."

"You got that right."

"Yes sir. You know, my old man served in the war. When I was younger I'd ask him about it; he never said nothing. Never told me nothing about his life. Yes sir, he was something else. Tough as iron.

Worked hard from sunup to sundown. Provided the needs. Never chased women. Demanding? Yeah, strict as hell. But I never figured him out. You know, he had a scar across his cheek." The driver pointed to his right cheek. "I asked him many times how he got it. Said he was born that way. Ha! Old photographs told me different." Paul Vere's eyes bored into the rearview mirror. "Why wouldn't he tell me what really happened?"

"I don't know. Maybe he got mixed up in something bad. Maybe he was ashamed of something."

"Yeah, maybe. But what the hell? Why keep it to yourself all them years?" Then Paul laughed softly. "Now my mother, she was different. She'd tell my sister and me everything. She'd tell us about rollerskating on streets as a kid and all about her crazy relatives and about her high school days. She loved to tell stories. But my father was as shut-mouthed as a mummy. But still, I looked at him like he was some kind of a king. You know, I always wanted *something* from him. Something important he could tell me. Something he had learned about life and could pass on to me. But nothing never come."

"Right," George said and wished he could think of something to say.

The taxi ride settled into a monotonous highway hum. Both men sat quietly as George let Paul Vere take him home to a father who had an outstanding public record.

———

George's boyhood home was old. In fact, the house was old when his parents purchased it. In this stretch of the state and on the outskirts of Providence, New Jersey, some houses date back to the late 1600s. George's father once claimed that their house was built in 1706, but his mother, Deborah, after some cursory research, said it was built in the seventeen seventies. Perhaps some historical society would know for sure. Over the years his father had refurbished and maintained the house and grounds. Yes, the house was old, but its foundation and construction were true and deliberate.

The taxi turned off the highway, made a few more turns, and came to an American farmhouse-style home set off a rural road on an acre of land. Really, the house stood in a gorgeous part of the state. Decades ago people purchased large lots — zoning ordinances dictated bigger parcels then — and the homeowners let many trees alone so that boundaries between properties remained natural. You might see your neighbor's house, but you kept a self-reliant distance. And although the town center was just three miles away, this hamlet stayed mostly unchanged. When the taxi stopped, George thought it strange how the house could look different according to the day, but he realized the difference was according to *his* mood. Some days the house looked cheerful; other days it looked gloomy. Today it looked a little lost.

"Here you are, Mr. Bowman," the cabbie said.

"Paul, we're the same pedigree, so call me George. What do I owe you?"

"Twenty-five dollars. It's a fair fare," the driver said with a laugh. "I don't thieve nobody."

George paid the fare and added a generous tip. Then he grabbed his suitcase.

"Your father don't know me," Paul said and touched his traveler's cap, "but give him my regards anyway."

"I will."

"Hell of a generation they were." The cabbie's expression turned solemn as he nodded slowly. "Yeah, those men were a tough code to crack." He extended a hand and George took it with a firm shake. With sadness, Paul looked into his eyes. "Listen, you know a change is coming, but, George, don't expect a change from him."

Now George nodded slowly and watched Paul Vere slide behind the taxi's steering wheel. The two men shared a final lock of the eyes before George headed toward the house — the back door that led to the kitchen.

Walking along the gravel driveway, he saw how much work the place needed. The kind of work George hated because he wasn't particularly handy, being more naturally inclined to make a living with paper and pencil. Here, weeds choked the grass. Vines strangled the bushes. On the remaining three apple trees in the deep backyard, branches crisscrossed each other or hung miserably like wounded arms. Paint flaked off the house's clapboard siding and signaled that the place needed a good scraping, priming, and painting. Even the American flag suspended above the front porch—a frequent sight in this part of the country—looked proud but ragged. The cloth had seen too many seasons. All of it made him wince with guilt.

The wooden side door stuck as he pushed hard to open it, which caused him to stumble over the threshold, but he kept his balance and stood inside the kitchen. Everything was familiar, as if it were a set from an old television show. A big porcelain sink faced a double-hung window that looked out to the backyard. Like museum pieces, the white refrigerator and gas stove stood unchanged, but a grey-black grime glazed everything and a stale, dull stillness tainted the air. Worn drawers, cabinets, and floorboards reflected an oily sheen.

George moved onto the living room with its large fireplace and hearth, and he smelled the airy remnants of burnt wood from hundreds of past fires. He always admired the geometric symmetry the builder created. A massive beam with knotholes and scars served as a mantel, and on it were pottery pieces that his mother bought from Colonial Williamsburg decades ago along with a clock and a small box containing long, thin matchsticks. On the opposite wall, flanking the windows, bookshelves held at least a thousand volumes. His father loved buying and reading all kinds of books, but now they stood lonely and dusty. On the south side, a picture window overlooked the long front porch, allowing plenty of light inside, and the afternoon sun fell against two wingback chairs, a round braided rug, a wide-planked, pine floor that showed antique nail-heads—not quite square—and an English rolled-arm sofa. On the sofa, asleep on his back, hands folded across his chest, lay George's father.

A colonial-styled end table next to the sofa held a ginger-jar lamp and a double picture frame. One frame showed his mother, a pretty woman in her twenties, her face in close-up angled perfectly to catch the photographer's light, and her hopeful expression looked luminous because of the slightly unfocused lens. The other frame showed his father, strong and confident, in World War II uniform complete with military cap and medals, sporting a trim mustache and a gleam in his eye that always reminded George of Clark Gable. Forever, those photos framed his parents as they were when starting their lives. The country was pulling itself together, standing tall, standing taller than all other nations. Everything seemed possible.

George stood over his father and saw right away that the man had grown thinner. Beneath the unbuttoned plaid flannel shirt and flimsy T-shirt, his father's chest rose and fell with its pattern of ribs. His legs, apparent even under the chino slacks, were too thin. How changed he was from the man in the framed picture. How changed he was from the last time he'd seen him. Watching his father this way, George's heart softened, and he wondered if the gaps between them were really any different from the gaps between all fathers and sons.

Gently, he nudged his father's shoulder. Frank's eyes, a solid brown, opened with a startled expression.

"No, there's nothing to be done," he mumbled.

After waiting a moment, George whispered, "Dad, it's me."

His father's awareness sharpened, and his face flushed. The man tried to snap his body to attention as he had done in the Civilian Conservation Corps, later in the war, and all the days George had known him.

"What time is it?"

"A little after four."

"Must have fallen asleep." His father smiled sheepishly. "Thanks for coming, George. How are you?"

"Fine."

"How was the flight?"

"Fine."

He didn't know what to add. Even as an adult, while around his father, George felt like a boy waiting for instructions. He touched the familiar red and blue print on the sofa, worn but stubbornly resilient. He looked aside and noticed yellowing newspapers and curling magazines piled haphazardly on the floorboards.

"This morning," his father seemed anxious to explain, as if he'd been waiting for the chance, "I put two frozen waffles in the toaster but couldn't finish them. Ended up in the damned garbage." He waved a hand toward the kitchen. "Years ago I went whole hog with those things. Hell, today, I didn't even want lunch."

"Your body doesn't need as much food, that's all."

His father looked at him as if catching a lie. "I'm dying, George. It's simple."

"Should you see Doctor Rush?" But George knew his father hated taking any medication; he'd even refuse a simple aspirin.

"No. He'll want to draw blood and take all kinds of tests. Add fuel to the fire. But Ben is a good man so I don't want to waste his time — or my money." His father, more alert now, ran fingers through his flowing white hair that showed only a small bald patch toward the back of his head. "George, did I tell you about my brother James and how he dreamt of his wife before he died?"

"You told me. And you've been having the same dream?"

"Yes. And sometimes I know I'm not dreaming. Sometimes your mother is standing in front of me."

"Well, Dad," George moved a hand to touch his father's shoulder but pulled it back, "visions aren't scientific logic."

"I know what I know," his father said firmly.

George knew the man's decisive mind, but he also knew that a lack of appetite was a tell-tale sign of the body's shutting down. His father had always been a good eater. Never overweight. Somehow the man's metabolism took in whatever he ate, kept the good, and flushed out the bad. Overall, his father was a wonder. Years ago when George's mother cooked breakfast, his father ate bacon and eggs six days a week, and on the seventh day he had pancakes dripping in syrup and butter. And he'd been smoking cigarettes since his late teens. George couldn't remember a time when the man even *tried* to quit. As a younger man, his father's frame could have been cut from an oak, and determination marked all his movements. Every stride had a purpose. On top of everything was the man's absolute certainty. How he could be right about so many things, George would never know.

"So, Dad, what do you want to do?"

His father let out a curt laugh. "For me, there's not much *to* do but face the music." The old man reached for a pack of cigarettes and within seconds had one lit and between his lips. George had never

26

gotten used to the smell. "But we haven't seen each other in a month of Sundays, and it would be a comfort to know someone was here." His father exhaled a cloud of smoke. "That *you* were here."

George frowned and asked himself who was with him when he had watched over Claire. But in fairness, who could have been? He had no siblings. Jack was in California and couldn't take a leave from his job for two to three weeks. So, that's how the world works. But *he* didn't work that way. Yes, a wall stood between him and his father, but after seeing his father so changed, George believed he might topple that wall. With patience and empathy—the same traits that had made him a fine teacher—he hoped to build a bridge.

"Well, I *am* here, Dad," he said with a faint smile. "Even brought a suitcase."

Upstairs in his old bedroom, George unpacked his case, setting socks and underwear in the lowboy dresser he had used years ago. Although the wood was pine and despite its nicks and bruises, the cabinet survived. Its wooden pull-knobs looked like the knots in bowties. Other than the dresser and the bed frame, nothing else that he had as a boy remained. Posters and pennants had been pulled from the walls. To allow more light, curtains had been removed from the dormer windows—an idea his mother had one desolate winter day.

Needing hangers, George slid open the closet door but stepped back when he saw his mother's clothes hanging in an organized way from the shortest to the longest garments. Ten years after her death, and his father couldn't purge his wife's clothing. On the shelf above the garments, he riffled through pillows and blankets, unwashed and musty. After finding extra hangers, he hung up four casual shirts along with a white dress shirt, a navy blazer, and a black tie.

In the kitchen and after taking a closer look, George saw that the countertop and floor were filthy. Stains on the stove were thick and many. While checking the food stock, he found the cabinet doors didn't close right, but worse, he saw that nearly all the cans and boxes were past their expiration dates. He turned to the refrigerator, dreading to look inside, but gripped the grimy handle and pulled. Standing like surviving soldiers were two bottles of water and a red plastic tub of coffee. A stick of butter smeared a glass tray, and thimbles of half-and-half creamers huddled on a side shelf.

George walked into the family room, across the uneven floorboards where his father sat on the sofa, and he was about to berate the man for letting things go, for the buildup of dirt, and for the lack of food. His father could have at least hired a housekeeper.

"You know, George," Frank held a cigarette, sat upright, and stared straight ahead. "I feel better now that you're here. Day after day with nothing to do and no one around, it wears you down. But I feel alive again."

"Well," George started but stopped, caught between anger and sympathy. "Well, I checked the groceries, and you need fresh food."

"Yes, you're right."

"I'll go to the A & P."

"Need any money?"

"No. The credit card will talk," George said with a smile. "I'll just use the bathroom before I head out."

"The toilet down here is busted." Embarrassed, his father looked up. "Can't get on my hands and knees to fix the damned thing. I'll tell you, it's a nuisance climbing up and down those stairs every time I have to go."

George wanted to ask why his father hadn't called in a plumber, but he knew the answer. Obstinate self-reliance wouldn't allow it. After stepping inside the bathroom, he saw a stained toilet. The sink, just as dirty, had a leaking faucet. He turned both sink handles hard, trying to stop the drip but nothing doing. He left and walked back upstairs to the full bath.

The original pink tiles had lost their luster and the sink, toilet, and shower needed a complete cleaning. On the medicine cabinet's miniature shelves perched a near-empty toothpaste tube, a muscle-ache cream, and an Old Spice aftershave bottle. George's feet straddled the commode as he unzipped and lowered his pants and then his briefs. He exhaled deeply, urinated, and felt overwhelmed with everything facing him. Seeing his father's condition and the state of the house and grounds made the situation real. Too real. How long did his father have? A few weeks? Of course, George knew this time would come, but, still, he wasn't prepared for it all.

Downstairs, his father sat on the sofa smoking his cigarette.

"Dad, I won't be gone long." George snagged car keys from a hook in the kitchen where they had always hung.

Outside, he walked across the driveway, which had never been paved. Gravel stones and grass ruts had been enough. As he approached the green Subaru Outback, George thought how his father loved station wagons. Whoever came up with the original wagon must have had men like his father in mind. Although his dad worked for a newspaper most of his life, the man was forever hauling things home from a hardware store or a lumber yard or a garden center for one project or another. That was typical of his father's generation, the men who fought the second world war and then built the suburbs. Men who sectioned off their land with split-rail fences and maintained them with power mowers. Their neighborhoods didn't need covenants because the men tended to everything with military efficiency and with a sense of right and wrong. To transport supplies from store to home, a station wagon was essential. The Subaru Outback, his father stated more than once, was the only surviving station wagon. But, of all the cars he'd ever owned, his father's favorite was a Chevrolet Malibu wagon. The old man put 150,000 miles on that vehicle. Frank let everyone know that he missed the American models and for years wished General Motors would produce a station wagon again.

George stepped inside the Outback, sat behind the wheel, and nearly gagged. The smell was horrendous. Cigarette ashes layered every inch of the car. In the backseat lay soiled afghans and throw pillows. He could barely see through the car's milky windows, and splattered against the driver's door and dashboard was a pebbled, plastic-like coating, but after looking closer and touching it, he realized it was dried mucus. Years of his father's phlegm, retched from a smoker's cough, caked the interior. George shuddered, and when he imagined cleaning the mess, he shuddered again.

His father would never let a car be so foul, but being older takes its toll. Then his cheeks burned as he remembered tossing taco bits onto his own floorboards. So, he wondered, how could he judge? Which led him back to the desire to know his father. One thing he knew for sure was that his father's strength was pride. On one side, people would call it being strong-willed; on another side, they'd call it being stubborn. George shook his head. Clearly, his father had been cut from a rugged cloth.

Behind the wheel, he rolled down the front windows, started the car, and calculated his route to the A & P, but then an unwelcome image of noxious clouds and a closed garage jarred him. George pushed the picture aside, backed down the gravel drive, and wondered if he should just forget everything and drive straight back to Colorado.

September 1922

Because no-one witnessed the incident, no-one knew what really had happened.

It rained hard the day that Frank's father died. The house and grounds were drenched and one hour earlier a lightning bolt had severed a monstrous tree limb, causing its branches to fall over the Bowman's chimney, the house's one source of heat. Josiah had to unblock the chimney so smoke would stop filling the house. It was a typical farmhouse anchored in the heart of rural Pennsylvania, halfway through the rectangular state and toward the northern border, not far from New York. What made the house uncommon was that Josiah had built it himself.

"I have to free the chimney from those branches," he told Abiah as he pulled his arms through a yellow rain slicker.

"You can't go!" His wife gripped her apron. "The storm is too strong."

He measured her words and detested thinking that something — anything — possessed strength greater than himself. Ignoring her, he buttoned the yellow slicker and buckled a pair of rubber boots onto his feet. From one of the pegs by the front door, he found his rain hat and jammed it on his head. He grabbed the doorknob. "I'll be careful." He turned to her and spoke with tenderness now. "I've been on that roof a hundred times."

"But not in a storm like this."

"We never had a branch block the chimney before. We need heat, and the house is filling with smoke."

"I've opened every window — a little."

"I know." He looked around as if to find another solution but saw none. "I'd better go before we all choke to death."

"You're too stubborn for your own good."

"Put that on my tombstone, woman," he said with a laugh.

Outside, the storm's severity startled him. It wasn't only the rain's intensity but also the wind's velocity. Josiah started, staggered, but righted himself, leaned into the storm, and forced one foot in front of the other. He was thirty-six years old; a tall, strong man with little education but endless ambition. If he wanted something, he pursued it and, more often than not, he gained it. Tucked in the back of his mind was his motto: "With Pluck and Luck." Now, like a younger version of Lear, he faced the splitting heavens.

On the house's south side lay his long wooden ladder. Luckily, this end of the house blocked the wind, so he blinked water from his eyes and took deep breaths. Rain had saturated the ladder and made it heavier, but without a direct wind to stifle him, he managed to hoist one end of it up to his shoulders while he braced the other end against the house's foundation. Then he walked the ladder perpendicular to the ground, but as it reached skyward its sides slipped from his hands, and the heavy rails banged against the house. With grit, he pinioned the wooden rails over the roof, angled the ladder, and stepped hard on the lowest rung to bury its feet into the spongy earth.

Positioning the ladder gave Josiah confidence and so he scaled the round wooden rungs until he reached the roof, but when his face rose above the shingles he felt the storm's wrath. Had he ever seen a tempest so powerful? With a cruel answer, the skies rumbled as lightning flashed and crackled close enough to singe him.

He pulled himself onto the roof and ahead of him lay the chimney, the gutter, and the broken branch. His rubber boots helped secure him to the wet shingles, but each step was treacherous. Steadily, he inched toward the severed tree limb. After reaching the roof's slanted pitch, he took two steps, slipped, fell, and landed on his back. By instinct, his legs and arms spread apart and stopped his slide after he thumped along the slick shingles for a few *feet. His heart pounded, first with fear and then with anger. "Of all the places," he demanded, "why did that goddamned thing fall here?"*

Glaring at the twisted bunch of branches, he made his way to them. Then with his toughened farmer's hands he lifted the limb off the flue. It was a maple branch, dense and heavy. Carefully, he moved to the roof's edge and saw that the splintered end had wedged itself into the wooden gutter. He peeped beyond the roof to the ground and saw two slanted, metal doors that led to the cellar. From this height the doors looked as if they lay flat against the earth. He knew they were bolted to a cement slab, and that he must dislodge the ten foot maple branch and heave it beyond the cellar doors.

After his gloveless hands gripped the tree limb, he raised the branch, but it clung to the gutter and, like stretched rubber, snapped back in place. Now the rain struck like pellets and the wind snarled like an injured beast. It swatted Josiah's hat off his head, blowing it toward his cornfield. With equal strength and fury, he wrenched the limb free and stood by the roof's edge, panting like a prey rather than a victor. From this angle, he reckoned that the branch, when released, would miss the cellar doors cleanly. All he had to do was let it fall. But anger vexed him. He felt insulted, as if heaven and earth had conspired against him.

Josiah remembered his wife's warnings, but obstinately set himself against the storm. In a mad rage he grabbed the branch and with all his might hurled it off the roof, but due to his violent motion and the storm's power, his weight shifted too far forward. His arms circled helplessly before he tottered and fell. Face forward, he plummeted through the air for several surreal seconds and then hit the cellar doors. Like a rubber ball strung to a paddle, his forehead smacked and bounced against the cement slab. Blood, thick at first but then diluted by rain, flowed from his head.

Having waited long, Abiah, fearful and weary, forced herself outside and found her husband's body. Because no one had witnessed the incident and because Josiah had been so smart and rugged, everyone assumed that it was a terrible accident, that he had lost his footing on the wet roof, and that he had died for the sake of his family.

September 8

George cleaned the frying pan after getting his father to eat a bacon and eggs breakfast. Actually, the man had done pretty well with it. Frank dipped wheat toast into the yolks and finished off the yellow centers. He ate two strips of well-cooked bacon, leaving a bit of fat behind. Now, George looked out the kitchen window that faced the backyard, sipped the last of his coffee, and studied the three remaining apple trees. Vines tangled and twisted the lower branches into a maze, but surprisingly the trees produced a handful of scrawny apples. Several oak trees edged the land and even though they had been there before his parents had purchased the place, George associated those trees with his father. Symmetrical and tall, because nothing had boxed them in.

George imagined that after his father's death he would sell the place and wondered if he should call in a landscaper, but he dreaded the cost. How expensive manual labor had become! He poured out the shallow pool of coffee and rinsed the mug. In the living room with the smoke-stained hearth, he found his father lying on the sofa, head propped by a pillow. Frank turned off the television with an angry snap of the remote.

"So much damned garbage on TV today."

George sat in a wingback chair. "I can find a station that plays older shows."

"Why would I watch those? If I don't know them, I never wanted to watch them. If I do know them, I've seen them before. I'll know what happens."

"Well, how do you argue with that?"

"Aw, hell," his father said. "I feel miserable because I can't do much." He sat up. "I always feel better doing *something*."

"I know, Dad. And you've done a lot."

"And that makes it worse."

George fidgeted with the armrest, waited a moment, and then said, "I know you made burial arrangements. The cemetery in Quincy."

"In there is a filing cabinet." His father pointed to the laundry room next to the kitchen. "In the 'C' file is a manila envelope for 'Cemetery.' Bring it here."

George returned with it and sat next to his father on the sofa so both could see the papers. "It's simple. Having served in the Army, I get a free burial in a military cemetery."

George had accompanied his father to Washington Cemetery in the town of Quincy after his mother died and was there when his father signed the final papers. This time it would be all on him, and he didn't want to fail. "Where Mom is buried. I know."

His father spoke wistfully. "After she died I'd drive up there once a week. Yes. I'd take a folding chair and sit by her grave. I'd stay for an hour or so and talk to her." He rubbed his chin and smiled sadly. "She never talked back though."

"Might be scary if she had."

His father nodded. "Might be at that. Well, it didn't take long for them to fill her row with graves and then a row before and after hers. *That's* scary—to see how many people die in a month. After awhile I felt like I was intruding, and the goddamn drive up and back got longer and harder. After a certain point a person's circle closes." His father stared off silently.

"Right." George stumbled but managed to ask, "And the mortuary?"

His father refocused. "When I die, contact Adams Mortuary. It's a family-run operation. Generations. They come and get my body, and they contact the cemetery. When you get to the cemetery all you do is show them these documents and sign some papers."

"Sounds easy."

"Easy as pie. And the mortuary is paid for, too. I took care of that years ago. You'll just need to finalize a few things. Your name is on my bank account, and you're the Executor. Oh, and my credit card, cancel it."

The word "cancel" struck a sharp chord. That, along with the image of a circle closing, made George blurt out, "Dad, do you think there's an afterlife?"

"I don't know." His father snatched a cigarette pack off the coffee table, tapped one out, clamped his lips around it, and lit it.

George thought that every time he broached a meaningful topic with his father, the man pulled back as if touching a piece of hot kindling. He wanted to know if his father had reached all his goals. Was he content with his life? And sometimes it seemed that the man wanted to open up but suddenly he'd slam the door shut.

George pushed ahead. "If there is an afterlife, do you think Mom is there?"

"*Somebody* better be there." His father inhaled the cigarette as if he were sucking the life out of it. "It would be a bad joke otherwise."

His father had never been a religious man. Likewise, George had doubts. "If there is an afterlife, what do you think it's like?"

His father sighed and shifted his tone. "You know, after the war when you met a guy—a stranger—and you had a feeling the guy had served in the war, you might ask: 'Were you in the war?' and he'd answer, 'Yes.' And that was it. You didn't need to say anything else."

"Dad, I'm only trying to…to understand things."

As if he were making his way through unknown land on a starless night, his father looked up, helpless and uncertain. How often George had seen that lost look in his students' faces when they tried to comprehend a mathematical concept beyond their grasp. Was his father, a man of infinite strength, now unable to grasp a realm beyond his reach?

Because of compassion, George pulled back. That was his strength and his weakness. He gathered the papers, tapped them against his knee, and set them back in the manila envelope. "I'll clean the inside of the car's windshield," he stated flatly. "It's clouded over from cigarette smoke." He headed to the kitchen, got the needed supplies, and left his father behind.

Inside the car George attacked the windshield with a rag and glass cleaner. Soot and smoke made the grime nearly impenetrable. He was frustrated with his father and with himself. He wanted finite solutions. He wanted his father to speak of things beyond the surface, but he knew the wall of silence between men was likely to remain. It would take more effort to build a bridge. Wishing not to lose heart, George sprayed and wiped the windshield, but the task seemed impossible. After ten minutes of slogging, he gave up.

_____   _____

In California, Jack Bowman sat sealed within a three-sided gray cubicle staring at a computer screen. For a modern office, there wasn't much natural light; only the workers sitting at desks adjacent to windows by the room's square perimeter knew the sky. Jack didn't have enough years with the company to be granted that view, so his desk and partial cubicle butted against several others. The digital time read-out on his screen told him that it was almost noon, so he turned his computer to Sleep mode.

"Click, click, click," Jack muttered.

He made his way through the maze of computers, desks, and chairs—assorted shades of gray. Most workers had gone to lunch; some never took lunch, which reminded him how peculiar web designers—techies—can be. He pinched past a desk but caught his cargo shorts on an open metal drawer. The young man sitting there looked up, annoyed for a moment, but then re-centered on his computer. Jack tugged his threadbare shorts free and re-tucked his T-shirt into his pants. His shirt featured a picture of a rock band from the '80s, and, if asked, Jack would be unable to name one song the band had played.

In the company's cafeteria he bought a hot dog and a Coke, the cheapest options. Then he spotted a table where three other web designers sat and ate. Two of them, Mark and Bob, had a sack lunch and a third young man, Bill, was squeezing ranch dressing from a plastic packet onto a garden salad. A tinge of despair twitched through Jack as he approached the group because he had been through this scene before.

"Hi, guys," he said and pulled up a chair.

"Hey, Jack," all three answered as one.

Bob seemed to be in the middle of an explanation: "At first I thought of purple and gold for the background, but then I landed on magenta and tungsten."

"Awesome choice," Bill nodded with genuine admiration while he chewed a tuna salad on whole wheat.

"Definitely," Mark chimed in.

Jack bit into his hot dog and wiped a dab a mustard from his lip with the back of his hand. He looked at his table-mates—his co-workers for two years—and marveled at how little he had in common with them. Even physically, he was different. Although they were all roughly the same age, Mark, Bill, and Bob looked like clones with their boyish bodies whereas Jack boasted an athlete's build. The men in his family tended toward trees rather than shrubs. He pictured his grandfather. Years ago, the man was an overwhelming presence. At times his grandfather could be gruff, especially with Jack's father, but Jack always got along with him. When he was very young—during the summer—he'd spend a day with his grandfather at the newspaper office. There, he explored the building from top to bottom. He loved roaming through busy rooms because excitement drummed from each worker's actions, and a common goal joined their various skills. Of course, the best part of the day was lunch when he and his grandfather walked up the street to a deli and ordered roast beef on rye—a sandwich so thick, it took his two small hands to balance it.

"Guys," Jack said after swallowing a gulp of Coke, "all you talk about is work. There *are* other things." No one spoke. He tapped the table. "Like football. Hey, the season just started. Anyone a Raiders fan? Chargers?" Shoulders shrugged. "Well, I grew up in Denver, so I'm a Broncos fan. Broncos anyone?"

Bob chewed his ham, cheese, lettuce, and tomato sandwich and said, "I haven't watched a football game since high school."

"Neither have I," Bill beamed.

"Me either," Mark added.

Bill shifted the conversation back to web design, so Jack turned to his hot dog. He thought of sitting at his station and whittling away the afternoon and wondered how many more mouse clicks he needed before reaching one million and if he did hit that number would he be awarded a prize the way airlines award travel miles. He gazed across the cafeteria and saw young men sitting at table after table, but they weren't men exactly and deep down Jack had a fuzzy notion that he fell short of some unwritten standard.

"Too bad we don't have more women around this place," Jack said, knowing he talked over Mark who was commenting about pixels. "They don't have to be stunners. Just female, you know?"

Silence. Then Mark said, "We certainly work in a male-dominated field."

"We certainly do," Jack echoed. "And what a field. We bang out all the ideas and work for peanuts while the guys above us do diddly-squat and rake in big bucks."

"There's always an opportunity to move up with the company."

"Yeah, and then what?" Jack reached a tipping point; his anger, building for weeks, erupted. "What the hell? Creating web designs? Fuck!" He slapped the table. "That shit isn't real. You can't *hold* it. And today's shit becomes yesterday's shit faster than you can flush a toilet."

The others sat dumbly, looking down or away. Then Bill cleared his throat and with a pained expression said, "Jack, it's clear you're not happy with this job. But we are. Instead of attacking *us*, why don't you find *yourself*?"

Jack's jaw dropped. The others nodded to each other, gathered their things, and left the table.

He sat and stared but saw nothing, trying to think of something to say, as if the others were still there, some justification or smart-aleck remark, but he couldn't think of a thing. Five minutes passed. He looked at the last chunk of hot dog and the sight turned his stomach. But he ate it anyway, making up for his not having breakfast.

Later, seated at his station, Jack alternated between glaring at his screen with half-hearted effort and surveying the office with complete indifference. He'd been doing this for the last four hours. Then, with a slow, barely audible shuffle, his supervisor, Robbie, approached. Robbie wore his usual attire: an untucked, collared shirt, jeans with designed slits, and expensive sandals. Jack thought his boss had the California-look down. Totally. At one time Jack found the West Coast lifestyle solid; now he found it hollow.

"How goes it, Jack?" Robbie asked and stroked his wispy mustache.

"It's going."

"Indeed. Well, did you get my email?"

"I...when did you send it?"

"Let's check your inbox and see."

Jack frowned and clicked onto his messages. "Looks like you sent it an hour ago."

"It looks that way."

The message asked if he and the other recipients could stay after work for an unscheduled meeting, and the message asked for a prompt reply. Because Jack no longer had a car and depended on catching a bus and because he didn't know when the later buses ran and because it was Friday afternoon, he shook his head and dropped his gaze, trying to check his anger. He noticed Robbie's bare feet swaddled in expensive leather sandals, and at that moment realized just how ugly a person's foot can be. Jagged toenails, random hairs, bumpy callouses, and brown silt coating a bunch of thin bones.

He looked up. "Kinda short notice, isn't it?"

"Yes. That's why I needed a quick response."

Such a smug bastard, he thought. "Robbie, I can't make the meeting. Because actually, I'm giving notice. I'm quitting two weeks from today."

The city bus shuttled Jack away from the tony center of town with its string of three-story office buildings, upscale shops, and elite restaurants that formed the backbone of life to the people living in compact mansions that perched on a bluff overlooking the Pacific Ocean. These seven-figure homes along the coast laid claim to views that a poor man would give his eyes to see. Moving on, the bus made its scheduled stops until reaching the town's fringes, the unprosperous part of town. Weary homes, cluttered yards, fast-food joints, liquor stores, and a Walmart. For the final stop only two passengers remained: Jack and an older man—a white man, unshaven, rheumy eyes— sitting across from him. Jack had ridden the bus for a month now and each time the same man was there. The passenger seemed oblivious to his surroundings. More than once Jack had started to say something to the man but stopped himself.

As his bus stop came into view, Jack jockeyed down the aisle, bracing his steps against the bus's shuddering halt; the older man, as he had done each time, remained in his seat. The doors opened, and Jack looked back at the man and then at the driver, a plump black woman with round dumpling eyes. She saw his hesitation, checked the large rearview mirror, and then looked again at Jack. "He rides the bus everyday," she said. "All day."

"How long has he been doing that?"

"Don't know. Long as I been driving this route, he's been here. I pick him up at the main terminal when I start my shift, and eight hours later when I finish, he gets off at the terminal."

"He just rides in a loop over and over? Every day?"

"Yup. Every day."

"Does he ever say anything?"

"No." The woman now looked at the open doors, and Jack felt her fixed eyes telling him that he must leave, she has a schedule to keep, and she doesn't have time to solve mysteries.

Once on the ground, he started his one mile walk through the seedy neighborhood. Along the way thought of stopping at Taco Bell but even the cheapest fast-food place wasn't cheap enough, so after walking fifteen minutes he reached a mid-century ranch house painted white and barely maintained for the last twenty years. Here, Jack rented a room. Two other young men rented two other bedrooms; they all shared the kitchen and family room. No connection existed among them.

Inside the kitchen he glanced at the particle board cabinets, Formica counter, linoleum floor, and grimy white appliances. From inside the refrigerator he rounded up peanut butter, jelly, and bread — none of which were his. He hadn't bought food for awhile and felt a little guilty pillaging but told himself it wasn't like stealing filet mignon. Besides, all the stuff was store-brand generic. The peanut butter too thick, the jelly too thin, and the bread softer than a damp sponge. The sandwich tasted as lousy as it looked.

After eating, he trudged to his room, an eight-by-twelve space with a small window, untied his sneakers, kicked them free from his feet, and peeled off a pair of dirty white socks. He tossed his baseball cap toward the open closet but missed. Drained, he ran fingers through his long, unwashed brown hair and then rubbed his forehead, eyes, cheeks, and chin. His mattress, without a boxspring, rested on shag carpet, probably there since Reagan was governor. The bedsheets were as raveled as his life.

He flopped onto the mattress, lay on his back, and folded a pillow behind his head. Looking at the ceiling, he noticed a crack that had not been there before and wondered if he had the wherewithal to fix it. He pictured spackling and a putty knife and fresh paint. But he couldn't hold on to the images because he couldn't stop his thoughts from circling back to the biggest mistake of his life: all the money he'd lost. For two months, guilt and anger trailed him like a Pinkerton man. And it was all due to Linda. Sexy, predatory Linda who had swindled him, had played him for a fool. He didn't want to think about that. But he had to face facts. He was nearly broke and completely finished with LA; likewise, LA was finished with him. He had to make a move. From his cargo shorts' pocket, Jack grabbed his phone.

———————————

Recently, Frank washed his flannel shirts because autumn's winds were not far away. But autumn has its songs, too, and he longed to hear them. He knew he'd never hear winter's silence again. Frank's father had worn flannel shirts on their Pennsylvania farm; he recalled the rich colors and fine patterns. He thought it strange how old memories were at hand when they should be the least retrievable. Over the years, Frank kept a half-dozen flannels because it was his staple shirt from mid-September until late April. Now, he needed only three. Switching off daily helped keep the shirts fresh and because he didn't sweat as much as he used to, the fabric lacked odors for weeks. The problem lay in getting the shirt on.

He had a classic, four-poster bed, the type Deborah wanted, with its cherry wood, its tapered and fluted posts, and its handsome chestnut color. The posts were equal length and rose three feet above the mattress. On the top of each, Frank draped a flannel shirt. Now, he stood in front of one and flexed his fingers.

"What are you doing?"

The sudden voice made Frank quiver, as if he'd been caught doing something he didn't want others to see. "Goddamn it, do you have to sneak up on me?"

"I wasn't sneaking. Sorry. So, what are you doing?"

George stood beside him now. Frank pointed to one shirt. "I like to wear these when the weather gets cooler, but I have a hard time with the buttons. Putting a shirt on and taking it off is a nuisance because I'm forever fumbling with the damn buttons." He hated to admit any weakness, especially a physical one, and he didn't want to talk about the constant ache in his hands or the way his fingers refused to follow his commands: couldn't feel, couldn't grip, couldn't navigate intricate movements.

"Okay. So, why do you have the shirts hanging on bedposts?"

"It takes time, but if I button each shirt now and leave its top button undone, I can pull it over my head to wear and then pull it off when I'm done."

His son didn't say anything for a full minute but a shameful look spread across his face. "That's a good idea."

"Well, it works."

Without being asked, George began buttoning the shirt. Frank moved to another post and started on a second shirt. He tried to grasp a button but his fingers lacked feeling. When he finally managed to secure it, trying to hold the button was like trying to pick a splinter from his finger with a pair of ice-tongs. But he kept trying. His hands, which used to be as strong as a steel vise, worked awfully hard to align the button with the hole and force it through the tight opening. Again and again he tried and at last succeeded, but by the time he fit one button in place, George had finished two shirts.

Frank stepped back, feeling in the way of things. He compared his present self to the man he was in the Civilian Conservation Corps. By God, he was a force to be reckoned with. He was as powerful and wild as the land he worked—the Adirondacks—and as free. Perhaps it was freedom he missed most. Freedom and wildness surrounded him. Lakes and streams cut their own borders. Animals bounded the woods; birds soared the skies. That expansive sky, immense as a man's dreams. So, he was unbound to any place or person; unfettered by vows or promises. And it all disappeared because of Carol. In a way, she had stolen his freedom, but Frank knew he had stolen much more from her.

"When I was in the CCC's," Frank said in a raspy voice, "there was a girl who lived on the edge of town." He touched the tail of a shirt that George had buttoned. "She was quite a looker. Caught my eye. Hell, she caught everyone's eye." He glanced up. George looked at him with a curious, eager expression.

No, he couldn't go on. Frank wanted to get it off his chest, but actually saying the words didn't feel right. Not now. Things—the house and grounds—were in terrible shape, and he couldn't leave them that way. Maybe after the house was in order and repairs complete. Maybe after everything was restored.

George said, "What about the girl, the looker?"

"She…sometimes she wore flannel shirts."

"Oh?"

"And she had a pleasant way of filling them out."

"And she lived nearby?"

"Well, not real close."

"So, did you get to see her?"

"Only a few times…in passing."

"She must have made a heck of an impression because you still remember her."

"Oh, just tricks your mind plays, especially when you're my age."

His son nodded and continued buttoning. After a moment he said, "All done."

"Thanks, George. I…I can't tell you…I…I'm just glad you're here."

"Right." As George left the room he reached into his pants pocket because his cellphone rang.

Frank touched one of the tartan shirts and thought about the Adirondack wilderness and how Carol had altered that nature, and his nature.

"Dad?"

"Is anything wrong?" This was George's first reaction because when Jack called there was usually something wrong.

"Not exactly."

That wasn't the response he wanted. George headed downstairs and sat in a chair by the large fireplace. He remembered reading somewhere that people of Jack's generation had trouble settling down, but, then again, his friends' children seemed to be doing all right. They worked steady jobs, had spouses, bought homes, had kids, and contributed to the Social Security pool. Not that everyone had to fit a cookie-cutter mold, but some sort of stability from his own son would be welcome.

"What is it?"

"I thought I'd come home for awhile. Take a break."

"You mean you're taking a vacation?"

"Not exactly."

George rested the phone by his hip, rolled his eyes, and took a deep breath. Then he said, "Jack, I'm in New Jersey, staying with Grandpa. Most likely, he doesn't have long to live, and he asked me to stay with him."

"So, you're there?"

"That's what I said."

"Okay. I get it. I need to stay with you guys."

"I'm not sure that's a good idea. Your grandfather can be hard to get along with."

44

"I always got along with him. If this is my last chance to see him, I shouldn't mess it up."

George thought of that retirement brochure and pictured the topic: "Spend Time With Family." Well, he told himself with grim amusement, having three generations together beats scuba diving. And he realized that Jack *should* see his grandfather a final time. "Right," he said and paced to the picture window that looked out to the neglected property. "All right."

"I'll book a flight and let you know when to pick me up."

George clicked off his phone and wondered about sleeping arrangements. The house had a third bedroom, so that would be easy. But things could get complicated. And when he reflected on the conversation, he circled back to "Not exactly." What the hell does mean? From Jack, he never got the full story right off, but he knew that stories have two sides and people have many sides. Starting with Jack's teenage years, George and his son had been drifting apart, and after Claire's death, sometimes it felt as if they were standing on different continents. He wanted a better relationship with Jack but didn't know where or how to begin. He frowned and thought that maybe it was too late to understand his father or his son—maybe it was too late for everything.

He stepped outside, needing some air. He marched to the side of the house, but slowed his steps, wondering where he was going in such a hurry. He came to the Subaru with its cloudy windshield and dirt-coated body. Taking it through a car wash couldn't hurt, but George didn't want to leave the house now. He pictured buttoning the flannel shirts and being aware of his father standing off to the side, as if he no longer existed. How would he—and Jack—handle the death? How would they face that day?

September 1922

To Frank, it was frightening having a casket in the parlor, but it was the time's custom in rural Pennsylvania, and people wanted to pay their respects to Josiah Bowman, who had died two days earlier. Upstairs in their shared bedroom, Frank's brother James, two years older, finished knotting a tie for him. The starched collar felt scratchy against his neck, but Frank's mother told her sons to wear Sunday clothes.

"How does that feel?"

"Tight."

"It's supposed to be."

Frank wiggled a finger between his shirt and throat to loosen things. "I hate wearing this stuff."

"Don't worry," James said with disgust. "You won't have clothes like these anymore."

"What do you mean?"

"You'll grow out of them, and that will be that."

"I don't understand."

James put his hands to his hips. "Mom told me not to tell you, but you should know. With Dad gone, we can't work the farm ourselves and we can't afford to hire people, so that means we can't make money. Without money we can't pay bills, and the bank will take our house. The bank will take *everything*."

Frank's eyes widened. "Everything?"

"Yeah. Mom said Dad tried to do too much and borrowed money from the bank, and then she said something about a mortgage and how the bank owns that, too."

"What's a mortgage?"

"I don't know," James said impatiently. "I just know that we're wrecked."

Later, Frank sat in the downstairs parlor for as long as he could, trying not to look at the coffin, often staring at the claw-foot table it rested upon. Most of their furniture was golden-stained oak, a sturdy and popular choice of farmers. People milled around while drinking coffee and eating sandwiches. Frank wasn't hungry and yet he was, so he left the parlor when Mr. Byrd, who owned the adjoining land, stepped out of the kitchen as Frank entered. Coffee sloshed from Bill Byrd's cup onto the plank floor, but another stain wouldn't matter.

"Franklin," Mr. Byrd touched the boy's shoulder with his free hand, "so sorry for your loss. Your father was an extraordinary man." Frank gazed at his neighbor's creased skin framing the man's face and wondered just how old Mr. Byrd was. "I knew you father from his first day here. Yes. Do you know that we established a boundary line between our properties?" The man stared off as if he could see the faraway episode. "Thankfully, many of the stonewall boundary markers remained. We added a few split-rail fences. That took some labor, I can tell you. And sometimes a row of pine trees served us well." He smiled astutely. "All of this happened before you were born."

"Yes, sir."

"But I can always check for facts and dates when I need them because I keep a firm record of my doings. You might call it a secret diary." The old man winked in a confidential way.

"Yes, sir."

"Ah yes, a remarkable man, your father. Exceptional with his hands. He could build or repair anything. Why, he could see a structure right to its bones, or he could imagine completing an unfinished project down to its details." Mr. Byrd shook his head in wonder but changed his tone. "Too bad he didn't buy life and property insurance. I urged him to buy both, but sometimes, well, your father could be rigid."

"Yes, sir."

"Franklin, as I said, I'm sorry for your loss; it was an awful accident. But now, you must be your mother's son." With that, Mr. Byrd walked away.

Inside the kitchen Frank made a ham sandwich, using the bread his mother had baked that morning and the ham she had cut into thick slices and set on a platter. Had she slept at all last night? He didn't want to sit in the parlor, so he set a stool against the wall by the icebox. If anyone came into the kitchen, Frank was small enough to be unseen.

Halfway through his sandwich, he wanted a glass of milk but as he hopped off the stool, the door opened, so he jumped back onto the seat. Two men, whom he didn't know and dressed in rough clothes that needed washing, headed for the bread and ham. They piled fat sandwiches together and slathered the meat with mustard. Then they refilled their coffee mugs.

"That poor bastard, Bowman. Head as thick as a brick," said the first man — lanky and thin as a razor — with a wad of food in his mouth. "No one could never reason with him."

"Sure, but look at all he had: pigs, cows, poultry," the second man said. "What's more, he bought up five acres last year and planted an apple orchard."

The first man bit off another chunk of his sandwich. "Hell, that's nothing compared to them two houses he owned in town. Rented them out."

"By golly, I've seen one of them renters," the second man — stout as a tree stump — said and slurped the hot coffee. "She's hotter than a two-dollar pistol."

"Can't get nothing with looks." The man wagged his sandwich at his friend. "It's money that counts."

"Ha! Can't never count out tits and ass."

The men didn't say anything for a few minutes, just ate and drank. Frank didn't stir.

"Wonder what's going to happen to his land and such?"

The second man grunted. "Everyone knows that Bowman was stretched. So, first the bank will take it, and then old man Byrd will find a way to get the land."

"That figures. Always has his eye out for land," the first man said and belched. "Shrewd bastard."

"Yeah."

The men chewed hard and smacked their lips. Frank thought of Mr. Byrd's hand on his shoulder.

"Wish they had some goddamned beer in this house. Coffee ain't enough for me."

"Can't blame them. Beer cost more than coffee," the man said in a worldly way and then his tongue pushed a lump of ham off his upper teeth. "And for them folks: no beer today, no nothing tomorrow."

The men snorted and laughed, and after a few minutes they left their plates and cups on the kitchen counter. Frank's stomach turned sour and he couldn't finish his sandwich. The ham suddenly looked like flesh.

Later that day around sunset, Frank stood on one side of his mother while James stood on her other side. With sadness Abiah looked down. Before them, Josiah's casket waited next to an open grave. The cemetery had started at street level but then, because of the town's growth and because of the increasing dead, rows of gravestones followed the ascent of one of those many hills in Pennsylvania. Frank's father would be buried toward the top of that hill.

A pudgy minister with pink, puffy cheeks held a Bible in his fat hands and waited for the caretakers to ready the coffin for lowering. Many mourners had gathered, black clothes and sunbaked skin, but Frank chose not to see them. He stared at the grass but then felt a shift in his mother's countenance. James kept looking down with glassy eyes. Frank watched his mother. With anger and disgust, she glared in a different direction, far from the coffin. He followed her line of sight — a line of sight that later in life Frank would understand to be the gaze of a woman who knows the secrets of another woman.

One hundred yards away, after the land dipped and rose, the ground was parallel to them, and there Frank saw a shapely woman watching them. She stood tall and defiant with a pretty face, raven hair, and olive skin. She wore a deep-red dress, deeper than the crimson sunset surrounding them all. Frank had seen her before and knew that this woman rented one of the houses that his father had owned.

September 9

The plane was filling up. Jack had a window seat while an older man in a smart navy blazer sat by the aisle. Passengers filed in carrying backpacks, bags, and anxious expressions. An attractive woman stepped out of the line and sat between Jack and the older man. A blend of light perfume and female scent filled the space with an aroma that Jack could practically taste. She wore business attire: a gray, pinstriped skirt and jacket that contrasted perfectly with her chestnut hair and caramel eyes. The woman removed her jacket and folded it across her lap, revealing a crisp white blouse. From her clothes to her hair to her face to her shape, she was an extremely attractive woman and close to Jack's age.

When the jet reached its cruising altitude and when seat belts unbuckled, the young woman pulled a laptop from her leather travel case. Jack had been stealing glances of her, had waited for an opening, and believed he had found it.

"I've done a lot of stuff with website designs," he said.

Her eyes, not her face, shifted to him but did not linger. "Oh."

"Yeah. I spent eight years in California tooling with websites and graphics." She did not respond, but Jack continued. "Do you work in California?"

"New York. This is a business trip."

"So, what's your business?"

Now she faced him. The beauty and symmetry of her features might evoke a Spenser sonnet, but her eyes leveled and her tone sharpened. "My business is none of yours."

Jack's jaw dropped and quivered as if he were caught cheating on a test. "I was just..."

"Look, I know exactly what you're doing." Her pretty eyes narrowed. "Men approach me a lot. That's okay because it's what they do. That's how it works." She moistened her lips. "Honestly, with some men I don't mind. I'll play the game. But..." She paused, stared right through him, and continued, "Have you even bothered to look in a mirror this morning?"

Jack stammered: "I was..."

"Sure. Tell me, is this the best you can do? A T-shirt, old jeans, sandals with socks? A sweaty baseball cap that's fit for the garbage bin? You haven't shaved in, what, three days?" Her upper lip pulled back over perfect teeth. "Hey, college is over."

"I..."

She raised a hand. "Sorry. I'm usually not this blunt, but the last thing I need today is to deal with nonsense." She turned to her laptop. "Look, I'm sure you're a nice boy, but you should shape up before it's too late."

An aluminum can couldn't have been crushed any better. Jack slid toward the window and wished he could jump out of it. A *boy?* he thought. She's my age and actually called me a boy.

Soon a stewardess came by with soft drinks and bags of pretzels. Jack passed on both, but the woman next to him and the man in the aisle seat accepted. The young woman took a ginger ale while the older man took a Coke, but he had trouble opening the small sack of pretzels. Like a daughter helping her father, the attractive woman opened the bag for him. She smiled and chatted easily.

He faced the window and watched pristine clouds cascade against a blue sky. The jet followed a course while every person on the plane seemed to have a path. Jack wanted to find a path, a trail that would take him to a place where he could produce something solid and good — but how to find it? Where to begin?

Through the tangle of highways and traffic, George drove to Newark Airport. He gripped the steering wheel and paid attention to roadsigns. So many roads crossed this part of the state, it was easy to take a wrong turn, and then, he wondered, who knows where you'd end up? Approaching the airport pick-up area, some men in business suits and a few women in stylish outfits hurried by, reminding him of how he always dressed formally for teaching, but most adults pouring out of the airport looked ragtag, as if they had fled a summer camp. Then George spotted Jack, so he pulled the forest-green Outback to the curb, shifted to Park, lowered his window, but kept the motor running. He stayed in the car as Jack opened the passenger's door and tossed a battered backpack to the rear seat.

"Is that all you have? No suitcase?"

"That's it." Jack plopped inside.

George took stock of his son's appearance and couldn't think of anything positive to say. Still, he tried to sound upbeat: "You look older."

"So do you," Jack said with a smirk.

George drove off with the window down, causing cigarette ash to fly. Jack waved a hand to keep soot from his eyes. "Geez, this car is a shit pit."

"It needs a cleaning," George said and maneuvered the Subaru through the web of roadways that crisscrossed the airport. After connecting with the exit, he glanced at Jack. "Your grandfather has let things go."

"Okay. But how is he?"

"Physically, he's weaker, but he maintains himself. Mentally, he's sharp. Pretty much the same person he's always been. But the house and grounds are in shambles."

"You can't blame him for that."

"I'm not blaming him."

Now, with the window up and the air conditioner on, the ashes stayed put, but Jack brushed a dusting off his T-shirt. "I guess this car never met a cigarette it didn't like."

"Right." Steadily, George drove beyond the cities and toward the suburbs. "So, how long will you be off?"

"Off?"

"From your job. You said you were taking a vacation."

"I said I was taking a break."

"So, this isn't a vacation?"

"No."

"Then what the hell is it?"

"I was fired."

"What?" George snapped his neck toward Jack so hard that the Subaru lost its lane. He jerked the car back.

"I gave that son of a bitch, Robbie, two weeks' notice," Jack snapped, "and the asshole fired me on the spot."

"Wait. You quit or you were fired?"

"What's the difference! I'm finished with California and all that computer shit." Jack coughed out a sarcastic laugh. "At first it was cool, being all laid-back and mellow, but after awhile everything felt like Jell-O. Everything is so goddamned mellow, it rots on the vine."

"Are you telling me," George tried to control his tone, "that you're finished with computers, your career?"

"Yeah."

He wanted to pull over and sort through this mess but kept driving. "So, what now?"

"Now? Now I need a new career. Something totally different."

"Do you think careers just fall out of trees?"

"You don't know what it's like feeling trapped," Jack spit out his words. "Why can't you ever see my side? I'm not cut out for a cubicle. I can't sit eight *billion* hours in front of a computer screen." Breathing hard, a whiff of ashes caught in his throat. He hacked but finished with another lash. "*You* always played it safe. A schoolteacher."

George's temples drummed. "Right, I had a profession and a *career*. Is that so bad?"

"Two ways of doing things: your way and the wrong way."

"I didn't say that."

"You're not listening!"

"What?"

"Forget it!"

"No, we can't forget it." Nearly missing an exit, he had to yank the steering wheel hard to the right. "What about your car?"

"I sold it."

"*Why?*"

"I had a situation."

"That doesn't tell me *anything*." His blood was steaming like a hot teakettle. "Why on earth did you sell your car?"

"I needed the money."

"Wait." George gulped and groped for words. "You still have your savings — the money I gave you after Mom's death — from her life insurance — the fifteen thousand?"

"Not exactly."

"What does *that* mean?"

"It means it's gone."

"*What?*" his voice cracked into a shriek. "How did you lose all that money?"

"You wouldn't understand."

"How can I *understand* when you won't tell me what happened?"

"Just forget it," Jack said and looked out the passenger's window.

George forced himself to stop talking and wondered how and why this could be happening to him. Even though he hadn't taken a wrong turn, he felt a twisting in the pit of his stomach as if he'd driven into a place never found on a map. After miles of silence he said, "What on earth will you do now?"

"I'll deal with it."

George heard another door slam. With Claire, this situation would never exist because she would know what to do with Jack — what to say. He prided himself on having compassion for others — so many students over the years — which made him feel guilty being unable to make allowances for his son; still, waves of defiance washed over him. "Whenever you said, you'll deal with it, it always meant that your mother and I had to take care of it for you."

"Well, Mom isn't here," Jack countered, still facing the window. "So, that leaves *us*."

George squeezed the steering wheel and looked straight ahead, realizing he knew his son as well as he knew his father.

Frank heard the Outback churn up the gravel driveway, but it took longer than he wanted to lift himself off the sofa and steady his balance. By the time he reached the kitchen, Jack had shouldered open the jammed back door and entered. Grandfather and grandson looked at each other. The same build, the same height, same brown eyes and same wavy hair, but of course Frank's hair had turned gray decades ago. He noticed that Jack's shaggy locks could use cutting. Although he didn't appreciate his grandson's shabby appearance: T-shirt, shorts, and cap, he thought it best to ignore everything. He reached out his right hand to shake and said, "Welcome home, Jack."

"Grandpa," Jack smiled, dropped his backpack, ignored the extended hand, and embraced him.

Frank, startled, hugged Jack in an awkward way. In a breath he smelled a blend of unlaundered clothes and unwashed hair.

George entered. Frank noted his son's similar hair and eyes but slighter build and inch-shorter height. In some ways he had taken after Deborah. But most apparent now was his glowering expression. Silence dominated the room as three generations stood looking at each other. Taking a step back, Frank recognized the tension between George and Jack. He knew that sensation firsthand.

"Well," he said, being the one to break the stillness, "I could show you up to your room, Jack."

"Don't," George said. "He's had enough help."

Jack picked up his backpack. "The spare room?" he asked, and Frank nodded. "I remember."

After his grandson climbed the stairs, Frank turned to George. "What the hell happened?"

"It doesn't matter," his son answered. "I've got to use the bathroom." George walked into the downstairs half-bath and closed the door. Immediately, he walked out, scowling. "Forgot. The toilet's broken."

George and Jack passed each other on the stairs without a word. Jack re-entered the kitchen as Frank sat down at the table and set an ashtray within reach. "What happened between you two?"

"It doesn't matter," Jack answered and turned to the window that overlooked the backyard.

Frank lit a cigarette, inhaled, and felt the soothing, burning smoke lick his lungs. It was an awful pleasure. He knew that nonsmokers didn't like the smell, but he wasn't about to quit because of anyone else's wishes, especially in his own home. He tapped a chunk of ashes into a black plastic ashtray while he clenched and unclenched his left hand to relieve tightness. Then he opened his hand and held it palm up before his eyes. Dozens of swirls and lines. Skin creases that ran parallel to his fingers or crossed diagonally down his hand or cut horizontally against his palm. He wondered what a fortuneteller would make of it. What could a clairvoyant tell of his future when all that remained was his past?

Just below his pinky against the base of his hand was a generous scar that ran four inches. He acquired it long ago. While working a two-handled saw with another man in the Conservation Corp deep in the Adirondacks, his hand slipped and caught one of the saw's shark-like teeth. It wasn't a deep cut, but the opening pulsed out a lot of blood. The two men stopped sawing and his buddy said, "You ought to go to the clinic. Might need stitches." Frank said, "It doesn't matter." Then he pulled a handkerchief from his back pocket, wrapped his hand, and kept sawing.

"The backyard," Jack said, turning to his grandfather, "it looks smaller than I remember."

"You haven't seen it in awhile." Frank exhaled cigarette smoke. "Things look different depending on where you are in life."

George returned. His son stepped toward the window but retreated; he stepped toward the table but stepped back. At last, he positioned himself at the kitchen's edge.

"Coming up on supper time," Frank said and snubbed out his cigarette. He tried to stand but the dull pain that constantly pulsed through his body ratcheted up a notch so he stayed seated. "You guys hungry?"

"I could eat."

"George?"

"All right."

"Your father restocked the kitchen," Frank told Jack, "so we're in the catbird's seat." He tapped another cigarette halfway out of its pack.

"Thought we'd have spaghetti. Everyone eats spaghetti. Hell, it's practically a national dish."

George said, "I'll boil the water."

Frank saw his grandson look flustered. "Jack, get a jar of tomato sauce—one with meat in it. Pour it in a pan and set the burner on Low. You'll need a wooden spoon."

Jack nodded but stood still. Without speaking, George set a pot of water over a high-flaming burner and then went about getting everything Jack needed. Each cupboard door stuck a bit, and he opened and shut them a little too hard.

Jack positioned the pan on the stove and looked over his shoulder to his grandfather. "How much?" he asked with the jar suspended over the pan.

"All of it."

Jack emptied the jar and with the wooden spoon stirred the spicy sauce. He clanged the spoon against the pan's edge to knock it clean.

Frank stood and rested his cigarette in the ashtray. Wanting to be of some help, he said, "Do we have garlic bread in the freezer, George?"

"Uh huh."

"I'll heat up a few slices."

George turned the oven to 400 degrees. "I'll get them out; you put them in."

"All right," Frank said and sat at the table again.

George pulled a small box from the freezer, opened it, and pulled the bread slices out from the wrapped plastic. He grabbed the bunch of stuck-together frozen bread and with a sharp, hard motion slammed it against the counter. The slices separated. Next, he spread a sheet of aluminum foil onto a metal baking tray—turned almost black from decades of use—and tossed the bread into rows like a times-table. "There you go."

Frank stood again and cleared his throat. "Shouldn't we let the oven preheat?"

"Can't if we want the sauce, spaghetti, and bread done at the same time."

"Ah, ha." Frank set the baking tray onto the oven's metal rack.

George opened a box of spaghetti, grasped the golden strands, and snapped them in half — all of them at once. He plunked the strands into the pot's bubbling water and lowered the burner's flame. After switching on the oven light, he said to his father, "You can sit at the table and still keep an eye on the bread."

The three men waited and watched, saying nothing. Frank thought to ask Jack about his flight, but knew it was of no real consequence. He ached to tell both of them about his plan for the house and grounds but knew the timing wasn't right with the silent squall between his son and grandson.

Jack moved back and forth from the window to the oven, checking the meat sauce as it burbled in the pot. George stood seemingly transfixed over the spaghetti. After fifteen tedious minutes, Frank said, "I think the bread is done."

George hunched to the oven's window. "Two more minutes. But the spaghetti feels right." He found a metal colander and set it in the sink. After shutting off the burner he used padded mitts to grip the pot's handles, turn it upside-down, and drain the water. Vapor rose and billowed. "Jack, grab some bowls." George's chin pointed to the upper cabinets. Jack opened one door, then another, and with the third try found the bowls and set them on the counter. With a large slotted spoon George divided the pasta into the three bowls. "Forks," he said to Jack and this time nodded to a drawer. Jack opened the right one and snagged three forks. He grabbed his pan's handle and then dowsed each bowl of spaghetti with sauce. Along with the food and forks, Jack placed paper napkins on the round kitchen table. George pulled the golden brown garlic bread out of the oven and put the slices on a separate plate.

"George," Frank said and pointed upwards, "in those cabinets above the refrigerator is a bottle of wine. Let's uncork it."

It was a long reach, but George opened the small, square doors, spotted the wine, and grabbed the bottle. "Sure is dusty."

"I was saving it for a wedding anniversary," Frank explained, "but things didn't work out."

George cringed but said nothing. After dampening a paper towel, he wiped the bottle clean. "Cabernet Sauvignon."

"Yes," Frank said. "There should be an opener in the third drawer to your left."

His son found a corkscrew and opened the bottle with a muted pop. Jack found three tumbler glasses and placed them around the table.

The spaghetti and sauce steamed as Frank filled the glasses with wine, and George placed a slice of garlic bread on the round edge of each bowl. Frank extinguished his cigarette and decided he wouldn't light another during the meal. He took a hard swallow of the wine. Its earthy taste held enough sting to ease some of his physical pain, but he wanted to feel emotional pleasure with the three of them—and only the three of them—together. But he knew everything was far from finished.

His grandson chewed a piece of bread and turned to him. "I didn't know what to expect, Grandpa, but you seem…all right."

The comment, so honest and inappropriate, made Frank laugh. "All right," he declared, "is the new great."

"Okay," Jack said with a smile, "let's go old school: you look great."

"Well, don't let looks fool you." Instantly, Frank saw his mistake and knew he had to fix it. "You know, when I think about it, I feel better now than I have in weeks."

Jack said, "For sure."

George said nothing.

The three fell back to eating as the food and drink filled them, warmed them, relaxed them, but they also returned to the safety of silence as each man hunched over his bowl.

Halfway through the meal, Frank knew he would never finish his portion and that his left-behinds would go to George and Jack. He sat back in his chair and furtively watched his son and grandson. Clearly, he didn't understand his grandson's generation. They seemed lax about everything, and he imagined Jack probably wondered why he was here, what he would do, and where he was going. The young fella looked clueless. His son, on the other hand, knew why he was here, but as far as Frank could tell, George was lost, too. How did things get this way?

Frank raised his tumbler as the setting sun caught the clear glass and brightened the dark wine. "I'm glad you're both here," he said, feeling the need to say something—to make the moment real. "It's better than being in an empty house. Hell, I bet the house is happier."

His son and grandson looked at him but remained silent. "George," he said, needing to unfold some of his plan, "tomorrow I want you to go to the grocery store and get a bunch of sturdy boxes. You know the kind." That's all he volunteered to say for now because he was afraid to tear any flimsy bonds.

"For vegetables and fruit?"

"Yes," Frank nodded. "So many things aren't right, and we have to make them right. There's more to do."

His son and grandson glanced at each other and then turned to their food. Without another word, the three men ate their unquiet meal.

September 10

Frank stood by the kitchen window and looked at the overgrowth that clutched the apple trees, and at the lawn that had mostly turned to weeds. It was nine o'clock. Jack entered the kitchen, making his first appearance of the day. Beneath a baseball cap, his dark hair dropped in all directions. He wore a purple *Star Wars* T-shirt and a pair of orange nylon shorts.

"Morning, Grandpa."

"It's almost *mid*-morning."

"Yeah," Jack said and rubbed his face with both hands. "Any coffee?"

"If you want coffee, you'll have to make it." Frank studied his grandson and shook his head. "What your father made this *morning* has been drunk or dumped down the drain."

"Where's Dad?"

"He went to the grocery store to get boxes." Frank wore a clean white T-shirt beneath a buffalo-plaid shirt and a pair of gray slacks. After shaving earlier, he splashed Old Spice on his face, a long-time ritual. "We could use them for packing and hauling things out of here."

His grandson gathered the coffeemaker, a filter, and a coffee can from a lower cabinet that didn't close all the way. After setting up the coffeemaker and putting the filter in place, he measured off tablespoons and looked up. "You want a cup?"

"I had mine already," Frank said but then added, "All right. I'll join you." With the coffee brewing, Frank sat at the table and lit a cigarette; Jack stood by the window. "We have," he said, "a strong physical resemblance. Did you ever notice that?"

"Yeah." Jack tapped the countertop restlessly.

Before the coffee finished percolating, Jack grabbed two mugs and started pouring. Without enough coffee to fill the second cup, he rammed the carafe back in place. From his shorts' pocket, he pulled out a cellphone, scrolled through names, and typed a text message. Absently, Jack brushed hair from his eyes. Then he thrust the phone back in his pocket and finished pouring the second cup. He sat at the table opposite his grandfather. The coffee mugs, bought at a garage sale years ago, were unique. Each one featured a maxim from the *Poor Richard's Almanacs* such as "Today is worth two tomorrows" or "Now that I have a sheep and cow everybody bids me good morrow" or "Death takes no bribes."

Frank sipped his coffee and stared at his grandson. "Why are you wearing that cap? You don't need a cap when you're inside."

"Because I like it."

"But it's filthy. And what purpose does it serve?"

"Purpose?"

"Yes, *purpose*. I mean, what the hell is a cap for? It keeps the sun off your head, and the visor shades your eyes." He repositioned himself erectly. "You know, I see fellas your age or thereabouts always with a cap, sometimes wearing them backwards. They look like fools."

"Grandpa, it's only a cap."

"What does *that* mean?"

"That it's not important. Who cares?"

"Oh? Well, maybe you're right." Frank puffed his cigarette for a moment. "But maybe one thing leads to another."

"Huh?" Jack looked to the door and then to the window.

"Something's wrong with young men today." Frank had formed his thoughts long beforehand but now had someone to hear them — someone he cared about. "It seems to me that women look better than ever, but men dress like ragged boys. Baseball caps, T-shirts, torn jeans, sneakers, and sweat pants — for God's-sake — in public! Do you know, the last time I was at the bank a young man in front of me wore pajama pants?" His lips twisted into a picture of disgust and disbelief. "It made me sick to wonder if he wore any underwear."

Jack laughed. "It doesn't matter. It's just what that guy felt like wearing."

"His clothes might not affect him, but they affect everyone around him. It seems like everyone has stopped caring about anyone except himself." Frank snubbed out his cigarette and immediately lit another. "I see men in their twenties and thirties who don't shave for two or three days. Like my grandson."

"So?"

"So, what's the *point*? It seems like males have lost their manhood and want to *look* like men, but instead they look like imitation lumberjacks."

"Shaving is a hassle."

"It didn't used to be a *hassle*."

"Times change."

"Yes, and all those small changes, when totaled, hurt men and they hurt society."

"Well," his grandson smiled, "I guess society has changed."

"That's my point. Young men have lost something because they don't want to grow up. They don't want expectations placed on them. Just play video games and turn everything over to the women."

"The women?" Jack smirked. "You make them sound like a different species."

"Maybe." Frank nodded thoughtfully. "Maybe they're destined to be the dominant race." He leaned toward his grandson as if to start an arm-wrestling match. "Look around. Women are taking over everything."

Jack sipped his coffee. "Yeah, there are more female bosses today, but men still control a lot of stuff and women don't make as much bank as men, overall." He rose, found milk in the refrigerator, and gathered a bowl and cereal from an overhead cabinet.

"I have nothing against women getting ahead," Frank clarified, "but why should men let themselves fall behind? It's just a matter of time. It starts small. For instance, when you see a man and woman in a car, who's driving? Usually the woman. You look at any TV commercial, and if a man and woman are in it, who's the idiot? Usually the man."

"That's just TV," Jack said and poured milk into a bowl of bright gold cornflakes.

"It's a model for behavior," he said, tapping the table with each syllable. "I'm not saying that men must be in charge, but it hurts society if they become helpless dolts. And a few years ago your father told me that some people want to change the reading lists in schools for boys."

"Reading lists?" With his spoon Jack forced the cornflakes down, dunking them in the milk.

"Yes, because boys don't read as much as girls today, they want to give boys other books to read—books that they would *enjoy*."

His grandson dipped into the pocket of his nylon shorts. "So?" Jack grabbed his phone.

"Your father told me those books are easier to read, so they just keep the boys behind, keep them stupid."

"At least they're reading." Jack placed his phone on the table and scrolled through messages.

"For the love of *shit*," Frank bellowed, "we're having a conversation. We know what's happening across the Pacific, but we don't know what's happening across the table. What is so damned important about your phone?"

Jack twirled his cap backwards and ate another spoonful of cereal. "Checking messages."

"Messages from whom?"

"Friends."

"And the way you spin through that thing, you have dozens of friends?"

"You *scroll* through it, and, no, they're not all friends. Just people."

"People? And they all have something important to say?"

"Not always."

"Then why bother with them or their messages? Why not send a message only when you *have* something important to say?" Frank saw his grandson gauge him as if he were from the Stone Age.

"Sometimes you just want to stay in touch...or just throw something out there...or whatever."

"People used to write letters. That took thought." He turned his face and blew cigarette smoke into the air. "We had a great system that transported those thoughts — the Post Office."

"We still have the P O," his grandson said with a wry smile. "It's called Snail Mail."

Frank frowned and finished his coffee. Jack finished his cornflakes. After a few minutes of calm and quiet, his grandson re-pocketed his phone and Frank said, "What do you want to accomplish today?"

"I don't know." His grandson's indifference quickly faded as worry filled his face. "I was kind of fired from my job."

"Really?"

"Yeah. But I'll level with you, it's okay because I wasn't into it anymore. So, I need a job." Jack's eyes searched the room. "But, Grandpa, I really don't know what I'm meant to do."

"Meant to do?"

Jack leaned in earnestly, and Frank saw his own features in the young face. "You know, I should have a *passion* for something. When you're young, everyone tells you to find something you're passionate about." His grandson threw up his hands. "I haven't found it."

Frank softened. "I've heard that sort of talk before. Maybe it's not finding a passion." He snubbed out his cigarette. "Maybe it's finding a purpose."

"Well, I'd rather like my job than hate it."

"It could be a blend of finding a talent and an interest, and then tying them to a salary that allows you to live the life you want, not the life others think you should want."

"Yeah, but where do I start?" His grandson thumped the table. "Why can't things be easy?"

"Because Easy never makes anything happen."

Jack stood, turned to the window, and gripped the counter. "Maybe if I take a break from everything? Chill awhile. Maybe I could figure it out?"

"You've got time."

Jack reached for Frank's mug. "More coffee?"

"No, thanks."

His grandson took the mugs and breakfast things and put them in the out-of-date dishwasher. Frank gently pinched his earlobe and altered his question: "Well, what should *we* accomplish today?"

"I could be putting a resume´ together."

"You'll have time for that soon enough." His grandson stiffened, so he shifted his thought. "What about this house?"

"It wasn't my idea to be here."

"I know. But you *are* here."

"So, you tell me."

"Build up, not break down." He studied his grandson's troubled face for a moment. "Jack, now tell me, it's not entirely about losing the job or finding a new career, is it? There's something else going on."

The young man's face crumbled. "Some girl totally screwed me over," he said and turned to the window again. "Grandpa, I lost a shitload of money."

Frank heard his Subaru roll up the gravel drive. "Do you know the best thing about money?"

"What?"

"The world never runs out of it. There's always a way to earn more."

He wanted to keep talking with Jack, to help his grandson find some answers, but George pushed open the jammed kitchen door and entered with a smile. "I managed to get a truckload of boxes."

"Good," Frank said and snubbed out another cigarette. It was time to state a plan that had been brooding within him, perhaps the real reason why he had called George. "Let's all sit down." He motioned to the table and shook a new cigarette out of its pack.

"I want to do a number of things around here," Frank said and noted the puzzled expression on his grandson's face and the wary expression on his son's face. But he knew what he wanted. "I'm not sure what this property is worth because I haven't checked its value lately. I'm guessing you'll want to sell the place after I die, and we all know that if it's cleared up and cleaned out, it'll be worth more. By myself, I can't do much, but you two can."

"What do you have in mind, Dad?"

"Well, I thought Jack could pitch in on both ends. Help me sort through things inside, and help you work outside."

"Outside?" his son asked with a sour look.

"The yard is full of weeds."

"It does look pretty bad," Jack admitted.

"A bag or two of fertilizer will do the trick."

George said, "All right."

"And the house needs painting," Frank stated. "The right way. Scraped, primed, and painted."

"That doesn't make sense." His son's eyes narrowed and his shoulders hunched. "That will take *time*. We should hire out that work; it would be more cost effective."

"Only the east and north sides need paint," Frank leaned forward. "It's the south and west sides that are flaking. Jack could help."

"I've never done that stuff."

"It doesn't take a great deal of skill to scrape and paint."

"But," his son said pointedly, "it takes time and *labor*."

"Let me tell you something, we've *never* hired *anyone* to paint this house."

"Too bad you didn't hire someone a few years ago," George snapped. "Things wouldn't be so bad now."

Frank's mouth opened and closed. He gathered himself. He had rankled his son and didn't know in which direction his grandson would lean, but he was determined to get his way. "There are two ways of doing things: the right way and the wrong way. Besides," he said quietly, "I'd like to see it through one last time." He rose, squared his shoulders, stood as tall as his aching back would let him, and then he walked away.

_____

April 1927

After Frank's father died, the family hit hard times. Frank didn't realize how poor they had become, but James did. The widow and two sons lived in a packed neighborhood along hard-working people with strange sounding last names. Middle-class merchants, who were doing well, lived within the town proper. In pre-Depression days the economy was good, and the coal that lay in the ground appeared to exist endlessly and the danger of dislodging it from the earth didn't matter because the mineral allowed jobs, which allowed careful spending for the poor and carefree spending for those who were not poor. The coal allowed the town of Vicksboro to keep a bank, a bakery, a hardware, a barber, a butcher, a grocer, a tailor, a furniture shop, and a men's and women's clothing store. The poorer people mostly provided for themselves while the richer people frequented the stores. Those who spent money in the stores had homes built of clapboard or brick, and they partitioned their properties with picket fences. Those who had money, of course, wanted more money, so they had poor people build tiny dwellings that the wealthy people could rent to the same people who had built them. In one of those rentals on the edge of town, Abiah Bowman and her two sons now lived.

Frank loved to roam the countryside. It didn't matter the season or the weather, he felt at home surrounded by nature. He roamed the austere fields of winter, explored the burgeoning flora of spring, and absorbed the vivid palettes of autumn. Of course, he enjoyed summer days most and he loved playing baseball with the guys, but sometimes he needed to go off by himself. He didn't mind being alone, nor did he feel anxious being in his own skin. His favorite spot was the forest where a shallow stream knifed its way through the black earth and eroded the land until tree roots lay exposed, looking like skeletal fingers clutching dirt for survival. He devised all sorts of adventures, imagining himself to be a Daniel Boone-like character. He blazed imaginary trails or killed ferocious bears or saved trapped women from peril, or he found a peaceful place to eat a solitary lunch, usually a cheese sandwich that he had made in his mother's kitchen, wrapped in brown paper, and stuffed in his back pocket. Also, he spent time in fallow meadows because with sharp eyes and some luck he often found arrowheads. They were different sizes and colors. He didn't know the names of the stones from which they were created; he didn't know the names of the Indian tribes that had made them. But he wondered about those people and what their days were like. They and he sweated under the same sun, gazed at the same moon, and explored the same earth. He imagined that what those people believed to be essential to life could not be tied to wealth. Things not tied to wealth, because they lasted, were eternally important. The arrowheads he gathered might be of some worth, but he probably would never tell his friends about them. Most definitely, he would never tell his brother. No, James would steal and then sell them.

By age eleven it was clear to Frank that he and his brother did not share the same outlook to life. One day James devised a plan that would net them free pies. Townshend Bakery did a good business and owned a delivery truck that would, for a fee, bring to the back door a delicious, fresh-baked pie or some other treat so that wealthier families could top off their suppers. James had watched the delivery man's route and it so happened that every week the fellow would park on a cross-through street, a street that lay horizontally between two vertical streets, ones that cut into those steep Pennsylvania hillsides. Instead of driving the truck along the inclined streets, the delivery man would park on the level cross-through street, load his carrier with pies, and walk to the houses that stood on the slopes. All told, it would take twenty minutes to cover one street before climbing back in the van, reloading, and delivering to the second street. For James, twenty minutes was plenty of time. He convinced Frank—through intimidation—to go with him, and the boys waited behind some bushes for the portly delivery man to lumber out of his truck and start his street descent.

"There goes fat-ass," James said, stood, and brushed dirt from his hands. "Come on!"

The next thing Frank knew, he and James were inside the delivery van with racks and rows of pastries. The sight dazzled and the smell of fresh fruit and warm crust overwhelmed him. Then James slid an apple pie from its rack and handed it to Frank. The pie was still warm; its heat transferred from the metal dish to his fingers. James snatched a blueberry pie and off they went. Ran. Frank's heart pounded, but it had nothing to do with the running. The idea of stealing something—the horror of stealing something—made his heart jump.

When they reached the school playground with its ball field and benches, the boys stopped running and panted like pirates with plunder. Nothing but open fields and wild trees surrounded them. Then James laughed in a thrilling, orgasmic way. "That was great!"

"We can't take these home," Frank said, and with trembling fingers set his pie on the bench. "Mom will kill us."

James frowned but then smiled devilishly. "We'll just have to eat them here and now."

He set his blueberry pie down and pulled out a pocketknife that had once belonged to their father. He cut a slice, held it in his hands, and took an enormous bite. Purple juice dribbled down his chin. He chewed and laughed but then, looking at Frank just standing there, he scowled. Angrily, James cut a piece of the apple pie and shoved it toward his brother.

"Eat it."

"I can't."

"Eat it."

"I feel sick."

"You make *me* sick. When will you understand? You think there are two ways of doing things: the right way and the wrong way, but nothing *good* happens unless you make it happen. You'll never get anywhere if you play by the rules." He slapped Frank's cheek, just hard enough to cause a sting. "People want you to do the right thing because it helps them, not you."

Frank looked at the slice of stolen pie with its apples coated in a gooey, sugary glaze. He turned and walked away. He walked the long way home.

George stood inside the detached garage that resembled a barn more than anything else. Years ago his father had set up a shop inside it, so the garage had a workbench, and a cache of tools hung in logical fashion. His father had fastened pegboard above the workbench so that all of his hand tools — screwdrivers, wrenches, pliers, hammers, levels, and clamps — had a designated place within easy reach. On lower shelves George saw oil cans, paint cans, and machine parts, and on the dirt floor he noted a lawnmower, a snow blower, and two spare tires with half-worn tread. He had to admit that the mixture of indoor scents and outdoor smells, made a not unpleasant aroma. Above him on a yellow, plastic-coated hook was his old bicycle. How he loved riding that ten-speed. A relic now. But still there.

The workbench was clear of everything except for dents, dings, and stains and, strangely, a cigar box. George recognized it immediately. It was a Phillies cigar box, decades old, in which his father stored drill bits, but the box always stayed on one particular shelf. He thought that the old man must have moved the box and had forgotten to put it back. George set it on the shelf. Tomorrow he would sort through the paint cans; today he needed a scraper and ladder. He frowned, thinking of all the prep work that lay ahead of him, and then the painting. He disliked the work, but in a way this task was his father's final request. Did he really have choice to deny it?

Outside of the detached garage George looked at the cement sidewalk that curved along the house's perimeter. He associated work around the house with his father, even if the man had earned his living at a newspaper. His father liked physical work, skilled work — work that belonged to the hands, mind, and heart of a man. In that, his father excelled; George did not.

As a boy, probably the first job George's father gave him one late afternoon was to sweep the sidewalk that followed along the house.

How old was he? Probably four or five. He felt proud, excited, and nervous, holding the heavy maple-handled broom and pushing the remains of his father's labor off the pavement. He worked carefully and slowly, feeling a sense of accomplishment as the day darkened, when suddenly his father touched his shoulder with one hand and snatched the broom with the other.

"I'll take it from here."

And he did.

It was a horrible feeling. Even today, George remembered that cold sense of failure and how the sun seemed to set immediately.

But now he lugged the aluminum ladder outside and set it against the house. Abruptly, he changed his mind and decided not to climb the ladder today. No, he was not fond of ladder work. He would start by scraping the siding that was reachable from the ground. A section of the house's clapboard that had flaked and peeled was now steeped in shade. George gripped the tool's handle and slid its sharp end against the siding. A layer of old paint lifted off and fluttered to the ground. George nodded, pleased. He slid the tool again, lifted old paint, but then more paint than he intended peeled off. He'd removed a layer that could have stayed on the siding. He stood back, relaxed his shoulders and tried again. This time he pushed the blade at the wrong angle and the metal tip sunk into the siding, causing the wood to split. Each try after that made things worse. He scraped and sputtered, making a mess of everything: too much paint, too little, too deep into the siding.

"For the love of shit." George hung his head.

Scraping drove him crazy because he could never do it right. Each wrong move multiplied itself. It was like doubling a number endlessly. But, stubbornly, George continued, more to prove his point than to do the job. So, for the next hour he scraped, stepped back to assess his work, scowled, and scraped again. Every time he stopped, the old house loomed larger, and the size of the job—the futility of the job—overwhelmed him. His stomach twisted with anger.

After another round of scraping, he stopped and set his hands to his hips. Just then, Jack came around the corner, waving another scraper as he approached. "Thought I'd help, or at least try. Anyway,

I need a break from being inside. I've been sorting through things in the attic. Whoo boy! It's hotter than hell up there."

"Right." George checked his son's shirt and saw sweat marks along Jack's chest and armpits.

"You know," Jack said in carefree tone that annoyed the hell out of George, "I don't see why it's a big deal to fix up the house. It's something Grandpa wants, and he can't do it. So, I'm all in."

"Uh huh. Have you scraped siding before?"

"No, but you could show me."

"Jesus Christ," George muttered. "Well, there's not much to it. I should have started with the higher boards," he felt obliged to explain, "you know, the ladder work, but…well, here, watch."

Several times he tried to show Jack how to do it, but, awkwardly moving the sharp-edged tool, George lifted too many layers of paint or dug too deeply into the wood. Jack cocked his head like a dog sensing something wrong. On the clapboard strip above the one George had scraped, without a word, his son started working. Jack positioned the blade at a perfect angle and instinctively braced his left hand firmly over his right to move the scraper with perfect force. George watched how smoothly his son's arms operated. He contrasted his own sloppy actions with Jack's smooth motions to someone who's right-handed trying to write with his left hand.

After five minutes George said, "Okay," dismissively and walked to the other end of the house. "You start at that end and we'll work our way to the middle." Fifteen minutes later he had scraped about eight feet. At that point Jack met him, having scraped about twenty feet, and George noticed that his son's work was damned near perfect. Jack smiled and turned back to start another board. When Jack started whistling, George felt so exasperated, he thought of jabbing a sharp stick in his own eye.

He stood there, frustrated; dazed by the amount of siding remaining and jealous of his son's work. With a sudden eruption, he threw his scraper to the grass. The blade stuck in the ground, but the tool tilted and slowly fell to the earth. He pivoted on his heel but stopped, turned back, and picked up the scraper. He would carry it to the shed and set it on the workbench. Jack, busy with his task, saw nothing. George called to him.

"I'm going to town."

"Why?"

Further annoyed, George barked, "Maybe I'll buy pizza for supper."

"But it's only," Jack checked his phone, "three forty-five."

"By the time I get there and back...what the hell do you care? You'll eat it." George wanted to fling the scraper all the way into the street, but he slapped it against his thigh as he paced to the workshed. Then he heard Jack whistling again.

Inside the kitchen George found the Subaru's key when he heard his father's voice behind him.

"Where are you heading?"

"To town."

"Why?"

"To buy pizza."

"From Enzo's?"

"Right."

"Make sure you get two."

"I will."

Something in his father's tone—some condescension, whether it was there purposely or not—needled him. The time between visits allowed George to forget the friction, but once together he and his father could rub each other like sticks starting a fire. But as he stepped back outside, a sudden thought came to him. Maybe his father *had* to be that way. To survive, Frank Bowman had to be tougher than everyone else because he had no one to fall back on. Jack had George and George had Frank. Their lives were easier. But his father had to establish himself the way a newly formed country must establish itself. He had to forge forward, no matter what. And George wondered what his life would be like after his father's death. Would all annoyances vanish, as if they had never been, leaving only good memories? Or would bitterness remain?

George chose to buy the pizza later because he had spare time, and on his last trip to town he had spotted a coffee shop that wasn't a chain-store and thought it would be worth a try. After a drive to what once was the rundown section of town but had experienced a revival, he pulled up to the place, The Day Owl, and found a parking spot. It was a charming brick building, very old, and the minute he walked inside he felt at ease. With its worn floorboards, exposed brick, and aromatic coffee, the place felt warm and homey. After a few steps he stood in front of a display case that offered a variety of pastries. At this time of day, late afternoon, customers scattered thinly and sat by eclectic tables that might have been picked at different flea markets. George remembered working at a diner—his first paying job, a summer job, when he was twelve—and every day the breakfast rush blended right into the lunch hour crowd, but after lunch the diner turned listless until four-thirty when the dinner crowd started drifting in. He enjoyed the in-between time, those quiet afternoon hours when he and other workers cleaned the place and ate a late lunch, but best of all was when the boss treated him to a glass of milk and a piece of apple pie. He pictured himself sitting at a window seat while a summer rain lightly tapped the glass, washed the sidewalks, and caused black umbrellas to glide by like pieces on a checkerboard. Inside the cozy, redolent diner, he was sheltered and safe with his hope-filled life stretching far ahead of him like an interstate highway. That was fifty years ago.

Now, George approached the main counter and behind it a woman with her back to him tended to an industrial-sized coffee urn, removing a gigantic brown paper basket of used grinds and replacing it all with a fresh batch. Apron strings tied behind her but he saw a white blouse and bluejeans that showed a trim figure. Her straight hair, gray with stray auburn strands, was cut an inch above her shoulders. When she turned, her bright green eyes widened as if she recognized him—perhaps was even expecting him—but then her face regained a calm but friendly expression.

"What can I get you?"

"A cup of coffee, please." George noticed the woman's slightly lined, slightly freckled face, and, oddly, he remembered an article from a *Reader's Digest* magazine that he read while waiting in a dentist's office that said sometimes you meet a person and instantly recognize a part of yourself.

"Happy to, but it will take a few minutes." The woman wiped her hands on her navy-blue apron and offered a confidential expression. "Between you and me, I forgot to get a fresh pot going sooner. Timing," she said with a laugh, "is everything." Subtle creases deepened along her eyes and lips, making it easy to tell that she smiled often.

"I remember hearing those very words several times in my life."

"So do I." They both smiled. "Now, how about a pastry to go with that coffee? Everything is baked right here."

"Well," George examined the display case and spotted a slice of cake with sweet, brown crumbs on top and a thick cinnamon swirl running through it, and next to it was a deep-dish slice of pie. He pointed to the piece. "Is that apple pie?"

"You bet it's apple."

"All right. Let's shoot the works." He handed her a ten dollar bill and she handed him change.

"Just take a seat," she waved to the rest of the shop, "and I'll have your coffee and pie ready in a jiffy. Maybe in a jiffy and a half because I want to get it right. After all, haste makes waste."

George found a table by one of the large front windows. The place was set up like a home's cozy family room or a country bookstore. Lazy newspapers lay in slanted stacks everywhere while hardbound and softbound books crammed dark wooden cases and shelves. Into the mix and within reach of every table were outdated almanacs — so old they could have been printed by Ben Franklin.

Soon the woman walked straight toward him, clutching the coffee mug and pie plate in strong, feminine hands. She kept her ample eyes directly on him.

"Here you go." She set the pie and coffee down.

"Thanks."

"You're welcome." She squinted as if to get a better look. "First time here?"

"Right."

"I thought so. I'll give you a chance to get going on these, and I'll be back to check on you." She nimbly wiped the tip of her nose with an index finger. "I get off soon."

Her round eyes and round smile reminded him of a bicycle in motion. Because she had to be close to his age, he wondered why she worked here. Could she be the owner?

Without much effort, George found a stray sports section from a local newspaper and skimmed the articles. The coffee was good and the pie delicious. He ate, sipped, read, gazed out the window, and wondered if that woman would return.

She did. Without the apron but with the same firm walk and warm eyes, she strode to his table and stood straight and expectant. "How was everything?"

"Excellent, especially the pie."

"My recipe," she smiled proudly, which caused a spray of freckles to push higher on her cheekbones. "Even the crust."

"Really? I'm impressed. Is this your place?"

"No," she winked, "although I have an inside connection."

She hesitated and ran a finger along the seat-back of one of the empty chairs. George sensed that she wanted something and then it came to him. "Would you like to sit down?"

"Yes!" A smile rolled across her face. All in one motion, she pulled out a chair, sat, and spoke, "This is my niece's store." She leaned closer. "My sister and I loaned her some money for a down payment on the place. Of course, Emily — my niece — and her husband contributed, too. Emily has a good business mind, and the shop is doing well. Three years now."

"The Day Owl. Good name."

"Emily thought of it. Actually, she came up with the whole plan."

"It's nice. Different."

"You might have noticed, we get an older crowd." Her eyes barely blinked. "The younger ones flock to the chains, but, as my niece would say, 'We keep things real.'"

"I like it. Classical music in the background," he waved a hand, "and the space between tables and all the books and newspapers. It makes you feel like you're in someone's home."

"Emily did a lot of research." Now the woman leaned back in her chair. "She knew that fewer tables would bring in less revenue, but she also learned that people would feel more at home. This is a large floor space and she's renting the building for a song because the place hadn't been occupied for years and everything needed work. This side of town three years ago," she made a face as if tasting something bitter, "well, there's been a lot renovation since then."

"Emily has a good eye toward the future."

"Luck?"

"Timing!"

She laughed in a quick, easy way and George pictured lightning tingling a key that's attached to a kite. "By the way," she said, "my name is Prudence but everyone calls me Prue—Prue Richards, to be exact."

"I'm George Bowman," he said and scolded himself for not taking the initiative. So out of practice. "How often do you work here?"

"Just part-time. It gives me something to do. Emily takes the busier, morning shift. She has two little ones, so I help out and watch them a few afternoons a week. It gives my sister a break, too, because she watches the kids a lot."

George glanced at Prue's fingers and didn't see a ring. He tried not to sound too reaching, "And does your husband help, too?"

Prue looked as if she had anticipated the question. "Oh, I never married." She brushed a stray hair from her thin lips and looked into his eyes. "I noticed you're wearing a wedding ring."

His face flushed. "Habit. My wife died about a year and a half ago. I don't know why I still…"

"No need to explain." Her expression filled with sympathy as her right hand reached across the table but pulled back. "I'm sorry to hear it."

He felt embarrassed. "I should move on with things, but I haven't done a good job of that."

"Who said there's a set time?"

"I know, but…"

"We heal in different ways and at different speeds. You're entitled to whatever time it takes. The important thing is to heal."

The words could have come from an ancient oracle, and George told himself similar words before but to hear them from someone else—from this woman—made the words comforting.

"So," Prue waved her hand as if to switch the topic and mood, "do you work or are you retired?"

"Retired."

"Ah. What did you do?"

"I was a high school math teacher."

"Well, that sounds rewarding. I never had the discipline to do something like that. Being a Pisces, I'm always swimming in two directions."

"What do you mean?"

"Well, take college for instance. I majored in art and minored in English. I wanted to be the next Georgia O'Keefe but, frankly, I lacked the talent. Of course, eating food and paying rent were pretty important, so I became a commercial artist."

"Really? Where did you work?"

"A bunch of different places at first but then I landed a job with the department store: Market Street. I worked at their main branch in Philadelphia for years. I sketched ads for all sorts of products. Everything from brassieres to placemats. After getting established, I did freelance work, too."

"Sounds interesting. And so different from my world."

"Your world was probably more steady. My world was at the whim of the economy: sometimes up and sometimes down. Then, not so long ago, people like me were pushed aside for graphic artists, people who could pilot a computer." She frowned. "I never got the hang of that. No, I'm a throwback artist."

"That had to be tough. What did you do?"

"I said goodbye to that career. Because I had saved my money—a penny saved is a penny earned—not a fortune but enough for a single gal—and I explored other roads."

"Such as?"

"Oh, I turned to oil paintings for a time. You know, 'Real Art.' Just to see if I could do it. I painted landscapes mostly." She hesitated and then said in a whisper, "I actually sold a few paintings."

"Hey, that's great."

She shrugged her shoulders. "About five years ago I moved here to Providence to be closer to my only sibling, my sister. We've always been true sisters, and I've always had a good relationship with Emily. Then I decided to tutor high schoolers in English. There seems to be a need for that, and it turns out I'm not half bad at it. I had a good thing going when Emily approached me about working here. I had to cut back on the tutoring, but I still take on a handful of kids each school year. I feel good about helping people. Say, that type of work is more in your world, isn't it?"

"Right."

"How long did you teach?"

"Thirty-seven years."

"Wow! When you retired, did you receive the Purple Heart?"

"No," he laughed. "Not even a gold watch."

"Such injustice." She shook her head dramatically. "So, did you teach here in New Jersey?"

"I started here but taught most of my years in Colorado. That's where I live."

"Oh," she looked disappointed. "You must be visiting someone."

"My father. He's past ninety and not in the best of health. The strangest thing is that my son, who's been living in California, decided to quit everything out there and is staying with us. Now, my father wants us to fix up the place, but I don't know if that's practical. Besides, it takes a lot of work. To tell you the truth," George felt his cheeks flush, "there's a lot of ladder work — painting — and I'm afraid of heights."

He wanted empathy from this stranger, this woman with a sharp mind and honest way. Instead, Prue's green eyes turned reflective, dreamy, and, at the same time, discerning. "You have a remarkable opportunity."

"Opportunity? To fix the house?"

"All right, the house." She checked her watch. "Oh lord, I'm running late." Prue stood as if prodded by electricity. "I'm supposed to watch Emily's kids. She's probably frantic, trying to call my cell phone." In a whirlwind she stood, brushed her jeans, and searched her bag. "Do you have a cell phone, George? I have one but seldom leave on the ringer. I can hear Emily now, 'Aunt Prue, why don't you leave on the ringer in case I need to reach you?' Well, she and I are just two different generations. Of course," she found her car keys, "a lot of older people have learned to make wonderful use of cell phones. Have you, George?"

"Well, I…"

"Indeed. Never make the unnecessary necessary. I don't know if that came out right. I try for maxims but sometimes fail. Well," she extended her hand to shake. He grasped it. "It was a pleasure to meet you, George."

"It was my pleasure."

"Do you think you'll be back — for coffee?"

"Yes," he said and tried to match that bicycle smile of hers before she sped away. "Yes, I will."

September 11

After poking through the paint cans in the detached garage, George found a gallon for the house siding: the creamy yellow that worked well against the white trim. It wouldn't be enough, but the local hardware store could match the paint. What he needed was a good exterior primer. The cans of interior primer wouldn't do and a new four-inch brush, he thought, would be worth the cost. He glanced up at his old bicycle and wondered why he'd stopped riding, especially in Colorado where summer days are clear and where mountain roads are enchanting. He touched the bike's front tire, flat but dangling free, and then he gripped the rim and gave the wheel a strong turn. The familiar whirring sound along with the spinning circle was mesmerizing, the straight lines of the spokes within a perfect circle. George let the wheel spin itself to a slow but steady stop and then touched the worn tire. How many miles had he pedaled on those tires? How many hours had he sweated happily under a summer sun? Was that part of his life completely over?

George returned to the business at hand. He set the paint can on the workbench and noticed the Phillies cigar box lying on the bench's edge. Could it have fallen there? Had he not placed it firmly on the shelf? Had Jack moved it for some reason? He would ask Jack about it later. His father was meticulous about keeping tools in proper places, so back on the shelf it went.

But holding the tattered cigar box made George think of the shifting poker nights that his father loved. Years ago a group of five men would meet every other week and rotate the hosting house so that the group would gather at Frank's house in the basement about five times a year. Finishing the basement by himself was, perhaps, his father's best personal achievement. Frank began with the cement floor and constructed a grid of two-by-fours, fixed them to the cement, and then attached three-quarter inch plywood sheets on top of the frame. That way he created a barrier space because he was determined the basement floor would not be cold. Over the plywood he laid a thick padding and a quality carpet, but before that final touch, Frank put up knotty pine paneling from the floor halfway to the ceiling. He stained it a honey color because, as he told George later, it reminded him of places he'd seen in the Adirondacks when he served in the Civilian Conservation Corps. His father completed the basement by adding a half-bath, a pool table, a sofa, a card table, and a bar, which he also built. Working on weekends only, the project took a year to complete, and George knew that the man was proud of his creation.

When George was seven years old, Frank gave him the sole job of cleaning the room in the basement where the men played poker, but first George had to light the auxiliary gas heater that took not only his hands but also his father's hands. It was one of those chores that he dreaded because the situation was dangerous and he didn't want to fail. Holding flashlights steady, gripping bolts with pliers, or hammering nails at odd angles made him anxious, but this job frightened him. The heating unit that stood against a wall was thirty inches high and twenty-four inches across. Behind that wall was the house furnace, and a copper pipe branched off from it to the rear of the auxiliary heater. In the center of that unit was a pilot light. From one side of the wall, the furnace side, George's father would lie on his stomach, reach across, and turn the valve that allowed the gas to flow. From the other side George would lie on his stomach, strike a stick match, reach across, and light the pilot. They couldn't see each other, which made the moment even more difficult. George focused on his father's hands, and that was reassurance.

Still, it was an unsettling moment. Just striking the match sometimes caused his fingers to fumble. Holding the tiny flame over the pilot hole had to be done just right, at a perfect angle, and then, magically, the gas flame would flare like fire from a dragon's mouth— like the beasts he'd seen in illustrated comic books. The scene of father and son lighting the flame might be pictured as a spark of life between two outstretched hands—something like an image from Michelangelo's Sistine Chapel. The spark of life undeniably existed between his father and him, and now when he thought about it, perhaps their similarities outweighed their differences.

Back then, as gas flames spread through the unit, George would pull the burning match out of the metal frame, hoping not to singe his fingers, and then blow the match out as fast as he could. Steadily, warm air filled the cold basement, and while his father went upstairs to shower, George set to work: wiping clean the bar his father had built, setting up the poker table with its two decks of cards and miniature carousel of chips. He would put a box of Phillies cigars on the bar counter and feel the heater drive out the final chill. When finished, he looked at the room with a sense of pride, as if it were as timeless and perfect as a placid sea. It made him feel good to light the furnace and to set the room—to succeed in his father's eyes.

Thirty minutes later the space filled with the tinkling of gambling chips, with laughter and the snapping, shuffling sound of cards and bets and boasts. The robust men ate sandwiches and drank beers; they smoked cigarettes and cigars that would cloud and spoil the pristine setting. What George remembered most about lighting the furnace was the warmth that drove out the chill within the space that engulfed him and his father.

And now, he had to drive out the chill between Jack and himself. He must be the one to make the first move.

October 1957

Frank had been working all day, scraping and priming the siding. He was beat. Sometimes George would follow him around like a puppy and this was one of those days, which was all right, but George could be distracting because a boy could get into anything and Frank had to keep an eye on him. Because Frank's father died when he was young, in many ways it was like never having a father. He never knew how to be a father.

So, his legs ached from trudging up and down the ladder all day and his arms ached from painting; meanwhile, he had to watch George. It was late October and Frank wanted to get the house painted before winter set in. The days were short and his time was tight. Finally finished for the day, he could wash his brush, put the ladder and tools aside, and give George the illusion of doing a job, so he gave him a broom and told him to sweep the sidewalk. After Frank stowed everything away, he watched George push the maple-handled broom slowly and deliberately. Too slowly. The sun was setting fast. It would be dark in minutes, and Frank could save his son from work. He took the broom from George and said, "I'll take it from here," and he finished the job. All Frank wanted was his supper, a beer, and a cigar. He was exhausted.

Frank sat at the kitchen table smoking a cigarette. His grandson poked his head inside the refrigerator and pulled out a half-gallon of orange juice. Jack shook the carton and found a glass. "You want some, Grandpa?"

"No, thanks."

Jack poured a full glass and drank off most of it in a single swig. His grandson wiped his upper lip with the back of his hand when his son traipsed down the stairs and swung into the kitchen. "Jack, come with me to the hardware store?"

"Uh...okay."

"We won't be there long. I only need paint." George grabbed the car keys.

"Let me finish this."

"Right. I'll be in the car. We'll see you soon, Dad." Then, seemingly as an afterthought, his son said, "You know, my old bike is hanging in the workshed. Would it be a crazy idea to take it for a ride?"

With George out of the house, Jack turned to him. "He hates hardware stores."

"I know."

"Anytime Dad tried to fix something," his grandson said in a low voice, "things went from bad to worse."

"I know," Frank smiled and added, "so you'd better keep an eye on him."

After Jack left, Frank walked to the picture window and watched his Subaru back down the gravel drive. He had lived in this house a long time and felt comfort in his furniture, in his books, and in all his possessions. He looked around and thought, Yes, I've made mistakes. I've done things I'm not proud of. But a man can't control everything. Could things have been different? Certainly. But I stayed the course, mostly. I was successful. Weren't my goals the right goals?

The front porch caught the morning light, so Frank decided to sit on one of the outdoor chairs. On weekends during this time of year before the Parkinson's tortured her body, Deborah sat with him on those wood-slatted chairs reading a newspaper and sipping coffee. They especially enjoyed the time between Labor Day and late October because the weather was mild and tinged with a sharpness that tingled a person's senses. Sometimes spring could be that way, too.

Now, Frank settled into a chair with a firm cushion and let the warm sun and cool air lap against him. He closed his eyes. Spring and newspapers and bicycles. A neighborhood of Victorian homes. Property hedges—boxwoods. Mature trees. Houses set back from the street to showcase picturesque lawns. A distance between the homes. No need to smell another family's cooking or to overhear intimate conversations. In Frank's mind, images appeared, wheeled, and disappeared. He was twelve years old, riding his bicycle on an extension of Main Street to the best neighborhood in Vicksboro, Pennsylvania. He was selling newspaper subscriptions.

April 1928

Twelve-year-old Frank Bowman received a letter from the *Harrisburg Herald* stating that he was authorized to sell subscriptions for the paper, and for each subscription sold he would pocket one dime. But the money would stay in a special account from which he could redeem his savings to buy merchandise from an exclusive catalogue owned and operated by the *Harrisburg Herald*. Basically, it was a way for the newspaper to use cheap labor and instead of paying money, the boys who sold the subscriptions were coerced to choose prizes instead. If Frank was being used, he didn't care because after scanning the catalogue of all the available items, the only one he wanted was an "authentic" Babe Ruth baseball glove. It would come with the Babe's autograph branded into the genuine leather and although it was modified to fit a boy's hand, and a left hand at that, it was as real as the legendary Babe himself. At two dollars and ninety-five cents plus shipping, he would need exactly thirty-one sales to buy the glove.

To sell those subscriptions, Frank picked the nicest neighborhood in town with the best houses because he figured if anybody could afford newspapers, those were the folks. Lining the streets were elm trees just beginning to bud. Each house sat fifty feet back from the street, each had an attractive, white-painted fence, and each property boasted lush shrubbery and promised rich lawns and gorgeous flowers to come. Frank hopped off his bike and started with the corner house. He moved tentatively up the slate walkway that led to a door painted ivy-green just like the shutters that looked aesthetically pleasing against the white house paint. He pressed the doorbell but also saw an expensive brass knocker hanging prominently in place. It glowed in the spring sunshine, and he couldn't resist touching it. He was beginning to understand the value of possessions.

A brunette-haired girl, probably in her late teens, with dark freckles and brown eyes opened the door. In an Irish accent she said, "And who might you be?"

"Frank Bowman."

"And what is your business, Master Bowman?" Her words were winter stern but her smile was summer warm. "Do you know the Saunders?"

Frank realized that "Saunders" had to be the family's name. "No, I don't." When she placed a curled fist against her hip, it was then Frank took full notice of her maid's uniform and understood that now she meant business. "I'm selling subscriptions to the *Harrisburg Herald* and want to know if the, um, if the Saunders would like to get the paper."

Over the years Frank learned there are two types of hired help. The first type deludes themselves into forgetting their origins, believing they possess the same privileges as their employers and will brush you away like an annoying fly. The second type remembers their roots and extends kindness. This pretty Irish lass was of the second type. She bent toward Frank and spoke: "You ought not to be comin' to the front door with this sort of business. Besides, the Saunders already..."

"Maggie, what's going on here?" A woman in her late forties suddenly appeared.

With a blush, Maggie's freckles seemed to merge. "It's a lad want'n to sell a newspaper subscription. I was just about to tell 'em that..."

"It's all right," Mrs. Saunders said in a pleasant tone. She also had brown eyes but a different hue than that of her maid's. Their color was like the sherry that a guest might leave in a glass. The woman's trim five foot three inch frame still looked fit, almost athletic. She wore a plain white house dress, and her reddish, chestnut hair was pulled back into two smooth bands, and draped over her shoulders was a delicate blue shawl. Frank felt as if a teacher were watching him. He smiled shyly and she smiled back. "So, you are selling newspaper subscriptions?"

"Yes, ma'am. For the *Harrisburg Herald*."

"And what is your name?" He told her and then it seemed her mind sorted through an invisible directory. "Bowman? Did your father die a few years ago?" she asked gently.

"Yes."

"A terrible accident." Mrs. Saunders frowned for a moment but then asked brightly, "Do you like tea and cake?" Frank nodded and said that he did. She smiled broadly now. "Maggie, prepare some hot tea and cut a generous slice of last night's cake and set it all on a tray, please. Master Bowman and I will be in the parlor."

Frank walked into the house and his eyes widened. It was beautiful. Carpet adorned the staircase steps while round Oriental rugs covered sections of the shining wood floors. The ceiling was high and the hallway wide. Dark, polished wood comprised doors and frames, but the walls, wainscoting, and moldings were painted light blue. White, fluttery curtains lightly caressed the floors. A small, round wooden table stood by the staircase and on it rested a large cut-crystal vase filled with roses. Frank realized that being early in spring, the roses had to be purchased. Everything smelled of flowers and polish and cleansers, but delicately and sweetly. The boy wanted to touch the lacquered wooden ball that topped the newel post but didn't think he should. As they passed down the hall, he longed to run his fingers across the textured walls but resisted; however, by the open French doors of a gentleman's study, he abruptly stopped. Inside were rows upon rows of books stacked on sturdy oak shelves. An oval rug covered most of the floor and on the rug, like a small fort, stood a magnificent mahogany desk.

"My husband's study," Mrs. Saunders said over Frank's shoulder. "Richard is a lawyer and sometimes works at home." In a kind voice she asked, "Would you like to go in and look about?"

The boy stepped inside the room and the scent of the leather chair behind the desk mixed with the smell of quality-bound books on the shelves excited him in a way he had never known. Loose papers lay on the desk but glass paperweights fixed them in place. The mahogany desk with its tight grain was stained a color not unlike Mrs. Saunders' tresses. The wood was hard yet soft, durable yet inviting. A leather tray with stitched sections divided paper clips from postage stamps, from tiny ink bottles, and from a single bottle of mucilage. There was a small photograph of Mrs. Saunders in a handsome silver frame, but no pictures of children anywhere. One paperweight was hexagonal and made of walnut. On it was a brass plate with the words: "Build Up, Not Break Down." Frank yearned to grasp one of the fountain pens lying on the desk, to test it in his hand. In all, the room nudged and awakened a sleeping desire within him.

Gazing at the bookcases, Frank compared the sight to the town's library, but even there the books did not reach *this* height. Almost all of the volumes in Mr. Saunders' study were leather-bound and uniformed in markings. Most dealt with law, but another bookcase enclosed authors' names that Frank had heard from teachers' voices: Shakespeare, Dickens, Irving, Hawthorne, and Twain.

Mrs. Saunders stepped inside and absently looked at a row of law books. "Richard works here sometimes at night and occasionally on Saturday afternoons. I try not to disturb him." Her face flushed. "I don't know much about any of this," she said helplessly. "It's his world." Her hand then reached out to his. "Come along."

Being not much smaller than her hand, Frank's fit nicely within her fingers. Her touch—it reminded him of rabbit's fur—was soft and warm as she walked him into the parlor with its large fireplace and lush sofa and chairs, with its expensive carpet and its expansive windows that let in buttery sunlight. Beyond the window a stately maple tree was imperceptibly engendering leaves that during the summer would lengthen, thicken, and shade this room from a harsh sun.

Frank sat opposite from Mrs. Saunders, sank into a plump chair, and had to prop himself up so that he wouldn't slouch. Soon Maggie carried in a silver tray with a burnished teapot, a slice of cake, a sugar bowl, creamer, silverware, and a white cloth napkin. Suddenly, Frank felt out of place. He looked at the cake but felt too awkward to eat it.

"Will there be anything else, ma'am?"

"No, no. Thank you, dear." After Maggie left the room, Mrs. Saunders looked at him with kindness. "Don't worry. It's just a piece of cake. Take your fork and eat the way you always do."

It was a white cake with a thick white frosting that melted in his mouth as only a homemade cake can. After Frank finished half of the large slice, Mrs. Saunders said, "So, why have you chosen to sell newspaper subscriptions?"

"I want to earn enough money to buy a Babe Ruth baseball glove."

Mrs. Saunders paused for a moment, perhaps understanding and linking newspaper subscriptions to a reward's system. "And for each subscription sold, you earn how much?"

"Ten cents," he said and then explained his plan and how the newspaper's catalogue worked. "Nobody I know has a new baseball glove." Frank tried to show her the bigger picture within him. "If I earn the money, I can buy the glove myself. It wouldn't be borrowed or given to me. It would be brand new." Frank tilted his chin. "And it would be mine."

"I see. And I suppose it would cause quite a sensation among the other boys? They might be envious."

"Well, they just might." He smiled again.

Mrs. Saunders smiled, too, and dimples highlighted her cheeks. "Believe it or not, I used to play baseball." She sipped her tea and then her expression turned playful. "I have two older brothers, and my father expected me to do everything that a boy could do. Well, almost everything."

Frank's jaw dropped an inch.

"Yes, indeed. I mostly played second base, and I was a good hitter," she said proudly. "What about you?"

"I play right field, but I'd like to play centerfield."

"That's a key position. It takes practice, but I imagine that you play a lot. From early spring through early autumn?"

"You bet." Then Frank asked what he hoped wouldn't be a silly question. "Do you still play?"

"Baseball? Oh my, no. Those days are far away."

"Then what do you do during baseball season?"

Mrs. Saunders appeared flustered and set her teacup down. "Well, I spend a great deal of time gardening."

"You mean like growing tomatoes and string-beans? Like that?"

"No, no. We have a gardener who oversees that sort of thing. No, I grow flowers. All sorts." Her sensitive eyes unfocused. "Different flowers have different personalities. You see, some are delicate, others are hearty, some are restrained, and others are wanton. Yet, they are all beautiful." Mrs. Saunders seemed to be looking at something that Frank couldn't see — perhaps something beyond her sight, too. She spoke in a halting voice. "In the afternoon I like to take tea and have a sugar cookie, or two. I have learned needlepoint. I have learned to play the piano. I read novels. Some twice. And, of course, the social obligations. The usual round of visits. Social circles. Yes, I turn in circles." She sighed. "And at night...I try not to dream."

Accidentally, Frank set his teacup on the saucer a bit too hard, causing it to clatter. It was enough to stir Mrs. Saunders from her troubled reverie, but she remembered where their conversation had stopped.

"So, if you earn ten cents from each sale, you will need approximately thirty sales to meet your goal." She took her teacup again. "How many subscriptions have you sold so far?"

"This is my first stop."

A short laugh escaped her lips, but her hand, pressing against her mouth, stopped the sound. "Tell me, Frank, why did you begin here?"

"Well, it's the best part of town, so I thought people would have money to buy the paper."

"Yes. But you see, that's also the problem. We already subscribe to that newspaper, and to a second one. I suspect Maggie was about to tell you that earlier. Yes, I overheard part of your conversation." She looked at Frank sympathetically. "Unfortunately, everyone in this neighborhood already receives the newspaper."

"Oh." Frank's eyes fell to the white cake that didn't look sweet anymore.

"Did that take the wind out of your sails?"

"Yes, ma'am."

"Don't let it. I admire your plan. It's a good one. You want to earn something for yourself, by yourself. Something no one can take from you. That's good." Her eyes sharpened. "However, are you willing to work hard in order to get it?"

"Sure."

"That answer doesn't sound as strong as it should, but I'll accept it." She leaned toward him. "If I may, I would like to pass along a few tenets to you that have helped me."

"Tenets?"

"Oh, some people might call them virtues, but let's call them key words to guide your actions. Would it be all right to share them?"

"Okay."

She took a sip of tea and then set her cup down. "Here are my four cornerstone words: education, industry, honesty, and discipline. Do you understand what I mean?"

"No, ma'am."

"Well, *education* is first because without it you will go nowhere. It's important to learn as much as you can. *Industry* is the ability to work for something. When something comes to us without much effort, we tend to under-value it. When we work hard for something, we tend to esteem it. We must possess the diligence to cut off all unnecessary actions and to keep at our goals. No shortcuts. Next, of course, you should already know the meaning of *honesty*, but the word can also pertain to a scale of justice. You mustn't wish to cause injuries to anyone."

Frank thought of his brother.

"And finally, *discipline*. It's the ability to stay with one's convictions. To do the right thing even when no one else is watching. Does all or some of this make sense?"

"I guess so."

"Perhaps the strongest advice I can give is to maintain your*self*. Shakespeare said, 'To thine own self be true.' Think of it this way: You must not lose the person you are."

Frank often reflected on everything Mrs. Saunders said to him that day, but especially that last bit of advice. Depending on how he heard those words, they could be interpreted in different ways.

She gazed again at a distant point. "You must widen your circumference."

"Ma'am?"

She smiled and explained, "If people here have the newspaper, you must go to the people who don't have the newspaper. People on the outskirts of town and those who live farther out — on the farms. Do you see?"

"Yes," Frank answered and wondered just how far his second-hand bicycle could take him.

"It will be harder and it will take longer to reach your goal, but if you stay with it, you *will* succeed. You must dwell in possibilities." Mrs. Saunders shivered and pulled her blue shawl tighter. "Without possibilities, life is narrow."

Frank looked into her sherry-colored eyes and then looked around the room again, mentally photographing all the details and pieces surrounding him, everything that totaled this room — everything that totaled this life that momentarily embraced him, a world that he would leave within minutes but a world that for the first time existed, and a world that he now wanted. He felt a sense of resolve and said, "I'll do it."

"Good."

Simply, Mrs. Saunders reached across the table that held the tea set and briefly touched his cheek. "And if you fall short of your goal, come see me again. Walk straight to the front door, Master Bowman."

Her fingers left a warm impression on Frank's face long after she withdrew her hand, but time and distance can cool almost any warmth. "Now," she said, grasped her teacup a final time, and concluded with a forceful nod of her chin, "finish your cake."

———————

Jack didn't understand his father. When he had tried to help with scraping old paint from the house, his father rejected his help and walked away. Now, the man asked him along to the hardware store — a place his father often avoided — and was as cheerful as can be.

As the Subaru made its way along the rural roads, his father glanced at him and said, "You can feel a trace of humidity in the air. Not like back home because we don't have much humidity in Colorado."

"I don't feel it."

"Maybe being in California you're used to some moisture? Maybe it comes off the ocean?"

"Maybe." Jack knew that his father was trying to make an in-road with him. He saw it in the man's body language and heard it in his voice. But Jack didn't want to make things easy because sooner or later his father was bound to bring up the fact that he'd lost a lot of money and had no job. Why else would he ask him to go to the store if not to create a chance to interrogate him?

"Right. Well, along the East Coast, September is a beautiful month. We should have plenty of good weather."

"I guess."

His father gripped the steering wheel harder and clenched his jaw. Jack turned to the window and regarded the old houses that sat back a good distance from the country road. He never saw colonials, Cape Cods, or saltboxes like these in California. Definitely, the houses were old but they looked timeless. And the land with its tall trees, changing grades, and dense foliage looked full and complete. It was strange but he felt more at ease here in a day than he ever felt on the West Coast. And because of the houses' ages, he wondered if they were filled with older furniture like his grandfather's place.

Eventually, the narrow road widened as it entered the town's boundaries. Although Providence had its share of shops and services, its buildings were no more than three stories high, the sidewalks were wide and clean, and people strolled along with faces upturned and expressions bright. Jack and his father drove past Clark's Garage, Enzo's Pizzeria, Dad and Lad's clothing store, The Cottage Diner, Song's Chinese Restaurant, Rowe's Stationery, and a dozen other shops. It wasn't a large town but it wasn't small either. It looked like a place that would welcome a stranger.

With luck, his father found a parking spot right in front of Randolph's Hardware and pulled the Outback between fading white lines. With a twist of the key, the engine stopped. Jack grabbed the door handle when his father said, "Wait."

"What?"

"I want to know what happened to the money, but…"

"I don't want to talk about it!" Jack moved toward the sidewalk.

"But!" His father gripped his wrist. "You don't need to tell me now."

Jack sat back in the car seat. His father released his wrist.

"I want you to know that you can stay with me at home for as long as you need. The situation might not be ideal, but it's better than nothing. All right?"

Without emotion Jack answered, "All right" and left the car.

Minutes later, inside the hardware store, his father went off to find the owner, Patrick Randolph, an old friend.

After taking a few steps, Jack froze. He didn't know how long Randolph's had been around, but he'd never seen a store like it because he was used to the big-box giants. This place had plenty of natural light from windows that spanned the storefront, and inside were a dozen long, narrow, rectangular tables that formed two dozen tight aisles. A hodgepodge of products lay on top of each table. Open to arm's reach was everything from hand whisks to wood shims to garden tools. The floorboards beneath the tables' edges were black, but the footpaths' boards were worn to their white oak. In one corner Jack spotted a bunch of five gallon barrels, each filled with different nails: common, box, finishing, casing, and brad. Instantly, he felt at ease and knew this store was the sort of place that wanted exploring.

As he wandered the aisles, he remembered what his father had said before they left the car, and it didn't take long to berate himself for being such a blockhead. When he was young, he had been close with his father, but he'd always had a better relationship with his mother. After she died, his father pulled back—retreated into himself—and Jack felt alienated. But now, wasn't he getting exactly what he wanted: to stay at home until he could figure things out? And wasn't his grandfather right? Money *can* be replaced. With a silent, mocking laugh, he told himself, I just have to figure out what to do with the rest of my life.

Just as some people are drawn to certain climates, some people are drawn to certain trades. So, when Jack passed by electrical parts: sockets, switch plates, wires, breakers, and fuses, he felt little interest. Then he meandered past washer and dryer parts: hoses, clamps, valves, and exhaust vents, but their shapes and functions sparked even less interest.

Thinking of his mother, he remembered how, years ago, she wanted a spice rack she'd seen in Tarrytown, New York, in an antiques shop. She never told Jack's father how much she wanted it until they returned home, and then she said the vacation in the Hudson Valley was expensive enough and buying a spice rack wasn't necessary. A few years after that, Jack was in seventh grade. His school was unusual because it continued a rare tradition of offering a wood shop for boys and a home economics class for girls. Jack's wood shop teacher, an ungainly yet talented man, knew the type of spice rack Jack's mother wanted.

"We'll build it out of pine," the teacher told Jack, "and give it a dark stain."

"Will it be hard to build?"

"No, but it will take patience because the side pieces have a lot of scroll work. The rest of it, though, will be one-inch dowels and flat pieces. Easy enough."

The shop teacher, glad to have a student who actually wanted to build something useful, guided him through each step. Jack learned quickly, and although the class met only once a week, the project moved along without a hitch. As Jack diligently shaped the piece, his teacher nodded his head with a look of appreciation and told him more than once he had a talent for woodworking. Jack remembered giving his mother the spice rack as a Christmas gift and how happy it made her. She laughed and hugged him, kissed him on the cheek, and he always remembered the scent of a special lavender soap that she used. Now, in Randolph's, he pictured the spice rack that still hung in their kitchen back in Colorado.

Jack moved along the old floorboards, some replaced over the years; he passed galvanized buckets, lawn hoses, and utility rope. When he reached the end of an aisle that displayed carpenter's tools, he walked toward them as if being guided by firm hands upon his shoulders. He stood before a wall of enticing tools— hammers of different sizes, shapes, and weights: claw, ball-peen, blacksmith, and hand-drilling; handsaws of different lengths and with different formations of metal teeth: rip, crosscut, backsaw, and carpenters; and an assortment of screwdrivers, chisels, pliers, and planes. Each tool hung fixed efficiently, each with a particular purpose. They glistened and practically capered before him. Without understanding, he felt a peculiar fusing of fascination and resolve, as a number of tools lured him to the point of lifting them one by one, from the wall display. He held each one individually, turned it, and appraised it in a manner that a chef might touch a cooking utensil or an artist might hold an exquisite brush.

"I'm all set with the paint." He heard his father's voice behind him. "Are you ready?"

"Yeah." Jack turned and set a shimmering steel chisel back in place. "And thanks, Dad."

September 12

Except for Claire and Prue, George had never told anyone about his fear of heights, and especially his skittishness with ladders. During the summer when he was thirteen, his father said it was time to paint the house and that he himself would paint the upper siding while George could paint the lower siding. Using the extension ladder would take the most time, but George needn't worry about that because his father said that on weekends he would handle that part. George would use the six foot stationary ladder that gripped the ground and allowed him to reach more of the lower siding. It was the extension ladder that his father told him not to use, to let it lie on the ground.

George decided to paint the house's north side first because it had the most shade throughout the day. The work went slowly but it went well, and by three o'clock his mother came by with a glass of lemonade.

"Here," she said, "you haven't had anything since lunch."

George took the cool glass and thanked her. He had reached an age when he could look at his mother through male, adolescent eyes. She was not beautiful in the way some women were beautiful, but his mother was pretty and gentle and kind. In those ways her beauty was unmatched.

"You're doing a fine job, George."

He nodded while drinking half the lemonade at once.

She stepped back and looked to the west. "You need to be careful. I'm sure a storm is headed this way."

He checked the sky. "I have time to do a little more."

"No more than a half hour."

"Oh, Mom."

"I mean it."

"All right." He finished the lemonade and handed her the empty glass. She smiled and George sensed that she wanted to hug him but denied the moment, perhaps thinking he might be embarrassed, so she turned and walked away. He knew his mother loved him and wondered why he didn't know what his father really felt toward him. With each passing year some distance, some wall, steadily built between them. Was that wall normal between a father and son?

On the ground lay the aluminum extension ladder. George noticed it, looked away, and looked again. What would his father think if he painted some of the upper siding? How impressed would he be? He pictured his father shaking his head in amazement and patting him on the back. Maybe praising him with words that sounded like love.

Even though the extension ladder was aluminum, it was heavier than he'd thought; however, with determination George hauled the parallel frames up and against the house. It leaned at a safe angle and its feet clawed into the earth. He'd keep the ladder at this height and forego raising it higher. He'd be smart about this. Besides, now he saw dark clouds moving fast and felt the west wind stir.

With the paint bucket, brush, and bucket hook, George climbed the flat rungs. Straightaway, he felt the difference between the ladders. As the aluminum frame wobbled, it reminded him of a tuning fork, struck and vibrating. He didn't dare lean back for fear of falling, Nor did he have enough hands to manage the bucket, brush, and hook. With each step up, his confidence dropped. His heart knocked and his throat dried.

George didn't reach the ladder's highest point, probably topping out at twelve feet from the ground, but that was all right. If he could paint even a small portion of the siding, it would be a success. He looped the bucket handle into the hook and twisted the coiled gadget's other end until it snared a ladder rung. Perfectly, the paint bucket strapped into place, but the weight of it altered his balance. He dipped the four inch wide brush into the bucket and reached to his right, which wasn't far because he kept his face close to the siding. He brushed a few clumsy strokes before jerking his hand back to the ladder for security. Into the paint can he dipped the brush again and then dabbed the clapboard siding, reaching farther this time; his arm stretched until his cheek pressed against the house. And now the wind whipped itself into a whirl. After rewetting the paintbrush, he reached as far as he could, but at the same moment the wind blew hard and George shifted his weight. Then, the ladder moved.

His first instinct was to grab something, but there was nothing to grab except the ladder. It was one of those surreal moments when time and perception lose themselves as George rode the ladder down, saw the earth rising to meet him, and jumped off. His left ankle rolled onto itself before his whole body slammed against the ground. Dazed, he didn't stir for a few minutes but gradually realized that aside from a few stars flashing in his brain and a throbbing ankle, he was all right. Because he could move his ankle, he knew it was probably sprained but not broken. He stood and gingerly put weight on his right side and gradually evened the weight of his body to both sides, which caused his injured ankle to fire a shooting pain up his leg. Quickly, he returned all of his weight to his right side. Then he saw paint splattered across the grass, as the bucket lay on its side. A garden hose, he knew, would wash the evidence away. But his father would figure out what had happened. And what would the man say to him? Or would a disgusted expression be enough to shame him?

Now in September, George, older but using the same ladder and tending the same house, wondered if he would ever stop trying to win his father's approval. Like before, as he ascended the aluminum ladder, its frame shook under his weight and with each vertical step his nerves jangled a bit, but he managed to feel more assured as he stood squarely and scraped an arm's span of siding. For a fleeting moment he felt good. But from this vantage point he saw another huge section of siding with flaking paint that needed scraping and rows of loose nails that needed hammering. Always more to do.

From within the house Jack heard a metal scraper assail part of the exterior's siding, a pause, and then the clanging of an aluminum ladder being repositioned. His grandfather stood next to him, smelling mildly and not unpleasantly of Old Spice, Ivory soap, and age.

Frank opened one drawer of a two-drawer filing cabinet. "You'll find all the important papers here: insurance, banking, Social Security, marriage license, birth and death certificates. All filed and labeled."

"Impressive."

"No. It's easy and it needs to be done."

Jack thought that if he were to die tomorrow, what scattered mess of papers would anyone find? Just debts.

"I've thinned out a lot of material over the years. Taken things to Goodwill or to nursing homes or to the junkyard," Frank said and rested his hands on his hips. "I know the house is rundown now, but I don't have the strength to keep it up."

"No worries, Grandpa."

"I've held onto some things in case you or your father might want them."

"I'll tell Dad and let him look first."

"As for those bookshelves in the family room," Frank wagged a thumb in that direction, "you'll find some first editions."

"Really?"

"Don't get excited. No Hawthorne or Twain. More modern things. But they might be worth something, so don't let them go for twenty-five cents apiece in a yard sale."

"I'll check before they end up in the bargain bin." Jack smiled.

Frank smiled too and then switched direction. "Let's see how your father's doing."

Jack followed his grandfather's slow gait and thought how different his own life was from his grandfather's. Facing facts, Jack knew he had lived mindlessly, but even with death a heartbeat away, his grandfather was deliberate about everything.

The first whispers of autumn had arrived with crisper temperatures, and as Jack breathed the sharp air, he saw that the old house, built honest and strong, was fit for the coming season. Jack's father descended the ladder and said, "The siding is in good shape for the most part, but there's a hell of a lot of scraping to do. A bunch of nails have popped out here and there, but I can hammer them back in."

"You'll need a wider nail to make them grip," Frank advised. "Pull out the old ones and put in new ones."

"Makes a lot extra work just to sell the place," Jack's father said and looked away.

"If you just push the nails in now, they'll pop out again before I'm in the ground." His grandfather hitched his pants and set off for the workshed.

Jack saw that something intimate had touched his grandfather. And he saw the tension between generations—his father wanting a reason; his grandfather wanting a way. It felt familiar. He also saw—instantly in his mind—hammering wider nails and sinking them into clapboard siding, fitting snugly.

His grandfather returned with a hammer, nails, and a carpenter's apron. His father reached for the apron, but Jack rubbed the stubble on his chin and spoke up.

"Let me try."

His words were so unexpected that his father's face screwed into a question mark. His grandfather said nothing and simply handed the materials to him.

"Put the nails in one of the pouches," his father said.

"I know."

And somehow Jack did know. He saw it all happening. Through the apron's loop he dropped the hammer's handle and then scampered up the ladder. His fingers gripped each ladder rung, alternating hands as he climbed. His feet found a center point on each step, and after he reached the right height, he spotted an errant nail. From the carpenter's loop, he pulled out the hammer and grasped the hickory handle. His grandfather had used the same Sears Craftsmen hammer since first buying the house. Jack liked the feel of its tapered wood, and with the curved claw he pried out the raised nail. Without looking, he reached into the apron's pouch and picked out a new, thicker nail. He set it in place, tapped a start, and took aim. With two on-target hits, Jack drove the nail dead into place. It didn't bend or lean because his hammer arcs were true and hard. The vibration that waved through his arm and shoulders made him feel strong, but it also told how much stronger he should be.

Jack repeated the process several times while his father and grandfather looked on, astonished. His movements were natural and instinctive. So, he continued, repositioning the ladder, climbing up and down deliberately, and hammering like a pro. After twenty minutes of flawless work, he finished a large section of the siding, and other than his right arm, he wasn't tired. Although the job didn't call for a bushel of skill, his talents were obvious.

After he descended the ladder for a final time, his grandfather whistled softly. "Now *that* was impressive."

Jack pulled the hammer out of the apron's loop, twirled the handle across his palm, and set it back through the loop. Comically, he thought of an old cowboy movie as the hero holsters his gun with a flourish. "I can do the other side of the house when you're ready, Dad."

Looking amazed, his father simply nodded.

"You know," his grandfather said without wasting a minute, "that door going into the kitchen doesn't close right. It needs to be planed down. Let's get a plane and see what we can do."

"We?"

"Actually, *you*, Grandson. Believe it or not," his grandfather chuckled, "the tool you need is called a jack-plane."

"Whoa," Jack said. "That kind of work is a whole different ZIP code."

"Well, you're in *this* ZIP code now."

"But shouldn't we hire someone to do it?" Jack asked, his eyes alternating from his grandfather to his father.

Frank grunted. "When I was young we never hired anyone. If we couldn't fix it, it didn't get fixed. But it always got fixed. Back in my day a man didn't have time to go jogging in a pair of silly shorts and push a baby carriage at the same time."

Jack had to laugh at that. "Well, I don't jog and I don't have a baby, but, Grandpa, I've never used a plane."

"So, learn."

"How?"

"I don't know. I can't show you because I can't do it anymore."
The old man clamped a hand on Jack's shoulder. "Be resourceful and figure it out."

"What if I screw up?"

"The door doesn't work now," the old man said with a twinkle in his eye. "How much worse can you make it? And besides, you're my grandson. You'll find a way."

He checked his father's bewildered expression and then turned to his grandfather who, as far as Jack could remember, had never looked so happy.

1937

The Adirondacks were as beautiful in the summer as they were devastating in the winter. In the summer the land's beauty was incomparable. In the winter the country was pine, sky, and snow. Forever, the pine trees stayed dense nearly to the mountain tops, the lakes were large, the sky close, and the air thin, so that a primeval feeling pervaded the spellbound region. It was stunning.

Buried within this landscape were many Civilian Conservation Corps camps of the late 1930s. The CCC's, a program created by Franklin D. Roosevelt, took out-of-work young men from farms and cities and set them to work by building dams, bridges, roads, and parks across the United States. The Adirondacks provided endless acres waiting to be partially tamed. The men earned one dollar a day, and at the end of each month the government required each man to send twenty-five dollars home.

Frank Bowman, nineteen and straight from rural Pennsylvania, father long deceased and without an education beyond high school, knew that he possessed an agile mind but lacked all introductions to doorways that would allow him to put his mind to use; however, by growing up with limited finances he had unlimited opportunities to put his body to use. Working the outdoors and repairing things indoors proved to be great training for the

CCC's. He liked working with his hands yet knew that he didn't want to earn a living that way. But how to open those doors?

He uprooted himself from a limited life. Everything had fallen apart in Vicksboro because of the Great Depression. Two years before leaving he had learned from a friend how to cut men's hair, but in a poor farm town one barber was enough. In a neighboring town he once took a job in a coal mine. Simply put, it was the worst job of his life. Descending into that black pit created a fear of being trapped forever. And once down there the air was dank and no amount of manmade light illuminated that kind of darkness. He could conquer the job's physical work but not the psychological strain. To him, it was completely unnatural, and after one month he quit.

After moving to New York City, hoping to find a wider field of employment, he tramped the pavement from morning 'til dusk. The one job offered was in a White Castle restaurant. Who knew that one pound of chopped meat made so many hamburgers? He handled the work and enjoyed the off-beat conversation with New York customers, but the manager kept shifting the employees' hours every two weeks. Eight hour shifts: midnight to eight or eight to four or four to midnight. His body clock never adjusted. So, when the CCC's called for more young men, he opened that door.

At six a.m. a bugle sounded revelry. Inside the cabin-like building, Frank, along with the other young men, rose. They immediately smelled the coalescence of a dying fire inside and a living forest outside. It was a smell so pure that a person might expect to find it in paradise. At six-thirty, breakfast: eggs, potatoes, toast, and coffee six days a week. On Sunday, pancakes and sausage. Seven o'clock, clean the barracks and camp. Seven-fifty, general assembly, raise and salute the flag, roll call, and work assigned.

The taste of coffee lingered on his lips each morning, and no matter how much food he ate, he lost weight — body fat — just like the other men. But there was something prideful in seeing your body transform from a normal frame to a lean, muscular, and powerful shape. For the first year he was assigned to forest fire control. These men were not fighting fires but preventing them. They built truck trails, fire lines, foot trails, bridges, fire towers, and even fire tower observer's cabins. They also strung telephone lines to the towers and cabins. Hard, physical work, but Frank was with a group of men that welcomed it. And it didn't matter if a fellow came from the Midwest farms or the Northeast cities or the Southern fields, they were young, American men *down on their luck due to circumstances they had not created and could not control. Black men, too, arrived from all parts of the country and were dispersed to all States, and if the federal government had a fraction of foresight, it would have integrated the conservation camps. No one would need to wait for a world war to see common humanity simmering beneath skin color. And because all the young men were poor, class distinctions did not exist. Also, because no one claimed a college degree, educational distinctions did not exist. Furthermore, each man's physical strength was clearly evident, so no one had to assert dominance. It was a natural division. The second division came with each man's innate intelligence, which was also evident, yet no man tried to lord over another because these men worked as a unit. The young men were destitute, yet they would never be so rich. That time and place — vast and unspoiled — are lost to us now.*

In the morning, low tones marked the men's talk, perhaps soft grumblings, perhaps a quick assessment of the terrain if they were creating a foot trail, or perhaps tactics and plans to outline the more complicated tasks. Frank would never forget the summer days with their deep blue skies nor the trees' green richness — the likes of which he would never see again — surrounding him like an ocean. No matter how far in time he traveled from that place, with closed eyes he conjured the scene instantly. The tools: mattocks, shovels, pickaxes, wheel barrows, and rakes to build walking trails. The dark soil, the dateless stones, the fallen leaves, the tough tree roots of oaks, maples, and poplars; the grass, the pine needles — all gave way to this "band of brothers" who individually worked as a whole. Air that a man could breathe; lake water that a man could splash against his brow. An eager sun that rose quickly in June and July, and gradually overreached the tall treetops — a sun that beckoned men to strip outer shirts and undershirts so that the muscles of arms, chests, stomachs, and backs hardened and glistened with sweat. Man at his best because his labor did not destroy but preserve. Their bodies of robust, masculine shape — bones and tendons and toughened flesh. Arms that cut down a tree with a two-handed saw. Backs and hips that dug deep into the earth with a pickaxe and pulled out the soil with a power that could unsettle the planets. Legs and loins that balanced a man on a two-by-four beam for hours. And for hours the work: the repeated motions, the heaving chests, and the rhythm of labor. The exquisite form of man, forming the earth to his vision. Channeling streams through newly constructed riffles to aid with aeration. Building towers, roads, and bridges. Afterwards, gazing with pride and gaping with awe at what their rugged hands produced.

The following year Frank was assigned to a crew that developed recreational areas, improved existing state parks, and built new campsites. His knowledge of carpentry allowed him to oversee a five man detail designated to build picnic tables. Their task called for ten tables per day. The work went slowly at first because each piece of the wooden table and its benches had to be measured and cut, sanded, attached, and finished. No exact measurements were given to Frank, only overall dimensions. During the first two days, the men produced just three tables. Then Frank thought to use the cut boards from one table as a template. He divided the men into assembly-line fashion so that each man built the same piece and duplicated the same construction steps. On the second day of using this method they had built six tables by noon. And noon brought their lunch break.

In temperate weather the men ate sandwiches, fruit, coffee, and candy bars outdoors. Their minds and bodies relaxed in the summer sun, rejuvenated; they felt the kind of peace that would elude them ever after. True, in the back of each man's mind lived recurring questions that would crest against him like waves, a thought that touched on the future and wondered where life would lead. Without education and without prospects, standing still in your late teens and early twenties would suffice for awhile, but at some point a man must move forward. Of course, by the late 1930s a distant thrum of war amplified to a distinct voice. But enveloped by a massive forest with the summer sun and a cool breeze rippling the treetops, there, eating a sandwich while sitting on the spine of an enormous, felled tree and surrounded by hardy companions, the future could wait a little longer.

Often during lunch the men's talk grew louder and bolder. They devised plans for after quitting-time. A challenge to arm-wrestle, play cards, listen to a radio, pitch horseshoes, or form baseball teams. They talked about the approaching weekend and checked with so-and-so to see if his car was running and figured out how many men would fit in the car so that they all could go to town. A small town, sure, but a town with a fair number of unmarried women. And their talk often turned to the names of particular girls they had met, to hair colors and eyes and lips and complexions, to legs and to the wonderful curved lines of a woman's body. Talk of possible sexual conquests, brash and boastful talk. Then, back to work until four o'clock.

In the winter the work was brutal. Hardwood trees had shed their leaves by late September or early October. Then it would snow. The snow seemed constant, as it either fell from a gray sky or lingered on the ground beneath a blue dome. Inches of snow. Feet of snow. A man couldn't wear enough clothes or have boots high enough to combat that snow. But the men did. They had to. On some days when the temperature plunged far below zero, the leaders postponed work until ten o'clock. Postponed but never canceled. How could Frank explain to anyone what it was like cutting down a tree in those conditions or ramming the sole of your boot against a cold steel shovel to displace a handful of earth. Yet somehow the men accomplished each assignment. They pushed through the snow and cold, endured the spring that teased them with feminine breezes and naked sunshine one day only to drop a foot of snow the next. Some nights in late spring they made a campfire and toasted peanut butter and jelly sandwiches. A Southerner showed them that trick. A simple, blissful luxury. Then by late May — Memorial Day usually — the snows surrendered, frozen lakes cracked and melted, and fields filled with wildflowers.

At night within their living quarters by the wood-burning stove, after the chores, after the outdoor contests, and after the indoor games of checkers and cards, the men's talk turned somber. They spoke of what they deeply wanted from life, of finding a woman who was sincere and strong and loving. Of owning a home, not on a farm yet not in a city. A place to raise children and to build a life that did not include want. And somehow, even though they pocketed only five dollars a month and so many doors remained shut, they believed in the future, in their country, and in themselves. What force could possibly defeat them — these men?

September 13

If George angled the scraper with its wooden handle and its metal face just right, if he emulated the motion of Jack's hands, a layer of paint would lift, surrender, and ripple to the ground like a falling leaf. Beneath the many layers of paint, the cedar siding with its brown tints and subtle swirls had been nailed in place centuries ago and now revealed itself to him as it revealed itself to the man who had originally touched it. George appreciated the continuity of man's labor. He had to admit satisfaction in seeing something take shape beneath his hands. And he felt more confident on the ladder. It was like getting used to a diving board; you must find your point of balance. Following the scraping would be the primer and then the paint: a new layer twining with the old.

While George descended the aluminum ladder, he remembered how Jack had bounded up and down the same ladder and how skillfully he had handled a hammer. Some kind of bond was forming between his father and his son. Was he jealous? Well, he was grateful for their connection. And yet, George was honest enough to admit it: yes, he was jealous. Why did his father deny *him* entrance? Why do men keep those who are closest to them at arm's length? Is it because they're afraid to appear vulnerable to someone who might no longer see them as nearly perfect? Why does a man talk to a stranger as a confidante and speak to his son as a stranger?

George shook off those thoughts and looked about him. He valued the East Coast's late summer and early autumn. Something dazzling about this time of year. Nature's clock was ticking, yes, but with trees and shrubs predominately green, with a tender breeze, with the blue sky, and now with the physical work that he was beginning to tame, he started to feel alive again, a feeling unknown to him for too long. And now, looking at the land from the ladder's height, George saw how weedy and bare the lawn really was, so he decided to visit Randolph's Hardware again that afternoon.

"Well," Patrick Randolph said to George, "it depends on what you want to do."

The two men had known each other since grade school. They were the same age, had played on the same Little League teams—even double-dated in high school. But Pat, instead of going to college, followed his father's and grandfather's path by running the family hardware store. It was a Providence landmark for eighty-seven years. George and Patrick stood inside the old store toward the back area by bags of fertilizer. Pat added to his thought: "And it's in-between time."

"I know," George said. "Too late for a fall feeding and too early for a winterizer."

"That's right, but…" The store's owner picked up a fifteen pound sack of fertilizer and flipped it around to read the instructions. Over the years George's friend had grown a potbelly and was bald except for the feathery hair that grew like a low crown, starting at his ears and winging to his shirt collar. In high school he was a wrestler, and with his tree-limbed arms and barrel-chested strength he rarely lost a match. "You know, I think with this brand you'll be okay with a fall feeding. It says late October, early November. You'll have to wait six weeks to put down a winterizer, though. If you're around." Being four inches shorter than George, Patrick squinted up. "Like I said, it depends on what you want to do. Short term or long term?"

"Short term makes sense, but it doesn't seem right."

"I understand. Hell, you can use this stuff," Pat pointed to a different bag, "and green up the lawn so's it'll look like Ireland. It's good for short term, but it won't help the grass's root system."

"Right. You see, my father's lawn is sparse and half of it is weeds. We're fixing to sell the place, so short term would be smart, but my father would never go for that. As a matter of fact," George felt pleased with his thought, "neither would I. It's best to subtract the weeds and increase the grass."

"A weed and feed." Pat's lips pursed. "Usually you drop that in spring, but let's see." The man scouted through his stock and muttered more to himself: "Been working here damn near my whole life; you'd think I'd know every product. But things change and times change. I'm all for change—positive change—but I can't keep up with *every* change."

George stood back and let Patrick ramble, knowing his friend was the type of person who talked and thought at the same time. The space where they stood had a musty scent of potassium and phosphorus, a scent of origin.

"Hey, this should do it." Randolph pulled a green and white bag up to his chest and read the packaging. "Yup. Late spring through early autumn. Takes care of weeds and boosts the lawn."

"Perfect."

"Do you want anything else?"

"Not today. I knew you'd have what I needed."

"Yeah. You'd never see a bag like this at one of them big-box stores." His friend handed the sack of fertilizer to him.

George set it by his feet. "Right. So, how is your place holding up against those tyrants?"

"We've been bloodied a few times, but we're fighting the good fight." Randolph's chest puffed a little. "We're a local store, and people like a place that serves the people." He slapped his hands against his thighs. "Hey, I'd better circulate. Never know when a gorgeous damsel might be in distress."

Knowing that Pat married just two years out of high school and that he and his wife had a pack of kids and grandkids, George smiled and said, "You're right about that, but you'd better not tell Elizabeth."

"Who's Elizabeth?" His friend winked. While walking away, over his shoulder, Pat called, "So, will you be back for the winterizer?"

Because he didn't want to say, no, George shrugged his shoulders. "We'll see."

With the size of his father's property in mind, George figured he'd better buy a second bag. With a firm grip on both sacks, he hoisted them under his arms and straightened himself. Yes, not as strong as he used to be, but he'd manage to get them to the front door registers. While steadying himself, another man walked near him and stopped. The man didn't notice George. In fact, he seemed oblivious to everything around him. George scrutinized the haggard face and bleary eyes. He scanned the graying, red hair and then made the connection.

"Jeff? Jeff Thomas?"

The tall, lean man stepped back. A startled expression turned to recognition. "George?"

"Yes." Excitedly, George grasped Jeff's hand to shake it, but the hand felt weightless. "Haven't seen you in years," George said. "How are you?"

Jeff blew out a low, soft breath. "I've been better."

George believed it. Standing before him was the valedictorian and star athlete of his high school's graduating class. Jeff Thomas was practically a renaissance man with a mind for science and math but also having a talent for writing, serving as editor of the school paper. Now, he looked exhausted and older than his years. His denim shirt was unbuttoned, untucked, and draped over a gray T-shirt. Both shirts were stained. He hadn't shaved in days; white stubble shaded his florid, blotchy skin.

"What's happened?"

"I lost Martha two years ago." His blank eyes blinked.

"I'm sorry."

"Yeah. Thanks." The man quivered and then suddenly seemed to realize where he was. "Came for a bag of fertilizer because the lawn is turning to shit. But walking to the back of the store, I asked myself, 'What's the point?' Been asking that a lot."

George touched Jeff's upper arm for a second. "I know about loss," he said. "Claire died a year and a half ago."

Hearing this, his former classmate's eyes glowed with interest yet the spark passed like a stick match that flares but fails to catch. "Sorry."

They stood silently. Then Jeff looked down. "You buying fertilizer?"

George nodded.

"Why? Did you move back here?"

"No, it's for my father's place. I'm staying with him for awhile."

"Really? How is he?"

"He's past ninety, but you wouldn't know it by the way he acts."

"Your father is a remarkable man." Jeff shook his head. " Hell, that generation was different."

"He's definitely a man of his generation."

"Those guys shaped the world," Jeff said sincerely. "You know, your father gave me my first job."

"I know."

"I was only a boy when my father died, so I appreciated how your dad helped me."

"Right, you worked for the *Courant*. Was it one summer?"

"Two. It fed my interest for news and history." The man's expression lightened. "Somewhere in college I realized I wanted to be a high school history teacher. I guess I was born for it." He became animated. "It was great working with kids, joking with them, getting to know a new crew every year and every year taking them on a journey. It was exciting. Rewarding. I remember setting up debate teams." He tilted his head with a look of marvel. "We'd take historical situations—critical moments in time—like whether we should break from England in 1776, and the students would hash it out. Or they'd argue if people are better off with a strong government or a limited one. The kids really got into it. Some even wore period costumes during the debates." Jeff chuckled and George guessed that his friend now reimagined the moments vividly. But his lightness darkened. The forward force within him stopped. Bluntly, Jeff said, "You taught math."

"Got some of my mother's genes. Although, Dad was always good with numbers, too."

"You must be retired now."

"Right. And you?"

The man looked distracted again, as if he had misplaced something. "I was going to finish my career with a program called Master Mentors. Older teachers working with the newer ones. It seemed like a good idea. But right before I signed on with the program, Martha died." He rubbed his unfocused eyes. "After that I...sort of drifted."

"I understand."

"It's easy to lose your way." Jeff hesitated and stared off. Then he started speaking but seemingly to no-one. "When you feel lonely and useless, you're liable to do...thoughtless things...unconscionable things."

George didn't know what memory the man saw or how far away it was. Did he see himself squandering money or using another person or hurting himself? George pictured his own closed garage and the car exhaust, and he trembled.

The two men stood silently again. His former classmate's face drooped and his shoulders sagged. "Guess I wasted a trip. I don't want fertilizer. Hell, what's the point?" He turned to leave but caught himself. "Nice to see you, George."

"Nice to see you." George forced the words and tossed out an obligatory offer. "Maybe we can get together sometime?"

"Sure," Jeff responded without emotion. "Sure. Say hello to your father for me."

His friend walked away with a shuffling stride. George, a bit dazed, stared in that direction a few minutes after Jeff was gone. Then he bent and gripped the fertilizer bags. It wasn't too late to revive the lawn. He didn't know about October or November, only about the work needed now, and he found it sad that the one time Jeff Thomas looked alive was when he had talked about teaching.

Another reason George left in the late afternoon was to stop at The Day Owl when Prue Richards would finish her shift. Because the store's large windows allowed the last rays of sunlight and because the building's awnings subdued any harsh glare, the place had an enchanting aura to it. Inside the coffee shop, George walked to the counter and Prue looked happy to see him.

"Coffee and pie?" she asked with a smile.

"Just coffee today."

"Find a seat and I'll meet you in a few minutes."

Soon, Prue, wearing a pink blouse and dark jeans, marched to the table George had chosen, one nestled against a spacious window. She had left her apron behind and now carried a full cup of coffee without looking at it and without spilling a drop.

"So," she said and sat down, "how are you?"

"Fine." He noticed that she had "doctored" his drink with a spot of cream and after taking a sip knew she had spooned in sugar, too, making it the same as he had prepared it the other day. "How are you?"

"I'm good. Glad to be off for the day. But I'm due at Emily's soon." Prue's thoughts, George discovered, could stitch from one topic to another, yet a unique thread somehow connected all of her patchwork quilt. "We get a younger crowd from now until closing, so a younger wait-staff—actually just two people—comes on. You may have noticed Shelley."

"No, I haven't."

"Oh. Well, she's pretty in a will o' the wisp way. A pale complexion with lonesome moon eyes, jet-black hair, and a thin, trim figure."

"No, I haven't noticed her."

"Hmm. Well, boys are drawn to her like English poets to nightingales."

"Oh?"

"Indeed. Only," Prue leaned closer, "between us, I think she prefers females."

"I see."

"How's your joe?"

"The coffee? It's perfect. Thanks for remembering how I take it. I couldn't do that."

"Many complain of their memory, few of their judgment." she smiled and waved her hand. "So, what have you been doing?"

"I just came from the hardware store."

"Randolph's?"

"Right. Funny thing. I ran into someone I knew from long ago. Jeff Thomas."

"Somehow I know the name...oh, wait, I remember now. It was awhile back. I read in the o-bits that his wife died...let's see...about two years ago?"

"That's right. How did you remember?"

"I might have a photographic memory," she shrugged her shoulders. "So, how is he?"

"Lousy, as far as I can see. Looks like he's given up completely."

"It's hard to lose someone you love."

"Yes, it is." He hesitated and looked searchingly at Prue, wondering if he could open a closed part of himself. He decided to take the risk. "Sometimes I feel disconnected from everything. Kind of useless." Then an odd comparison popped into his mind. "I've got an old bike hanging on a hook in my father's workshed. I haven't ridden it in years, and it's just wasting away. I'm kind of like that."

"You know what you should do? Take that bicycle *off* the hook, clean it up, and *ride* it."

"I guess I could."

"Nothing's stopping you. You're closer than you realize."

George wasn't sure what she meant by that. He watched her chin nod firmly to emphasize her words. After a long moment she said, "It's a good thing you're in the fixing-up trade."

Again he felt confused but managed to say, "It gives me time to think."

"Yes, but there's a difference between time spent thinking and time spent doing." She arched her back as if preparing to pitch a baseball. "Too much reflection can work against us. But *doing* things challenges us. It changes us. Work, even if it doesn't reach your heart, reaches your mind. It takes you out of yourself—your concerns." Prue opened her hands toward him but kept them closer to herself than to him. "Your concerns are important, but when your mind is somewhere else, those concerns recede and find perspective. They become less urgent, more tolerable. And if we're lucky enough to do something we savor, it touches us deeply. I feel it when I paint, or when I tutor kids and see the lightbulb flash in their minds." Her freckled fingers spread against the table's distressed wood. "Only living things change."

George remembered Jeff's haggard eyes just before the man walked away.

"So," her tone shifted and shook the image out of his mind, "how is the restoration going?"

"The house?"

"All right," she said with a laugh, "the house."

"It's okay. Mostly, I've been scraping the siding, removing old layers of paint. What's strange is…" He wanted to say how annoying it was to see his father and son getting on so well and how Jack was demonstrating a latent talent for working with his hands and how damned cheerful his son was lately and how alienated *he* felt. But George sipped his coffee and swallowed his thoughts. Besides, what could he tell her about scraping siding that would be the least bit interesting? So, he was stymied. "…How time runs by."

Without a logical transition, Prue said, "I just thought of my grandmother—my mother's mother. Her name was Alma."

"But," George tried to re-track things; however, Prue sprinted ahead as if her words were trying to catch her thoughts.

"Good ole Grandma Alma. According to my mother, Grandma was strict with her—sour and scolding—but with me she was such a sweetie. Honestly, the sweetest, most tender person. Yes, she was the one who taught me how to bake. And she was patient with me. So childlike with me." Her cheeks dimpled as her eyes beamed. "She told me secrets."

"Secrets? What kind of secrets?"

"Oh, silly things. Boys she had crushes on when she was young. All the faraway places she wanted to see but never would. Ah, she and I were very close." Prue locked fingers of both hands and stretched out her arms straight from her breasts. The delicate skin along her throat and upper chest peeked through the unclasped top button of her blouse. The pink shirt, reflecting softly, added a glow to her cheeks. "But my mother and I were never close. It's funny, but I've always imagined that if I had children they would be close with my mother. Grandparents and grandchildren. Isn't that how it works?"

"I don't know."

"Of course. You have siding to scrape."

Befuddled, George was speechless again. He didn't know anyone quite like Prue Richards. One moment her thoughts eluded him, and the next moment her thoughts touched him. He looked away to regroup himself and to understand her rambling mind. Then he looked back. A smile peeped from her lips and then unfolded fully — warm and tender. "Oh, George," she laughed and sighed at once. "You're not making this easy. How many layers are left?"

"Layers? You mean of paint?

"All right. Paint." Impulsively, she checked her watch, and this time George knew exactly what she would say: "I'm running late. Sorry, but I've got to go."

September 14

Jack and his grandfather worked on the back door that opened into the kitchen, tapping pins out of its hinges. For a long time it needed repair, and it was this door rather than the front door that saw the most use. It was a solid door, as old as the house, with four, equal-sized raised panels. It was so weighty that both men had to handle it.

"When I was young, I didn't have a lot of choices for earning a living," his grandfather said. "The other day your father asked me about being happy in life, and I suppose I didn't answer him."

"*Were* you happy, Grandpa?"

"I had a good job, made a positive difference, and put food on the table. Maybe happiness isn't the right word for that. Maybe my generation didn't think of finding happiness as much as it thought of finding employment." His grandfather looked at him squarely. "What do *you* want, Jack?"

With a gruff laugh Jack said, "I want to be happy."

His grandfather offered a wry smile. "Do you think it works like this: you hop in your car, find a highway, and look for an exit marked Happiness? You turn off, park the car, and there you are—you've found Happiness, and you stay there forever?"

"No."

119

"Then how does it work?"

Jack shrugged his shoulders. With a claw hammer he tapped the base of a screwdriver, its tip wedged against the door's center pin. Having been in place so long, the pin was hard to loosen. He wanted to talk about Linda, her calculations, and how she'd made a fool of him, but he kept silent.

"As far as I can tell," his grandfather picked up a thought, "happiness comes in small moments. Sometimes they're life-changing moments, but mostly they're not. Some pleasant feeling might come to you while drinking coffee or watching a rainstorm. It could be some little thing you've accomplished—something you can hold in your hands or something you can't hold. Life is constant transience. We reflect on certain moments and try to repeat them. Meanwhile, a whole lot of nothing fills the gaps between those moments."

Jack let everything out in one breath. "I'm almost broke. Some girl screwed me over. It's complicated."

"It's probably not as complicated as you think." His grandfather braced the door as best he could. "Do you want to talk about it?"

"Not now." Jack tapped the final pin free. Even with all the pins removed, the door was stubborn. Both men understood the situation. They clutched the door, shook it loose, tilted it, and carried it to the garage. That door was more solid than Jack had imagined. No molded fiberglass here, and walking it from the house to the shed, he noticed that his grandfather's feet wavered. "Set it down, Grandpa."

Without argument the older man let the door slide through his grip. His breath came fast and Jack realized that his grandfather's strength and health were definitely dwindling.

"One of us has to open the shed door," Jack said, refusing to embarrass his grandfather, knowing how much the man linked physical strength to self-worth. With an unsteady but determined effort, Jack lifted the door himself, balanced it, and carried it off. His grandfather followed and opened the workshed's wide door. With newfound vigor, Jack managed to ease the kitchen door into the big wooden vise bolted to the workbench.

Setting hands on his hips, Jack mentally reviewed the process that brought him to this point. He had prepared for it by finding how-to videos on-line and downloading them to his phone. The first step was to take the jack-plane his grandfather had given him and while watching a video on how to clean a plane and sharpen its blade, he carefully disassembled the tool and then followed the how-to steps. It was a simple idea. He knew nothing about tools but knew a lot about accessing information. He made the two worlds meet.

Yesterday he took apart the plane and cleaned each piece: the lever cap, the frog, the lateral adjusting lever, and the blade. Of course, the blade was the most important piece and this one was coated with rust. He switched to the second video that showed how to remove the rust and sharpen the blade. A 0000-steel wool pad lifted the corrosion in no time. In the overfilled shed, sifting through the workbench's drawers, he found a sharpening stone. Then, watching the demonstrator's technique, he angled and moved the blade's steel tip in a firm motion, and after trial and error and many turns, it was perfectly sharp. Reassembly of the plane was not as hard as he had feared.

Next, Jack found a wooden yardstick that would be his straight-edge. It was a quarter inch thick and although worn and blotted, it remained straight and true. On it was printed the name and address of a hardware store from upstate New York, probably no longer in existence, a store so old that the address lacked a ZIP code. Before he and his grandfather dislodged the brass pins, Jack had placed the yardstick against the door and with a sharp pencil marked where the wood needed planing.

"I'm going back to the house," his grandfather announced. "I've done enough grunt work for one day."

"Abandoning ship?"

"Something like that, Captain." The old man held a hand against his chest but managed to wink and walk away.

Jack watched his grandfather amble to the house, the man's blue and green tartan shirt, untucked, trailed over a pair of faded jeans. The clothes fit too loosely over his thin body, and in seeing that, a strange awareness crept over Jack. His grandfather had only one child, and that child had only one child. And he was that child — that son. His flesh and blood derived from them; his spirit linked to them. The generations' hopes, failures, and dreams were all connected. So, what hindrance could one kitchen door present?

It had been a few years since George last visited the cemetery. The gate to the military burial ground was open as he knew it would be, and he had memorized the days and hours of operation without even trying: Monday, Wednesday, and Friday from nine to six. The town of Quincy was a one hour drive from his father's house and while growing up, he had little reason to visit this town. Now, he hadn't told his father or his son where he was going.

Compared to the spacious West, eastern roads were awfully narrow, but George didn't mind. Out West a person could drive an interstate and see pretty much the same thing for hundreds of miles: wheat fields or cornfields or mountains or prairies, but here every turn and twist brought forests or farms or neighborhoods or towns. You had to stay alert.

Nothing had changed about the cemetery. It gobbled up a corner lot and continued for several acres. A wrought iron fence staked its boundaries. As he drove onto the grounds, a squat, brick building stood like a sentry. It was inside that building five years ago when he sat by his father and watched him sign papers that allowed his mother a place in the ground. His father, of course, was entitled to a free burial, but George wasn't sure if it cost anything for his mother to rest there. He was sure, however, that soon he would be inside that windowless structure again, and he would be the one signing papers.

He steered the Outback through a roundabout and then took an offshoot west before stopping. He was wrong; something had changed. His father told him how quickly the ground had filled with the newly dead, and before him stood so many fresh grave markers, he couldn't get his bearings. Naturally, being a military cemetery one marker resembled all the others, and the straight rows, vertically and horizontally, made the puzzle more perplexing. He had to leave the car. In the near distance, he noticed a backhoe at rest and wondered how fast that thing could dig a grave.

After several fits and starts and searches, he found the right marker and read the name Deborah Bowman, then the dates, and then the words: Loving Wife and Mother. Yes, that was permanence; however, it was always at this point that George felt lost. He had come all this way to see a small marble slab lying flat against the earth. No burial mound because flat ground was how the military did it here. The words, the marble, and the image were exactly as he remembered, so after the hour's drive he needed to do more than just stare. But speaking aloud to a piece of ground always made him feel self-conscious, and he wondered if his speaking, or, even if his thinking, ever found a receiver.

But he forced himself to say, "Mom, I hope you're at peace. If there is a heaven, I know you've found it. Dad says he'll join you soon. Well, I'm living with him for the time being, and he can be such a pain." George laughed softly. "No one knows that better than you. He was always so powerful, like a force of nature that runs its course and bends anything in its way." He stared hard at her name and murmured, "What could a flower do against a frost?"

He stopped, not liking his thoughts. Yes, his mother was soft, gentle, warm, and giving. Perhaps he took after her more than was good for him. But George also realized that just as nature needs tenderness, it also needs strength.

"Jack is with us, too." He said in a positive way. "Maybe it's for the best."

All at once everything seemed foolish: standing solemnly, speaking secretly, as if this were hallowed ground. Wasn't it just government land that developers couldn't get snatch? Weren't cemeteries just a business — as necessary as prisons? Mechanical, exact, and efficient? He leaned forward and whispered, "Goodbye, Mom...for now."

Turning away from the grave, he saw a man in well-worn overalls striding along the row of markers. At first George feared he was standing in a restricted area and would be told to leave, but that couldn't be. Then he remembered the backhoe. The older man strode with resolve and soon stood five feet from him. "Good afternoon," said the workman with flowing, white hair in a hearty accent.

George returned the greeting and then asked, "Do you operate that backhoe?"

"Aye sir, that's me job." The man's ruddy complexion flared above his canvas shirt. The denim overalls were tattered but rough-hewn and seemed to robe the man with authority.

"I have to say — and I mean no offense — grave-digging is a strange job."

The man shrugged his shoulders. "Ya git use't ta it, and it's steady employ if ya know what I mean." He looked at the marker by George's feet and nodded at it. "Y're mother, is it?"

"Yes."

"I could tell by the dates. But I'm guessing she weren't military, so I'm wondering about y're father."

Despite the rough clothes and manners, the man's astuteness impressed George. "He's still living."

"Aye. But won't be fur long, eh?"

"That's right."

"Well, judging by *her* dates, I'd say he's lived longer than most." The men stood silently for a moment while it seemed to George that an eeriness filled that silence. He wished the worker would move on. But he didn't.

"So, why are ya here?"

"It's hard to say." Such a blunt question made George flinch. "I'm not sure."

"Hmph." The man inhaled deeply through his nose, turned his head, and spat onto a narrow strip of grass. "Ya probably want to reacquaint y'r'self with death."

"What?"

"Y're mother died years ago so ya don't need ta think about her passin' but now y're father will go soon and ya have to reacquaint y'r'self with the idea that a living, breathing, and talking person will soon turn ta dust. So, ya have ta visit the buryin' ground."

Something stuck in George's throat, and he coughed to clear it. "I guess you're right, Mister...uh..."

"Matter." The older man extended his burly right hand. "Colin Matter." The hand with its many callouses felt like a roughed-up leather glove. "Originally from Scotland, but I'm a New Englander now. Got waylaid here several decades ago."

"Right." George looked back at his mother's grave and after a moment mused, "Death is a strange business."

"It's strange because we only do't once. There's no repeat performance." Matter chuckled. "And no one comes back to give us details."

The old man put things in a bizarre, unsettling way. George stared at the flat, ubiquitous gravestone. "It's hard to factor that no matter what a person does or accomplishes, they're destined to fill a small sliver of earth." He ended with a bitter tone: "The eternal rest."

"Oh, I wouldn't be too certain of that." Colin Matter's cheeks puffed scarlet and then his lips formed a haughty smile.

"You mean an afterlife?"

"Aye, but not in the way y're thinking."

He really wished this gravedigger would return to his job. If the man was taking a break, it must be over by now. Trying to end the conversation, George said dismissively, "I don't know anything about an afterlife." He took one step to signal his leaving.

"No one knows for absolute sure, but I seen strange things."

The older man left an opening and George, although wanting to leave, couldn't resist taking it. "What do you mean?"

Matter chuckled and grinned. "I seen things in this graveyard over the years. At twilight. It's always at twilight. I seen what might be called spectral evidence."

"What?"

"Aye. I seen spirits rise from the earth and cavort like drunken dryads."

"Like what?"

"Like crazed women and wild men." He nodded confidently. "It happens most in late autumn and through the winter. The nether beggars grow weary of their cold sepulchers, so they rise and dance like demons and maenads."

"Nonsense." George shivered. "That sounds like illogical superstition."

"Ah," Matter laid a finger aside of his nose. "There are more things in heaven and earth than are dreamt of in philosophy. Do ya know who said that?"

"No."

"Then I won't be troubling ya with the knowledge. But all I can say is, keep open to possibilities."

"Thanks." George scowled. If the workman wouldn't move on, then he would. "I have to leave. I've an hour's drive ahead of me."

Again, the strange old man honked phlegm into his throat and spat it out. "Maybe it's a wee closer than ya think." Without saying goodbye, he turned and walked toward the beast-like backhoe.

Nearly unnerved, George drove out of the cemetery.

Bordering the military ground was a natural preserve and because he had never been there and because he wanted to shake Colin Matter's words from his head and because it was a gorgeous day, he decided to go. Thick woods covered the acreage, and from the facsimile map of the park that was carved and painted into a large rectangular wooden signpost, he saw that the place didn't have fields or lakes, only woods. That was okay with him. Keeping the map in his mind and driving along the main thoroughfare, he discovered the auxiliary turn-outs that led to trailheads. With nothing more challenging than hills in the area, George knew that the trails wouldn't be too difficult to hike, so after passing the first turn-out, he chose the second.

The curved parking lane looked as if a Titan from a different age had swung a gigantic scythe to clear away the trees, and for an epoch nothing had impinged the natural growth that bordered the parking area. When George opened the Outback's door, tranquil silence greeted him. He heard only the intermittent call of a bird. After quietly closing the car door, he spotted the trailhead and started his trek. The path was three feet wide and margined with a forest so dense that it seemed primeval. For a moment he wondered who had built the trail, but then his senses over-brimmed with that unique smell of decay and growth that emanates from a forest. Tall treetops blocked most of the sun so that everything fell into dreamlike shadows. Engulfed by hoary trees, a cobalt sky, and a marked path that guided him like a goddess, feelings of ease and wonder filled him. In spring this forest offered promises, in summer it blurred to greens, in winter it stripped to starkness. But now, in this shift of seasons, undergrowth thinned, leaves streaked, and ripeness returned.

It had been ages since he'd walked an East Coast forest, but it all looked familiar, and then, of course, he remembered his first date with Claire when they walked another forest. He also remembered the time Claire told Jack about their first outing. Everything came back vividly.

They were living in Colorado, in the same house that George had left several days ago. He pictured himself sitting at the kitchen table grading papers while Claire and Jack were in the family room with the television tuned to an old-time comedy but with the volume low. Jack, age twelve and curious about how couples meet, asked his mother how she had met his father.

Claire laughed when she explained: "Well, it took several connections. It was like those lights you wrap around a Christmas tree," she said. "One string is never long enough, so it has to connect to other strings. One end plugs into another end."

George imagined that Jack understood what his mother meant, even when she explained things in screwball ways, but his son pretended to be confused. "You're telling me that people are like Christmas lights?"

"No, no, no," Claire giggled. "Johnny, we had a *teacher* connection. Your father had a teacher friend who had a wife with a teacher friend and *that* teacher knew me. So, after a half-dozen phone calls and two full moons, voila, your father and I had our first date."

"Where did you go? To the movies? To dinner?"

"We went to the Delaware Water Gap."

"What's that?"

"It's a big section of land with dramatic cliffs and green forests where the Delaware River runs between Pennsylvania and New Jersey. It's either a state or a federal preserve; anyway, it has beautiful hiking trails and dense woods. There's nothing like it here in Colorado because the forests are different back East."

"You're kidding!"

"What?"

"*That* was your first date! A hike? How unromantic!"

"It *was* romantic.'

"No way."

"*Way!*"

George stopped grading papers and stood by the edge of the family room, listening with delight as Claire told the story.

"It was a beautiful spring day. Mid-April. Your father drove to my door and picked me up in a little blue Chevette."

Jack interrupted: " A Corvette? Dad had a Corvette?"

"No. A *Chevette*—they don't make them anymore. It was an economical car. Dowdy for sure." Claire snickered. "I called it the orthopedic shoe of small cars. So, your father picked me up and asked where I wanted to go. Because I had never been there and because it was a silly request, I said, 'The Delaware Water Gap.' You should have seen the look on your father's face. I'm sure he calculated the mileage, time, and expense in his head."

"How far was this Gap?"

"Oh, about an hour and a half."

"You're joking."

"I'm not joking."

"What did you do all that way—talk?"

Claire giggled again. "Can you imagine your father talking all that way, Johnny? No. I talked a little but mostly we were quiet, and I watched the scenery along I-80. A lot of green along that road in northwest New Jersey. Very pretty. Besides, I took pity on your dad because I suspected that he was terribly shy and awkward with women." With these last words Claire raised her voice and mischievously lifted her eyebrows toward George.

"Hey, wait a minute," he pleaded with mock anger, "can't I defend myself?"

"No!" Claire and Jack bellowed as one.

Claire sighed and said to George, "Remember when we started walking one of the trails and you tried to impress me with your knowledge of trees?"

"Knowledge of trees?" Jack asked incredulously.

"It worked, didn't it?" he said. "I mean, in the end?"

Claire nodded with satisfaction. "Yes, my math-man. It did."

Now, as George hiked the preserve near the cemetery, his first date with Claire played in his mind along with the forest and the day and the world that surrounded them: the numberless trees and the spring sunshine that coaxed dormant bushes and brambles, and how it dappled and nuzzled new growth. The timeless process of re-creation.

Yes, looking back, George admitted that he was shy, especially around Claire at first because he knew immediately how special she was. And no, it didn't take long for him to feel at ease with her, but as they started along the trail he tripped over his own nerves.

Although it was a spring morning in the Delaware Water Gap, brown autumn leaves littered the path. George knew little of trees or of their leaves, but he recognized oak leaves because of the trees around his boyhood home. Here, in this unspoiled forest, lay enormous leaves and he saw a chance to impress. After snatching a six inch long tan-brown leaf from the ground, he held it up. "Do you know what kind of leaf this is?"

Claire gave it a cursory glance. "Yes," she said assuredly, "it's a *big* leaf."

Deflated, George tossed the leaf to the ground. "Well, actually, it's an oak leaf."

"Of course," she said and walked ahead so that he couldn't see her blushing smile.

The hiking trail in the Gap was never steep, but it seemed a long way to the top. Finally, when they reached the trail's summit, their faces glowed with perspiration and their breath came fast. But the view was majestic. Far below, the blue Delaware River rushed between two green swaths, one of Pennsylvania and one of New Jersey. From this perspective, George and Claire felt like wardens of a Brobdingnagian estate. It was fantastic, and being far from society's cries and whispers was fantastic, too, so that gradually, as they talked, their uncertain conversation turned secure. Sitting on the secluded ground, they talked for two hours, chatting about everything from politics to religion, beliefs to superstitions, and plans to dreams. George had never spoken so many words at once. Neither he nor Claire spoke the word "love," but as stealthily as time moves across the sky, it silently emerged.

After talking and then after a long silence — a silence that filled them with comfort — a silence that filled them with hope — George stood and stretched his arms. "Should we head back?"

"Should we?"

He looked off. "It's a long way down and a long ride to your house."

"I guess we'd better go." Claire stood and brushed the bottom of her jeans. "Or we'll wind up like Rip Van Winkle." She laughed. "How would you like a twenty-year beard?"

"How would I look?"

"Ready for a barber," she poked his arm and then stepped closer to the overlook for a last view. "Amazing, isn't it?"

He studied the river's steady flow. "I've seen maps that show this spot, but from here we can see where the river actually divides the two states."

"That's a typical thing for a man to say."

"What?"

"Why must the river divide? Why not think of it as joining?"

George saw no argument. He reached out his hand and she took it.

The walk up had been long, but he knew the way down would be easier. Yes, something wonderful had transpired between them. Perhaps the setting engendered their relationship or perhaps two people, similar yet dissimilar, knew they had found each other and together formed a balanced equation. Whatever the Logos, the warmth within their hearts surpassed reason.

After forty minutes of descent, they walked along the level, lower path, tired but near the trailhead. The way was strewn with big brown leaves, so he couldn't resist. After picking a large one off the ground and holding it up, he said, "Do you know what kind of leaf this is?"

"Yes," Claire said with a smile, "it's an oak leaf."

"No," George said tenderly, "it's a *big* leaf."

From that day, George and Claire walked the same path.

Now, after trekking for half a mile in the forest preserve adjacent to Washington Cemetery, George noticed a slim off-shoot, a span of ground only a few inches wide but worn bare to the tawny earth, so tapered that it might not be a path at all. He wondered if he should keep on a certain path or move to an uncertain one. An imaginary sign flashed in his brain: Stay on the Trail. That would be the smart thing to do, and it would be his norm. But George left the trail.

The undergrowth snagged his jeans; however, he walked confidently, despite not having a clear destination. He went along, telling himself that he wouldn't be lost, that he could always retrace his steps, and, unexpectedly, the farther he went, the wider the path grew until he rounded a bend and stopped. Before him the land dropped to an elfin glen and in it stood a group of pine trees. At least four dozen, each standing no less than forty feet high and branchless until the upper third of their trunks where limbs sprouted. The trees, their height, and their branches were as normal as daylight, but he found it inexplicable that the trees formed a geometric pattern, a grid with rows about four feet apart, north to south and east to west.

Then, like an explorer on newly discovered land, he wandered among the pine trees, checking their unmarked lines. Were the rows, like a checkerboard's, true? He roamed the area, examining angles, following one column of pines after another, and no matter where he stood, the view was geometric—not perfectly symmetrical like those grave markers in the cemetery. Yet the pattern was close. Then, perhaps because the area was so unusual, his thoughts traveled an unusual path. George wondered if he could locate a nexus—a place where, if he stood without moving, all the trees would align. And if that alignment existed and he stood in that spot, perhaps he could find the place where everything in his life would align, too.

On the edge of this forest-within-a-forest was a fallen tree, a log now, its topside worn smooth. George sat on it as many people must have done. He considered the natural formation— or was it natural— surrounding him and told himself that nothing like this could grow on its own. His logical mind wouldn't allow it. So, how did it happen? Perhaps a man—perhaps a group of men—planted the pines. That would make the most sense. But if it didn't happen that way, some other force was responsible.

Since Claire's death—even before—he had questioned God's existence, His intervention and indifference. Was everything planned or random? He knew that people have faith, and no one has absolute answers. And yet, these trees. If they had not been planted? The symmetry...the odds. More things in heaven and earth than in philosophy. Would the old gravedigger know?

George remembered Claire. She had harmed no one, had asked for little, had given a lot, and she had died too soon. Too soon? For whose timetable? Who decides the span of life? And what is the final effect of that life?

Of course, George knew how ripples work, how one life touches others, but now his thoughts drifted into a dangerous realm. If a person had never been born, what difference would it make? Are all people connected, or are we like individual leaves on a tree? Leaves that bud, unfold, thrive, wither, and die. One of a finite, alienated number. What difference does one leaf make? Or, more directly, what difference has *my* life made? That first date with Claire and the years we had after. Didn't that count for something? But he told himself that if Claire had never met him, she would have met someone else. Probably someone better.

George picked a stone off the ground and threw it into the woods. It hit something and the sound echoed. He lowered his head into his hands and told himself that he was past his prime and all ripples were behind him.

The forest lay hushed and peaceful. George raised his head now and looked around. He wanted to linger in that odd plot of ground and link nonlinear thoughts. To smell the primal pines that aimed at the heavens. He wanted to stay until shadows stitched across the stillness and knitted themselves into a protective cloak. The idea didn't seem so far-fetched. He remained motionless: eluding time, breathing quietly, losing himself in a luxurious darkness.

Then he remembered Prue, that quirky, spirited woman in the coffee shop. And then he pictured his father and son. In a curious way, they seemed closer than he had imagined. So, not with complete reluctance, George stood and stretched his limbs. He must return to his father's house, and he must be there before darkness.

Inside the workshed, Jack grasped the plane. Nothing in his world—no gadget or electronic device—carried the substance of this tool. Instinctively, he liked it. Something made for the hands, apparently for *his* hands. But when he held the plane over the kitchen door and was about to begin, he stopped. He had never done this before. What if he bungled it? He had bungled a number of things in his life. He looked around. Outside, the September sun was gentle and golden. Light poured through the shed's open gate-like door and seeped through the siding's cracks. Earthy scents encircled him. He was alone.

Suddenly, he wanted his grandfather there to support him, but then he realized that his grandfather had left him alone purposely, not to embarrass him if he did fail. He rested the plane on its side and took a deep breath. After a moment, a plan opened to him.

His grandfather apparently had a piece of all creation in this shed. Jack wouldn't be surprised to find an Aldabra tortoise shell hanging in the rafters, so it was easy to find a long piece of wood to use for practice. After lifting the door from the vise and guiding it to the ground, he found and then secured a practice piece into the vise. The board was common pine, a softer wood than the birch door, but it would do. He gripped the knob and handle of the jack-plane and ran it against the wood. Thunk! The blade bit too deeply and the abrupt stop shook his shoulder. He readjusted the blade, remembering how to change the depth and being thankful he had used a practice board. Now, he worked the plane against the wood, over and over, gaining his point of balance, gliding the cleaving blade through the pine gracefully, lifting a ribbon of the yellow-white wood, watching it curl like an ocean wave, hearing the slick-slack sound of lumber sliced by steel, smelling the Christmas-like scent of pine shavings, feeling the power within his arms while, in an artist-like flourish of repeated motion, he became the craftsman and the craft. Nothing he had ever done felt this natural. He lost himself in a magical movement as he commanded one pass after another against the glistering wood. His muscles swelled as if he were lifting weights in a gym. Sweat beaded on his forehead. Now, being aware of his trance, he stopped.

At his feet lay his labor's proof. It was real. Jack reached down and grasped one of the wood ribbons, delicate but firm. He held it against the sunlight transpiercing the shed's open door and knew that the shaving was certainly alive—as alive as he was—and what his grandfather had said about happiness and small moments returned to him. Yes.

He removed the practice wood and re-set the four-paneled piece into the vise. No doubts or fears. Confidently, determinedly, Jack planed the kitchen door.

September 15

Jack stood by the kitchen window, drinking coffee. His grandfather had walked to the property's boundary where the apple trees stood. Jack would catch up with him in a few minutes and see what repairs to tackle next. A morning chill detached a few leaves and whirled them to the ground. Although Jack was young, autumn forced him—as it does most people—to reflect on life. Perhaps lengthening darkness troubles everyone, as it did him. He glanced at the kitchen entry door and knew it shut perfectly now that he had repaired it. He had planed it, sanded it, stained it, and varnished it. The work wasn't hard, but it took longer than he had imagined. It was like moving back in time and living at a slower pace. It surprised him to know that he didn't mind.

Because his grandfather knew much of tools and repairs and especially of life, Jack wanted to tell him about Linda and how she had bilked him. He had only wanted to help her, but having sex with Linda affected his mind more than it affected his body. What would I gain by telling it? Would it help just to get it off my chest? He frowned and thought: I can align a door but can't align my life.

Frank ambled along the house toward the back property because he wanted to check the apple trees. When he turned the corner, he saw the aluminum ladder raised to its highest point with George standing on the top rung. His son pinioned himself against the siding and stretched his hand to paint the boards. This side of the house really didn't need painting, so Frank felt proud that his son was doing it anyway. He saw that George was immersed in the work and part of that absorption had to be caution—perhaps fear. Frank didn't want to startle his son, so he coughed just loud enough for the sound to travel far enough. George cocked his head, looked down, and squinted.

"You're doing a fine job." Frank called up and then spoke under his breath, "I know how you don't like heights and ladders."

George looked puzzled for a moment but then said with a laugh, "If it looks good from there, you don't need to see how it looks from here."

Frank smiled and waved his hand. He readjusted the wide brim of his straw hat and walked on. As he came closer to the apple trees, his thoughts shifted from the past to the present and back again. It was amazing how those trees survived years of neglect and how, if George and Jack weeded the area and pruned the trees, his son and grandson could turn things around. The apples grew to half their natural size, but with the right care they would grow properly again: full and rich and abundant. With the right care. But what was it that he wanted to tell George? Yes, he must set things right. Every day he had the chance but every day he failed. Why did he keep silent? Was it shame? Pride? But the cigar box was on the workbench. And some things, of course, don't matter. In a person's life only a handful of things truly count. Yet, how to tell it? What to say?

Suddenly, something squeezed his heart; it felt like some beast had gripped it, a beast that could snarl and cleave, a beast whose strength he couldn't match. His right hand clutched his chest while he gasped for air. Unable to stop himself, Frank dropped to his knees and then fell face-first against the ground. Pain kept a steady pace, almost like contractions. He had to ride it out. He refused to lose consciousness.

He had no idea how much time elapsed—ten minutes?—but eventually the sharp pricks subsided and his breathing found its normal rhythm. After pushing himself up, he righted himself on his haunches. No one had seen him. A good thing because he couldn't bear the embarrassment. He stood and walked forward slowly.

In the shade of the apple trees stood a cypress bench. It had a firm back and seat — old, weathered, and splintered but sturdy enough to bear his weight. Frank sat with a groan as the creaking wood matched his creaking bones. Sweat popped from his pores as his body reacted to the jolt his system had weathered. He held his hat and gently fanned his face.

His body had changed over time; that was natural. But what about his mind? Of course, the mind changes, too, but if unchanged, it locks in secrets forever. He set his summer hat back on his head with a tilt and then stared off. Images and words tumbled and turned but joined easily enough. Yes, the words came easily because they had always been inside of him, and inside of him they would always stay.

June 1937

Frank Bowman was young and strong, never to be that young and strong again. His Civilian Conservation Corp camp was in upstate New York in the Adirondacks near the small town of Speculator. He had been there a year and a half. It was a strange existence, a life and world unto itself. Surrounded by men. That life was comfortable but also discomfiting at times. Because he was enterprising and because writing had long interested him, Frank started a small-scale newspaper, a monthly publication of six pages that documented the camp's work, but it also featured the men. He would interview a man and then write about the fellow's life: where he was born, how he grew up, his interests, and his hopes. The guys loved the stories and each man, although he wouldn't say it, wanted to be the next guy that Frank featured.

It didn't cost much to print the paper, and the camp's captain was a literary sort and subsidized the production. To make it work, the captain used some of the canteen profits. There was never a charge for the paper, and besides, it was good for morale because the guys got a boost from reading it. Along with the interviews and reports on their work, Frank tossed in cartoons that some of the boys drew. They had talent. The illustrations focused on the men's tasks but with a humorous slant. He also included nature pieces that a few fellows wrote. Perhaps they were trying to be Thoreau. Additionally, Frank wrote sports columns and made predictions for camp baseball match-ups and horseshoe tournaments. Made up horoscopes. Predicted the weather. Put in sayings from the Bible or Shakespeare or Poor Richard's almanacs—anything he could remember or what he found in the town library, although the building was a good walking distance. He went there once in awhile and skimmed a book of quotations that one of those old-time librarians handed him. The women in that world of hardbound, beautiful books were as wholesome as oatmeal.

In a way, Frank was riding high. So, one day he walked to a different part of Speculator—with its necessity stores that included a hunting and sporting goods shop—and he bought a pocketknife. Because his father's knife ended up in James's hands and because Frank had always wanted one, he put money aside a little at a time and bought a good one. It had two brass plates, one on each side. He had his initials engraved on one side and CCC engraved on the other. He was proud of that knife because he had earned it through honest work, and it made him feel more like a man; it was a way of being resourceful. He felt good about himself with running the newspaper and with being in great physical shape. He thought about the future and even worried about it sometimes, but he mostly lived in the moment and without fifteen dollars to his name, felt rather invincible.

Once a month the town put on a dance. A local band played—mostly country and western music. As long as it was something a man could dance to and hold a girl close to, the type of music didn't matter. One night Frank saw a new face. Every guy saw that face. The girl had light skin and high cheekbones, dark eyes, and long, straight, jet-black hair. She was tall and angular with a tomboyish, loping stride, but there was no denying the female aspects of her body.

Like dogs catching the scent of cooking meat, guys sensed her presence. Word was that the father had walked out on his wife and daughter, and that he was a white man who had or had not married a Native American woman. The mother wasn't full-blooded, but she favored the Indian side of her heritage. Physically, the daughter blended the best of both cultures. Rumors claimed that mother and daughter moved to town looking for a new start because they had distant relatives in the area. It was an old story, and old stories never end in new ways.

The daughter, the men had heard, was eighteen. At the dance, while the rest of the guys tried to get a read on her, Frank hung back. A couple of times he walked past her, coming on and off the dance floor, once carrying two bottles of Cokes, one for him and one for the girl he danced with a few times. But Frank came in close with his eyes, let her know he was alive, that everyone else didn't count.

He didn't talk to her that night, and the next day he heard what the guys had to say about her: didn't seem too bright; seemed stuck on herself; probably knew she was too pretty for her own good. They said no regular guy was going to hook that fish.

A month later there was another dance. The number of men swarming around the new girl had thinned, but even with a closed lid, that honey pot would catch sticky fingers. Later that evening Frank made his move. The first thing he had to do was get her out of that dance hall. It was a late June night, still cool in those mountains. She agreed to take a walk. They shared small talk for awhile, and Frank played it smart, not pushing, and soon enough she opened. He learned quickly that, no, she wasn't book smart, but she was far from stupid.

"What have you heard about me?"

He told her.

By this time they had walked a circle outside of the dance hall and had reached the front porch, but neither wanted to stay in the light of the music so they walked to the back again by a loading dock where garbage drums waited for the weekly pick-up. They sat on a boulder that girded itself on the forest's fringe. Earlier Frank had asked her name. She said, "Carol Appleton."

Behind the dance hall building with thin moonlight and dense shadows, it was hard to see her face. Her voice, though, sounded thicker than the shadows. "I've heard all the talk," she said. "People think that my father left my mother and me a few months ago. Bullshit. He left so far back, I barely remember him. A floating face of white skin and black stubble. A cheap aftershave smell." She looked into the forest for a moment, and Frank wasn't sure if she was real or not, but her profile could have been featured on a movie screen. "My mother and I have been bouncing around ever since."

"I'm sorry."

"Don't be. I hate when people pity me."

"It's not pity. It's one person feeling something for another person."

She tilted her head back. "And what do you feel toward me?"

"I don't know yet."

"An honest answer. Tell me," Carol ran fingers through her hair, so black that the strands were lost against a starless sky. "When you're done with the CCC's, do you want to find a job working outdoors?"

"No. I want the type of job where I shower before work, not after it."

She seemed to weigh his words, smiled sadly, and said, "My mother made a big mistake eighteen years ago, and I'm that mistake. Ever since I was old enough to understand how a woman could let those mistakes happen, I promised myself that it would never happen to me." He moved closer while the moonlight made her dark eyes glisten. Mystery shrouded her. "Do you have a cigarette?" she asked.

Frank took a pack from his shirt pocket and tapped out two; he gave her one and took the other.

"Can I trust you, Frank Bowman?" Carol put the cigarette to her red lipsticked lips. He struck a match that glowed orange-red against her face, highlighting her jutting cheekbones and gleaming eyes. The match flame touched the cigarette's tip and then she pulled her head back and sucked in the smoke so deeply that he saw her throat stretch and her breasts rise.

He wanted her. Knew there was no love to it, just desire. Without even trying to stop the lie he said, "Sure, you can trust me."

139

It happened about a week later. Her place. The mother worked two menial jobs, so she wasn't around much. The sex between Frank and Carol wasn't tender but it was deep, and he knew that she thought of him as a man who could turn her life into something better. Someone who would get a good job one day and have one arm holding her, hoisting her up with him. He let her think it, but he didn't see it that way. They met two or three times a week for an hour or so, and their time together always ended with the same moment. Frank remembered those times and how he walked back to camp surrounded by more pine trees than a man could count and being hungry enough to eat whatever food the cook would slop on his plate.

How did he feel about the situation? Well, he was young and strong, and it was sex. Once in awhile he thought about love, tried to imagine a future with Carol, but the picture never focused. After a month and a half of seeing her, he stopped by one early evening, their usual time. She was waiting for him, sitting on the front porch of that ramshackle place, but her fingernails were digging into her skull. When she heard him, she looked up with tears and disgust.

"I'm pregnant."

In the back of Frank's mind the danger was always there, but he had ignored it. He spoke the only words that came to him: "Are you sure?"

"I'm late and I've never felt this way before." She glared at him, blaming him.

"I thought you wouldn't let this happen?"

"Yeah."

"I thought," building his own anger now, "you were taking precautions."

"Yeah."

"What about the goddamn diaphragm!"

"Yeah, what about it? Almost foolproof." She gnashed her teeth. "You're the goddamn fool that got through!"

Now Frank ran fingers through his hair. He took a breath as if emerging from the deep end of a pool. "We have options."

She had a blank look but then her eyes sharpened. "Abortion?"

"Well, yes."

Carol curled hands around her knees and tucked her knees to her chest. "Do you think I would do that?"

"It might be the best thing." Frank tried to sound reasonable and compassionate. "We can't take on a child now. We have to get our own lives started."

"What if my mother had an abortion?"

He stumbled. "That was a different situation."

Her eyes turned wide and wild and she punched her knees. "I could never do that. I could never just erase my child's life!"

"All right." He let a minute pass and then thought of another tack. "What about adoption?"

"Just give up without trying? Just say, I can't handle this. I don't want you. Live with that the rest of my life? No. I've got more guts than that." She pulled loose hair from her wet lips. "I thought you did, too."

Frank sat next to her, faced her, and grasped her legs. "Okay." Something started rising in his chest and even though he was sitting, he felt as if he might fall. "Okay, we'll go through with it. We'll have the child."

"Are you just saying that?"

"No. I mean it. We just have to figure out how to manage everything."

Immediately, Carol became calm and rational, as if she had already considered every angle, as if her rage had been an act, a calculated play. "After the baby is born I can get a job," she said matter-of-factly. "My mother could help with watching the kid. You could quit the CCC's. It's only for single men, right?"

"Right." Another wave of dizziness hit him, and Frank suddenly wondered if *he* was the father. How many men had slept with her? How was he to know?

"You'll get a job," she said, "and we'll get by."

Get by. The phrase choked him. He pictured his life as an elevator shaft plunging into a Pennsylvania coal mine. He knew that kind of darkness.

Quietly, he sat next to her for awhile. Maybe it was three minutes; maybe it was an hour. Before leaving, he told her again that everything would be all right and that he would stop by once a week, which he did. But as Frank walked back to camp that day all he thought about was finding a way out of that pitch-black mine.

Months passed while Carol plumped and swelled like a gourd, became more excited each week, and each week that Frank visited, he listened to her ever-expanding plans for their future and noticed her mother eyeing him as if he were a roasted turkey on a platter. He dealt with the guys at camp, their grins and wisecracks, and felt a rope tighten against his throat. He had to cut free. But it wasn't like cutting coarse rope with a pocketknife. It wouldn't be that easy.

At times Frank fantasized about killing Carol. He pictured poisoning her but figured some smart coroner would trace the toxin back to him. He imagined drowning her. With so many lakes in the area, it would be natural to go boating some Sunday afternoon. He could find a way to push her into the water and pictured himself holding her down while she tried to surface. He saw the air bubbles and her frantic face and then her sinking body. But he realized that people would wonder why she had gone boating in her condition, and why he had been unable to save her. And where exactly would he do it? Strange thing about that place was even though it's so isolated, someone always seems to be watching everything that happens. And Frank questioned if he had the courage or the vileness to go through with it. The answer was simply, no.

So, on it went. Carol continued her plans. They would all live together at first: the mother, the baby, and the two of them, and Frank would find a job and eventually they would get a house. He reckoned a crummy place located nowhere and surrounded by nothing. Maybe in a year or two, they would have another kid and the coffin would be nailed shut.

With Carol eight months pregnant, Frank had to do something. He thought of leaving camp, going AWOL. Guys did that sometimes. There was supposed to be some penalty, some price to pay, but in those days it was easy to fall off the edge of the earth, and the federal government had no time to look for a runaway nobody. He could leave one morning before sunrise and head north—out of the country completely—-to Quebec or Nova Scotia. He heard they were nice places. There might be some fast talking along the way, but he could make it work.

And yet, sometimes things happen in queer ways. Some people believe in divine intervention. Frank believed in luck, both good and bad. One Thursday afternoon, a letter came from his brother James. Frank learned that two months ago his brother secured a bank loan and now rented store space in Newark, New Jersey. James was starting a haberdashery shop and was just stocking the place. His brother figured it would be a two or three man operation, and he wanted to know if Frank would work for him. If a man had a job waiting for him, he could not stay in the CCC's, so he could leave with a clean break and legal paperwork.

It was then Frank thought of Mrs. Saunders. Every so often, for no reason, that stunning afternoon played in his mind. It was his only visit to that grand house and it happened years ago, but he recalled each detail vividly. Mr. Saunders' study: the harmony of intelligent order, the smell of expensive books, and the touch of a polished desk. Of course, he remembered sitting across from Mrs. Saunders and sipping tea from a china cup. Mrs. Saunders, attractive and willowy, leaning across the table and talking of tenets. The individual words wanted to return now, but he knocked them away.

Frank moved faster than the devil and was out of Speculator inside of a week. And if he were to tell George about it, he would have to say, "No, there was no love to it. I never said goodbye, and I never looked back."

——————— ———————

"Oh sure," Prue said. "It's from *Hamlet*. It looks like your gravedigger knows his ghost stories."

The Day Owl's background music played Sinatra this afternoon, and the faint lyrics spoke of flying away to distant clouds. George said, "I guess the quote fits the man's occupation."

"Indeed. So, is there more to the world than physical reality?"

"Should there be?"

"I think so. The way to see by faith is to shut the eye of reason."

"Maybe that's why you're an artist and I'm not."

"Maybe." Prue's pretty eyes looked into his. She had a way of delving inside of him with a delicate boldness.

"Do you keep it up, the art work?"

"Yes. It's funny how things move in a circle. The most powerful forces of nature move in circles. So, I've returned to watercolors. That's where I started." Her lips pursed. "Was it high school or earlier? I don't remember. But I'm back to watercolors again."

"You enjoy it."

"I do, and it's challenging."

"And it helps fill your day. Along with working part-time here and with tutoring."

"Mm hm. And for the record: I also like to bake, read books, do crossword puzzles, and go for walks."

"Sounds like you've got it figured out."

"What's that?"

"Life."

She let out a brisk laugh. "Oh, no. No, life is too big of a crossword puzzle. Too many squares."

George liked being near Prue and felt as though he could fall inside of her and not be lost. And with afternoon shadows multiplying, the coffee shop's furnishings blurred like a faded Daguerreotype so that the edges fell from focus while the center stayed clear. Prue was the center.

"But you fill your days. You seem content." He lightly tapped the round wooden table.

"At the risk of sounding sexist," her fingers fluttered through her hair and swept strands from her forehead, "men have a tougher time adjusting to retirement because they lose their working identity. Most men define themselves by their jobs. Not all women do."

"You're probably right."

"And your wife died not long ago, so you've lost another identity: husband. It's disconcerting."

"And you...you never married."

"No, I never did."

George hesitated, inwardly parsing his words. "Being single. Do you find it difficult?"

Her eyes shifted away. "No. But being lonely is difficult. I've been lonely sometimes, but no more than anyone else. Heck, you could be in a marriage, in a sewing circle, in a book club, or in a crowd and still be lonely." She looked back at him and touched his forearm. "Do you know what I mean?"

"Yes. But it's not so much that I miss people."

"Exactly. Everyone needs people, but everyone needs something else." Both hands lifted and waved the air. "Oh, I've had a couple of romances that I thought would take me to the altar, but for one reason or another I never heard those wedding bells. And I've had other close encounters," her cheeks blushed, "but we'll leave those to your imagination." She smiled shyly and then gathered herself. "More than anything, people need to be needed."

"Like helping your niece, here."

"That's right. Even though she could do without me because someone else would fill my place. But every morning a person needs to wake up to something. Something to look forward to, something to keep him going. Spouses or partners may alter, but people need something solid that stays fixed."

"Right. I wonder if I'll find it again?"

"It's closer than you think." Again she grasped his arm and stared into his eyes. He tilted his head, wanting to pose an intimate question. "No," she laughed gently. "It's something else."

He understood the coolness of her words but felt the warmth from her fingers. It spread through his senses.

September 16

Outside, scraping sounds echoed inside to the kitchen where Jack and his grandfather stood.

"Maybe I should help him," Jack said. "I know he hates scraping siding."

"It's up to you. But you did a fine job on the kitchen door, and there's more to do in here. Your choice."

Jack had been fiddling with the kitchen cabinet doors that didn't shut right. Over time the pieces had moved or had swollen or the floor had shifted. Whatever the cause, the doors did not meet the frames flush. He said, "I've tried to help Dad around our house, but it's frustrating. He's not that handy."

"I know." His grandfather lit a cigarette.

"Dad thinks he knows what he's doing, but when I tell him how *I* see things, we argue. Or if we try it his way, things usually fall apart and we argue anyway. I've learned to stay clear of it."

"I understand." His grandfather walked to the kitchen window and rested his hands on the sink. His chin dropped open and his eyes turned to a blank stare.

Jack ran his finger along a door's edge. After a moment he said, "How would I take this down?"

"Sometimes you don't see it coming. Sometimes it's just there...in James's store on a dead-end day...or riding the bus on a Tuesday morning."

Jack stopped what he was doing and watched his grandfather who seemed to be speaking in a dream.

"It's there right in front of you, and you have to...to respond. You must do something...even if it's not what you should do."

"Grandpa?" When Jack touched his grandfather's shoulder, the man shivered and looked around sharply.

"I... Sorry... What was it? What did you say?"

"I asked how I should take this edge down."

"Oh. Well, you could use a table saw," Frank explained, "or you could use a router."

Jack grasped the door and pushed it in place. "The screws are loose. We'll need to get those tight to see how much to shave off the door. Should I drill new holes for the screws?"

"If you do, it will throw off everything else. Tell you what," his grandfather said and laid his cigarette on the counter. "We'll get some wood glue and stick matches. It's an old trick."

"I like tricks."

"We'll put glue on the end of a stick match and push it into the hole. Plug in as many matches as you can. Wait for the glue to dry and then snap off the ends. Then sand down the matchstick stubble. That way the screw will have something to bite into. Just what the doctor ordered."

"That's a neat trick."

"Life is full of them."

Jack set off for the workshed to get the wood glue and stick matches and once again felt a touch of awe toward his grandfather. He didn't know anyone who had lived such a wide-ranging life. He did know tension existed between his father and grandfather, but toward him, his grandfather lacked all friction.

Thirty minutes later, inside the kitchen and with the cabinet doors unattached, Jack dipped one end of a matchstick in glue, and then set the stick inside the screw hole. So many thoughts had been racing around inside of him, he knew it was time to let them out. Keeping his back to his grandfather he said, "I blew my savings."

Frank dipped a second matchstick in glue and handed it to Jack. "You wouldn't be the first."

"I totally screwed up, Grandpa."

"And you won't be the last. Man is the only animal that can be skinned more than once. Tap those sticks in."

Jack lightly struck the hammer's head to the thin pieces of wood. The decades-old hickory handle felt just right. Explanations didn't. "I took out loans. There was a girl. It was a royal fuck-up."

"Women," his grandfather said with empathy, "can impair your judgment."

"I'm afraid to tell Dad about it."

"Does he need to know?"

"He probably has ideas." Jack began plugging another hole. "Maybe he thinks something worse?"

"Sometimes a man's business is only *his* business."

While the two men waited for the glue to dry, his grandfather lit another cigarette, grabbed an ashtray, and sat at the kitchen table. Jack joined him. He caught a whiff of menthol liniment and thought how feeble his grandfather was at times and then suddenly how strong he was. Now the old man's eyes seemed to drift to a different place. "I suppose because there's so much of it, I've been thinking about the past lately," his grandfather said with a shy laugh. "Now tell me, Jack, have you learned anything from what you did?"

"Sure."

"Can you put it into words?"

"Maybe not." He thought for a moment. "I might be less trusting. More cynical. But I don't know if that's it."

His grandfather nodded slowly. "I guess every man learns lessons throughout his life. Usually they come through experience." The man flicked ashes from his cigarette and then put the filtered end back between his lips. His grandfather inhaled deeply and looked at him. "Sometimes a person might stumble on some philosophy — maybe in an essay written long ago or a line from a play, a poem, or a novel —

and he's amazed that someone who lived in a different place and time truly 'got it.' Completely understood."

"I read stuff like that in college," Jack said. "One philosophy professor asked the class if there's a difference between knowledge and wisdom."

"What did you think?"

"I thought that knowledge is just surface, but wisdom is deep."

"Yes, that sounds right. And experience is usually the way to wisdom. A man has wisdom when all of his experiences — what he's read and thought and done — come together at a particular point. It's like a geometric pattern where everything lines up."

"I guess that takes time."

"Yes, and the sad thing is we can transfer knowledge but not wisdom. Not to another person, not to the next generation. Each man must discover it for himself."

"Dad always told me to be careful with money." Jack frowned. "I had to learn the hard way."

"That's right. Now here I am at the end of my life and I could tell you what I've learned about politics and religion, about love and betrayal, about heartbreak and joy — and about loss. There is *always* loss." His long arm reached across to the cabinet frame and snapped off the end of a matchstick where the glue had dried. "Living is loss."

"Physical loss?"

"Physical and emotional," his grandfather said. "And just when we have it all figured out, we realize there's nothing we can do about it. We have no control. With every day we lose a moment of what we once possessed. Then, after we die…"

Jack understood his grandfather's words, understood the deeper level that the older man intended. He finished the thought: "The next generation comes up."

"Only to be cut down eventually," his grandfather said with a wistful smile, "by indifferent reapers. Yes, it's quite a system."

Jack stared at the matchsticks poking out of the wooden cabinet frames and wondered if he should tell his father what had happened. Try to explain. Or should he fall back on the steadfast silence between men?

He stood, snapped off the rest of the matchstick ends, and then, with a half-sheet of fine sandpaper, sanded the stubble flush to the frame. His grandfather handed him screws, and with a Phillips head screwdriver Jack pressed and turned each screw in place, reattaching the door so he could measure the exact excess to trim. The doors would be easy to fix.

Now, Jack faced his grandfather and looked into the man's eyes. He said, "Build up, not break down."

George did not like the scraping — but no longer hated it — didn't mind the priming, and actually liked the painting. To see finality gave him an unusual sense of fulfillment. That's something teachers don't see because their students are never a finished product. He wondered if a person is ever a finished product. Then he remembered feeling finished, completely played out. After Claire's death he had staved off depression for a long time, but, like a bird that mistakenly traps itself in a house and batters against all possible exits until someone opens a window, despair finally escaped.

George finished scraping one side of his father's house, and to give himself a change before tackling the other side, he decided to prime and paint this side completely. Standing on the ladder and extending his right arm, he brushed on the primer and watched the white paint seep into the bare brown wood. Although he felt more confident now, he needed a break soon because his calf muscles ached from arching on the ladder's steps.

Once his heart ached just as much, and he felt hopeless. He might compare himself to the apple trees on his father's grounds with an undergrowth that smothered his spirit. After reaching his lowest point, he thought of ways to end his life — many were brutal and violent. But a painless and certain way pointed to monoxide poisoning. With his garage door shut and with his car running, it wouldn't take long to succumb to the fumes. And it didn't.

Descending the ladder, George worked a different set of muscles. Overall, his strength was increasing and although he wouldn't have chosen this work, it made him feel good. Using his body, completing a project, and surrounded by September — the mixture of elements was an elixir. He moved the ladder five feet to his left in order to prime the next section of siding.

George had positioned himself on the cement floor by the car's rear tire and next to the exhaust pipe. The fumes didn't smell as foul as he had imagined, and he couldn't think of a single thing in this world he would miss. He didn't know if he would see Claire again or if an afterlife existed, but even those things didn't matter. He just wanted to end the endlessness of living. To extinguish the exhaustion of endurance. He sat on the cement floor, knowing his actions were wrong but telling himself to be silent and still. Poisonous clouds swirled and enveloped him, and within minutes he was coughing and feeling drunk. So light-headed and so light-limbed, he passed out. And then, unexpectedly, he was sitting on his front lawn, gasping like a man nearly drowned, leaning upright against Sam, his neighbor.

"Hey, buddy." George felt Sam holding his shoulders. "Are you all right?"

He finally caught his breath, embarrassed and puzzled, and looked at Sam.

"I came by to borrow your twenty foot ladder," his neighbor explained, "when I saw smoke coming out of the garage. I punched in the code on the box. Remember when I watched your place a few years back?"

He nodded stupidly.

"Well, I remembered the code. Never thought of it since, but it came to me in a flash. What the hell happened, George?"

"I don't know. Must have slipped and hit my head. Thought the car was shut off." He felt so foolish. "I don't know."

Sam squinted suspiciously. "I don't see a bump on your head."

"It's on the back of my head." George touched a smooth spot on his skull.

"Well, how do you feel now?"

"Fine." His fingers brushed the lush grass beneath him as deep breaths of clean air filled him. "Thanks, Sam."

It looked like his neighbor was about to say something but stopped himself. George stood and gained his bearings.

Now, positioned high on the ladder, from his back pocket George grasped the metal scraper and slid it across part of the siding he had missed. Paint peeled off like a wood shaving, exposing the brown board beneath. *Take it down to the bare wood,* he heard his father say from years ago. It was the only way to do the job right. To restore. He re-pocketed the scraper and dipped his brush into the primer. A metal hook held the bucket to the ladder. With a few strokes the white primer coated the bare wood. He was doing everything right.

"You have the right to forgive yourself." That's what the psychologist told him during a therapy session. For all of its triteness duplicated in magazines and television talk shows, the statement stayed with him. He and the psychologist talked about a number of things during those seven sessions. The therapist said that George had fallen through an imaginary trapdoor, had fallen through darkness, and had landed in a spectral graveyard.

"Everyone makes mistakes. Of course, this incident was quite drastic—a moment of severe depression. But you had never been there before, and you have not been there since. You came here, to this clinic, for help on your own accord, and reaching out in that way is a positive action. You've taken steps to help yourself. We must take care of ourselves before we can take care of others. The first step is forgiveness. Then we can start anew."

It sounded simple enough. Yet the horrible memory lingered like the fumes that had filled the garage, their scent lasting even after the large door stayed open for an hour. George had thought that the outside air would obliterate that odor quickly, but it didn't.

Now, George made his way up the aluminum ladder again, not so disoriented by the vertigo of height, more accustomed to the lack of stability. Standing on that ladder high above the ground isolated him yet liberated him, too. He felt apart from everything yet a part of everything. His thoughts worked like a flowchart. He knew that sometimes marriages run into ruts. Sometimes people tire of each other. Sometimes one person thinks he'd be better off without the other person because she drives him crazy with little demands—

something must be done around the house—or she makes plans for them without telling him first—or she forgets something across town and he must go and get it. Sometimes he takes her places because she's frightened to drive on highways. How all of that flustered him. But not having Claire beside him was a terrible feeling. And besides, he told himself, what's the point in living if you're not providing. So, if Claire were with him today, and if she asked, he would drive her to the end of all roads.

Time to stop for the day. The primer worked well. Later, the house paint would cover both old and new work. A fresh coat over everything. George started down the ladder and thought of Prue Richards and how alive she made him feel. What would Claire think of her? What did Prue think of him?

His feet touched the green grass, already showing effects of the fertilizer that he'd applied. Bracing himself on the land he knew well, George examined the restored siding and realized it would never be as good as new, but no one would expect that. It was good enough.

September 1940

Frank sat on an uncomfortable wooden chair inside his brother's clothing store. Because of that nightmare with Carol, he knew he had to leave the CCC's, and his brother's job offer, at the time, was a godsend. Besides, James had promised him that they would be partners after a year. His brother said he'd figure a way to make that happen, even if Frank didn't have the money to buy into the business. Frank sometimes speculated about how James found the cash to start a business in the first place; however, he chose not to question the past, only the future. And here it was, two years gone, and he wasn't a partner. He was still sitting on that bone-hard wooden chair.

It was a small shop that sold casual clothes for men. In that time hats were popular, and the store stocked boxes and boxes of them. The brothers stacked boxes four-high on shelves six feet off the ground and then used a hatbox-reacher to snag the exact box they wanted. To steam-clean the hats, James bought a small machine that one man could operate. The brothers never charged much for the cleaning, but it was an easy two-bits per hat. But steaming the hat released mercury vapors that impregnated the felt. Breathing those vapors, Frank soon realized, could make you screwy. Mad as a hatter. He hated the smell, and he had cleaned a dozen hats that morning.

As for the overall job, he especially didn't care for waiting on people who had a superior attitude. In the Adirondacks he had built things. In the store he sold things. Frank desperately wanted something new and challenging; he wanted to use his brains and to make a difference. During slow days, especially in July and August, he sat on that hard chair because it didn't face the store's large clock, and that way he didn't have to see his life ticking away.

But being idle wasn't good because his mind rambled. Sometimes he thought of Mrs. Saunders and everything she had said. At times he questioned if she were happy, but somehow he knew that she was lonely in that grand house despite all the furnishings, the elegance, the maid, and the gardener. And he often wondered why she had been kind to him that day; why had she revealed her personal feelings; what had she seen in him; why had she married Mr. Saunders; why had her life turned out the way it did? What were her choices, her circumstances? Could he ever explain or justify to her what he had done to Carol? How would his actions line up with her tenets? Could he make her see he would have been trapped? Maybe she'd understand that—a fear of being trapped. But no matter how much Frank rationalized, he knew that what he had done to Carol was wrong, and yet, conscience, with time's passing, often turns weak and fragile. And so, when the next strong conflict squares up, it's a little easier to ignore tenets.

In late August business picked up because people looked forward to cooler days and, of course, school started soon, so folks bought fall fashions. James's store was located in downtown Newark, which in those days was an upper-tier city. Good restaurants, good businesses, the state's largest newspaper, the *Star Ledger*, was based there, and people paced the sidewalks with staunch strides. But Frank was stuck in that chair.

It was just after Labor Day and the seasons seemed to transition overnight. Business was good and after steaming all those hats, Frank went to the stockroom for more hats and ties. His generous arm-span let him hold two hatboxes under each arm, and if he kept his arms straight and rigid, he could wedge three necktie boxes between his armpits and wrists. When he reentered the shop's sales floor, a distinguished looking man and a young woman stood there, and Frank knew by their amused expressions that he made a most awkward, ridiculous appearance.

"Mr. Reed, Miss Reed," James began, "I'd like you to meet my brother Frank."

Onto the nearest counter Frank set all the boxes and extended his right hand to Mr. Reed. "Pleased to meet you." An assured expression filled the older man's dark eyes, and it was matched with a firm handshake. However, Frank knew if he squeezed the man's hand with his true power, he could crush those fingers, but he let Mr. Reed think that he possessed the greater strength.

"Mr. Reed," James stated, "is the editor of the *Star Ledger*."

Nothing could have impressed Frank more. He marveled to think that this man was not only responsible for a payroll of workers, but beyond that, he influenced so many lives by overseeing which articles to print and which editorials to publish. While he appraised Mr. Reed, without knowing it, his life's course, like a mountain stream, switchbacked and found a different direction.

Mr. Reed's hand gestured to his right. "This is my daughter, Deborah."

"It's nice to meet you," she said and held out her hand. Frank grasped it earnestly and gave it a single shake.

Deborah had brown hair and brown eyes, a plain face and figure. Yet Frank found something attractive about her. Probably her poise. She stood erect and composed, wearing a worsted wool skirt of forest green and a cream-colored blouse. Around her neck and dropping to her upper chest hung a tasteful, expensive cameo. Her demeanor, similar to her father's, indicated an air of formal education that included knowledge of manners and culture.

"Well," she said with a smile, "by the way you carried those boxes, your arms might have stretched an inch."

Frank wanted to respond, but Deborah's smile disarmed him completely. He knew then that she had a kind heart.

James stepped forward. "Don't let that stunt fool you. Frank is a regular handyman, but his real talent lies with writing. He's done some newspaper work of his own." Frank looked at his brother with astonishment because it was rare for James to praise him.

"Is that so?" Deborah said. Her hands primly folded by her waist. "Please tell us about your newspaper experience."

"My brother is being too kind."

"And you're being too modest," James stepped closer. "Frank was editor of his high school paper, which may not sound like much, but it gave him a great foundation and a chance to discover his talents. Then, when he was with the Civilian Conservation Corps he did some hot-shot writing for a newspaper that he created. Wrote some topnotch pieces. He's a natural."

Frank's jaw dropped due to this avalanche of praise. He knew that James's wife was pregnant, but it wasn't until later that he learned his brother was looking to cut him out of the business altogether. In fact, James was thinking of hiring a young black man to take Frank's place, a man who would work for half the wages.

"Perhaps we can do business sometime, young man," Mr. Reed said. "I have great respect for men who worked in the CCC's. They had grit. You might show me a few of those articles you wrote if they have survived." Mr. Reed's attention shifted. "Now, James, I'd like to look at an assortment of new hats. My wife tells me that my fashion is out of date."

"Sure, Mr. Reed. If you'll follow me?" James turned back. "Frank, when you have a chance, set those neckties in the front case, please."

James spoke, not in his usual brusque manner, and Frank understood why. He glanced at Deborah Reed. She had picked up a necktie box and seemed to be studying its white, glossy contours.

Her eyes turned shyly to the handsome, unpolished stranger. "Father is a fine newspaper man but has no fashion sense at all," she said. "Mother usually accompanies him, but she's under the weather so she sent me in her place."

Frank carried three slim necktie boxes to the front counter and let Debbie carry the one she held. That way he could keep talking to her. Over the years his baritone voice mellowed, and he adopted a folksy manner of speaking that people found appealing. "Do you have fashion sense like your mother?"

"Of course."

"A natural talent?"

"Yes, just like writing." She handed him the rectangular box and smiled coyly. It was a perfect smile — perhaps expensively provided — that made Frank a bit self-conscious because of his own imperfect teeth. Deborah asked, "Do you have a talent for writing as your brother claims?"

"I'm not sure why he was gassing on about me. That's not like him."

"That doesn't answer the question."

He set one tie in the case, allowing its bold stripes to show through the glass. "I'm nowhere near as good as your father, but I like everything about a newspaper." Frank's enthusiasm poured out. "By reaching so many people, you have a chance to make a real difference. It's a world in itself. Yes, I have talent, and I know how to work hard and how to learn. If I had the chance, I would succeed." Perhaps vestiges of mercury vapor stayed with him and caused his bold words.

"Yes, I'm sure you would." She handed him the fourth box. "By the way, call me Debbie. I sign my name Deborah, but in conversation it sounds too formal."

They talked for awhile and soon Frank realized that her voice reminded him of Mrs. Saunders', refined and gentle, yet Debbie Reed's voice had a lightness to it, an aspect that Mrs. Saunders lacked, and Debbie's laughter came easily. Perhaps because she was younger. He suspected Miss Reed realized he didn't match her education or her background, but he hoped by the way she was looking at him that she might believe those things don't matter. For him, the more they talked, the more attractive Debbie became, and the more his mind set a plan in place — one that would crack his conscience in two.

After Frank shelved the merchandise, after Mr. Reed purchased two hats, and after Deborah selected accent feathers to slip into the hatbands, he stepped close to her. She pulled car keys from her pocketbook, keys attached to a rabbit's foot. Rabbit's foot keychains were popular in those days, but her face flushed when she saw him assess it.

"Silly, isn't it?"

"I've seen sillier things."

"When I was a girl," she explained, "Father and Mother took me to the Boardwalk in Atlantic City. I was allowed to play one wheel of chance, so I put a penny down and the only time I've ever played such a thing, I won."

"You chose a rabbit's foot for the prize."

"Yes, some of my friends had them, so it wasn't terribly unusual."

"A rabbit's foot is supposed to bring luck. Has it brought you luck?"

"It depends on your definition of luck."

From the corner of his eye he saw Mr. Reed gathering his purchases, so Frank worked fast and stepped even closer, now breathing a mixture of her perfume and a lingering trace of mercury. "Debbie, I hope this isn't too forward, but would you be willing to have dinner with me this Saturday?"

Later, years into their marriage, Deborah told Frank that she knew his intentions all along. Not of a dinner plan only but of a deeper plan. Conscience, promises, and tenets. Frank swept them aside as if they were meal scraps meant for the trash.

"Yes," she answered with a charming smile. "I'd be willing."

And so was he.

September 17

Jack had never taken advantage of anyone. That's why being used by Linda was such a slap in the face.

Outside, a foggy mist steeped the morning, continued, and prevented his father from working the house siding. Jack stood inside the detached garage, which had never housed a vehicle. It had always been a workshop, and now with the rain and dampness, the oversized, dark outbuilding softened his senses. Limited vision, muffled sounds, indistinguishable scents; but touch was certain. He placed his hands upon the workbench top. Its smoothness and distresses felt exactly as they had always felt. Perhaps more distinct now. Perhaps, as he stood in shadows, the bench's surface felt reassuring. Every item in a workshop has its fusion of inaction and action. Every tool at the ready, waiting to perform its appointed function. Gradually, his eyes adjusted to the darkness, his ears discerned each sound, his nose traced origins, and his hands rested on a wooden surface that knew the touch of older hands. A fragment of words floated in his mind: season of mists. It felt familiar yet he couldn't place its origin.

Earlier, the misty fog and light rain had lulled his grandfather to sleep, and when Jack reentered the house, the man was snoring on the family-room sofa. All at once, Jack had a craving for the past. Perhaps it was the soggy weather that caused a remembrance of rainy afternoons and a craving to eat something sweet and warm. In the kitchen he searched through cabinets but found nothing. In the refrigerator he was surprised to see a tube of ready-to-bake chocolate chip cookie dough. His father must have bought it at the A & P and hadn't mention it. No, he and his father hadn't said much of anything since their trip to Randolph's Hardware. He was honest enough to know that since then he hadn't made much of an effort.

Jack held the cookie tube and then sidestepped his normal way of doing things. He read the directions. After preheating the oven, he spooned out cookie chunks and dropped the dough onto a baking tray. While he waited for the oven to warm, he thought of his mother. She loved to bake, and she baked everything from scratch. Her favorite cookie was oatmeal raisin, but she always indulged her son with chocolate chip, his favorite. It was this time of year on a day when summer skies turned autumn gray or when the sun burned off morning mist or when a cold rain glazed the ground that his mother marked the seasons' transition with her first batch of baking.

He pictured her wearing a gingham apron, letting him help when he was young, letting their fingers slip "accidentally" into the batter and licking off sweet lumps. Sometimes she sang a song that her mother used to sing. But most often, especially when mixing that first batch of cookies, she recited a poem. Now, Jack tried to remember the words that his mother half-chanted, but the oven in his grandfather's kitchen chimed to signal it was heated, so he laid the tray of cookies on a steel rack, shut the door, and set the timer.

Without disturbing his grandfather, he stole into the family room and started hunting the bookshelves. Suddenly from behind, his father whispered, "Do I smell cookies baking?"

Jack turned. "Chocolate chip cookies."

"From that tube I bought?"

"Uh huh."

His father nodded. "It's a perfect day for cookies. Believe it or not, when I was showering I thought of baking some."

"Beat you to it."

"Right." Jack's father placed his hands on his hips. "Are you looking for a book?"

"Yeah." Without sounding apologetic, he said, "I was thinking of Mom."

Sheepishly, his father smiled. "Coming down the stairs with that scent in the air, I thought of her, too. But why a book?"

"When Mom baked cookies she usually recited a poem. I'm trying to find it. But I don't know how to find it because I don't know the title."

"Do you remember any of it?"

"It had a ton of imagery. I remember a woman walking through fields and stopping by a cider press."

"I thought so." His father nodded. "It's called 'To Autumn.' It's by Keats. We need an anthology of British poets."

The two men set to searching and soon Jack came across a tan, hardbound book from the Everyman Library. "Hey, look," he said and read the title, "John Keats, the Poems."

"That'll do it."

After checking the index, Jack turned to the right page. While skimming the poem's lines he said, "Yeah, this is it." The oven's timer started beeping. He carried the book to the kitchen and his father followed. Wearing a hefty oven mitt, Jack lifted out the baking tray and set it on a cooling rack.

"They look perfect," his father said.

"Amazing what you can do," Jack tried for irony, "when you follow directions."

His father said nothing but pulled a plate from one cabinet and a spatula from a drawer. He turned each cookie onto the plate. "We'll let them cool a few minutes."

Both men sat at the kitchen table. Jack opened the hardbound book and flipped to the poem. "Hey, how did you know the title?"

"It was your mother's favorite poem," his father explained. "She read it to me once a year midway through September."

"She *read* it to you?"

"Yes." His father's face reddened as he held up his hands in a defensive gesture. "Hey, she insisted on doing it that way. And to tell you the truth, I didn't mind." His father's tone turned reverent. "Your mother would pick the day and we'd go to Winchester Park—the one with all the old trees, the stream, and wetlands—late afternoon, and she'd read the poem out loud. Funny thing is, she held the book but never looked at the pages because she knew the words by heart."

Jack didn't know what to say but pictured the moment. Then he checked the poem. "It's just three stanzas."

"Right."

As if he were a boy attempting to leap over a puddle, Jack readied himself for a challenge and began reading the poem.

"You're going to read it out loud?"

"I want to hear Mom's voice."

His father nodded and Jack started again from the beginning. Sometimes he hit the rhyme too hard and sometimes he stumbled on a phrase, but he pulled through. When he finished reading the first stanza, he looked up. "Your turn."

"Me?"

"Why not?"

George rubbed his chin. "Just keep in mind that poetry isn't my strong suit." He cleared his throat, took a breath, and began. His father read of a winnowing wind lifting soft hair and of gleaners keeping steady while crossing a brook and of apple pulp oozing from a cider-press. His father finished the second stanza and cleared his throat again. "You can see why your mother liked this poem. It's beautiful." He handed the book back.

Jack read the third and last stanza aloud, better this time because he went slowly and calmly and followed the poet's rhythm. He visualized the litany of autumn songs: full-grown lambs bleating, red-breasted robins whistling, hedge crickets singing, and swallows twittering in the skies.

"It's beautiful for sure," he said, "but I don't understand all of it." He put the book down. "What do you think?"

"Whoa, I'm a math guy." His father tried to wave off the question, but Jack kept looking at him, wanting an answer. "Well, I don't understand all of it either." George straightened himself in his chair, and Jack imagined his father might have done the same thing when a

162

student asked him a difficult question. "I think the poem says that autumn moves along and things fade, but something else will follow."

Jack, greater than ever, wanted to tell his father about Linda but didn't want to jostle the moment, so he circled back. "Why do you think Mom liked the poem?"

"Oh," his father started but stopped. "Hey, those cookies aren't going to eat themselves." Jack moved the plate of treats off the counter and placed it on the table. His father asked, "Should I make coffee?"

"I'd rather have milk."

"Milk it is." His father opened a cabinet, pushed aside the Poor Richard's mugs and grabbed two tumbler glasses. Jack filled them both.

"Dunking," Jack announced as they sat back down, "is allowed."

"Like this?" His father dipped a cookie into his glass, paused, raised it, and bit into it.

Jack chuckled and did the same. To him, the blend of flour, sugar, chocolate, and milk tasted almost like the past. "Not bad," he pronounced, "but not as good as Mom's."

"No, but don't forget that she baked everything from scratch."

Jack took another bite and one cookie was gone. "So, tell me, why did she like this poem?"

His father finished his cookie and half shut his eyes as if reaching for a memory that was hiding in a dark chamber. "I remember asking her about the poem, what it meant, and she told me not to look for a definite answer, as if it were a math problem. 'Just enjoy the poem's beauty,' she said. 'Enjoy its beauty.'"

Jack stitched those thoughts with his father's earlier thoughts and felt bolder now. "Maybe the poem just talks about autumn's beauty. Maybe it's not the beginning of things like spring, but autumn still has something. Even though it's later in the year, there's a chance for something good."

"Yes," his father nodded slowly. "And I remember now... she said, 'Every season has its beauty and every beauty has its truth.'"

"I sorta get it. And that definitely sounds like Mom."

"Right." His father smiled. "Your mother had her creative moments. She'd laugh that gentle laugh of hers and call those moments her 'flights of fancy.'"

"Too bad you and I don't have that pilot's license."

"You have it, Jack. An artistic flair. I saw it in your web designs and see it now in the way you handle tools. Me? I'm Mister Black-and-White." His father stared at the table. "But no one was quite like your mother."

Jack nodded and thought that he and his father would never have his mother again, but they still had each other. He wanted to say something meaningful, something that would suspend evanescent motion, but nothing came to him.

His father pointed toward the window. "The mist is burning off."

Jack peered beyond the glass. "Skies are clearing."

"Right."

Silence filled the space between them, but without saying a word Jack believed that that space had diminished a little. He picked another cookie off the plate. His father followed. They chewed the soft, crunchy sweetness just cooling, yet warm enough to make the moment last a breath longer.

Later that afternoon, George arrived at The Day Owl when Prue Richards' shift ended, and she joined him at a table near a large window that opened to the sidewalk. He had a cup of coffee.

"You actually baked cookies from a tube?" With comic exaggeration, Prue rolled her eyes.

"I know, it's heresy, but what do you expect from two clueless men in a kitchen?"

"Well, when you put it that way..."

They chuckled and George said, "It turned out to be a good moment."

"How so?"

"I don't know. Things felt different. Better. I think Jack is taking hold of something. He's more assured, and I sense that he's moving toward something. I don't know what that is, but maybe he does."

"And how are things with your father?"

George felt that Prue absorbed everything he said. She listened and somehow knew his mind more than he knew it, yet this question took him by surprise. "What do you mean?"

"Remember I said you had a great opportunity? Well, you didn't return just to fix up a house."

He never told her of the distance between himself and his father or of his wish to close that distance. She faced him with open eyes and, he was sure, with an open heart.

"My father is very closed-off."

"Most men can be that way."

"Right, but I'd like to know him better."

"Men and melons are hard to know." She smiled but then turned serious. "Why is it important for you to know him?"

"Sometimes I think that if I don't know my father, I can't know myself."

"I'm not sure that's true."

"Maybe." George waved a hand, wanting to move his awkward feeling aside. "And maybe I'm making too much of it."

"Well," her eyes widened and challenged him, "if I asked you to describe him, what would you say?"

George looked down at the table's spiraling wood grains. "He's sure of himself—sure of everything. Whatever the situation, he sees right through it. He knows what to do and how to do it."

"Always?"

"That's just it." George sipped his coffee. "If he wasn't sure, he'd never let on."

Prue looked out the wide window as people passed. Her chin pointed beyond the glass. "All those people walking in separate directions. We could say that some are heading home from work and others are running errands. Couldn't we?"

"Sure."

"But what else do we know about them?" She pointed discreetly. "That young woman is hoping the man she's been dating will ask her to marry. That older woman is thinking of piano lessons she took as a girl and wondering why she stopped playing." Then Prue nodded toward a man in a blue suit. "He's thinking of cheating on his wife with the young secretary his business partner hired recently. Which scenario is true? All of them?"

"I don't know."

"All right. But, more importantly, what does each person think about it? How would each person portray himself?"

"I'm not sure."

"Don't you see," Prue persisted, "that if each person stated his feelings, even under oath, his words would be incomplete? People can never say everything they feel. Our emotions are too complicated. Too contradictory." She leaned toward him intently. "I can tell you what Walt Whitman said: 'I contain multitudes.' Yes, people's testimonies would be untrustworthy."

George gazed out the window and reflected. "Strangers are one thing," he said, "but family is another. Shouldn't we know them?"

Prue laughed gently and eased back in her chair. "Perhaps we know them least because we see so many sides to them. So, let's play Twenty Questions, only I don't have that many." She lightly tapped the table with each question: "Is your father cruel or kind; is he vengeful or forgiving; is he cold or warm, is he talkative or tight-lipped?" Now she tapped the table as if simulating a ticking clock. "All?"

"All."

"See what I mean? We keep the core but add layers. Who is the true Frank Bowman? How did he behave around his close friends? Did he tell jokes? How well did he know their personal situations? How did he interact with people at work? Was he fair or unfair? Did he enjoy or hate gossip? How did he behave with your mother when they were alone? Was he romantic? Did he ever cheat on her?" George dropped his gaze, but Prue finished at eye level, her green eyes probing. "Describe your father."

"I can't."

Now her hands touched his. "We only know the cusp of people. Look for his virtues, not his vices. Maybe you don't know if your father accomplished his goals or failed a few. And you don't know how he reacted to setbacks or successes." Once again she leaned closer, creating a thin space between them. "But you know that he lived a life. He is part of us, and we are a part of him."

His hands enclosed hers. She said, "Perhaps it's enough to know only what we know. Besides, that may not be what you need."

A quiet moment passed. George felt content with the touch of her fingers and the beat of her pulse. Then in an altered, upbeat tone, she said, "Are you still scraping siding?"

George nodded. "But I started painting, too."

"Painting is a better stage than scraping?"

"For me it is."

"Yes," she smiled, "a fertile stage usually follows a fallow one."

"I suppose it's a cycle."

"Hey, that reminds me," her expression turned playful, "have you taken that old bicycle of yours out for a ride?"

"No, but I will."

"Mmm," Prue set her lips, held his hands, and peeked out the window. George's eyes followed her vision.

Beyond the clear, broad glass the September sun descended sooner than it had set yesterday, and the sky, which minutes earlier was an unbroken blue, gradually shifted to a palette of richer shades.

————— ——— ——————

July 1962

"Happy birthday!" Debbie and young George wished in unison. It was Frank's forty-sixth birthday, and the three of them spent it in Colonial Williamsburg, a place Frank had longed to see. They were dining in the heart of the refurbished town inside King's Arm Tavern, a tavern that once served meals to George Washington, Thomas Jefferson, and Patrick Henry. Debbie and George lifted their glasses of apple cider while Frank lifted a mug of beer. The scoured dining area was filled with well-to-do people: women in wool dresses and men in tweed jackets. Although the room was crowded, it felt intimate because of the dim lighting and because on each table a solitary candle burned.

"Did famous men really eat here?" young George asked.

"Yes," Debbie said.

"Well, no," Frank qualified, "this is not an original building. In the 1930s," he explained, "after a great deal of research, people renovated this tavern to resemble the original structure."

George looked deflated.

"But," Debbie said, "it probably looks precisely like the actual tavern. With some imagination on our part, we might hear a person like Peyton Randolph or Patrick Henry talking politics at the next table."

George glanced at the next table while Debbie looked at Frank with an expression that said, Why must you ruin this?

"I know they have Ghost Walks at night," George said with wide eyes as he turned back to his mother. "Do you think spirits really exist?"

"Of course they do," she said, as if explaining a simple math formula. "Certain spirits are allowed to intersect with the living. It may happen briefly, but God has mysterious ways of working. We must believe in something greater than ourselves."

"Do you think spirits were here when the Revolution started?"

"Yes. For all we know, great people are great because of God's invisible intervention." Deborah spoke with firm conviction. "Sometimes people are shepherded whether they know it or not. The Founding Fathers were probably influenced by what they called Divine Providence."

Frank couldn't be quiet any longer. "Actually, most of our Founding Fathers were Deists, people who believe in God but also believe that God keeps out of most people's business."

Now Deborah glared at her husband and adopted a civil yet peremptory tone. "God may intervene whenever He pleases, for as long or as briefly as needed."

Frank let it go and at that moment their salads arrived. The three ate fresh greens, onions, and tomatoes and waited for the main course. His would be a filet mignon, ordered medium-rare. It was an occasion to indulge and enjoy; however, cynicism nagged him. He knew that Debbie and George delighted in Williamsburg, but honestly Frank was disappointed. Anyone would know that a pre-Revolutionary inn would never be this spotless. To him, the whole town was like a Colonial Disneyland. While his wife and son enjoyed watching costumed people perform crafts like silversmithing and coopering, he remembered living in rural Pennsylvania and being poor and watching people make or mend things because they couldn't afford to buy new ones. Families often went without meat and lived on potatoes and bread. The days were long and hard, the nights were cold and dark, and soon enough another day followed. In this reconstructed town everything was well-maintained like the gardens and houses—even the lower-class homes—but the reality of desolate farm life never looked that way. Gray, weathered siding; overreaching rot and vines; threadbare nerves; bone-bare hopes—that was a reality neither Deborah nor George ever knew.

George looked to his mother. "What will we do tomorrow?"

"Well, I've been looking at the events schedule," Debbie said, "and I think we should take a tour of the Capitol Building first."

George's face lit up. Frank saw his son's happiness and felt that he should be happy, too. What else could he possibly want? He was financially successful with an important job. He had used his position at the newspaper to take editorial stands that promoted improving low-income housing districts, creating summer programs for kids, updating the town's hospital, and much more. He had gained respect and a standing in the community. More than that, he believed he had a good marriage and that Deborah loved him.

The waiter cleared the salad dishes and left a small basket of breads and muffins. George took a muffin and smeared it with butter. Debbie demurely selected a roll and bit delicately into it. Her social manners were perfect. Looking at her, Frank suddenly felt the strangest mix of emotions. Does her manner endear or repel me? Then, a confounding question: Am I capable of loving someone completely?

I've worked and built and provided, but wouldn't I have done that for myself? What's missing? *Is* something missing? He reflected on his house and possessions—all that he had accumulated, but asked: To what end? He remembered Mrs. Saunders in her appointed house and the empty circles she followed. Did she and her husband have a good marriage? Was their love tender yet passionate? He looked at Deborah again.

The entrees arrived. George and Debbie had ordered fried chicken. Frank told himself, Yes, George is his mother's son more than he will ever be mine. His features and personality favor hers.

Mother and son bit into their food and looked at each other with identical, satisfied expressions. Frank cut into his steak and saw that it was cooked medium-well. Only a person who enjoys his steak medium-rare would understand the colossal difference. He couldn't have the waiter take it back. The chefs couldn't re-cook it. Once something exceeds its peak, its course cannot be reversed. He didn't want to start over with a new order because that would take time he didn't have. So, there was no point in doing anything.

As the family finished their meal, Debbie rested back in her chair and touched her upper chest. "I cannot eat another bite."

George said, "I might have room for dessert."

"Only a growing boy would." She looked at him with pride. "I believe your meal comes with a choice of ice creams."

"I'm thinking vanilla."

Deborah turned to Frank. "I thought of ordering a small birthday cake ahead of time," she explained, "but I know how you don't like anyone to make a fuss over you."

"That's okay," he said. "The steak was enough." He looked at the barely-eaten cut of meat.

"Happy birthday, darling."

Deborah was sincere, and the glow from the steady but dying candle made her look quite charming. In a few minutes the waiter set a pewter bowl with two scoops of vanilla ice cream before George. As he and his mother ooh'd and ah'd, Frank ruminated on Deborah's wish. Instead of the sweet ice cream mounds, he watched the waning candle flicker.

The mahogany cabinet measured thirty-two inches high, thirty inches wide, and thirteen inches deep. It had two small doors above two smaller drawers. Jack liked the look of it. His grandfather said it was built in the seventeen hundreds, and that he'd bought it at an antique shop because he, too, liked the way it looked. For years his grandfather stored liquor in it but later it held prescription medicine that he administered to Jack's grandmother. After Deborah Bowman died, the piece stood in its same place next to the bedroom window, but too often his grandfather left the window open, forgetting to shut it when a summer storm rolled in. Over time, rain that splashed through the window-screen damaged the top of the cabinet.

After viewing on-line videos, Jack hauled the piece to the workshed and stripped the remaining varnish from the top piece. It was a messy, smelly job brushing on the potent remover and scrapping off the gummy old finish and he learned that next time he'd need more drop cloths, but uncovering the original wood was like unearthing buried treasure so the smell and the scraping were worth it. In the shed Jack found a Sears Craftsmen finishing sander and attached a sheet of 100 grit sandpaper to it. The decades-old machine vibrated his arms, but he commanded the motion. Any remaining particles of the finish, he sanded away and at the same time lifted the stain.

He switched to a 180 grit sandpaper and repeated the process. The intricate and uniformed pattern of the cocoa-shaded wood mesmerized him. Brown sawdust coated his fingers. It felt like flour, and Jack reasoned that it should feel that way because it, too, contained life. The wood had come from a tree that once rooted in the earth. It grew in the manner that people grow. And like people, its essence could pass to others. It lived, and now, in the form of fashioned wood, it may always live. After sanding a final time with a 320 grit, the top was as smooth as polished granite, yet alive, perhaps alive as the apple trees that fringed his grandfather's property.

On a visit to Randolph's Hardware, Patrick Randolph showed Jack a manufacturer's display of a dozen stains and how they would look on oak or pine.

"What you got to realize," the owner said, "is that oak and pine are light woods. People who don't know, think that oak is a dark wood. Now, you want to match a stain on mahogany, which is a dark wood, so that can be tricky if you just go by these samples."

"Yeah, I need help and that's why I'm here." Jack smiled and pulled out his phone. "Take a look at this cabinet and see what you think." He showed Mr. Randolph a picture he'd snapped a half-hour earlier.

"Hey, kid, that's slick. I can't tell you how many people come in and want me to match a stain and give me nothing to go on. But with this, we have a fighting chance."

Jack pointed to the photo. "The finish is dark, but it has red highlights, too."

"I see that." With certainty, Patrick said, "You need a red-mahogany stain. This one." He pulled a small can, papered in yellow, off the shelf.

"Will it be enough?"

"Oh yeah. If you were to refinish the whole piece, this would do it."

In the workshed Jack dipped a clean cloth into the red-mahogany container, and with a deft, sweeping movement, spread the stain into the cabinet's top piece. He loved the way the liquid darkened, embellished, and enlivened the wood. It was like transforming a blank canvas to a watercolor painting. After ten minutes he wiped the wood with a different cloth to soak up any residue, and then he'd let the stain dry completely.

While Jack worked on the cabinet, he thought of his grandfather and how being around the man gave him a new understanding of things. He couldn't put it into words; however, Jack knew that he related better to his grandfather than he related to his father, although that relationship had been better lately. Jack believed, as a man, he could never match either of them, yet during the course of a handful of days, he now believed he might surpass them.

So, how to finish the cabinet? A varnish, a polyurethane, or a Tung oil? What type of brush? Or should he spray the final coats? The cabinet top must match the cabinet bottom. Jack likened the challenge to creating a symmetrical web design, but it was more important than that because every detail must be deliberate. He was through with happenstance.

He decided on a polyurethane spray with a satin finish. Before spraying the cabinet, he worked a practice piece and learned how far away to hold the spray can and how slowly and steadily to move his hand in order to create an even coat. With a little practice, he felt satisfied enough to handle the real job, and the job went well—not perfectly, but he was learning. Between coats, after letting the finish dry, he sanded lightly, and after three coats the top piece matched the rest of the cabinet just fine. He completed the project over a day and a half, and most of the time was spent waiting for either the stain or the finish to dry. He didn't mind.

With the work done, Jack headed to the upstairs bathroom to wash up. There, he let the hot water run in the sink because it took a minute to warm. He imagined how much longer it would take in January and wondered if installing solar panels on the roof and connecting their energy source to the water heater might help the situation. He knew nothing about solar panels or water heaters, but the idea interested him. With water warm, he lathered his hands using his grandfather's only soap: Ivory. The white rectangular cake. He didn't know anyone else who used it, so, in a way, it made the plain soap special.

Grime, sweat, and sawdust flowed off his skin and swirled down the drain, tangible evidence of his labor. After scrubbing his hands, arms, face, and neck, he felt renewed. Jack slapped his stomach once and felt pleased to hitch his belt a notch tighter. Before leaving the bathroom, he grabbed his grandfather's bottle of Old Spice cologne and patted a dash of it across his cheeks. He changed into a clean white T-shirt and a new pair of indigo jeans.

His father had gone to town, having become enchanted with a coffee shop there, and his grandfather napped on the sofa—something the man was doing more often. So, Jack decided to sit on an Adirondack chair on the front porch. Outside, beneath his feet, the eight inch wide plank boards were in good shape, but their gray paint could use a fresh coat. Above him, four inch wide strips of pine comprised the porch's ceiling. A tongue and groove joint kept the pieces tight. During the warmest part of the day, the roof blocked the sun's heat, but now the setting sun slanted horizontally onto the porch. But being midway through September, it was a mature sun so Jack let the tender warmth lap over him.

From its bracket attached to one porch-post, an American flag hung breezeless. Somehow, Jack felt just as breezeless, and so he lazily studied the sky and land. Everything was incredibly quiet. No electronic distractions. No bird songs or animal scutterings or leaves rustling. Keenly aware of the stillness, he suddenly felt uneasy and instinctively reached for his phone but realized he'd left it in the house. That rattled him even more. Anxiously, he gripped the chair's wooden arms and pulled himself up. But then he wondered, Where am I going? Without his father, grandfather, or a car, he had nowhere to go. Instead of troubling him further, the realization actually calmed him because, however strange, it was liberating to know that he didn't need to be anywhere. He could relax. And now with a silent whisper, the wooden chair invited him to remain, so he slid back in the seat. After awhile, he could breathe his own breath.

It was here his grandfather had sat many times and watched the sky alter gradually or swiftly from morning to afternoon or from afternoon to night. Around him now, the land, trees, and fields stood as boundaries but also as bridges. Jack closed his eyes. Yes, there were no sounds— except for nature's softest murmur: the thrum of transience. And yes, he had things to do, but everything could wait. Time would pass at its own pace. It would engender, ripen, and fall.

In a surreal sense, Jack felt completely at ease, as if he were rising out of his flesh, as if he were floating and drifting. And then, although his eyes remained closed, his mother appeared, an arm's length away, wearing her denim jumper, cotton blouse, and cardigan sweater. She was young and healthy. She smiled and said: "If you build onto someone's work, you'll shape a legacy."

Jack shuddered, opened his eyes, and realized he had drifted into a shallow dream. Beyond the porch's roofline, the sapphire sky and cirrus clouds converged to harmony. He pictured the refurbished cabinet within the workshed — although he had plenty to learn, the piece *did* turn out all right and he felt good about that. Then he pictured other sheds on other properties. The vision was like a kaleidoscope shifting into dazzling focus. He told himself that this part of the country has many old sheds, barns, and homes, and those structures hold many old pieces of furniture. A number of owners would want those pieces repaired or restored.

Something was taking shape.

September 18

High up on the aluminum ladder, George smelled steaks cooking and his stomach growled. Earlier in the day, Jack bought fresh charcoal, cleaned the grill, and now had three steaks sizzling at once. George knew Jack had his work cut out for him because George's father wanted his steak cooked medium-rare; he wanted his well-done; and Jack wanted his medium. Turning back to his work, George dipped a paintbrush into a bucket of primer and thought how the imminent passing of his father did not seem possible. Perhaps the feeling was common, that a father who existed from a son's beginning can never be replaced and whose nonexistence can never be imagined. But his father was dying, and he wondered which memories would live.

Around him, the trees and grounds gave shelter as their green foliage steadily altered to remarkable colors. East Coast trees have no match for their brilliant autumn shades. Years ago, he and Claire lamented the lack of fall color in Colorado. Late September in the Rocky Mountains, being all pine and aspen, only aspen leaves turned gold. And during that time of year when summer visitors departed and winter skiers had not yet arrived, he and Claire usually went to a mountain resort for a weekend and rediscovered themselves. Those were the only times they left Jack behind, always with a colleague of

Claire's, someone like her: a responsible, caring teacher with children of her own.

For the weekend, they rented a condominium at a resort, complete with a full kitchen, dining room, family room, bedroom, fireplace, and a balcony enclosed on two sides facing a meadow that stretched west, framed by majestic mountains. They had a top floor unit of a three-story building. From one window they could watch the Blue River whirling and swirling its steady swath. On the building's east side and centered within the cluster of condos was a beautiful indoor pool. Its southern wall of glistening glass rose twenty feet high and caught the sun's westerly movement.

Up on the ladder, George applied white primer to the clapboard siding. He didn't mind the painting now because he was getting better at the work and because it brought the final product closer. While he dipped the brush, painted the boards, and periodically moved the ladder, private moments of his time in the mountains with Claire flashed in his mind.

Morning coffee, opening the sliding glass door to the balcony, allowing cool air in; bacon frying, eggs and toast cooking; quiet words; sunrise tracing the mountains; syncopated breathing; a chill; last sips of coffee.

Then they walked to the indoor pool. George in the water; Claire on a lounge chair reading newspapers or magazines. Swimming. Emerging. Glimmering sunlight through glass. Stepping out of the pool. Water beading on his skin. Sitting beside her in a parallel chair. Hands touching.

Later they roamed alongside the pulsing river, treading the soft soil, following the meandering pathway through the airy forest, breathing the earth, and submerging in the sound of rushing water. After awhile they'd sit in a shady spot along the bank as warm, midday sun splashed through pines, willows, and aspens.

"After all the rain last week, the river is running high."

"Amazing how the stream keeps flowing."

"No end to it."

"And yet, the Earth's water is finite."

"Man can't create water."

"The rain cycle keeps it going."

"Yes."

"If nothing interferes."

"If nothing stops the cycle."

"Everything renews itself."

The September sun was warm enough to dry the water-based primer soon, but George still had a wagon-load of painting ahead of him and letting the paint dry completely was best. Meanwhile, he checked for spots he may have missed. His father was right; repainting the house this way was the best way. In fact, George had decided the whole house could use a fresh coat. After seeing some boards that needed priming, he moved the ladder several feet to his right and climbed up.

Up the condominium's stairs George and Claire climbed until they reached the top floor, and then entered the coolness of the rented unit. Between three and five o'clock in late September is an odd stretch of time because the day seems suspended forever yet passes faster than it should. It calms and startles.

After stripping naked, George and Claire moved to the open, sheltered balcony and draped towels across the outdoor chairs. With backrests angled and frames nearly touching, they lay face up, exposed to the unfettered afternoon. Claire's eyes as blue as a Colorado sky. A late breeze brushing their bodies. The swollen sun pushing against sharp mountain peaks. Perhaps a shadow. Soft breathing. Her pale breasts falling and rising; his skin goose-pebbling. Fingers reaching without and within. First a shiver, then warmth.

He missed those intimate moments, and he missed the security of knowing who he was.

Finished for now, George tapped the paint can's lid in place. The sun was sliding toward its setting point. He glanced at Jack tending the steaks and wet his lips in anticipation. He and Claire always had anticipation for *someday*. They would see all parts of the United States and they would visit Europe and they would gather memories. But none of it happened. And yet, he had memories of the mountain resort. He had known a real and lasting love. He and Claire never traveled far and wide, but what had they truly missed?

The ladder felt a bit lighter today as George rested it on the ground. He stretched his arms above his head as he sometimes did in the school hallway just outside his classroom door during passing period. A teacher across the hall poked fun at him for doing that, but soon she started doing it too. He pictured the woman's sleeveless, supple arms stretching above her head, and her pointed breasts rising. Her wavy brown hair framed her face perfectly. She was shapely and pretty and fifteen years younger. Sometimes she'd smile at him in a leading way—an unmistakable way between a man and woman—and sometimes during unbridled moments, George wondered what might happened if, on a given day, he stopped by her classroom after school or if they met coincidentally in the parking lot. What would happen if he stepped close and lightly brushed against her?

It would be wrong. And he didn't need it.

The paint can's metal handle found the new-formed callouses on George's hand as he carried the bucket back to the shed.

————   ————

August 1984

Physically, Deborah had been limited for several years, the Parkinson's doing its work. It was dreadful for Frank to see how a healthy person could deteriorate slowly and painfully each month. Deborah lost some of her balance and part of her will. He cared for her and did for her and in his way loved her, not without a sense of guilt because he also resented her at times. At this stage of his life, sixty-seven and retired since 1983, he wanted to travel and do frivolous things like hot air ballooning in New Mexico or zip-lining through a rainforest. However, he prepared meals and cleaned house and laundered clothes. All without complaint. But beneath a patient composure he questioned things and wondered "what if's" and knew that nothing would reverse Deborah's condition. Certainly, his wife would grow worse until she would be immobilized completely, and after her body stalled, what would become of her mind?

On Tuesday of every other week, Frank arranged for a woman to stay with Debbie. Her name was Marie, a retired physical therapist, who worked part-time for the Meals-on-Wheels program. Frank paid her to stay, and she was kind to Debbie. This made it easier for him to escape to the only place he wanted to go, Atlantic City, which he realized didn't make any sense because the city offered nothing cultural to see and nothing fulfilling to do. Nothing except casinos. First and fundamentally, he was not a gambling man when the odds were against him. Second, he hated losing money. Third, it was a ninety minute drive each way, and as the saying goes, time is money. Yet it offered an escape. The lights, sounds, and drones of activity distracted and coaxed him to forget the past, the future, and even the present. He lived in the moment of magic wheels spinning within slot machines. He didn't play poker or roulette, only slot machines. For him, the best part of it was to be surrounded by people without interaction. Perhaps a quick exchange now and then, but Frank remained almost exclusively within his own world.

To make the enterprise more practical, he kept a log of each outing, measuring how much he had won or lost and then tallied the afternoon against the others. If he took a conservative approach and walked away from the machines after winning a small pay-out, he discovered that during the course of a month he came out ahead. The thrill of winning money, he admitted, was stimulating and it took discipline to turn away. When it came to money, he possessed discipline, a trait that he believed allowed him to succeed in many areas where other people failed.

To break up the repetitiveness of gambling, Frank walked away from the Siren machines, away from glowing, frantic rooms without clocks, where he ate a buffet lunch and went outside to a boardwalk that connected one casino to another. Along the way, the city had placed benches with curved backs that overlooked the ocean. Few people walked the boards, leaving the temperature-controlled palaces, and fewer sat on the wooden benches, but Frank spent thirty to forty minutes watching the waves, ever constant and ever changing. They broke in a steady rhythm, but suddenly one wave would rise higher than the others and smash against the shore with unquestioned authority, reaching its fingers far and deep, greedily clasping its gritty haul and then turning back to its eternal home. He wondered what provoked that single wave to work against the common pattern. Why did that wave seek something different? Was it forbidden? Or was it simply the melding of current, wind, and shore at that particular moment?

Spellbound, he stared at the ocean, that infinite engine that contained all of the past, present, and future—all of the secrets, joys, and miseries in its sounds and shiftings. While sitting there, he sometimes reflected on what had been and wondered what would be.

Once every fourteen days, always a Tuesday because traffic on the New Jersey Garden State Parkway and the gamblers at casinos were lightest, Frank drove to Atlantic City. Three hours total driving. Three hours at the casinos including forty-five minutes for a lunch halfway through. One particular Tuesday, however, was different because on Monday evening while heading home from the grocery store, the car's oil light came on. This had never happened, so next morning Frank drove to Clark's Garage, a place he had used for years. Indeed, it was one of the oldest gas stations in the state. When Louis Clark opened the place, this part of the country was uncharted territory for gas stations. He kept four overpriced pumps outside while the real business was inside repairing vehicles, and Lou Clark, a top mechanic, did great work. Everyone appreciated him.

As he stood by the front counter, Frank hoped the car would be ready after a quick oil change. With a sad expression, Lou limped up to the shop's counter. The man suffered a hunting accident years ago that left one leg shorter than the other. Louis Clark wore slate-colored pants, a grease-blotted T-shirt, and a slate-colored work shirt, unbuttoned with a white oval patch over his left breast with "Lou" stitched in red thread. It was a short walk to the counter from the lifts, but for Louis it probably felt like a journey.

"Mr. Bowman, you got a doozy of an oil leak," the owner announced with a grimace. "One of the rings is bad."

"How expensive is the repair?"

"The part itself ain't expensive, but it's gonna take time to do the job. Labor is what costs you." With the calculator in his brain, Lou set his price. "Two hundred bucks ought to do it."

"How long will it take?"

"I got about five jobs ahead of you. Thought you only needed oil, so I snuck you in. But I got others ahead of you now. With them, figure it'll be some time this afternoon. Late afternoon."

Frank winced. "Don't worry," Lou said, "I'll give you a bottom price for a top job."

"It's not that. I wanted to go to Atlantic City."

The shop owner looked at things through the eyes of a person used to navigating tough terrain. "You could take a bus," he said and wiped his hands on a grimy rag. "The station is two blocks down, and they run buses to and from Atlantic City every day."

Frank knew a solution when he heard one. After a call home to Deborah and Marie explaining the situation, he was at the station paying for a roundtrip ticket. While boarding the bus, he checked his trousers and found his pocketknife but realized he had left Debbie's lucky rabbit's foot in the car. She'd taken it to Atlantic City the few times they'd gone together; she never enjoyed going but went for his sake. When Deborah stopped going, she gave him the rabbit's foot for luck. For the first time he was without it.

Frank hurried to reach the bus and was the last person to board. For a moment he thought he'd stepped into a Hollywood movie because, like a script, he saw just one open seat—next to an attractive woman reading a paperback book. She looked a few years younger than Frank, and with no other option, he sat beside her and said hello.

"Hello," the woman answered in an amiable but pragmatic way. She returned to her book.

Soon the bus left the station, made its way through cross-streets, down Main Street, and eventually entered the Parkway for an uninterrupted trip. Clandestinely, Frank glanced at the woman's auburn hair streaked with gray and her ruddy complexion, but her skin showed a smoothness that should belong to someone younger. Perhaps she sensed his glances because the woman raised her eyes. "Do you go to Atlantic City often?"

Startled but regaining composure, Frank said, "Yes, but never by bus. I always drive."

She nodded. "I haven't seen you before, and I take the bus down and back every two weeks."

"Do you visit someone?"

"No. It's just an escape." She faced him now and clasped her hands over the closed paperback. "I go to a casino, play the slot machines, have lunch, play some more, and then go home. You?"

He shook his head, amazed that her routine was identical to his. "Believe it or not, I do the same thing." He checked her hand for a wedding ring but found bare fingers. "I took my car to the shop today and had to leave it for a few hours. Decided to take the bus."

"What shop? Clark's?"

"Yes. You know it?"

"Of course I know it. I live in town."

Frank wondered why he had never seen her before, but the thought was absurd. With so many people in Providence, why would he have seen her? Yet if he had seen her, he would certainly remember because, although her features were not striking, they were indelible. She possessed tomboy qualities mixed with feminine traits. To him, for some off-beat reason, she looked like a New Englander.

"Do you work in town?"

"I work part-time at the Veteran's Hospital. I'm a nurse." Her hazel eyes blinked. "How about you?"

"Recently retired. I worked for the *Union Courant*."

"Oh, that sounds interesting. Were you a reporter?"

"Editor."

"Well, that's impressive."

"Worked my way up to it," Frank said but knew how Deborah's father had made everything happen. Besides hiring him to work at the *Star Ledger* years ago, his father-in-law was integral in helping him when an opportunity came along at the *Courant*. Frank had worked hard for Mr. Reed and learned every aspect of the newspaper business. He never asked Reed to cut him slack, and Reed never did. However, when the owners of the *Courant* wanted to sell, everything changed. It was a small, local paper—something Frank could manage and do well with financially. Mr. Reed gave him the down payment to secure a loan. That's how he became editor. Then he and Deborah bought the house in the country on a one acre lot. Things fell into a pattern after that. Thinking of it all, he shifted the subject and motioned toward the woman's book. "How's that going?"

"I've read it before." She showed him the cover.

"Ethan Frome. I know the title, but I've never read it. Good story?"

"Yes, and it's well written. As a matter of fact—and this might interest you—the idea for the story was based on a news article that the author once read."

"News article? Those usually don't end happily. How about the book?"

"No," she laughed lightly. "This story would not fall into the Happy Ending category."

"Then why do you re-read it? Most people want an upbeat ending."

"Because I'm not like most people," she said firmly. "Besides, things that don't end happily give me something to think about. Being a nurse, I see a lot of unhappy endings. You can't get too close to patients; can't let your feelings run away. But with a book, I can let my emotions go and not be…"

She stopped but he finished her sentence. "Hurt."

"Something like that." She fingered the bookmark. Her hands, though small, looked strong. She seemed athletic, and he had always been attracted to athletic women—a trait that Deborah lacked. The woman opened her book and intimated that she wanted to cease their conversation, but he wouldn't let her.

"I know exactly what you mean. Working for a newspaper, you come across all kinds of stories that trip your emotions, but you must keep a distance. You can't make everything personal because it will weigh you down."

She looked up. "Overall, I'm a logical person. Orderly. I go to Atlantic City twice a month, and I go to gamble." She spoke without pretense. "Maybe it's to remind myself that life has its element of risk."

"A sort of calculated risk?"

"Yes. I maintain, well, almost a regimen of eating at a certain time, sleeping eight hours, exercising, going to work, doing weekly chores, or riding to Atlantic City with a book that I can read on the roundtrip ride. I'll even read Shakespeare," she said with pride. "But at the casino with those crazy slot machines, I never know what might happen."

"I understand," he said and then saw the inevitable. He had never thought of it before, nor had he ever wanted it before. He offered a formal handshake. "I'm Frank Bowman."

She accepted his hand and said, "Erica Greenfield." She smiled carefully and locked her eyes into his.

At that moment Frank understood why a random wave rises higher than the others and why it breaks the pattern of conformity, but despite having a talent for words, he could never state the reason clearly.

October 1984

Waves broke on the Atlantic City shore, laving and smoothing the sand. In early October the summer crowds had long disappeared. Even the flow of people at the casinos had tapered. Perhaps the autumn weather was so fine that people wanted to be outdoors savoring the season's colors and scents and the last warm light before winter's darkness.

Unlike other people, Frank and Erica sat on a boardwalk bench that overlooked the ocean. Most people used the wooden walkway to link one casino to another without having to use their cars. They had no interest in staring at the ocean.

It was their third trip to the city, including that first bus ride. Living in a town of a certain size where eyes and gossip were ever-ready, Erica insisted on walking to the bus station as usual. There she met Frank and slipped inside his car, eliminating the chance of someone seeing him drive to her house.

Frank tried to tell himself that he was not doing anything wrong. Just two people sharing a ride and traveling to the same destination. For that matter, Erica chose not to break her reading habit, which kept their driving time mostly silent. All was innocent enough. However, the emotions that stirred within him signaled a clear warning, one he tried to ignore. He was attracted to her. She was attracted to him.

While in the casino, separately, they played slot machines in the morning but were always within view of each other as if losing sight of one would be worse than losing money to the one-armed bandits. Their pattern was to stop for lunch and gamble again in the afternoon, but on this day they decided to sit outside after lunch and neither one seemed anxious to go inside again. Perhaps it was the weather's sharpness; perhaps it was the ocean's pull, its timeless sound and cadence.

From a pushcart vendor Frank had purchased a bag of peanuts, and now he opened the package, cracked apart a shell, took one peanut, and offered the other to Erica. On a wooden bench that looked out to the ocean, they sat close enough for their bodies to touch. She opened her handbag, searched it, and found a tiny, self-sealing plastic bag.

"We can put the empty shells in this."

He was not surprised that she would have a tiny sack available and actually appreciated her odd, swift efficiency. To reach the bag, she first had to remove the paperback she had been reading. It was *Macbeth*. He nodded toward it and said, "I know that one."

"It's one of my favorite Shakespeare plays."

"Did you know it was Lincoln's favorite?"

"No, but I know he liked Shakespeare and the Bible."

"Yes." Frank opened another peanut shell. "It was a strange, terrible irony," he said, drawing on his knowledge of history. "Lincoln had read Shakespeare—could even quote long passages—before arriving in Washington, but he had never seen the plays on stage. That's why he loved going to the theater."

"It was such an undeserved end for him. And he was so unlike Macbeth."

"It's been years since I've read that play, but I remember how the main character feeds on power."

"A lot of double-dealings, blood, and death."

The ocean, with its surging and swishing, along with the pungent smell of sand and salt, both soothed and stimulated, and Frank wanted to deepen their conversation. Perhaps because he and Erica were late middle-age or perhaps because Deborah's physical condition preyed on his thoughts. Without tact, he said, "Do you think about death?"

Erica took a peanut. "In my job I see a lot of it."

"But do you think about how we're approaching it?"

"Yes and no. I think more about adjustments along the way."

"Adjustments?"

"That's what happens. You can't see as well, so you wear glasses. You can't hear as well, so you buy hearing aids. Will you need a walker? Will you have a stroke? Cancer? How will you adjust to the small and large changes?"

Naturally, Frank thought of Deborah, and then he remembered his CCC days and how strong—how nearly invincible—he had been. "It's sad to realize how the body declines."

Erica shrugged. "That's what happens." She pointed to the ocean. "It's as inevitable as those waves reaching the shore."

"Yes, without doubt." He continued to crack open and share peanuts. It intrigued him how Erica sometimes put a shield between herself and what she was saying. He admired her stoicism, yet it troubled him, too. "Do you think there's an afterlife?"

"No. Why should there be?"

"Oh, you know, a system of rewards and punishments."

"With so many religions, beliefs, and value systems in the world? I don't see how it makes sense. Besides," she gathered empty peanut shells and scooped them into the plastic bag, "what would a person do for eternity?"

"You wouldn't be a person anymore."

"Then what's the point in having been a person? If something— call it heaven—removes our humanity, then why did we have humanity in the first place?" She brushed a few seed coats off her skirt.

"We all have desires. Desire for money or power or creativity. What's the point of existence without it? Desire makes us human."

"And achieving those desires makes us happy?"

"Yes, as much as one has the ability to be happy. Once we lose the capacity to be happy or sad or inspired, why would we want to exist?"

"So, we just die. Like a dog, a bird, or a rat?"

"I guess you want something from me that I can't give." She sighed. "In my world of nursing—of science—we are no more than those animals that you mentioned except we have a highly developed brain. A brain that can imagine everything. But we are simply organisms that age, break down, and die. We are subject to whims of chance and nature, as are all living things. We're different only because we have an awareness of the processes at work."

"Nothing more?"

She held up the plastic bag now half full of peanut shells. "If I were to toss these shells into the ocean, and if each shell represented one thousand lives, each shell would be swallowed by the waves in an instant."

They sat in silence for a moment and then he said, "If there is no reward or punishment, why bother with morals? With right or wrong?"

She looked deeply into his eyes, and he sensed she understood that this is where he had been subconsciously going all along. "I believe we determine for ourselves what's right or wrong. Not because a law states it or a religion decrees it." She touched his hand. "We make our own morals."

"No judgments?"

"We are creatures of instinct and impulse." Pointing to the bag he held of remaining peanuts, she said, "If I were to take the rest of those peanuts and scatter them on the sand," her small hand spread wide, "it wouldn't take long to see them devoured by thoughtless scavengers, either for need or want."

Transfixed, they sat on the bench upon the raised boardwalk. Before them, the strip of sand led to the edge of that vast boundary, the immense ocean with its churning waves. Abruptly, after several minutes, as if responding to a command, they stood and left the bench.

They passed through the casino, directly to the parking garage, and into Frank's car.

"Your house?" he asked.

"Yes."

Erica unpacked *Macbeth*, found her bookmark, and prepared to read. Frank started the car and drove off. He held the wheel, aware of a movement's beginning but unaware of the movement's end.

———— ————

April 1922

"James, Franklin, time for prayers!" Josiah Bowman's voice boomed through the house.

Six-year-old Frank dreaded the harsh ritual of evening prayers, and he knew that this night would be worse. He followed James down the steep, narrow stairs until they opened to the parlor with its faded wallpaper of purple-printed flowers. In this part of Pennsylvania, nights on the farm alternated between chilly and cold, so a fire often blazed within the large fieldstone hearth. The parlor was a tight, constricted room with one small window that allowed a meager amount of air and light. At this time of day there was no outside light at all.

Frank's mother sat on the sofa while his father commanded in a wooden armchair and read aloud from the Bible—the large, black leather-bound book he engulfed in his left hand. His voice was deep, mellow, and threatening. He had repeatedly told his sons: "Religion will save your souls" and "Jesus forgives," but the Jesus that Frank knew was life-size, locked in the Vicksboro church, and forever crucified—a statue of an emaciated man nailed to an un-rotting plank of wood. Jesus might forgive, Frank thought, but if he ever did anything wrong, his father would never forgive him. The Bible's words and his father's actions contradicted each other. By reading the Bible, his father tried to fill his sons with faith and wonder. He failed.

While Frank's father read passages, the man paused at the verses with more authority than any priest could summon. Frank's mother sat with her head lowered, knitting steadily, usually a scarf or sweater — something to keep the boys warm later — and when the old man paused in his chant-like reading, she would proclaim, "Amen!" or "Yes!" or "Praise God!" Frank never knew if she listened to the words or if, like a trained parrot, she spoke when a void existed.

His father's right held a rod. An actual branch broken from one of their oak trees, planed down to a keen surface. The Bible in one hand, the rod in the other, and the sons kneeling before their father. Kneeling on that wooden floor. Frank's knees whimpered into numbness every night when he heard the solemnity of his father's voice and the cadences of the King James' verses.

"As the Lord said, 'Simon, Simon, behold, Satan hath denied to have you, that he may sift you as wheat.'"

Being a boy and going to school — especially school in those days when teachers held authoritative sway — and then walking three miles home and then doing chores around the farm, eating supper, and then maybe having an hour to throw a baseball back and forth with a friend, and then doing homework, by the time of evening prayer, Frank was dead tired. Right in the middle of a hectoring verse it was easy to nod off, practically fall asleep even with your feet tucked beneath you. That's when his father used the rod. Whack! On top of his sons' heads or against their shoulders. His father made sure they stayed awake while reading about Jesus's mercy.

One night Frank couldn't keep his back straight while kneeling. That day he and James had had a fight. For doing their chores, the boys received a weekly allowance; Frank earned twenty-five cents and James received thirty. James often taunted him: "We both like money, but you save it and I spend it." Frank learned not to trust his brother because James was cunning and deceitful. He was not above stealing, and a few times he stole Frank's money.

Like his father, Frank was innately handy so to thwart James, he altered one of his dresser drawers. The drawer was five inches deep, but he took it apart and cut grooves one inch above the original grooves so that he could raise up the bottom. He then cut a piece of wood to make a second bottom. This gave the drawer a false compartment in which he could hide his weekly coins. He reassembled the drawer so that it looked untouched, and he was careful, never opening that hidden section when James was in the house because his brother had found other hiding spots and had robbed him before, and Frank did not want that to happen again. But it did.

One day after chores, Frank discovered his money gone, so he confronted James in the barn. It was a gutsy thing to do because his brother was older, bigger, and stronger.

"Go ahead and tell Father," James said. "I'll say that I didn't take it. I'll swear on the Bible, and he'll believe me."

"All right," Frank said. "I *will* tell him." He moved for the barn door. James grabbed a wooden bucket and charged. Frank ran; James threw the bucket. It hit Frank's feet, causing him to trip and fall. His brother pounced on him, rolled him on his back, and sat on his thighs. Frank's arms flailed, but James caught both wrists. Like a bronco bucking its rider, Frank's hips bounced wildly until the older boy lost his grip and balance. In a split second, Frank's right hand cracked James flush on his cheek. Maybe he had thought about doing that before. Maybe in the back of every brother's mind there is an indelible, rivalrous stain. James had never been kind to Frank, lording his physical strength over him. At times he was abusive. Frank sometimes wondered if that was normal for an older brother.

James was stunned but not hurt. More than anything Frank had wounded his pride. James pulled back, stood, and staggered. Frank squirmed free and ran. He was an arm's length from the open barn door when something cold, sharp, and hard stabbed his lower back. Three metal prongs. James had grabbed a pitchfork and, with all his strength, rammed it into Frank's back. The pain was lethal. Frank screamed, stiffened, and fell. Then he fainted.

When he came to, James hunched over him. "Are you all right?"

Frank saw panic in his brother's eyes, and not knowing if he really was all right, nodded yes.

"Don't tell Father. If he finds out, he'll whip us both." James' words sounded as desperate as a prayer.

Frank nodded again. He didn't believe his brother, but he believed in not betraying someone. And he thought that if he did tell, James would get revenge later, and that if he didn't tell, James would owe him something. So, that night kneeling for prayers, he couldn't straighten his back.

"Franklin," the old man instructed, "sit up straight."

As their father continued reading, the boys looked at each other. Fear shimmered in James's face. Because of the wounds in his back and the heat from the fire and the fatigue and the rock-hard floor, Frank swayed and felt himself floating forward. The reading stopped. Then an oak rod cracked his shoulder. An intense explosion shot through him, touching every nerve in his body. It was an appalling agony, one he would never forget. Somehow, Frank straightened his back.

The reading resumed: "And he said unto him, 'Lord, I am ready to go with thee, both into prison, and to death.' And he said, 'I tell thee, Peter, the cock shall not crow this day, before thou shalt thrice deny that thou knowest me.'"

Frank glanced around. His father chanted scripture. His mother knitted furiously as flames writhed in the hearth. James, with whatever conscience he possessed, must have realized he owed his brother something. Frank tasted tears and knew that whatever life he would live, it would never include his father's kind of religion.

George set the half-full paint can on top of the workbench and felt tired after working for hours, but it was a different kind of tired. Not at all unpleasant. Really, it felt good to extend his muscles beyond their normal range. And it wasn't like cutting his lawn. No, with power-drive wheels, the lawnmower practically cut the yard by itself. But now, with his body tired, his mind followed. His thoughts didn't ramble so much. And he felt satisfied in knowing he had done something tangible. Something positive. And a flurry of Prue's words fluttered inside his brain. Perhaps that's what people need: a purpose—something to rise to each morning and to wrap in a pillow each night. It could provide a reason to endure. However, after cleaning brushes with a garden hose and now walking toward the house where Jack was grilling steaks, George knew that this type of work, although worthy, was not his work.

He approached the house. His father sat serenely and, it seemed, stared at something beyond everyone else's vision. His son smiled and gave a quick salute-wave. And as George strode forward, for a moment, he felt nearly weightless, as if existing in a different plane, as if seeing things in a new way, as if on the verge of comprehending something meaningful if only he could set his watery thoughts to solid words. Then Jack said, "The steaks are done." And so, the exact phrasing — the specific sounds that would unlock the secret — escaped him. It was like trying to catch a leaf in a swirling autumn wind.

September 19

The calendar said it was still summer but the days felt like autumn as George sensed a decisive shift in seasons, a movement he couldn't see but knew. He stood on the ground and kept a five foot ladder by his side so that he could rest the paint can on the ladder's bucket holder while he painted. All of the high work was finished. Now, he took wide swaths with a four inch brush and applied the pale yellow paint over the siding. As he painted, golden sunlight warmed him, and his arm's motion reminded him of a similar motion. It happened in the classroom during those intense times when, at the chalkboard, he demonstrated a math formula for the students. Working furiously against the slate, the chalk he held slashed with a staccato pace — sometimes chips flew off like sparks from a fire — sweeping from arm's length to arm's length, he solved an intricate problem. He was completely immersed — aware yet unaware — forming numbers and signs, watching their outlines glow, and aligning all components equally. It was during those moments he was most alive. His true self, George believed, existed most in the classroom.

Now, his arm moved horizontally over the clapboard with a certain rhythm, not a painter's rhythm or his father's rhythm or even his son's rhythm, but his own rhythm. After dipping the brush into the bucket, he spread the fresh paint over the old siding. He thought of Jeff Thomas and how the man seemed more dead than alive. "Only living things change." Jeff was a teacher and a good one. He had more to give. There is always more to do.

Jeff did, however, mention one thing that stayed submerged in George's mind but now swam to the surface: a mentor program. He stopped painting. The thought came to him, stark and clear. Something sparked inside of him, so he set the paintbrush in the shade and hurried inside.

He didn't bother tracking down his cellphone but instead used the wall phone in the kitchen. He knew his former school district's number by heart. After several rings a woman answered. In less than a minute she connected him to the Master Mentors program. The woman in charge of that program knew George, having been an assistant principal at the high school where he taught last. They exchanged warm greetings and small talk, and then he asked questions; she answered, and with each answer, scattered pieces repositioned themselves to deliberate places. Before the call ended, the woman had offered George a job.

After hanging up, George didn't move but believed that a margin of possibilities — possibilities he hadn't felt in months — had suddenly widened, and he realized the mentor position could provide more than a job. It could provide a purpose. Then he thought of Prue. He thought of her often and his feelings toward her surprised him because they had come quickly and deeply, and he realized that by opening one door, another door must close. That's why he hadn't accepted the job straightaway but asked if he could think things over for a few days.

George checked the kitchen clock, but, even without checking, he knew Prue wouldn't be off work for awhile. So, he had to fill the time. He should go back to painting the house, but he didn't want to do that just now. He wanted a new direction — a new movement — something that he could shape and control.

"George," his father said and stepped into the kitchen. He looked thinner, which made his prominent eyes even more pronounced. He carried a wooden hanger that held a shirt and a pair of pants. "I want you to iron this shirt and press these pants. The ironing board is in the study."

For a minute George couldn't believe his ears. Just when he was on the verge of framing something important, his father disrupted things with a mundane, domestic chore. He thought of making a joke about it but didn't find it funny. "Of all the...why on earth do you need those things ironed?"

His father's expression fell with hurt but then he turned his chin up. "I wonder if it's possible for you to do something I ask without making a federal case of it?"

"For the love of... Dad, what's so damned important about that shirt and those pants?"

"Nothing. They're a dime a dozen." Frank laid the garments on the kitchen table and turned to leave. "They're only important to me."

George shook his head, watched his father walk away, and took up the clothes.

In the study he grudgingly opened the ironing board and plugged in the iron. As he waited for the appliance to warm up, he thought maybe his father was losing his senses. After so many years and pathways, it was only natural to falter. And how many roads had the man taken? George knew some but not all of them. Which were worthwhile? Which were mistakes? He couldn't answer, but he knew that his father's final road rendered no options.

Around him, the room nearly burst with shelves of books and one roll-top desk that George had first seen in his father's newspaper office before the period piece found its way to this study. His father seldom used the desk for writing or even for paying bills; he mostly used it for storing papers, supplies, and paraphernalia. His mother, poking fun, used to call her husband a "hidden hoarder" because he squirreled away so many things, and when the roll-top was closed, no one could see all the stuff he'd stashed. George thought it was the perfect desk for his father.

Now, with the iron warm, George lay the pants on the ironing board and separated one leg from the other. The trousers, a charcoal gray, were made of worsted wool—perhaps the finest and nicest pair of pants his father owned. But as George glided the iron back and forth, his thoughts stayed in a negative groove. How could his father be so selfish to ask him to do this? Well, he told himself, the man had always been that way. Often putting himself before anyone else.

He finished pressing the pants and as he draped them over the hanger's wooden dowel, his father walked in carrying two more items.

"Put these with the other things." Frank set a navy blazer and a striped tie on the roll-top desk's flat surface. "You'll just need the one hanger for everything."

Instantly and unnervingly, George now understood his father's intentions.

"This sports coat," Frank said with a touch of pride, "was the first expensive purchase I ever made for myself. Still fits. Even with the weight I've lost lately."

"I remember it." George wanted to sound unruffled. "You know, I have a blazer a lot like it."

"Every man needs a navy blazer."

George spoke softly and felt light-headed. "It's the foundation of a wardrobe."

"Yes. You know, I have a nice Harris tweed sports coat that's seen me through a lot of rough weather, but I thought you or Jack could use it."

"Probably Jack." George swallowed hard. "He's more your size."

"Yes." Frank nodded slowly and then with a lighter tone, said, "I'll bet you've never seen this tie."

George gave the red and navy striped necktie a good look. "No, I haven't."

"This was your mother's first gift to me. Sort of a joke between us. When we met I was working in James's store, hauling some boxes like a pack mule. I must have looked like a buffoon. She and her father stopped in to buy him some hats."

"Mom told me about that first meeting many times."

Frank smiled wistfully. "Long time ago."

"The tie still looks good. Only it's…"

"Too narrow?"

"Right."

"That was the style then."

"Styles change."

"Yes. But some things should never change." His father looked at the desk and then seemed lost for a moment. Absently, he licked his lips and then regained himself. "Well, like I said, everything should fit on one hanger."

"It will."

"Thanks, George. I appreciate it."

Alone in the room, George imagined his father's unspoken plan. The clothes that would bind together, that would hang cloistered in a closet, would wait patiently for an eternal purpose. After being transferred to the Adams Mortuary, his deceased father would be fitted into those clothes by an undertaker and then the embalmed body would be laid inside a coffin.

George pulled the white cotton shirt off the hanger and spread it over the ironing board. There was something different about touching the shirt's fabric now. Something more tangible. He held the iron and began the horizontal, pressing motion and wondered how *he* could be so selfish. His hand started shaking. He stopped ironing. He needed to catch more than his breath.

———————

July 1986

Frank told himself that he hated leaving Deborah when the Parkinson's was really bad, when it gripped her like a pair of pliers. Every morning she tried to read the newspaper. Some mornings were all right, but most were not. She would sit in a stupor, her limbs twitching involuntarily and her eyes staring blankly. When Deborah was like that Frank couldn't reach her. When she felt the tremors coming, she folded the newspaper and set it on the side table next to her chair. It could be any part of the paper except sports, which she never read. Frank gathered the paper and glanced at the page she was reading. He wanted to believe it was a silent way of communicating with her. Perhaps she folded the paper to a headline or article that she wanted to share with him.

On the days when Frank met Erica, he hired Marie. When Marie worked for the Meals-on-Wheels program, she and Deborah formed a friendship, but Marie was tired of driving "all over creation" and said she had enough contacts to hire herself out as a daytime aide and companion to housebound people. Frank paid her to cover the time he needed for Atlantic City and Erica, and each time before leaving he would ask, "Do you have everything you need, Marie?"

One day she answered in a shrewd tone, and Frank knew something—perhaps some form of gossip—had surfaced.

"I have everything *I* need."

He looked inside the refrigerator. "Lunch?"

"I'll make a tuna salad. I bought all the fixings—fresh."

"Sounds good."

"I could make *you* a sandwich. You won't need to spend money on a casino lunch."

"The casinos keep food prices low to stop people from wandering off."

"I guess there's something to be said for not 'wandering off.'"

Frank said nothing but walked to Deborah and grasped her hand. For some reason his touch made her jump. Quickly, he kissed her cheek and turned away.

"You must be having a string of good luck down there," Marie said. He moved to the door, not wanting the conversation, but she continued. "You used to go every two weeks and now it's *every* week. Probably two years now."

"That sounds about right."

"That's some lucky streak."

"Who said it's been lucky?" "I suppose I did."

"You may be right; you may be wrong."

"Right or wrong, I know that streaks *end*."

Frank pulled the door open but looked back. Deborah's eyes, and only her eyes, like those of a wooden doll, swiveled toward him. That image and Marie's words made him shiver. He knew it was wrong. Everything was wrong. But he couldn't stop.

Most of the border land along the two-lane road through the north end of Route 206 remained pristine and rural, but when towns like

Flanders and Chester crowded against the narrow road, clogging traffic, the drive was challenging. Jack wondered how things looked years ago when his parents traveled this same road on their first date. Now, when he reached the junction where Route 206 intersects with Interstate 80, Jack followed the signs guiding him west and soon appreciated the interstate's wide lanes and its greenbelt that separated the eastbound and westbound roads. He relaxed a bit and thought of the earlier conversation with his father.

"Mind if I take the car for awhile?"

His father frowned. "I was thinking of going to town for an hour or so."

"The coffee shop?"

"Right."

"It's just that I've been feeling cooped up lately. I haven't been anywhere since forever."

"You're right." His father's expression changed. "You need to get out, and I've been hogging the car."

Jack reached for the key hanging by the kitchen door. "You don't mind?"

"No." His father opened the door that moved easily now. "Hey, where are you going?"

"Haven't decided." He smiled and felt the sense of freedom that comes with a car and open roads.

Actually, in the back of his mind, Jack had planned to reach the Delaware Water Gap because he thought it would be fun to retrace his parents' first outing from years ago. On a map the destination didn't look far, but the snarling traffic along Route 206 had slowed him down. Still, he wanted to track his parents' steps. But as the Subaru rolled along the interstate, Jack wondered what he would do once he reached the Water Gap. He hadn't thought that part through. The grounds must have a dozen trails, but would he hike one and then try to get back to his grandfather's house in time for dinner? The answer was no, and that made him second-guess the whole idea, and that led him to question why he couldn't feel certain about things and why he was so restless.

After driving twelve miles along I-80, Jack saw an exit sign for two towns: Blairstown and Hope. He thought, No way. How could a town be named Hope? He remembered his grandfather's pointed scenario about finding Happiness. If he took a side trip now he probably would never make it to the Water Gap, but with a laugh he thought, Well, if Hope is just off this highway, I'd better find it.

The exit ramp led to a standard, barebones junction: a right turn for Blairstown, straight ahead for the interstate return, and a left turn for Hope. He turned left and drove along a country road without another car in view, and because of the unbroken foliage and the bending road, he had limited sight. And yet, the land was beautiful. It became even more beautiful when it opened to the small town— a village, really—where modest, colorful houses looked like storybook sketches that stood like wildflowers, acting as if they had grown out of the land. Although the homes were old, they were well-maintained with fresh paint, green lawns, and charming landscapes. He wondered if the town council held an annual contest for the best-looking property where the first place winner would be exempt from his yearly taxes.

He turned right on Water Street, which appeared to be the main avenue. The road paralleled an unhurried river, and soon Jack came to an old stone structure. By the roadway he saw a square wooden sign, painted white with black lettering, hanging from a post. The sign stated that the rustic, fieldstone building in the background began as a water mill in 1859, was abandoned in 1923, was rebuilt ten years ago, and turned into a restaurant, now called Water Mill Tavern. The place looked rugged and proud.

He drove slowly past antique buildings that probably had been repurposed a number of times. On the side of a barn-like building with faded red siding, he read large white lettering that said: Hope & Pray Engine Repairs. He passed a burly man gripping a socket wrench and pulling himself out of a truck's engine compartment. Grease smeared the man's forehead and arms. One building down was a two-story Victorian house with a wraparound, covered porch. The house was painted light blue and all of its gingerbread lattice and railings were white. Inside and out, the place was stuffed with collectables. Above the porch was another sign, this one painted pale yellow with pink letters: Lost But Hopefully Found.

Then he came to a low building with a log cabin look. It had a spacious front window with fancy gilt lettering: The Deli of Hope, and in smaller print: Established 1976. His stomach jumped with hunger. After parking the car smack against the curb, Jack stepped out onto the sidewalk, and because he hadn't driven a car in awhile, he felt stiff, so he pressed his hands to the small of his back, rocked his torso, and then stretched his hands over his head. He tossed his ball-cap onto the carseat and smoothed a borrowed coral-colored T-shirt from his father into a pair of jeans.

Walking to the storefront, he noticed the building's trim work and its four-paneled door were painted a Union blue. A layer of silt coated everything. He wondered how many generations had passed or entered this building, and peering closely, he appreciated the old-fashioned millwork encasing the windows. Beneath his feet, the cement sidewalk with its big black flecks looked like it could have been mixed from the first batch of Portland cement. Grasping a brass, patina-tinged doorknob with anticipation, Jack opened the deli's door.

A conical bell, rigged above the door, jingled. Facing the storefront window were two steel mesh tables and matching chairs, each piece painted flat black. With two steps forward, the savory onslaught of fresh meats, cheeses, and breads assaulted his nose in full force. Walking in farther, he was drawn to the showcase that displayed—along with cold-cut food staples—mounds of egg salad, potato salad, and tuna salad, each throned on large lettuce leaves. Everything looked old-style wholesome. The plank floors, he noticed, were once painted a Confederate gray but now were worn to the bare wood, except for corners and crevices where feet couldn't tread.

From the back room a plump, short woman, whose head barely reached a post office calendar tacked to the wall, hurried out to greet him. She wore a navy-colored housedress that had small, red geometric shapes floating on the cotton fabric. Although Jack figured her to be around fifty years old, the woman wore her dark hair parted in the middle and curled it coquettishly by her chin. "Hello there, young man," she said with a glint in her eye.

"Hello," Jack answered and hesitated because he wasn't sure how this old-time deli worked. No electronic menu board with numbered options glowed above him.

The woman adjusted her white apron that tied at her waist and hung to her ankles. After a pause she asked, "Are you in the mood for a sandwich or a snack?"

"A snack."

"Why, sure. We have all sorts of tasty things," she beamed, "especially for a handsome young fella."

Jack dipped his head with a blushing smile and then a different, stronger voice sounded. "Don't be buffaloed, young man. She says that nonsense to all wayward strangers."

When Jack looked up he saw a tall, lanky, homely man with unkept dark hair and an angular face that could have been shaped by a hatchet. He thought that this man would look better with a beard, but the sparkle in his blue-gray eyes belied his stern expression and suggested a sense of humor beneath a mournful appearance. The man's feet moved like shovels as he took his place behind the counter next to the woman.

"Oh, Amos, can't an old hen flirt with a young rooster?"

"Ah ha," the man said with a grin, "is that what you call it?"

The woman looked lovingly at the man who stood eighteen inches over her. The tails of his forest-green corduroy shirt with two breast pockets disappeared at his trim waist and tucked haphazardly into a pair of coarse trousers. "How else am I going to make a sale this late in the day?"

The man, who looked about ten years older than the woman, laughed. "You have me there." Now his attention turned to Jack. "Are you new in town or passing through?" "Passing through."

"Well," the man nodded gravely, "I suppose that's true for all of us. Anyway, my name is Amos Hanks and this here's my wife, Mary. When we stand side by side like this, you get the long and short of it."

"Pleased to meet you. I'm Jack Bowman." He took a breath and glanced around. "Cool place. How old is this building?"

"County records," said Mary, "show it was built in 1809."

"Wow! Do you know what it was originally?"

"It was the Pierce family home," Mr. Hanks stated with a deadpanned expression. "Franklin Pierce was born here."

"Oh, for goodness' sake," Mary poked her husband's ribs. "Would you stop telling those tall tales?"

The man laughed. "All right, Mother. Actually, it was a blacksmith's shop, but through the years it changed over to a number of things." Suddenly, his expression darkened. "At one point in our lives we hit a rough patch." Amos' eyes shifted quickly toward and then away from his wife. Then his voice changed back to a light-hearted tone. "We needed a new direction in our lives, so we bought this place and have been running it as a deli since the bicentennial."

"Long time. I guess you get a local crowd?"

"Indeed," the man said, "and we always have people humming off the highway because they're curious to see what Hope actually looks like."

Mary's eyes rolled dramatically. Jack smiled and said, "That's my story, too."

"Ah ha. Yes, it's a remarkable road, that I-80." Amos Hanks waved an enormous hand the length of his wide wingspan. "It's the only road that connects the whole country from east to west. New York to California."

"I didn't know that."

"Over the years we've had people from almost every state stop in. From all walks of life. Young and old. Rich and poor. One time or another, it seems, everyone rides Interstate 80."

"Where are you going, young fella?"

"To the Delaware Water Gap."

"Why?"

"Well," he was thrown off by the direct question. "I guess it has something to do with my parents, but actually…actually, I don't know why I'm going there."

Husband and wife exchanged glances and then Amos said, "Where are *you* going?"

Within that man's homely face seemed to dwell a breadth of understanding that Jack associated with his grandfather, but Amos' entire countenance appeared to run deeper, and Jack realized that the man wasn't asking about a highway destination.

Briefly, Jack explained his situation: being down on his luck because of his own foolishness, quitting his job, and now staying with his father and grandfather. He mentioned the tasks he had accomplished around the house and ended by saying, "I'm toying with an idea, with a type of work I might do, but that type doesn't bring in much money. I guess I'm looking for answers."

Mr. Hanks said, "And I imagine that the job you potentially have in mind involves working with your hands."

"Yeah."

"Well, people might look down on what I'm doing, but this job fills a need. And when you think about it, many jobs involve working with your hands. Isn't that what a dentist does?" Amos chuckled but then added soberly, "Society arbitrarily decides status, and arbitrary status decides salaries."

Jack heard the words but shook his head. "I'm just not sure."

Amos Hanks stooped forward and hung his head over the counter. "You know, being on this back road, we often get folks who are lost and they stop here for directions." The tall man spoke in a firm and steady voice. "But they're not really lost because at least they're looking for something. I've always believed that the people who aren't looking for something—those who think they have it all figured out—are the lost ones. The main thing is to live for something beyond yourself. A person who gets all wrapped up in himself makes a mighty small package." Again, Amos waved his huge hand. "Naturally, self-purpose is necessary, but it's best to look for a greater purpose. Something that transcends and connects us to others." He paused and then looked squarely into Jack's eyes. "You'll be all right."

"Hey, you might like living here," Mary said abruptly. "It's quiet and we don't get much traffic. I *hate* traffic."

Her husband's brow knitted, but then an amused expression lit his face. "Certainly, Mary, just when I'm imparting wisdom for the ages, you must interject your opinion on traffic." He winked at Jack. "So, what will it be? Did you say a snack?"

"Yeah. What do you have?"

"Mother makes the best apple-filled doughnuts."

"I've never had an apple-filled doughnut."

"No one else makes them; that's why they're the best."

Mary smiled and gently pushed her husband. "Out of the way, you old coot." As she moved to the opposite end of the showcase, she pointed to a wooden table painted white with an ornate sterling silver tray on top of it. A sheet of butcher paper lay over the tray and two doughnuts rested on the paper. "I make two kinds: plain and sugar sprinkled. And I have one of each left today."

"I'll take the plain one."

"My choice, too," she said and with a square wax-paper sheet, she snatched the doughnut. "Just plain."

"That's why she married me," her husband laughed. "Could a person look more plain?"

"Oh stop," she said. "You have plenty of handsome qualities."

"Like my dance steps?"

Mary giggled and turned to Jack. "Amos and I met at a dance and unfortunately at the time he didn't have much dancing experience."

"But I saw this here pretty gal and had to meet her. So, I walked up to her and said, 'Excuse me, Miss, but I'd like to dance with you in the worst way.'"

"And that's what he did. Danced with me in the *worst* way."

The older couple both laughed and so did Jack.

"Now," she held up the wrapped treat, "do you want this to go or do you want eat it here?"

"Here, if that's okay."

She set the pastry on a plate and handed it to him. "Tables and chairs by the window. Would you like a drink with that? Coffee, tea, soda?"

"Just water, please." He walked to the table and set one chair to face the street. The windows gave a good view of the rural road, the houses, and the storefronts. Across the way he spotted a restaurant that offered a complete turkey dinner for a fair price and then a hardware store that, from its display window, featured a sale on sturdy work clothes. He wondered if he should take a look at them.

Jack bit into the doughnut. "Whoa," he murmured and couldn't imagine anything tasting better. The crust was crisp and flaky. The filling was loaded with luscious apples and swaddled with a gooey, seasoned coating. It was perfect. And the husband and wife running the place? A little odd, but they seemed content. What did his grandfather say about finding a purpose and a talent? And making enough money to live the life you want, not the life others think you should want?

"Here you are," Mary said and placed a tall glass of ice water on the table. Before turning away, as if by habit, she glanced at a framed photograph hanging on the wall that Jack hadn't noticed. It was an eight-by-ten black and white picture of a boy—perhaps ten years old—wearing a jacket and tie and bearing a handsome physical blend of Amos and Mary.

Alone now, Jack looked at the boy and wondered why his picture was there. Then a terrible feeling crept across his skin. Without really knowing, somehow he knew. The boy had been their son and he died not long after the picture was taken.

Jack leaned back in his chair and took a few quiet breaths. He wondered how many chances a person gets in life, and he thought that perhaps Amos was right. People must always search for something. But Jack added more to that thought: whatever that something is, it can't be someone else's goal. Each person must discover his own way.

While finishing the doughnut, Jack felt grateful for the moment. He had found this off-the-path place by himself. He had created a memory for himself. He didn't know if he'd return to this secluded village someday, but he would not drive to the Delaware Water Gap. There was no need.

207

September 20

After emptying one paint can, George lifted another onto the bench inside the workshed. Over the clapboard siding, the creamy yellow paint had gone on smoothly and covered nicely, and using the same color helped, so that if he missed a few spots of the siding, no one would notice. Getting every drop of paint from the bucket wasn't possible, but he came close because ringing in his ears was his father's voice from years ago, instructing him not to waste anything. Although his father was a product of the Great Depression, the advice was timeless.

From the outbuilding's open door, sunlight glossed the paint can's metal lid. It seemed a shame to pry open the lid and stir the paint because the can and its label were spotless, and no matter how careful a person was, paint will drip, streak, and spoil the pristine. George grasped the paint can opener and wedged its curved pry-edge against the lid. Methodically, he worked the bucket's circumference with steady pops until he skated the lid free and away. Then, like a mythology story retold by Edith Hamilton, he saw a silhouette of Prue Richard's visage in the paint. Only a moment. And then it receded.

George knew that people uproot and move all the time. He could name a half dozen people his age who had moved in the last ten years.

His house in Denver, once on the market, would sell quickly. He could buy a small place in New Jersey — of course, taxes would be higher — but he could return to a world that had always been a part of him. Perhaps Prue would become a part of that world, too. He looked back into the open can but only saw paint waiting to be stirred.

Carefully, he dipped the stir-stick into the paint and swirled the mixture. Despite his precaution, rivulets swelled over the rim and ran like thick tears along the paper-coated can. Wiping a rag against the drips would only spread the paint and make things worse, so he let the overflows run their course. Gripping the metal handle, he carried the can toward the house, trying not to jostle the bucket so that spilled paint wouldn't blotch the lawn.

Then George worked purposely, coating his father's house with fresh paint, yet his mind moved with the flow of his brush, back and forth. Yes, it was easier to paint the same color than it was to try something new. He didn't mind the work now but understood that he would never be especially good at it. Did he want to be with Prue? What did *she* want? Autumn is ideal for painting. Temperatures too hot or too cold will thin or thicken the paint, but September days are perfect. Autumn isn't spring, but it's not winter. Jeff Thomas was an educator. His wife was dead. His life was wasting. The sun touched George's shoulders, and when he moved horizontally to follow the siding, half of his body fell into shadow. It was a delicate balance. A mentor program. Prue. The paint's dense texture and pungent smell. Pale yellow lapped the weary boards. Blue sky. Mums and other late flowers bloomed into sensuous colors. A one-acre plot of green grass sprinkled now with fallen leaves like freckles on her fingers. As a mentor, he would work with five to seven new teachers, providing feedback, being a sounding board, offering advice or commiseration. In a way, it would still be teaching. The old helping the new. The new paint melding with the old layers. He could start with the upcoming semester in January, when the Roman god Janus looks in two directions, when students revert to or become entrenched in their habits — good or bad — and days pass slowly for unseasoned teachers as their auspicious hopes fade. He could help. The paint will dry and make the siding look good again. The Day Owl. Eclectic tables and chairs. Prue walking toward him with firm, gentle eyes. Soon the work would be finished. But he knew that this work would never be his work. Needing a break, he rested the brush across the circular top of the paint can.

Wearing a wide-brimmed straw hat, his father ambled alongside the house, his gait unbalanced, and when he reached George, his breath uneven.

After a moment he squinted through the hat's brim. "I have a final request."

"You don't need to be so dramatic." George set his hands to his hips. "Let's hear it."

"I want you and Jack to take care of those apple trees out back."

"You mean cut them down?"

"Hell no. Those trees were here before we moved in. I mean trim them properly." His father's hands moved as if directing the work. "Cut out the dead branches, reshape the trees, and dig out all those choking weeds and vines."

"Dad, why bother? The new owners may not even want those trees."

"What the new owners may or may not want is of no interest to me."

George shook his head and chuckled. Then he scrutinized his father's steady gaze. After so many years, the steel had stayed strong. He knew that rescuing the trees was the right thing to do, but just for the heck of it, he didn't want to give in so easily. "Let me think about it."

After his father walked away, George picked up the paintbrush but set it down again. On such a beautiful day — he wondered how many days like this remained — and with a restless feeling, he didn't want to do another lick of painting because it could wait. But what to do? Where to go? Then it came to him. "*Enough!*" he said. After washing the brush clean, he headed for the workshed.

Although it was dark and dank inside the detached garage, it was also enticing with its persistent odors of lawnmower, grass, gasoline, oil, mineral spirits, lumber, and paint. Overhead, suspended from one plastic-coated hook through the spokes of its rear wheel, hung his old bicycle. When did he ride it last? It had to be a few years into his marriage, after Jack came along and life's must-do's filled his world. He thought of those obligations as a liquid inside a bottle. No matter the shape of the bottle, the must-do's will fill it.

Lifting the bike from the hook, he felt its hefty steel weight; perhaps that's why it ended up in his father's garage. Outside in the sun, he flipped it upside-down to rest on its saddle and handlebars. After checking the bike's connecting points he found them secure. He turned a pedal, worked the shifters, and watched the chain jump along its gears.

A ten speed. That was high-tech back then. The chain and chainrings needed cleaning, but what would work best?

Along with the grease, dried grass and weed fragments had floated in, found, and clung to the sticky surfaces.

May as well use the old standby.

Back in the garage he rummaged and found a can of WD-40. Outside he shook the can, pointed the nozzle at the chain, and sprayed away. Particles and grease dripped off, as if some heat source melted the gunk. After wiping everything down he sprayed again to lubricate the parts.

Too bad the bike stayed unused for so long. What happens to something that lies fallow? Lucky it didn't rust. He made a mental check of his own muscles. Now, about those tires. Because the bike had been suspended off the ground, the tires had no dry rot, but they had lost elasticity and were certainly flat. He snapped the frame-fit pump off the bike, secured its tip onto the rear tire's valve, and started pumping. Ten, fifteen, twenty-five strokes. He wiped sweat from his brow and pinched the tire.

Five more strokes should do it. Are the new pumps more efficient?

After the second tire was full, he inspected everything again. The tires *were* a bit brittle, but they should hold for one ride and everything else looked fine. George maneuvered the bike into the Outback's cargo space and after going inside the house and changing clothes, off he went. Wearing a navy T-shirt, red shorts, and white sneakers he headed for Echo Lake Park. The roadway through the park was mostly flat—a couple of climbs—but he wouldn't have to deal with traffic lights. He hadn't been to the park in decades and almost without realizing it, he felt excited, as if he were embarking on a journey — no, an adventure. Silly? Yes, it was silly, but he liked the feeling.

In no time he was there, pleased to see the place had not changed. In the center of the twenty-four acre park nestled a natural lake. A two-lane road cut through the park, keeping the lake on one side while forests or fields bordered the opposite side, creating a backdrop — for most of the year — of blue and green. Although it was a curving, two-lane road, George felt safe cycling here because a good-sized bike lane flanked both sides of the road, and drivers gave riders a wide berth. Taking it all in, he felt anxious to start, so on top of a hill he pulled the Outback into a paved turn-out with several parking spaces. Years ago he had parked there for the same purpose. His ride would end with a climb but begin with a descent.

With the bicycle upright and ready, he checked the sky and, being on this rise, saw that dark clouds had suddenly massed in the west. He remembered the forecast called for a chance of late afternoon showers, but above him the sun was bright and the sky clear, so he reasoned the storm would not come for at least an hour or it might shift direction and miss him altogether.

George gripped the handlebars wrapped with black tape so worn that it barely offered a cushion for his hands. His left foot touched one pedal and with a push his right leg straddled the saddle and he was rolling. For a few seconds the world shook before he found his balance. Getting the feel of things, he circled the turn-out a couple of times, stretched his arms to the handlebars and his legs to the pedals. It felt new yet familiar. And then he wondered why he hadn't taken a helmet. Well, he told himself, the loop around the park was only ten miles and he'd be careful. After steering to the main roadway, he released the brake levers and let the bike go.

The downward slope and rushing wind made it seem as if he were moving fast, but George knew it was an illusion. The land leveled and his legs pedaled awkwardly at first but soon found a circular rhythm. Echo Lake Park was a good choice because he remembered each straightaway and turn. He clicked the gears and, although he had told himself that he would take it easy, the thrill of riding at a fast speed was too alluring. His heart drummed, his body broke into sweat, his hands gripped the bars, and even the vibration through the old steel frame forced his senses alive. Like an out-of-focus movie, roadway and nature whirled past him. He felt—but couldn't put words to it— that he, nature, and some other force merged into a whole, as if he were rising out of his flesh, floating and drifting. The transcendent feeling was similar to being in the classroom, alive to the moment.

While riding a bicycle, perspective changes. Each swell and dip in the road become tangible. A person's pace is faster than walking, yet each passing object is distinct. The human eye can even isolate individual trees, and now each tree's leaves were transpiring to autumn's ripeness, would pass to winter's expiration, and then reappear with spring's resurgence. Transience and eternity.

One lap along the roadway equalled roughly ten miles, and as George pedaled past the entrance sign for the park's small nature museum, he figured to be six miles into the loop. Not feeling winded, he imagined riding forever. In a Walter Mitty moment, he thought of taking up biking again and pictured himself logging thousands of miles per year. He thought of cycling across Vermont in the fall. Why not bike across the Rockies in the summer? What's to stop me?

As if to answer his question, he heard a pop followed by a hissing sound as air burst from his front tire. In seconds the rim bumped against the pavement. After braking, he pulled to the shoulder and realized that the tires and their tubes were indeed too brittle.

Now what? Why didn't I plan for mishaps?

He turned to the saddle bag and remembered how, inside it, he usually carried a spare tube and patch kit.

What are the odds?

He unzipped the black bag, didn't find a spare tube, but found a patch kit. The little plastic green box.

But what about the glue? Wouldn't it be dry?

He unsnapped the plastic box and inside, miraculously, the glue had *never* been opened and he saw plenty of patches.

"Geez, who would believe it?"

George separated the tube from the tire, pumped up the tube, and felt where air blew out of the puncture. He let the air escape, roughed up the injured spot with the kit's sandpaper, and then opened the tiny tube of glue. After spreading the translucent stuff on the wound he grabbed the tire to search for the culprit, and while running his finger along the inside of the tire, he found the felon with a prick against his skin. A thorn. In one way or another, he told himself, there's always a thorn. After pulling it out, he tossed it far from the road.

After he set the patch in place, George realigned the tube inside the tire and pumped. The patch held. So, he thought, the bike has life to it yet. The repair took close to twenty minutes. He had been sidelined but not stopped, and he felt satisfied about solving the problem. Now he had to calculate the remaining distance, which he quickly figured to be around three miles. He hit that target, but missed seeing that the western sky had turned gray and a fast-moving thunderstorm was rolling toward him. While repositioning the bicycle, he looked up.

"Damn!"

The storm charged head-on; not too far off, skies rumbled. His one option was to keep going because he couldn't turn back, and what was the point in stopping?

Maybe I can make it to the car before the storm hits. I don't have far to go.

The front tire sagged a little as he hopped on the bike, but it would do. He felt strong, pushed the pedals hard, and soon moved at a good pace. With each stroke he cut the distance, but the approaching storm, like a relentless pursuer, stoked a sense of panic.

With his mathematical mind measuring the distance, George figured that now he had two and a half miles to go, but by checking the sky he knew that the storm moved with hellish speed, so he raced along. Then, as if to herald an army, the wind with a trumpet-like blast announced the foe's arrival. It was the fastest moving storm he had ever known, but now the wind actually pushed him along as the sky turned to slate. Two miles to go. His heart thumped; his legs churned. Ahead, a constant climb to the car.

Why didn't I park on level ground?

Halfway along the hill, his lungs couldn't keep up. His breath came in shrieks. Rising off the bicycle seat, as he had done years ago and riding in a standing position, his legs turned to jelly while his heart pumped with pain—a pain so sharp that he thought it might be serious. Then, the storm hit.

The wind that moments ago aided him now goaded him as it whirled like a hurricane and wrapped around him. The sky rumbled, cracked, and opened. Rain pelted the road with drops so big they bounced off the pavement. His clothes quickly became saturated, his pedaling even tougher. And just when he thought he had taken the worst of it, the rain fell harder and faster. It battered his head, back, and arms, as if he was being sprayed with pellets fired from a hundred rifles. He could barely see two feet ahead of the bike, making him feel trapped in a dark night. And now, his thoughts and fears betrayed him, so that the worst part of him emerged.

Why did I ever try this bike ride? I wasn't ready for it. I'm not ready for anything because I've failed at everything. No matter what I try, it won't work. I'm alone and there's nothing ahead of me. Only dwindling days.

Although he tried to pedal, the wind and rain whipped against him until he felt pinned in place like a displayed insect. He could barely breathe and his body ached with stinging pain from head to foot. He wanted to give up. He was tired of pushing and fighting, not only through this storm, but through his life. He wanted the struggle to end.

But then something broke inside of him, deep inside. It was no tangible part of him, but it was the best part of him. A part that belongs to all who push against an immovable wall. George shook himself the way an animal shakes off water. Then he righted himself, hunched his shoulders, and forced his body to propel him forward.

At last the Subaru was in sight. His legs convulsed but somehow his mind tamed his thrashing heart and heaving lungs. George surged ahead. So did the storm. Again, the wind's changing current worked with him, pushed him along, as if through a tight, wet tunnel, because everything around him was a rainy blur. His head tilted up toward the storm as he unleashed a primal wail, as if it were the first time he smelled the air.

Twenty feet from the car, the thunderstorm rushed past him like an apparition on horseback with hair trailing like a woman's, as long as desire and brief as pleasure. After four more pedal strokes, he stopped, dismounted, dropped the bike to the ground, fell to his knees, and then collapsed onto his back.

Minutes passed. Slowly, he swiveled his torso and sat up, arms propped behind him, legs stretched flat, and clothes drenched. His mind performed a physical inventory: legs wobbly but okay, arms fine, and heart calm. Yes, he had wanted to avoid that storm, thinking it the worst. And it *was* bad being stuck out there alone, but he had made it. He was not harmed. And then he laughed. He laughed until his body shook, until he felt every muscle, every tendon, and every ligament. George knew that crying and laughing create the same release, but he sure did miss the laughter. He couldn't remember the last time he felt so giddy. And in this heightened frame of mind, he told himself that he may not have everything aligned, but he was alive. And that was good enough for a start. Then he thought, Why not ride the Rockies?

The tempest passed as quickly as it had come. Gray skies broke to blue. George unlocked the Subaru's hatch and lifted the weighty steel frame into the vehicle. With the bicycle stowed, he opened the driver's door, peeled off his soaked T-shirt, and tossed it onto the passenger's floor mat. The newborn sun felt warm and welcome against his flesh. He removed his sneakers and socks. Looking around, he saw no one, not a car or person in sight. So, he stripped off his drenched shorts and wet underwear and pitched them on top of his T-shirt. Ridiculous? Yes. Risky? Yes. But, he told himself, So what? I've played it safe all my life. It's time for a new play.

He drove back to his father's house as carefree as a child and innocent as a lamb.

"Well, it looks like you went for that bike ride."

George's mouth dropped. "How did you know?"

"You look different," Prue Richards said, "in a good way."

George sat across from her in what had become their usual table. "To tell you the truth, I feel different. In a good way. But how did you know?"

"Haven't you ever heard of woman's intuition?"

"Sure, but...well, never mind." Prue always surprised him in one way or another. It was part of her beauty, of her mystery. But unresolved questions still wriggled in his mind. He let a moment pass and then said, "You never taught full-time?"

"Oh, no. Like I mentioned before, I never had the self-discipline." Prue laughed. "Here's an example: over the years I'd try to master living a healthy lifestyle. Well, just when I managed to stop drinking Coke, I gave up exercising." She laughed again and shook her head. "No, in order to be a good teacher, you have to be regimented. I flit from one thing to another."

"But you held a steady job when you were sketching ads."

"Yes, but I did most of that work from home. I kept my own schedule — or not."

George decided to move his Windsor-back chair parallel to her right shoulder. He mumbled something about the setting sun giving off a glare. She offered to close the window's curtains, but he asked to leave them open. "How about tutoring? You've always liked that."

"Sure. But, there again, I'm not taking on the world. A few students here and there never tied me down."

"I guess what I'm saying is, you've found ways to fill your time."

"Lost time is never found again."

"Maybe that's what I'm feeling: I'm losing time."

"You're putting in time."

"You mean on the house?"

"No. But I think you're trying to lead up to something, so go on."

"Well, I've been thinking of Jeff Thomas."

"The man you met at Randolph's Hardware?"

"Right. I remember how lost he looked, and worse than that, how defeated he was." George took a breath, buying time, wanting to broach the idea brewing inside him and knowing that choosing one direction would eliminate another. He felt as if he were standing on the edge of an ocean with the wet sand shifting beneath his feet, but he stepped forward. "Jeff mentioned something that didn't register at first, but it came back to me."

"The mentoring program?"

"That's right." His eyes widened.

"And you called your district to see if they have one."

"How did you know that?"

She scrunched her shoulders. "Lucky guess. So, what's the scoop?"

"They have one."

"Well, now."

Something tugged at his heart as he gazed at her face. "I talked to the woman in charge of the program, and she offered to hire me for the spring semester. I'll need to earn a specific certificate, which involves taking a few classes." He paused but pushed himself to say, "I'm thinking of doing it."

"I see." Prue glanced toward the wide window as a summer sky, with imperceptible persistence, inched closer to an autumn blue. "So, any obstacles?"

"What do *you* think of the idea?"

"Ah." Her cheeks reddened. "Let's back up a little. Tell me why you want to do this."

Now he glanced at the same window, sensing the passing day. "I want to feel useful." And then words escaped like water through a cracked dam. "Teaching was my work. It filled me. It completed me."

"Yes? So, why the reluctance?"

"Well, shouldn't I leave that life behind and find a new one? That's what everyone does." He waved a hand toward her. "You moved on."

Prue ran fingers through her graying hair, lifting locks and shaking them free. "Maybe I could have stayed longer—learned computer tricks; asked for changes—but I felt it was time. And things fell into place when I wasn't looking. But, my goodness, I never thought I'd be helping my niece or serving coffee. I never dreamed of being part of the business world."

"I know what you mean. I'm not the business type."

"No, you and I are not aggressive people; we're pleasers. We're not takers; we're givers." She leaned toward him in a simple but significant way. "And that's what I'm doing here. Perhaps it's what I should be doing. For now. Providing for people, for my family, and for myself."

"Maybe that's what *I* need to do: provide." He looked to her for more than an answer. "Do you think that my returning, I mean to the teaching world, is the right move?"

"I don't have the power to say."

"Do you think," he began and knew his question implied more than the words, "I should go back?"

"Doing something that makes you feel useful is never going backwards. Besides, there is no going back. Either we stand still and wither or we move forward and change."

It was, all things considered, a fair answer because George realized she would never tell him to stay. Again, he shifted his chair closer. Prue's hands—freckled, tapered, artistic—lay on the table; her soft hair framed her discerning face. He should have checked the tables nearby to see if the moment was safe, but he didn't. Besides, perfect moments never exist. So, he moved closer and kissed her.

When their lips parted she whispered, "I thought you were afraid of heights."

"I am."

"Don't be." She gripped his shirt at his breastbone, pulled him in, and they kissed again.

September 21

After that bike ride and on this gold and blue morning, George felt rejuvenated. He had prepared breakfast for himself, his father, and his son, and after eating the meal, he herded Jack to the workshed to gather tools. Then they made their way to the apple trees on the property's far corner. Between the two of them, they carried a shovel, a pickaxe, a tree pruner, shears, loppers, and a bow saw. They aimed to cut away dead branches and to uproot brambles, weeds, and vines. Yes, they would reclaim the old trees.

Looking over the crisscrossed mess when they reached the three trees, George said, "Geez Louise, this is a bigger job than I'd thought."

"Why don't you cut the dead branches," Jack said after grasping his father's shoulder, "and I'll dig out the weeds and vines?"

George liked how quickly Jack evaluated the situation, and he knew that digging out the undergrowth was the harder work, so he had to appreciate his son's willingness to take it on in order to spare him the struggle.

Many of the trees' lower branches had rotted, which would make for easy cutting, so George left them for last and started on the higher branches. His son worked on the weeds and vines, using a pickaxe and shovel to loosen the soil; then he could tear up the brittle dead and stifling growth. Jack wore a new pair of work gloves and a long-sleeve shirt with a thorn-thick fabric that George recognized. Years ago his father had purchased it from an L.L. Bean catalogue.

The three apple trees stood about thirty feet high. Each had a half bushel or so of scrub fruit. With the proper care the trees could replenish and thrive. Again, George wondered if the new owners would keep the trees, but it didn't matter. He wanted to do this job, so he stepped back and found a good angle to check the first tree's upper branches. After zeroing in on a group of limbs that crisscrossed each other, he extended the tree pruner to its maximum length. His gloved hands gripped the tool's pole as he guided the sickle blade against one limb. With a rocking motion, he swung the cutting edge back and forth, forcing the blade to bite into the branch. After a series of steady strokes, the wood cleaved. He worked the steel teeth for an even cut; the branch conceded and fell to the ground.

For three and a half hours, father and son worked beneath an autumn sun that could deceive them into thinking that warm days would never cease. With all of the dead limbs gone, George examined the trees. He to wanted to create symmetry, to eliminate branches shooting at odd angles. With a new blade in the bow saw, he'd cut through each branch swiftly and cleanly. Feeling his muscles respond to physical labor pleased him, but knowing he could reshape and renew these old trees pleased him more.

Jack liked the way his muscles rippled as he carefully separated the dead from the living, believing that a change from without could cause a change from within. By winnowing the past he could find the future. He saw his father standing back from a tree, gauging it as if the thing grew against a geometric grid. Then his father stepped forward and cut a limb so that the now-balanced tree could best revive. At that moment Jack longed to tell him how he had lost his money. But he couldn't find a starting point. So, he said nothing, and his inability to open himself to his own father upset him more than ever.

George tossed branches into a heap and thought that he and Jack could cut them down further for firewood. Even the dead has a purpose. The dead. As he watched Jack pull the weedy overgrowth, some of it going stubbornly, some of it apparently knowing its time was up and surrendering easily, he remembered his foolish suicide attempt. He wanted to tell his son what had happened in that garage and why it had happened, but instead he silently stacked the cut limbs.

"We could use those pieces for firewood," Jack pointed to the pile of branches. "But we'll need to cut them into shorter lengths."

"You read my mind."

Jack nodded. "The trees look much better."

"Getting there."

"I should have brought trash bags for those weeds and vines." Jack glanced toward the house. "I'll get some and then help with the trimming."

George wiped sweat from his brow. "What do you want for lunch?"

Jack chuckled. "How about we start with an apple?"

"You know, I remember eating apples from these trees years ago." George felt a tinge of nostalgia. "They're Cortland apples. Delicious. Good for eating and good for pies."

"Good enough for me," Jack smiled, walked away, but looked over his shoulder. "I'll make sandwiches."

Inside the house Jack found his grandfather sitting on the living room sofa. The TV wasn't on, but the man stared in its direction. Jack approached. "Grandpa," he said softly, "I'm going to make sandwiches for Dad and me. Do you want anything?"

His grandfather started as if he had been struck by a wooden rod. "What's that?"

"I'm making sandwiches," Jack repeated patiently. "Do you want one?"

"She liked tuna salad sandwiches. I never cared for the taste."

Jack hesitated and then said, "We have turkey and ham. Some Swiss cheese, too. Do you want a sandwich?"

"No. No, there's nothing to be done. It happened, that's all." His grandfather settled into the sofa. He stretched his legs, folded his hands across his chest, and closed his eyes.

Jack made two hearty sandwiches, snatched a big bag of pretzels, and lifted two bottles of beer from the fridge. After grabbing a box of plastic trash liners, he rejoined his father.

November 1996

Erica was diagnosed with pancreatic cancer. Like quicksilver it snaked through her body—its speed and destruction, astounding. Between detection and death, she lived only three months.

"No, there's nothing to be done," she told Frank over the phone.

He visited when he could. She was home and down to her final days as a Hospice worker watched over her. The aide, a plain-looking woman in her mid-thirties, answered the door.

"I'm a friend," Frank said. The house felt unnaturally quiet and smelled like wilted flowers left in a vase.

The aide barely acknowledged him. "This way," she said and led him to Erica's bedroom, a room he knew in a different way so recently. Now, the curtains were drawn because any sunlight bothered her. The deep shadows, plastic vials, tissue boxes, stale scents, and cold blankets gave Frank a coffin chill. Death was lurking. Erica lay on her back, gaunt and fragile, her head on one pillow.

He stood before her. She waited to speak until the aide left, and said, "I'm glad you're here."

"I wanted to be here."

He stepped closer, sat on the edge of the bed, and grasped her hand. For a long time they sat silently as gloom gathered because the November sun was setting fast. Sensing the day's passing, Frank felt anxious. Touching her hand, his hand trembled.

"What's wrong?"

"It's so unfair," he said in a voice not unlike a boy's.

She smiled faintly. "This isn't a ballgame; no rule book or umpires, and if I compare this brief time of illness against all the good health I've had, how can I say this isn't fair?"

"Aren't you bitter or angry?" His emotions unleashed. "Don't you feel cheated?"

"Of course," she said with a weak laugh, "but no one promised me I'd live forever."

"Yes, but it's too soon."

"Probably." Erica strained to push herself upright. His strong arm guided her. "What makes it hard," she said, "is the awareness. Man is the only creature aware of his own passing. So instead of saying, Some cells inside of me went haywire and they're crowding out the good ones and that can happen to any organism, we say, Why me?"

Again the clandestine lovers sat silently for a long while. Darkness steeped the room so that he could barely see her pale face. A frightful thought had been running through his mind, and now he let it out. "I keep wondering if what we did—our relationship—somehow caused all of this."

Sitting upright was too much for her. Erica struggled to reposition the pillow, and Frank fumbled at first but set it right. She sank further down. "No, it happened, that's all. Two people found pleasure or comfort in one another. It lasted years, but it's only a moment." She labored for breath. "It was a gamble and I have no regrets. Do you?"

"No."

"If it's natural, it's good." She shut her eyes and whispered, "It's only death. Rot gives way to..." Erica stopped speaking and sank deeper into the pillow. Her breathing was faint.

"She seems quite tired, sir." A hushed voice sounded by the bedroom door. The aide had moved like a specter. "Perhaps we should let her rest."

Erica's hazel eyes closed.

Frank gathered himself, stood, touched her cheek, and then kissed her lips.

Outside, while starting his car, he knew he would never see her again. Ocean waves broke against his brain. He thought how unjust the situation, and how he would miss her, and how dying alone would be most miserable.

The weedy growth was cut and cleared; the tree branches removed. George and Jack sat with their backs against the base of the same tree, eating and drinking, while their legs spread straight upon the ground that was now clear of dead and tangled roots. A blue, cloudless sky hung over them and the air, as in happens in late September, grew crisper as the day passed its midpoint.

"Dad, I don't know how to put this, but you seem different."

"Oh?"

"In a good way. Yeah, you seem—I don't know—less tense."

"Maybe changing my routine has helped." George paused and then admitted: "I fell into some bad habits after your mother died."

"It was hard to lose her."

"Right."

His son swung his legs around and faced him. "I've thought about this for a long time and maybe I've reached a point where I can say it. I know how much Mom meant to you. Mom and you always had a special thing. But you don't know how much her death hurt *me*." Jack spoke in a level tone. "You took on all the grieving, Dad. You pushed me away and never let me in."

The unemotional words hit George harder than passionate words could match. And what Jack said was not only true, it was wrong on his part. George couldn't avoid seeing the irony. He had treated Jack as *his* father often treated him.

"I didn't realize," he blundered over words. "I'm sorry."

A moment or two passed.

"Well, I could have done more," Jack offered. "I could have said something."

"No. It shouldn't have been on you to say anything. It was on me."

"Maybe we were hurting too much to say anything."

"Maybe you're right."

Silence settled between them in a familiar, complacent way.

Jack sipped his beer and took a bite of his sandwich. "Do you think Mom is with us in some way?"

George didn't know what to believe, but he looked at his son as if seeing him for the first time. No, not quite. It was the first time seeing his son as a man. George didn't know all the answers, but he knew what to say now. "Yes. She will always be a part of us."

Purposely taking extra time, they gradually finished their lunch. And suddenly, George wanted the day—this moment—to last. He wanted his father, his son, and himself to live in suspended time a little longer. He didn't want to confront duties, decisions, or deaths. He wanted to capture this late September moment more permanently than the power of his memory would keep it.

He drained the last drop of his drink and with a contented sigh said, "I can't remember the last time I drank a beer in the afternoon."

"I can," Jack grinned; however, his expression turned serious. "But all that's going to change."

"Oh?"

"I know it's only been a couple of weeks, but I've *found* something, Dad."

"What do you mean?"

"I like working with wood and tools. I like repairing things, and I'm pretty good at it." Jack picked a blade of grass, looked aside, but plowed straight ahead. "There are a lot of old houses around here with furniture in need of repair, and the people who own the furniture need someone to do the job. That could be me."

His son's excitement was genuine and George didn't want to dampen it, but his linear nature couldn't be suppressed. "There's a lot to know about fixing furniture, and about business."

"Don't worry," his son smiled. "I'm learning my limits. First, I'll only take jobs I can handle. I won't go in whole hog. Second, the Internet is full of resources — videos — that show how to do practically anything. Third, I know there's not a lot of money in this, but I'll be okay. And finally, I know you're thinking this isn't what *you* would do and this isn't the way *you* would do it, but people take different roads." Jack nodded a drumbeat. "I can't *be* you, but I *can* do this."

George saw a half dozen flaws and hurdles to the plan, but he locked into Jack's eyes and asked pointblank: "Is this want you really want?"

"Yeah. I can *feel* it," his son said with conviction and kept his father's gaze. "It's as clear as the sky."

From years of teaching, George knew that people, unlike apples, don't ripen at the same time. He wanted to caution Jack, but then he thought that perhaps his son had found a path and the best thing he could do was not block it. "Well, let's see how to make this happen." He stood and clenched his son's shoulder.

"One day," Jack said with a laugh, "I'll have a whole crew working for me."

George smiled. "But for now?"

"For now, let's cut those branches so they'll fit the fireplace."

George braced one end of a stocky branch. His son gripped the bow saw and rhythmically cut a perpendicular line. The saw blade's teeth spit out wood bits as Jack leaned hard into the work. Equally, George set his strength to hold the branch in place. So, two men stood poised in perfect balance: shoulders, arms, chests, hips, and legs. They were as close as any two men could be.

———————

"I lost my mother to emphysema," Prue said, looked to the wide coffee shop window, and then back to George. Beyond the window the September sun slipped behind a row of cirrus clouds.

"That's a miserable way to die."

"Yes. It seems people die too young in a horrible way, or they live too long in a slow decline."

Prue had a way of speaking and listening that most people lack, and George was drawn to her more each time they met, but he knew that nothing stands still, even when waiting. "We leave the world humbled."

"Yes, but humility can make great people twice honorable. Too bad we couldn't go out in a flame of bursting beauty like maple leaves."

He smiled. "Only an English major would say that."

"English minor."

After a pause he said, "Claire died in a car accident. Careless driver. A total injustice. You wonder why it happens."

"At first I asked questions like that, but then I realized that some questions don't have answers. I decided that most things happen without rhyme or reason."

"No justice?"

"Justice isn't perfect." She smiled faintly. "You, former math teacher, want all the columns—everything—to line up. Like a chessboard. You want definite answers." She shook her head. "Well, it's not like that. The longer we live, the more our life becomes like a sonnet that loses its meter."

"You're right. Sometimes nothing makes sense, and we can feel really down."

"Yes, those are days of despair, but over time the intensity passes. It's gradual, so gradual that you can't distinguish the movement. It's like that magical day in late February when you suddenly notice that daylight lasts longer. You know it's still winter, but you feel a little closer to spring." Switching moods, she said, "Well, today was really autumn. You could feel the change."

"Right. Summer is just about done."

"How are things with your father?"

Prue's flow of thought baffled but never lost him. "They're no worse. Maybe better."

"What's changed?"

He thought for a moment. "I have."

She smiled, then stretched her arms and legs parallel to the floor. "Oooh, long day. This old gal has been on her feet too much."

He leaned closer and feeling bolder than before, said, "Have dinner with me tonight?"

She puffed her cheeks and blew out a breath. "I'm pooped. Besides, I have to help Emily with the kids."

"But I thought..."

"Oh, well, let's see..." Prue's eyes widened and she playfully set one finger against her cheek. "Dinner tonight? Why, today is Tuesday, isn't it?"

"Yes."

"Well, that takes care of this Tuesday, but what about the Tuesday one month from now? And two months from now?"

"Well, I..."

"George, I'd love to, but," Prue's playfulness disappeared as her eyes sharpened, "should we start something we can't finish? You must make a decision."

"You mean, after my father dies."

"Yes."

"To stay or to go."

"Yes, and it must be your choice. Somewhere in that numerical mind of yours, only you can solve the equation."

"Ah, hell," George sighed. "Why can't things be…"

"Black and white?" She chuckled. "Oh, I know, let's buy a copy of *Consumer Reports* — the 'All Conflicts' issue. Instead of deciding which refrigerator or car to buy, we can read about having children or remaining childless, being single or getting married, and, of course, staying or leaving."

"Very funny."

She sat back in her seat and gazed sympathetically. Delicate creases by her lips and eyes, to him, made her more attractive. In a softer tone she said, "Sorry. I know this is a big-time decision and you want to do the right thing, which perhaps in your mind is the rational thing, but people are a bundle of memories, thoughts, and feelings. We're not always rational."

"I guess choices are a combination of facts and feelings."

"No," Prue moved closer. "Instead of a choice between two things, it's a choice between two visions: who you are and who you want to be."

"They're not the same?"

"I don't think so. I think choices come down to commitment." Her hands raised. "No, not a commitment to another person. To ourselves. We must commit to the person we want to be, and that usually means reaching beyond ourselves."

George wondered why his life moved in a switchback pattern. Why couldn't his steps follow a straight path or rigid grid? And if he stayed in New Jersey or returned to Colorado, did he have enough time to start over?

"Is it too late for everything?" He felt like giving up again. "We have more of the past in us than we have of the future."

"The past doesn't bind us." Prue edged forward. "And, yes, we're beyond life's midpoint, but our sun hasn't set. Possibilities exist. The restoration isn't complete."

She moved toward him and tilted her face. Her flushed cheeks and warm breath caused a current to cascade through him. They kissed, parted lips, and kissed again.

September 22

No one asked or told him to do it, but Jack opened all of the Subaru's doors and sat sideways behind the steering wheel with a sponge, paper towels, cleanser, and a bucket of hot water. He had already emptied and discarded the plastic ashtray that sat by the gear shifter — the ashtray his grandfather had "borrowed" from an Atlantic City casino because he said they had taken enough of his money to cover the cost — and Jack had vacuumed every inch of the car's interior with a Shop-Vac. He had sprayed, wiped, and cleaned all the windows of smoke and grime. Remaining were the seats and doors, and on them, along with normal dirt and smudges, was a layer of phlegm, as if sprayed through an aerosol can. Because of his grandfather's cigarette habit, over the years the man had sneezed, coughed, and hacked gallons of phlegm. He understood that his grandfather had reached a point where he couldn't clean the car anymore, but the layers of dried mucus *were* disgusting.

Jack thought about the cleaning he had accomplished throughout the house and it wasn't surface cleaning, as he had done while living in Colorado or California, but deep cleaning; the old elbow-grease, as his grandfather called it. He had assailed the kitchen: getting the porcelain sink to gleam, ridding the freezer and pantry of expired products, forcing baked-on stains to disappear from the stovetop and oven, cleaning and polishing cabinets, and reviving the plank floor's luster. He also helped his grandfather strip closets to their minimum and persuaded him, at last, to take his grandmother's clothes go to Goodwill. Then he reduced his grandfather's garments to a wardrobe's size of a man just starting out, which would make the circle complete.

Diligently, Jack had made his way through all the rooms: sorting and sifting; eliminating newspapers, magazines, accumulation, clutter, dirt, and dust. He even helped his grandfather recycle receipts and statements. It appeared that the man kept nearly all paper transactions from large purchases like a washing machine to trivial purchases like a pair of scissors. The two of them spent hours dividing and discarding old receipts. At one point, holding a stack of papers, Jack asked, "Should we buy a shredder for these old bank statements?"

"Let me have those," his grandfather said. With some of his former strength, the man tore the papers in half and tore them again. "Okay," he declared, "now they're shredded."

Jack remembered other repairs he'd made like replacing washers in the handles of the downstairs bathroom fixtures and replacing the entire flush system in the toilet. As his grandfather said, "No repair is difficult once you understand how things work."

Now, inside the Subaru Outback, Jack sprayed the driver's door and scrubbed it with the rough side of a wet sponge. It was the car's final section to clean and where the dried phlegm was worst. His grandfather, each time before sneezing or coughing, must have turned his head to his left. Weeks ago the task would have made his skin crawl, but now Jack faced it head-on and reasoned that body fluids are as natural as stains, rust, and death. Unpleasant but inescapable. A part of living. And an obligation of the living is to give attention to the dying.

June 1997

Erica had been dead for seven months. Meanwhile, Deborah's Parkinson's disease had advanced, and slowly Frank emerged from his torpor, as he dealt with Erica's passing. What, if anything, had he learned? If nothing else, he realized how much Debbie meant to him.

He returned home from a beauty supply store with a pair of scissors for cutting hair. After retiring from his newspaper career at the *Courant*, one of the few things he took home from his office was a roll-top desk that he had purchased years ago at an estate sale. On that desk he opened the new package and slipped the sales receipt in the top right-hand drawer. The scissors were exceptionally sharp and Frank felt a bit intimidated because it had been years since he'd cut anyone's hair, and he had never cut a woman's hair. But he thought that if he botched the cutting it wouldn't matter because no one would see it. Then he thought, Yes, it does matter because Deborah is my wife, and she means more to me than anyone else. I owe it to her.

By this time, Deborah stayed on the first floor of their home. She sat in a wheelchair, and Frank guided her to the half-bath. He folded a towel and set it against the sink's edge and then tenderly tilted her head back so that he could shampoo her hair. Her eyes, so clear and honest, looked at him with a mixture of trust and apprehension. He didn't know what she knew about his affair with Erica. At that moment it was enough for *him* to know and to feel ashamed.

Deborah was a true brunette with naturally straight tresses although now her hair showed more gray than brown. As Frank's fingers gently lathered the shampoo and touched her scalp, he recalled seeing Debbie for the first time in his brother's store. He remembered carrying boxes and looking foolish, her smile, her cultured manners, her concern, and her sincerity. He remembered falling in love with her. Perhaps not the deepest love, but it *was* love and he wanted to restore their relationship. He wanted to be there for her in every way possible. More than anything, he selfishly wanted redemption.

Frank continued massaging in the shampoo. The Parkinson's had affected Deborah's speech so that she didn't talk much but now, and as his fingertips soothed her scalp, she moaned softly. He ran warm water through her hair, rinsed out the soap, cradled her, and raised her upright. After toweling her hair, he set a hair blower on Low to complete the drying.

Standing behind Deborah, he combed her straight hair even straighter. Her delicate strands streamed through the comb's ivory teeth, and with his thumb and forefinger cocked through the scissor's eye rings, Frank snipped a horizontal line along the plastic comb. Each contraction of the scissors made a distinct snipping sound that echoed against the bathroom tiles.

Frank didn't know what came over him. Something about that sound, something about the cutting. Was he cutting more than hair? He thought: Deborah believed in me when no one else did. She took me into a better world. She never asked for anything. She didn't deserve this god-awful disease. She didn't deserve my betrayal.

Then in the magazine rack at the base of the toilet, he noticed a folded newspaper. The obituary section of the *Courant* showed prominently, and the way it was folded allowed him to see the date, a few days after Erica's death. He didn't dare pick up the paper but was damned sure he had spotted the name "Greenfield" and felt just as sure his wife had set it there for him to find.

Deborah could not sit steady. Her limbs, flesh, and soul quivered. Suddenly, Frank's hands shook like an earth tremor, and he set the comb and scissors down. Like a child, he grasped her shoulders and started to cry. His tears fell onto her hair.

"I'm sorry," he whispered again and again. "I'm sorry."

Deborah's left hand reached across her chest and touched his right hand. "I know."

Frank stood before his bathroom mirror, naked from the waist up, and smeared a sharp-scented menthol balm along his left shoulder, biceps, and triceps. The white ointment eventually vanished as he forced it into his flesh but the smell lingered. His left hand repeated the process against his right arm. He whispered something that was neither a word nor a sigh—a sound that lacked meaning to anyone but an older man.

In his bedroom he fumbled with a flannel shirt draped over one of the four bedposts. After three attempts he fished the shirt free. Then he slid it over his head, the shirt's buttons all fastened except for the top two. He gathered his breath and waited. After a moment he fastened the second button from the top.

Down the hall was a small room that Frank had added year ago and used as a study although he seldom did anything there connected to his newspaper job. Mostly, he used the room to sit in a tan leather club chair and read books. For brief time he smoked cigars, which made the room perfect as a hideaway place; however, he always kept the door open. When he retired from his newspaper career, he had two men haul his roll-top desk out of his office and up to this room. Although he used the desk to write checks and pay bills, it became an all-purpose storage bin for receipts, stationery items, and odds-and-ends.

Now, Frank rummaged through one drawer with its hodgepodge items. His weathered hands had a tough time grasping things, but he willed his fingers to obey. One by one, he picked up four arrowheads. They were each about an inch long flint, umber-colored, and as sharp as the day they were created. Forever, a cold, hard feel. After examining their facets and feathered cuts along the edges, he set them back in the drawer. Next, he pulled a pair of cufflinks with amethyst-colored glass in the shape of a jewel. They were remnants from James's clothing store. Then a salt-glazed mug purchased at Williamsburg, Virginia. The mug was engraved with a colonial flag. Then several Mercury dimes and wheat pennies given to him by farmer's wives when he sold newspaper subscriptions and transported himself across unpaved roads on a ramshackle bike. Then a black-and-white, crinkled photograph of young men in khaki clothes sitting around a campfire, their faces in shadows and ancient trees encircling the primitive site. Then a paperback copy of *Macbeth*. Smudged, fragile pages. Then an editorial he'd written decades ago on the importance of civic duty, the newspaper yellowed.

Jack had been standing by the doorway for several minutes, silently watching. Although he couldn't see what his grandfather examined, he could tell that the man was emotionally affected. His grandfather always maintained a guarded front, and now Jack imagined when his grandfather thought no one was watching, his guard dropped. The man's shoulders sank and his body slipped. Even though Jack rapped gently on the door, his grandfather jumped a little. When he turned, Jack saw tears welling in the man's eyes.

"Didn't mean to scare you."

"You didn't. I was just going through some things. Nothing important." His grandfather stood erect now.

Jack nodded slowly. "Nice desk."

"Yes, but it needs a thorough going-over. Some repairs and cleaning."

"How long have you had it?"

"Long time."

"Well, that narrows it down," he said with a laugh.

Jack came up to the desk and started to inspect it. He checked the top, sides, and base. Carefully, he opened and closed each drawer. "Looks like the guide for this drawer has split. Maybe I can repair it or make a new one. What should I do?"

"It might be easier to make a new one. You could use the router, or, you know, if we had a table saw—one of those small, portable ones—that would make the job a lot easier, and it would open new possibilities."

Jack heard his father coming down the hall and then saw him standing by the open door. "What are you two doing?"

"Just checking this old roll-top," Jack said. "It's in pretty good shape."

"I remember, as a kid, seeing that in your newspaper office, Dad. I always liked it."

"Yes, it's a solid piece."

Instead of work clothes, Jack noticed his father was wearing a T-shirt, shorts, and sneakers. "Where are you going?"

"For a bike ride. I'm trying to sneak one in while you guys are slaving away." The three men shared a laugh.

Jack raised an eyebrow good-naturedly. "And then off to a certain coffee shop?"

"Perhaps."

"Well, have fun."

"Indeed," George said, started off, but turned back and looked at his father. "You know, the other thing I remember from your office is that old baseball glove you had in a frame. Do you still have it?"

"Not sure. If I do, it's probably buried somewhere in the basement."

"Right. Okay, gentlemen, don't work too hard."

Jack heard the kitchen door close and then he faced his grandfather. The man looked drained and distracted. He stared at the desk and said, "George and I are getting along better. Have you noticed? Maybe the work has helped. So different. He never realized. He never knew how much I..." The man's eyes watered again. "It was a mistake. I was young, but it was a terrible mistake."

Cautiously, Jack touched his grandfather's shoulder. "Grandpa?"

Frank shivered and looked about him. "Huh?" A moment passed. "Oh. Well, this desk needs some attention."

Relieved, Jack tried to reconnect their conversation. "These old roll-tops must be scarce."

"I imagine if you fix it up, you could sell it and get a good dollar for it."

"Seems a shame to sell it. Don't you have a sentimental attachment?"

"What if I do? Once I'm dead my attachment ends."

"Well, maybe I'm getting attached to it."

"That's your affair."

Jack appraised the desk: "It's solid oak. No veneer or particle board. It's got cut-glass drawer pulls and nice trim touches. It's a quality piece of work."

"Look," his grandfather said, "I wouldn't mind if you took the desk, but where would you put it?"

"Good point." Jack looked away and knew what his grandfather meant: he had no place of his own.

"Sorry."

"No worries. Hey, did Dad tell you about my plan for restoring furniture?"

"Yes, he did."

"I've been thinking." Jack felt a flutter of excitement. "On the outskirts of town some of those old buildings have spaces for lease. I can rent space cheap, haul the tools from the workshed there, and set up a shop. If I rent a one-bedroom apartment, I can make a go of it. What do you think?"

"Yes, that might work." Then his grandfather was distracted again, staring off with his jaw dangling. In half a minute his focus returned. "I need to talk to your father."

"But...he just left."

"Oh, that's right. But I must talk with him."

"What's up, Grandpa?"

"Never mind." He added with a wink. "Just fix the desk. "

"You're a strange old man," Jack said with a smile.

"I'll be even stranger if I don't get a sandwich for lunch."

"I'll get you one."

"No, it gives me something to do. You want one?"

"Later."

"You know, it *is* strange," his grandfather mumbled, looking lost again. "Sometimes I think of the generations: my father, me, my son, and my grandson, and I try to line things up. But it doesn't work." He headed to the kitchen.

———————————

April 1970

It was a good office. Tight, but that was his fault because he hoarded things, and he thought that keeping possessions and secrets had much to do with losing his father at an early age—and then losing their house and property. Those were hard lessons. From those lessons Frank learned that anything could be taken from him at any time.

Happiness and complacency are illusions. So, he clung to a number of things.

His newspaper office was in a corner room on the top floor of a five story building. The original bricks and mortar of the walls had been untouched. Modest-sized windows flanked the corner, and the floor measured twelve feet by fifteen feet. Frank had cluttered the space with filing cabinets and stuffed the shelves with books and papers. On the walls hung memorabilia, framed maps, and sketches of transitional moments in American history along with more recent photographs of prominent people. Some shots included Frank standing next to those famous people. There were personal pictures, too, of his past and of Deborah and George.

From an estate sale years ago, he'd bought a roll-top desk because he wanted to create an image that existed in his mind. He didn't try to duplicate Mr. Saunders' study because he couldn't re-create that setting even in his own house. But where did the image originate? It might have appeared in a movie or play he had seen: a news office, a roll-top desk, a hard-working, hard-boiled, and honest editor. In his mind, as editor of the *Union Courant*, he had served the public well. Always supported school bonds, health care for the poor, road and bridge improvements, and tax breaks for the middle-class; always supported the police and fire departments, the building and maintenance of parks; held the justice system to the highest standards. Frank thought of it as building a legacy, not with his hands as he had done in the Conservation Corps, but a legacy constructed with his brains and the good-old power of the pen.

He remembered how years ago the co-owners of the *Union Courant* had irreconcilable differences and parted ways. With enough capital a person could secure a loan and buy a controlling percentage of the paper's interest. With Mr. Reed's network and money, Frank was that person.

Did he deserve the opportunity? Had he earned it? The larger part of him claimed, Yes. He had slugged through a hardscrabble life, served his country, and learned the newspaper business thoroughly. But the smaller part of his conscience proclaimed him false because he had gained too much through nepotism. But Frank learned to lean on the larger part of his conscience.

Outside, a gorgeous spring day had unfurled, the type that arrives after a dreary winter, but also the type that offers fickle hope because early April weather has a way of abruptly changing. The temperature can shift from warm to cold, the sky from fair to foul. It was close to lunch time now and as Frank sat by his roll-top desk he wondered if he should go to Monroe's, a terrific deli where they piled thinly sliced meat on rye bread or should he go to the Highlands, a Scottish-styled pub that served a delicious shepherd's pie? Frank believed he had reached a point in life at age fifty-four where he should indulge himself. What places did he want to see? What things did he want to buy? He sat smugly in his swivel chair with hands locked around the back of his head, elbows flared out like wings.

Stella, Frank's secretary, knocked and entered. Because she was usually unflustered by anything, her distressed look was jarring.

"There's a young man here to see you."

"Who is it, Stella?"

"He wouldn't give his name." She shut the door behind her but kept her hands against the wood panels. Her eyes were wide. "I told him that he should make an appointment, but he laughed in a nasty way and said he wouldn't need one." She hesitated.

"Go on."

"He said to tell you, 'Carol Appleton.' He said that you would know."

Frank's heart sank to his stomach, but he tried not to show it. "Send him in."

Stella left and Frank took a deep breath. Not wanting to be sitting down for this, he stood up. In walked a young man, tall and lanky. He wore a black leather motorcycle jacket with too many silver zippers, a soiled undershirt, dirty jeans, and scoffed boots. The fellow looked like a personified cliché, but his menacing air declared that nothing was for show. He was hellishly real.

Frank recognized the man's dark, penetrating eyes, the same as his mother's. He tried to control the situation, the way he had controlled so many situations. "Who are you and what do you want?"

The young man didn't flinch. In fact, he sneered. "You know who I am." For a full minute the stranger examined Frank as if scrutinizing a counterfeit bill, and then became diverted by objects on the walls. Sauntering around the office, the haunting figure inspected the photographs. He stopped and tapped the glass that sheltered a black and white framed picture. "You look so young there."

The picture showed Frank stripped to the waist, arms crossed beneath his chest, almost a body-builder's physique, and two other young men who bookended him with a similar pose during their time in the CCC's.

"Had your whole life ahead of you." He turned: black eyes and jet-black hair. "But you didn't have one minute for me."

Frank's knees buckled but he gripped the desk. "You're Carol's son."

He grinned and said, "Your son, too."

The young man sat down across from the roll-top desk and motioned for Frank to do the same. "My name's William Appleton. I live near Speculator, New York." He spoke as if he had memorized a script. "I'm a mechanic. I work on cars but mostly fix motorcycles. I do all right for a thirty-two year old." His eyes flashed around the office. "Of course, not as good as some folks."

Frank swallowed the young man's bitter tone and thought that William Appleton looked like a time-battered man rather someone in the prime of life. "And your mother?"

"She died three months ago. A drug overdose."

"I'm sorry."

"Are you?" His head tilted.

"Yes." Frank sat rigidly. "I never meant her any harm."

"What *did* you mean?" William drew a deep breath. "Yeah, she wrote down the whole story. Don't know when, but she shoved the papers in her night table drawer." The young man leaned forward but not with kindness. "Never told me anything before, even when I asked. But I guess she had a bad feeling about where she was headed. Yeah, she wrote how you disappeared. Her being eight months pregnant and *you*, like a shit-heeled coward, just bolted."

"I was young," Frank's hands opened in appeal. "I made a mistake."

William scowled. "Well, now you can rectify your *mistake*." He stopped with a simple-minded look of delight. "Hey, I like the word 'rectify.' It goes good with 'mistake.'"

Frank slapped his desk. "What do you want?"

"Whoa there, boss man. Take it down a notch. If you don't know what I want, you ain't much of a newspaper man. Of course, I've done some checking. You've had this job a long time. Rich in-laws. Yeah, I got all the facts." William nodded as if peering into a different dimension. "You have a wife and another son who live in a nice house not far from here. I have the address with me somewhere." He started a mock search of his pockets.

"Don't bother." Frank's anger rose. "How much do you want?"

"Five thousand dollars."

Blood rushed to Frank's forehead. "That's a lot of money. What makes you think I'll pay it?"

The lanky scarecrow of a man leaned even closer, and Frank clearly saw Carol's face. "You've built up a nice life for yourself and a good reputation, but I can destroy both of them things just like that." William snapped his fingers. "For starters, I'll ride my motorcycle right up your front lawn and say hello to Debbie. Then I'll pay a visit to the *Star Ledger* and see if they'd like to print a story. A touching piece about a pregnant woman and a gutless man. Ought to sell real good, and we'll see what happens to that spotless reputation of yours." He settled back in his chair and smiled. Frank recoiled after getting a good look at the man's yellow teeth and gaps where teeth should have been.

Like mad bees, thoughts swarmed in Frank's brain: I could come clean and tell Debbie; she might understand. But there's George to consider. And if I did tell them, what's to stop this devil from going to the *Star Ledger* anyway?

Frank opened the roll-top desk's thin middle drawer, pushed aside his pocketknife, and pulled out the newspaper's ledger and checkbook. In less than a minute he wrote a check for five thousand dollars and handed it over.

William scanned the check and nodded. "Thanks, *Dad*." Frank didn't have the strength to stand again. "You should be grateful that I'm a thoughtful guy," William said and grinned. "I came here instead of your home because I figured you'd use the newspaper's funds." He winked. "You can cover your tracks that way." William stood and walked to a window. "Nice view." He cocked his head to see the western sky. "Hey, clouds are rolling in. Might rain. Might snow. Never can tell with April. It's a fucked-up month."

"You have what you came for. Now you should leave."

"You're right." William reached the door and gripped its handle. "I won't be back. Or maybe I will."

"What?"

He grinned that ghastly grin again. "Hey, we're just getting to know each other. I might stop by again or I might not. You'll never know." He opened the door. "But if I do come around, tell Stella not to ask any more questions. I'd hate to have to answer them."

It was a punch to the gut and Frank took it. Afterwards, he sat at his desk for a long time, lifeless. At some point, for no reason, a line from a novel came to him. He couldn't remember the novel's title, but the words were: There are some debts that cannot be paid like money debts.

He nodded slowly and knew he would go on paying this debt for this the rest of his life. He glanced up and saw within a framed case his Babe Ruth glove with its proud marks of wear. It looked tattered and terribly distant.

Jack didn't know what to make of his grandfather, and it frightened him to see this once stalwart man so feeble. There was no way to restore him. He turned to the desk and assessed the years of bumps and bruises the sturdy oak piece had sustained. His right hand grazed the desk's top. "You've seen better days, my friend." While checking the faded finish and worn spots, he thought of refinishing the whole desk; it would be a job and a half but he could take it on. And yet, something about this tough old roll-top made him think it would be better off left as it is. Just fix the drawers and give the rest a good cleaning.

Jack needed to see a functioning drawer work to use it as a model, so he extended one drawer to its full opening; it stopped in place perfectly. He reached for the drawer's backside and felt a metal catch. After two attempts, he unhooked the lock. When the drawer came out completely, he emptied its contents onto the desk's flat surface and found two small spiral notepads, old postage stamps, brittle rubber bands, and paperclips.

He flipped the drawer over to examine the runner, and caught in the crevice between the back and bottom pieces was a weathered slip of paper. Carefully, like a pair of needle-nose pliers, he positioned his thumb and index finger, clasped the fragile paper, and pulled it free. On this side, the torn sheet was blank, but the opposite side revealed an elaborate-looking bill of sale. The top left part of the sheet featured a detailed sketch of a roll-top desk exactly like his grandfather's. To the right was someone's cursive handwriting: September 25, and then a typeset: 189___. In the blank was a handwritten numeral, but a watermark made it illegible. In the center of the sheet, a bold and ornate font in faded red ink noted: *A. Cutler and Son*. Jack figured this was the original sales receipt.

Setting the drawer aside, he hurried to his laptop and found that Cutler and Son desks were once the gold-standard for roll-tops. Jack discovered that the company started in the 1820s with Abner Cutler who later brought his son into the business. The enterprise was bought out in 1930. But the company had flourished for more than one hundred years. Remarkable. After searching farther, Jack found that a number of Cutler desks survived and were still in demand. The work of father and son far outlasted their lives.

He turned to the desk again and soon was lost in one of those moments when a person does something but unconsciously thinks of something else, so while he scrutinized the drawer, other images crystalized magically and completely. They appeared in the way a new melody appears to a songwriter without trying to create it. Jack pictured a computer-generated logo of a roll-top desk centered on a page. The desk would be sepia-brown. Yes, other and older types of furniture existed, but just about everybody would recognize a roll-top, and it seemed to him that that type of desk symbolized not only the past but also craftsmanship. Around the desk logo, in richer colors, he would include the name of his business and phone number. He would design and print a flyer and post it in the local grocery and hardware stores so that he could start his business on a small scale.

He had been christened Jonathan. When he was young, his mother called him Johnny; his father called him John. Beginning in high school he insisted on being called Jack. Now, he decided that on the business flyer his name, in a bold and ornate font, would read: Jonathan Bowman.

September 23

On this chilly night, George could have closed the windows, but there was more life in having them open. His father and son didn't mind. Because the Boston Red Sox were playing the New York Yankees in a tight division race, it made a good night for baseball. Jack had suggested pizza, and Frank insisted on beer. The small, square television belonged to a previous age, but the picture faithfully reflected baseball's timeless quality. As with all sports, baseball divides into wins and losses, but ironically baseball's norm is failure. Even failing seven out of ten times at bat makes for greatness. Part of that thinking transfers beyond baseball. Because every man fails in life, people esteem the men who fail less often.

The score was tied at two runs apiece going into the bottom of the sixth inning. Boston had made a late-season surge, winning nine of their last ten while the Yankees dropped seven of their last nine. Their once comfortable lead dwindled to a single game.

Jack said, "Good thing they're playing in New York. Boston crowds are toxic."

"Fans have become despicable in both towns," Frank said. "Years ago, people would cheer or boo, but they weren't obnoxious. Now, anything goes."

"Maybe," George offered, "they don't know better."

"That's the problem," his father summed it up.

Jack said, "You know, it would be cool to visit Boston."

"I've been to Boston once a long time ago," Frank stated. "It's a great city."

George said, "You probably couldn't throw a stone without hitting something historic."

"Have you been there?"

"No. Claire and I talked about visiting but never did."

"I'd like to go," Jack said and looked at his father.

George looked at his father. Frank said, "Don't look at me."

George turned to Jack. "It would make an excellent road trip."

Jack smiled as the game shifted to the seventh inning.

The mood in the house was peaceful—so different from that first night's spaghetti dinner. Now, the three men sipped beer and ate pizza while the baseball game moved slowly, as if it were a story that any person could tell by heart because he had heard it so often. George knew that the game they were watching didn't matter; it was the game itself. He thought that baseball links each person to his past, to a time when he was young and watched grown men play a boy's game and believed in his own unlimited future. And, sadly, perhaps it is the link that determines exactly when illusions end.

George remembered his father telling him that growing up in rural Pennsylvania, he, his brother, and the neighboring boys played baseball all summer long with salvaged bats, taped balls, and ragged mitts. His father, however, had been enterprising from an early age and decided to sell newspaper subscriptions in order to earn his own glove—a brand new glove with the name "Babe Ruth" emblazoned on it.

Frank had so much going against him. First, it was a poor county filled with hard-working immigrants who scrimped pennies. Second, most people lived on farms spread across miles, not like today's suburbia with homes stacked like dominoes. So, Frank traveled the dirt roads as far as his battered bicycle took him, which was as far as his legs could pedal. Each day he set out, taking in parts of the county that were once simply names on gas station maps but then became real. He enjoyed meeting other people and seeing other places because the world no longer confined itself to a shared room with his brother inside a rented house. Being taller and stronger than most boys his age helped Frank to project credence in what he was selling and in himself. And perhaps subconsciously he understood that most people really don't know what they want but will follow someone who does know.

After months of pedaling that bike and selling subscriptions and after mailing in receipts and coins, the glove arrived. It proved quite an event beginning with a special package delivered through the post, which usually brought only bills. It even impressed his brother James. In all, the glove, so perfect, seemed too good for use. Its tanned leather was stained a golden color and its stitching was flawless. Other boys gazed at it with wonder, more amazing than a newborn calf or baby. They had seen those things before. But this was an unblemished baseball glove branded with an autograph of the legendary Babe. Miraculous. And Frank had earned it penny by penny and mile by mile. In the process, the world became less mysterious. It had, because of baseball, become more certain.

How could he explain the significance of that glove to George or Jack? Something they would view as common, for him, meant much more. On the one hand, it was an end of innocence. He would know forever the importance of money, and he would know how money was the only certain means to success. On the other hand, the glove represented baseball. And for him, baseball was ecstasy. It was a game that boys played without training or coaches. No one tied it to scholarships or discipline or state titles. It wasn't tied to school or to home; it was freedom. The boys played from early spring through early autumn. They played after chores until the ball was a shadowy sphere against a darkening sky. They played it with their hearts and souls because the joy of it was the only joy they knew.

Frank longed to share the feeling with George but realized that some things cannot be passed to another. And he wanted to share his secrets with George but told himself that his son, who knew a sheltered world, would not understand. George never faced poverty nor — as far as Frank knew — did George ever fight his way through a dark night with both fists. Of course, Frank felt ashamed of some things he had done, and those things would be difficult to lay bare. So, why reveal them? He believed his son had a certain way of looking at the world, a calculated safeness to every action. He believed George had never sacrificed his principles. But *he* had. And yet, he told himself, if some kind of celestial scale weighed his deeds, wouldn't the good exceed the bad?

Between innings Frank said, "They get a good crowd every game, but I've read that baseball isn't as popular as it was."

"As a kid, I remember seeing men working outside their houses and having a portable radio tuned to a baseball game," George said. "Go to a hardware store or to a gas station garage during the summer and the game blared through radios."

"Football is big now," Jack said. "A lot of heavy gambling on that sport."

Frank said, "You can bet on baseball games."

"Baseball's too slow."

George said, "A baseball game and a football game take about three hours."

"Maybe it's the pace of the game?" Frank wondered.

"Maybe it's football's violence that attracts people?"

Because of his father's interest in baseball, George had been to the old Yankee Stadium many times. Seeing the new stadium on TV made him long for the past. In some ways the old ballpark resembled a castle with its green-blue facade that trimmed the third deck. One might expect knights on horseback to charge out of the field gates. No other place matched its grandeur. Other teams played in fields or parks, but this was a *stadium*, closer to the glory of Rome's Coliseum, and, of course, the legends who lingered within the confines, began with the monuments of Miller Huggins, Lou Gehrig, and Babe Ruth in the farthest reaches of centerfield— so far that no baseball struck by a mortal could reach them without first touching the earth. And new legends stepped from the dugout—or perhaps descended from the heavens—stood by home plate, smacked a ball into the seats, and trotted the bases while cheers embraced them.

As a boy, George idolized Mickey Mantle. One of his lasting memories of baseball came not from playing the game but from watching it with his father. It was the summer that Mantle and Roger Maris chased Babe Ruth's home run record. It was that summer in the room where they all sat now that George had learned the game by watching the Yankees and by asking his father questions. Frank would sprawl on the sofa, and George was small enough so that he could lie next to his father and rest his head on his dad's arm. A warm closeness existed between them. George never ran out of questions about the game, and his father never ran out of patience for answering those questions.

In August, Frank bought tickets to a game. He and George had great seats several rows behind the Yankees' dugout. His father always managed to work in some games during the summer, but they never had seats like these before where they were close enough to touch the players as they loomed onto the field like gods transformed into flesh.

Both pitchers were on target that day, but Whitey Ford had missed with one pitch and Cleveland's Rocky Colavito launched it into the left field seats. Throughout the game George kept an eye on Mickey Mantle. He watched the Yankee star jog to centerfield at the start of each inning and then trot back again, all with that odd, hobbling gait he had acquired after a series of injuries and surgeries.

By the bottom of the ninth Cleveland still led one to nothing. Mickey had been to bat twice and both times, batting left-handed, had driven the ball to the warning track in right field. Each fly ball turned from a teasing possibility into an easy out. The Yankees opened the bottom of the last frame with Bobby Richardson knocking a single up the middle. On a hit-and-run Tony Kubek grounded out to the second basemen, but Richardson reached second. The next batter, Joe Pepitone, managed a ten pitch at-bat but struck out. When Mantle stepped into the batter's box, the crowd knew the moment was at hand. He batted from the right side now, and everyone knew his average was better as a right-handed hitter. A home run would be great, but all the Yankees needed was a single to drive Richardson home and tie the score. It was one of those magic moments in sports when thousands of people — in this case forty thousand people — share the same jolt of electricity, the same twinge of excitement at the same instant. The crowd, without prompting, cheered madly. The pitcher worked a three-two count with a couple of loud strikes, deep into the seats but foul.

George, on the edge of his seat, couldn't clap or cheer because his heart was in his throat. He didn't want Mickey to fail. Heroes shouldn't fail. George focused on the navy-black pinstripes, on the number "7" adorning the jersey, and on the rugged profile of Mickey's face as the sun coated it with a golden glaze. Mantle adjusted his helmet and re-set his stance. He flicked the bat rhythmically to synchronize his swing. The pitch came. On a fastball count, the pitcher threw a change-up. Mickey's swing came a fraction too soon: an awkward, harmless miss.

That was tough, but George understood that the season was long, and this was not the most crucial game the Yankees would play. Even if heroes fail, they can be forgiven. It's a matter of how one faces defeat. Then, on the field in a fit of anger, Mantle grasped the bat with both hands as if it were a club, raised it over his head, dropped to one knee, and smashed the bat against the ground. It cracked and splintered — broke completely through. It was a terrifying sight. But what frightened George most was the expression on Mantle's face as he swung the bat. It was a look of primitive rage. A murderous, hateful look. It stunned George to know that, even within a baseball legend, vile forces live. A darkness hides in all of us.

It was a swift, simple act but one that should not have been witnessed nor was it one to forget. George thought that he would never do such a thing and was certain that his father wouldn't either. Instinctively, he edged closer to his dad in their box seats and perhaps that's why at the same moment his father's arm draped his son's shoulders. Along with the shattering of the bat came another rupture, intangible but deeper.

Watching the television, George knew that his life had not been as tough as his father's nor was it as easy as Jack's. Parts of their lives touched; however, distance remained among the generations. Now, he assessed both men. Whatever Jack did to lose money could not be as bad as his own suicide attempt. Money can be replaced. He imagined that his father had not lived a saint's life, but George believed that

Frank had never been so weak as to throw his spirit away. So, George decided that nothing would be gained by telling his secret. Not his father or his son would benefit; nor would he be absolved.

"Two slices of pizza left," Frank said.

George turned to his son. "Jack?"

"I'll split one with you."

His father cut a wedge in half. "Bottom of the ninth and down by a run," George stated. "Time for heroics."

"These fellas get a good buck for playing a game," Frank said. "We'll see if they can earn their dollar."

Unlike his father and grandfather, Jack didn't enjoy baseball the way they did. When he was younger, he had tried to play, but he just wasn't cut out for it. The turning point came when he was twelve years old and his Little League team made it to the semi-finals. With a victory they would go to the final round. The coach assigned Jack to right field, a spot that allowed the worst player to do the least damage. It was the top of the sixth, the last inning of an abbreviated game, with his team, the Mustangs, holding a one run lead. The other team, the Raptors, had runners on second and third with two outs.

Looking back, Jack understood the fantasy of it. He was of a generation that from birth was overly praised. No matter how small or large the action—from taking his first step to tossing tissue in a trash can—he was congratulated: "Good job!" or "Way to go!" or "That was great!" He stood on a sandy foundation, raised on rubber dreams. The baseball team was an extension of that high-praise world where rewards and fist-bumps came for wins as well as for losses. Trying was as good as succeeding.

So, the Raptors had runners on second and third with two outs and a right-handed batter at the plate. Because he was the clean-up hitter with a tendency to pull the ball, Jack's manager shifted the outfielders to their right about twenty feet. Although Jack was on-the-ready, he believed the ball would never find its way to right field. But it did. The hitter sliced a pitch off the end of his bat, and the ball headed Jack's way. He raced toward it and although the ball curled away from him, his speed cut the distance and as he reached for it, he over-reached, because instead of hitting the glove's pocket, it popped against the glove's heel and dropped to the ground. Jack heard a collective groan from the Mustang fans. He scooped up the ball and threw it somewhere near home plate, but the batter had raced to third base and the damage was done: two runs had scored.

Baseball has a way of providing a chance for redemption because the game possesses symmetry. In the bottom of that inning, the Mustangs' first batter drew a walk. Actually, he was hit by a pitch after a clever body maneuver. "Great job!" the crowd shouted. The next batter flied out to centerfield. The third batter rapped a single to left field. The following batter watched a wild pitch bounce to the backstop, which allowed both runners to advance. Five pitches later the batter sat on the team's bench after striking out.

Jack stepped into the batter's box. It was a thorny situation because only a base hit would do, and Jack was a mediocre hitter. Could he draw a walk? Not if the pitcher threw strikes, and the first pitch ripped the heart of the plate. Fans from both sides were clapping and screaming, each wanting their side to win. Something about rabid parents yelling at twelve year olds can be more than unsettling, but Jack kept his cool because he knew that this was his moment, as if it were scripted: one swing to earn heroics and redemption. However, it took two swings, both mistimed — both missing the baseball completely.

Afterwards the coach told the players they were great and they had tried hard and they had fun and those were important things. No, they would not move on to the next round because the brackets didn't work that way, but it was all right. Yet something in the coach's voice and something in the way the boys glared at *him* told Jack that sometimes trying just isn't enough.

After all the other boys left, Jack turned to his coach and said he was sorry, and to this day he remembered the sick feeling in his stomach and what the coach said: "It's not your fault. A bird can't fly without wings." Jack didn't understand what his coach meant, but now it was easy to decipher. It was as clear as the sound of a fastball smacking a catcher's mitt.

As Jack finished his beer and recalled that failure on the baseball field, it made him recall another failure. He looked at his father and grandfather and refused to believe that either man could do anything so foolish as to lose money the way he had. On top of that, when it was happening, when Linda was playing him for a fool, he knew something was wrong, but he wanted to be his own man and didn't want to follow what most people would do. Sitting in his grandfather's family room, he shook his head. No, he would never tell them. While staring at the small television, he thought how baseball links generations the same way that silence links men. The game and the girl: both times he wanted to be a hero, but life had other plans.

"I want the Yankees to win," Frank said, "but I feel for the Red Sox manager because this is how you get fired. Here we are in the bottom of the ninth and the closer walks the lead-off batter in a one-run game. The manager makes the right move, but the player doesn't deliver. It's like getting a piece of gum stuck on your boot heel."

George said, "He probably has ulcers."

"Now the Yankees have their slugger up."

"*This* guy," Frank said with derision. "I've read he's mixed up in a steroid scandal."

"He denies everything."

"They all do."

"Fans are on their feet," George remarked.

On the second pitch the right-handed hitter crushed a fast ball, sending it into the left field seats. The crowd exploded.

"People only care about results," George said. "Who wins, who loses."

"Baseball isn't the same."

"The player has to live with himself," Jack said. "Some people are strong like oaks; others are weak like pines."

The words impressed Frank and reinforced his decision. After snubbing out his cigarette, smoke curled the air.

"I'll wrap up that last slice."

"Hold on, George. Let's lay out our plan for Jack."

George returned to the sofa and smiled eagerly.

"Plan?" Jack said.

Frank wasted no time. "Your father and I have decided to leave the house to you, Jack. You can start your business right here and not worry about paying a mortgage, or a rent for that matter."

The words came so unexpectedly and forcefully, Jack forgot to breathe. He looked to his father who nodded decisively. Dumbfounded, Jack was silent but finally said, "That would be great. But, Dad, if you sold the place you'd make a pile of money."

"And let someone else reap the benefit of our hard labor?" George said with a laugh. "No way!"

"Your dad will be the estate's executor," Frank explained. "He's already set up a joint checking account with both your names on it. When I die he'll pay the current bills, but after a month or so, *you* will be responsible."

"Grandpa has paid the taxes and insurance for the coming year," George added, "but next year those costs will fall on you."

"Oh."

"Don't worry," Frank winked. "I've left enough in savings to cover taxes and insurance for awhile. Your father will be in charge of that account, and if things go as they should, you'll be on your way."

"Are you guys sure about this?"

Frank and George smiled. Jack, although overwhelmed, smiled too.

"I guess you can wrap up that slice of pizza now, George."

"I will, and then you and Jack can fight over it in the morning." Three generations shared gentle laughter.

Soon each man was in bed. Each felt content; however, each man held a belief of the others that was both true and false.

1928

It was an age about to disappear forever. In the late 1920s most people had steady work, and at the end of each month some money remained after paying bills — even the small farmers could find extra pennies and nickels gleaming in a Mason jar. By the decade's close, however, the world receded beyond the common man's grasp and even beyond men with a longer reach.

A few years before the Great Crash, through the spring and summer and early autumn, young Frank Bowman was a knight-errant, determined to sell thirty-one newspaper subscriptions, redeem his credit, and buy a Babe Ruth baseball glove. Mrs. Saunders had told him to go to the people who did not already have the paper, and that's what he did. By riding his bicycle he covered more ground, and he started with the small rental homes, each with a brood of children. Even though the families had emigrated from Italy, Ireland, Germany, and other countries, all the mothers were similar. They pinned up their hair and wore long aprons with pockets that held everything needed to face all situations. These women were a curious blend of personalities. One minute they barked commands to their children like drill sergeants and the next minute they soothed a scraped knee like kind nurses. If a person were to look into each mother's eyes, he would see pride and strength. She instinctively knew what was best for her family, and she would fight bare-fisted through a winter storm to get it.

Fittingly, each small home had its distinctive cooking scents. Cabbage in one kitchen, garlic in another, sausage frying in one skillet while potatoes boiled in someone's stockpot. What bridged all the homes was the stimulating smell of baking bread. Not a house went three days without the rising of loaves. With so many stomachs to feed, bread was the cheapest way to hush hunger. Mothers patted hands against aprons to wipe away flour; they looked admiringly at Frank because of his ambition and offered him a slice of warm bread with a dab of butter, and they would smile, an indomitable smile, that pushed them through today and toward tomorrow.

When Frank showed the mother or father that a newspaper subscription would cost them only pennies a week or when he mentioned names of wealthy people like the Saunders who read the paper every day — names of families that the poorer folks wanted to emulate — or if he stated that encouraging their children to read a newspaper would make them better Americans, he found a way into their pursestrings. And yet, his words were not dishonest because he believed them. Perhaps that belief helped tip the scales. He, along with everyone else, believed in a great nation and in great possibilities.

Beyond the town's boundaries lay the fields and farms. Mostly backbreaking places, yet not so formidable that a man couldn't maintain them.

A man with a strong wife and strong children that supplied enough hands to help with the planting, tending, and harvesting of the prolific soil.

Frank rode his second-hand bike along dirt roads, each week widening his circumference, as Mrs. Saunders had suggested. He pedaled past the limits of what he had previously imagined. He pushed beyond the buckeye trees, the oaks, maples, and pines — past the numberless cornfields and wide wheat fields. He felt physical exhaustion and mental clarity. He thought of the tenets that Mrs. Saunders had spelled out. He thought of his classroom education but wanted more. So, a few weeks earlier, he had concocted an aspiring plan of using the town's small public library and of measuring one foot of shelf space and of reading all the books on that shelf space over a two week period. It didn't matter the books' content; he would read until he had conquered all of the library's shelves. He believed in this life, a life of tenets; he believed in living it and never straying from it. Weren't his beliefs everyone's beliefs?

On he went. Every week farther. Making a sale here and there. Waiting for the husband or wife to say, "Well, sure, I guess we can afford that." Excited, he bounded out of the broom-swept house and down the dirt path bordered by geraniums or marigolds while towering hollyhocks grew along the fences. It was a world on the verge of vanishing. Never again would streams surge unspoiled, never again would trees spread as plentiful, never again would skies stretch as soundless, and never again would as many men be linked by laboring hands so proudly to their own piece of land.

Frank checked the ever-changing sun as weeks passed, checked its point of descent so that he had time to re-trace his lengthening journey before the road back home turned too dark to see. In those days only the sun, moon, and stars provided light. As he pedaled, he saw vast forests and wide fields, wider than dreams. The verdant land over-brimmed with life. And as the sun lowered, it embossed everything with a golden glimmer: himself, fields, forests, and even the road that was merely dirt. His legs beat a rhythm against the sun's decline, against time itself. He was winded but never tired. He would outrun the present and claim his future. He knew no fear. His physical existence would encounter the earth, inhale it and exhale it, as ordained. He churned the battered bike in the same way he would vanquish the universe and bend it to his vision. He would subdue everything in sight and hold it in the palm of his hand. His bicycle tires whirled dirt into the air, and when he pedaled fast, a silty plume first enveloped and then trailed his fleeting figure. It coated him, the landscape, and his memories in a sepia shade forever.

Over time, Frank changed as the land changed as the people changed. Natural shadows stretched, met, and unexpectedly transformed into electric light.

September 24

It was a calm, cool morning that held a promise of becoming the type of day that, if photographed, would find itself on an illustrated calendar. Morning shadows lasted later. Windows stayed shut an hour longer. Coffee tasted richer.

George walked into the kitchen and found his father already there, standing by the window, gazing toward the apple trees. "Good morning," he said quietly.

Frank quivered as if waking and spoke not so much to George but to himself. "She looked so wholesome in that chambray dress. She was young and pretty, and her arms were reaching to me." His father kept staring out the window.

Unsure of what to do, George raised his voice. "Dad?"

His father turned and looked confused but then appeared to recognize his son. "You're up early."

"Couldn't sleep anymore."

"Same with me."

George maneuvered around his father within that tight kitchen, getting to the coffee-maker. It never seemed right for either man to touch each other, not even an accidental grazing. His father set a black plastic ashtray on the kitchen table. In a few minutes George poured

258

him a cup of coffee in a ceramic mug with a maxim from *Poor Richard's Almanac*—"God Helps Those That Help Themselves"—and did the same for himself. His father stirred in sugar and a splash of cream. "Started drinking coffee in the CCC's," he said and sat at the table. "Those winter mornings were so damned cold."

"The Adirondacks, right?"

"Yes, near a town called Speculator." His father lit a cigarette.

"You've never talked about it much."

Frank shrugged his shoulders.

"Well," George said like a curious student, "what did you do up there?"

"You name it. We built roads, which meant first cutting down a hell of a lot of trees. We constructed bridges. We built tables and benches for parks. You can look all that up." His father sipped his coffee with a proud expression. "For that time period, with the equipment we had—the primitive tools—it's amazing what we accomplished."

"Are all those things still there?"

"I don't know."

"If they are, I'd like to see them."

"I took your mother there on our honeymoon." His father tilted his head thoughtfully. "On our way to Niagara Falls."

"Niagara Falls," George echoed with a touch of wonder.

"It was a popular honeymoon place in those days."

"What did Mom think of Speculator?" George sat down opposite his father.

"She liked it all right. But it was hard for her to imagine what it all looked like before we cut down and built up."

George had not heard this kind of serenity in his father's voice since the summer Mantle and Maris chased a ghost, and his father answered every question that he asked.

"We drove up there at the end of June," his father spoke nostalgically. "Everything was so green and the land so immense. We were young. And the country—well, the world—was different. Niagara Falls, so powerful and majestic. Inspirational, too. Lord, anything seemed possible."

"I might take a ride to Speculator one day," George said defensively.

His father set his cigarette in the ashtray. "I suppose that's something you and I should have done a long time ago."

"Why didn't we?"

After a moment of silence his father said, "I remember one of the men in charge at the CCC camp. I can't remember his name. The workers — guys like me — were in our late teens and early twenties. The fellas in charge, the captains, were probably in their forties. They seemed old to me then. Well, on a Sunday afternoon one of the older men and I played horseshoes. You know, it was a September day like this when the early morning and late afternoon are alike. The sky blue and the air clean, so that you feel alive and think nothing will ever change. So, this captain and I were both very good at horseshoes. Soon we got into a rhythm, pitching those shoes inches from the stakes or tossing one ringer on top of another. The horseshoes clanged like fire bells. You've never seen anything like it."

"No, I guess I haven't."

"We threw until our arms ached. Until we couldn't throw anymore. When we finally quit, he turned to me and said, 'Thanks, young man. I honestly enjoyed that.' And he clapped my shoulder."

"And?"

"Well, after that game I wondered what my life would be like when I was his age. But time rolls on." Frank flinched. "You end up going in directions that you never imagined. You do things that you'd never thought you'd do. Sometimes you end up doing what you *must* do instead of what you *should* do. And 'must' is a tough nut to crack. At least that's what you tell yourself."

George thought he understood what his father was trying to say and suddenly realized how easy it is to blame someone else for life's disappointments while unknowingly *you* might be the actual cause for someone's altered plans.

Silence lingered between them. He noticed his father's cup was empty. "More coffee?" he asked and the mood shifted.

"Sure."

"Pancakes?"

"You bet."

"We have a box mix."

"With enough butter and syrup, they'll taste fine."

George got the griddle going and stirred up the batter in seconds. "Couldn't be easier," he said. "Just add water."

"Yes, that's how everybody wants things today. No one understands that quality takes time."

"'Quality' doesn't factor into the equation."

"No. People are imprisoned by time. They want everything fast."

"Faster and faster." George tested the griddle's heat and found it ready. He poured three circles of batter.

"And it's sad that people will grow up with instant pancakes and never know the difference."

"They already have." George flipped the cakes and watched them rise. "Besides, if they don't know the difference, they won't care."

"I suppose you're right. A pebble and a diamond are the same to a blind man, and every generation gains some things and loses others." His father lit another cigarette. "Speaking of the next generation, where is that lazy son of yours?"

"He's *your* lazy grandson."

Both men smiled. "We'll give him another half hour."

"Here you go." George set a plateful of hotcakes on the table; steam swirled from the golden-brown discs. "I'll leave enough batter so Jack can make a batch, if he wants," George said as his father put butter and syrup to work, sparing neither.

The second batch of pancakes cooked quicker than the first and because his father ate slowly, George could set his plate on the table and join him. They sat as men often sit while eating, in silence. Their thoughts could be far and wide, or they could be focused on the here and now, or just the food and its taste. In ten minutes both plates were empty and the coffee low. While his father smoked, George found that the smell didn't bother him. He thought of odd moments when he passed by someone who would be smoking a cigarette. It might happen outside a hardware store or a grocery store or when a neighbor three houses down worked outdoors. That aromatic scent would link him to his father forever.

"Will you finish painting the house today?"

"Right. Jack and I should be done by noon or so."

"Nothing left to fix?"

"We've accomplished a lot—for two amateurs."

"I'm pleased that Jack is using the old tools."

"Right."

"He has a natural talent. You can see it in the way his hands move." His father flicked ashes into the tray. "He has the skills."

"I guess talent skips a generation," George said bitterly.

"Probably."

"Is that it?" Something finally snapped inside of him. It flared like a rifle shot. He was glad to have the emotion out but at the same time embarrassed, knowing he was being foolish, as if witnessing the moment from a high, distant point. "Is that what you've always wanted from me?"

"What are you talking about?"

"What you see in Jack. How he works." George stood up so suddenly and forcefully, his chair fell over. "Isn't that how you measure a man?"

"Oh, for the love of God." His father's eyes narrowed and his jaw quivered. "How the hell do you know what I think?"

"That's just it. I don't. I could make a list things you did, but I couldn't list *you*. We've never had one serious talk in our lives!" He slammed his plate into the sink, half-hoping it would shatter. "I ask questions, try to open you up, but you close me off. Always."

"Don't you think I *know* that?" His father stood up with arms outstretched, one hand holding his coffee mug. "I want to tell you so much, but I can't!" George turned and all at once saw that the man was empty, as if the air within him had vanished or a flame had extinguished. "I just can't," his father mumbled as the mug slipped from his hand, landed on the plank floor, and broke into pieces. Frank followed with a slow-motion drop, first to his knees and then to his hands.

George rushed to his side and guided him back into a chair. He held his father's shrunken shoulders. "I'll call 9-1-1."

"No," Frank pressed a hand to his chest as his head sagged. "I'm all right." After a few minutes his staggered breath regulated and he waved away his son's support. "Just light-headed for a minute."

"Dad, I'm sorry. I thought…"

"You think too much." His father looked up, exhausted, but his face showed no anger. Soon enough, he regained himself. George shifted his weight from one foot to another. After another minute, his father sat tall in the chair and looked at him squarely. "George, everyone finds his own talents," he said. "I only wanted you to be happy."

"I know." He picked up the fallen chair and sat next to his father. "But that's not what I mean." His voice was calm but firm. "I wanted to know *you*. What made you proud. What brought you happiness. What you lost or gained." He folded his hands together. "You were always a mystery locked in a fortress."

"I'm not what you think," his father said as his head sank again. "I'm just a man."

"Right," he sighed, "but I thought that by knowing you I could know myself."

Frank brought his eyes level with George again and smiled sadly. "Son, most of my life has nothing to do with you at all."

"But…"

"No," his father said and fixed his fingers on the table. "Move on and attend to yourself."

The two men sat like boxers on stools in between rounds of a long fight, neither knowing that the final bell had sounded long ago. Then his father looked at the pieces on the floor. "Well, I made of mess of things."

"I'll take care of it." George checked the damage. "Maybe I could glue it together?"

"If you want." Frank pulled the cigarette pack from his pocket but after a pause tucked it away again. "I had that mug a long time, but it doesn't matter any more. Fix it or toss it. It's up to you."

George gathered the pieces and placed them on the counter. He took the dirty dishes, rinsed them, and set them in the dishwasher. Now, without seeing, he sensed his father rising and moving toward him. Then his father stood close — close enough for George to smell the man's essence. One hand touched George's shoulder while another pointed past the window.

"Those apple trees were covered with weeds and vines. You and Jack cut away the rot. Now the trees will thrive, and they'll find their natural strength." His father nodded deliberately but kept peering beyond the window.

George looked in the same direction and indeed the morning had transformed into a fine autumnal day, and looking out that window, for an instant, he thought he saw a woman standing with her back to him, her blue chambray dress billowing and her long brown hair swaying with a breeze. His father turned to leave, but then did something he had never done. He turned back and embraced George in a brief, manly way and said, "I'm proud of you, Son."

As his father walked away, George trembled.

The ladder work was done, so George and Jack stood on level ground and finished painting the house.

"I can handle the trim around the windows if you'll do the siding," Jack suggested.

George knew that painting the trim, especially around the windows, required more skill than it did for painting the siding. It was Jack's subtle way of saying that he was the better painter, but that was all right with George because it was a simple fact.

"That works for me," he answered. "We should be done around noon."

"Just in time for lunch."

He took a deep breath. The crisp, autumn air held a tinge of decay in it and at the same time a hint of life. His arm stretched a full span across the siding while only the tip of the brush dipped into the paint. Years ago his father showed him how to do it properly. Now, he brushed a final coat onto the clapboard pieces and admired the paint's luster. He glanced at the cement walkway bordering the house and noticed how house scrapings and fallen leaves had cluttered the path.

After painting, he would sweep the cement walk. All of the work would be complete. In a curious way George felt that his time in New Jersey might be complete, too. He should return to Colorado. But he wasn't sure why. Because the idea of being a mentor intrigued him? Because he had built a life there? Because he had his own house to maintain?

Then he thought of Prue and instantly imagined what a new and different life would look like with her. His hand whisked back and forth against the siding, while his decision whisked back and forth in his mind. He stopped and gazed around. Then without a logical connection, he wondered if Sam had been cutting the lawn in between Starbuck's runs. He had to smile at that, and he felt grateful that Sam and Sammie were his neighbors.

The September sun warmed his back, not the intense summer heat, but a balance against the autumn chill. In this moment of harmony, George realized that he was, as Prue had said, a giving person and that in giving to others his life had served a purpose. Without the giving, his existence would be meaningless. For the first time, he truly felt good about repairing the house. Two days ago, during a second phone call to his former school district, George asked for the paperwork he needed to enroll in a mentoring class and for the application needed to get his new certification. Everything would be sent to his house. He could start mentoring with the spring semester. He pictured the white cardboard boxes in his basement stuffed with teacher files and thought that perhaps he could find use for the material after all. He could pass along a few old tricks to new teachers. Yes, he could try that pursuit, and if it didn't suit him, well, even at his age the world still held possibilities.

Yes, again Prue. Her listening intently. Her words, her arms, her smile, her touch.

"How's it going?" Jack asked.

George left his reverie. "Fine."

Jack seemed to be examining the work but said, "Dad, I'm excited about this new business thing, but I'm kind of scared, too. I mean, I've got to find out about insurance and liability and maybe about being bonded. I've never dealt with stuff like that."

"You might contact a lawyer who specializes in small-business start-ups and get advice."

"Yeah, good idea." He hesitated. "Just when I'm feeling good about this, I start thinking I can't do it. That I don't have the talent. What do you think, Dad?"

George thought that a question might work better than an answer. "What makes you think you can't do it?"

"There's so much to it. It's a huge step."

"Well, like you said before, you'll take one step at a time."

"It's risky."

"Everything's a risk. Doing nothing is a risk."

He knew Jack was anxious, but he saw the glint in his son's eyes and also knew that his son's confidence, at least most of it, had returned. George felt proud. "And you have margins for error. There's me and there's this house."

"I still feel funny about taking the house."

"Don't." George set his hands on his hips unconsciously emulating his father's way of standing. "If an outsider bought this place, yes, we could make a nice profit, but what would be the cost?"

His son frowned. "He probably would change everything."

"Right. He might even scrape off the house completely and put up something that would be all right for awhile, but it would never be lasting."

"That would stink." Jack set his hands on his hips. "This place has character."

"Because it's been through so much." George touched a piece of the siding as if the house were a living thing. "Through all the winter cold and summer heat, through the additions, subtractions, and amendments, this structure has endured."

Both men felt a surge of pride because the words suggested more than the span of generations, even more than the people. It was as important as a divine principle or a sacred document. A heritage.

"I'll take care of it."

"You will." His expression lightened. "Maybe one day I'll see a grandson running around here?"

"Hey, don't be totally surprised."

"Would you name him George?"

"*He* might be a *she*," his son smiled. "Georgiana?"

"All right. That will work."

"But I've always liked the name Ben."

"Then you'd better hope for a boy."

Jack laughed and then checked their progress. "We should get back to it."

George grasped the paintbrush but realized the moment. "Things are changing for both of us," he said. "We have to see things differently. We have to see each other differently."

"Let's stay connected."

"Yes."

"Have you ever sent a text message?"

"No."

Jack stretched his arms behind his back and said with a wink, "I'll show you how."

Hours passed. Frank felt light-headed and bloated. Had he eaten too much breakfast? He hated this constant monitoring of his body. How wonderful it was to be young and strong — strong enough to tackle any physical labor all day without aches or cares. Yes, the newspaper business was rewarding, but it was business. Physical work was pleasure. And he couldn't do it anymore.

Outside he saw his son and grandson painting, and he noticed the cement walkway. It should have been flagstone or brick, but years ago money was an issue and cement was the cheapest solution. For some reason the walkway remained that way. Now, the simplest job left to him would be to sweep it clean. It required no skill and little strength, and he would be doing something helpful and physical.

Inside the workshed Frank lifted the old broom from its hook. It felt heavier than he remembered. He saw the Phillies cigar box, took it off the shelf, and placed it on the workbench. Tenderly, his fingers rested on it as if it contained treasures. He looked around for masking tape but only saw a roll of blue painter's tape. It would do. It would be even better. After tearing off a six inch length, he attached it to the cardboard lid. Then he left the cigar box on the bench as he had left it there before.

When George and Jack finished, George volunteered to clean the paintbrushes. Jack went inside to wash up. Overhead, the noonday sun was warm and gentle. George washed out the second brush when he saw his father sweeping the cement sidewalk that curved along the house. His father pushed the broom slowly. Frank wanted to go faster, but his arms wouldn't obey. Still, he kept working and felt good about what he was doing. Suddenly a hand touched his shoulder.

"I'll take it from here."

Frank didn't want to let the broom go, but what choice did he have? His fingers released the maple handle. He stood there for a moment, bewildered. Then he turned and walked to the house. Every man wants to feel useful. He felt useless.

Upstairs, after George and Jack had cleaned up, Jack said, "What should we do for lunch?"

"How about McDonald's?"

"Just when I've lost a few pounds?"

"Hey, McDonald's is the all-American cuisine."

"Should I tag along?"

"Sure. Why don't you drive and I'll pay the bill?"

"Deal."

"I'll see what your grandfather wants."

They came downstairs. Jack took the car keys and headed for the door. "See you soon, Grandpa."

Frank stood by the kitchen window, seeing the grass and trees and sky, but not seeing Deborah. He longed to see her again. Now, he was dimly aware of peripheral sounds, but they were only sounds, not words.

"Dad, we're going to McDonald's. What would you like?"

Someone was speaking to him, but he couldn't pull himself away from the window. He felt that he was close to seeing her again. Then, a hand touched his arm.

"Dad?"

Frank turned, expecting Debbie, but it was George. His son must have said something. "What's that?"

"Jack and I are going to McDonald's."

"Oh."

"What would you like?"

"Nothing."

"Nothing?"

Frank pictured McDonald's and its hamburgers and fries and Cokes. Then he remembered the old Coca-Cola bottles. Yes. Yes, once a month the CCC leaders bought two cases of Cokes for the working men. Those little green bottles fit perfectly in your hand and the drink tasted sweet going down your throat. He remembered that unique time in his life when he stood alone. When his muscles and sweat earned their way to a pocketknife and to pocket money. It was a time of pitching horseshoes and building bridges. It was a time when he was like the land: rugged and pure.

"Dad?"

"I'll have a small Coke."

"Is that all?"

"Yes."

"All right. We'll be back soon."

He watched George move for the door but abruptly turn back. Awkwardly, his son embraced him and whispered in his ear. "I love you, Dad." George stepped back. "Did you hear that?" His son spoke in a choked voice and then left the house.

Yes, I heard you. Maybe it's easier for the younger generations to say things like that. My father never said it to me. But, then again, he died so young. And maybe by not having a father after the age of six, I never learned how to be a father. But why? I've been granted more time than most men. Is there a weakness to saying intimate things? All right, what if there is? A simple vulnerability. But that's just it. What George never realized—what no one realized—is that because I had nothing handed to me for the first part of my life, I had to fight for every scrap. A tough life branded a fighter's toughness into me. Any sign of weakness would be blood in the water for sharks to scent, stalk, and attack. Let my guard down? Never.

A watery nausea washed over him, but Frank managed to pull a coffee mug from a kitchen cabinet and then remembered he already had coffee and didn't want any now. Every morning he looked forward to that first taste of coffee. More than the sun, it signaled a new day. And for him, each day began with a plan. Other men let life happen to them. They were nothing but tourists. He, on the other hand, knew exactly what had to be done and how to do it. Always a plan. Always accomplishments. He learned to think that way on the farm and after losing the farm and in the CCC's and in the Army. All of it. He told himself that his way had been the right way. Slowly, he walked to the family room and thought of watching television until his son and grandson returned. His recent plan had worked well, and it was good having them there.

I saw it through. Yes, this time I saw it through. The house, inside and out, looks fine—fine enough to pass along. That's what I wanted...but there's something else. Something I need to do before leaving.

And now, he didn't want to leave. He wanted to stay...a little longer. He gripped the television remote but then remembered the broom being taken from him and that horrible, useless feeling rippled through him again, and he wondered where all of his accomplishments had gotten him. And he wasn't thinking of possessions or wealth. No, it was a hole far deeper than those things could fill. He held the remote, sat on the sofa, but did not turn on the television.

No, George doesn't understand me completely, but I never wanted to be completely understood. I was hard to get along with sometimes and I was hard on George sometimes, and everything had to be done on my terms. I needed it that way. Anyone who knows me would understand that. But does anyone know me?

Goddamn it, my thoughts are flying in crazy directions.

He felt dizzy.

For some reason Frank thought of his father and how strange it had been for a strapping, athletic man to lose his footing on a roof where he had stood at least twenty times before. Only a storm, and a savage storm at that, could account for his father's fall. But what commotion in the clouds could have jarred the bearing of that colossus? Then Frank saw a woman in a red dress defiantly watching a funeral service. He remembered pedaling his bicycle on dirt roads, past farms and fields—the stomach-churning scent of baking bread. He thought of hot coffee and cold mornings in the Adirondacks surrounded by enough wilderness to last eternally, and he thought of shaping pockets of land so that people could take part in that primeval existence. He thought of serving in the Army and winning a war. He thought of his newspaper career and of his house and of keeping things going—the visions and revisions. But other thoughts pressed against him, thoughts he didn't relish. He needed a Border collie's agility to fend off those shameful thoughts. Now, on a polished table before him, Frank saw a silver tea service. He had just finished a slice of cake and perhaps he had eaten it too quickly because his stomach felt awfully full. Mrs. Saunders asked if he was all right. He had trouble swallowing but nodded yes. She looked at him with sad, soulful eyes. Her skin was soft and unblemished. He wanted to say her name but realized he had never learned the woman's first name.

How on earth could I not know her name?

God, he felt so full! His heart seemed to rise in his throat. His brain swelled. Did he release the television remote, or did it fall from his hand?

I'm going to vomit.

He stood but the floor moved. He stepped but lost his footing. He lurched and hit the sofa. Then he was on the sofa but slipped off of it. It felt like falling off a roof, plunging to an abyss, falling and falling until his back hit something solid and his eyes glared at the ceiling.

My God, so this is it. George, where are you?

His breathing was heavy. His eyes were glazed. He wanted George but a different person appeared. Yes, one who did not look or act like George, but a person who was more like himself. This wretch was not there to give; only to take. Selfish, self-centered. His mind summoned a hideous image. This person—this thing—opened its mouth while Frank poured some sort of golden liquid past the gaping lips, but there was no end to it, no satisfying it. Because this monster could not be satisfied, it reared up, fingers fitted with talons that aimed to slaughter. William would have his revenge. Frank raised his hands for protection, but the figure swatted the weak flesh aside. He wanted to scream but could not. His eyes closed and the face disappeared as another took its place. Erica.

Is she coming to save me?

Frank reached for her, but she did not reach for him. He called to her, implored her, but she remained unmoved. Her eyes were chips of stone. "We are organisms that crawl upon the earth."

"No, there must be *more*."

Frank's chest sank under an incredible weight. Then Deborah appeared with arms at her side and an expression that was neither kind nor unkind. It conveyed a sadness he had never known. It transcended pity.

"Where's George?" she asked.

"Gone," Frank whispered.

"Yes, they're all gone."

"You know them all?"

"I've always known."

"I never understood."

"You understand now. What it's like to have everything taken from you and to be completely alone."

"My sins don't equal this injustice. To die alone, misunderstood. I don't deserve it."

"Yes, you do. You didn't stay true to things greater than yourself."

On his back Frank lay as helpless as a stunned creature. He could not move or speak or cry. The ceiling came into a strange sharpness. He noticed a small crack in the plaster that he had never seen before.

It must be repaired, he thought. I must fix it.

September 25

Sunrise. A gorgeous day. Sun and dew create a mist.

Breakfast. Coffee and toast. Narrow conversation between George and Jack.

The house stands unattended.

The mail arrives with store flyers and two utility bills that George will pay later.

Shower and shave and dress. Drive to town.

Wait in the bank's lobby for someone to help with revising accounts and transferring the safe deposit box.

Back to the house. Unease trickles through their bodies because they possess life but have nowhere to channel it.

George leaves the house and walks to the property's edge, and then walks farther. Beyond the rutted trail, a patch of forest remains. He remembers sitting in a child's wagon and his father pulling the black metal handle on their way to the woods. The red wagon rumbled along the frozen earth. He wore a woolen jacket, cap, and mittens because father and son within the December forest will find an evergreen tree to chop down and then erect in the family room and decorate with lights, ornaments, and tinsel. Not much of the forest stands now. Half-acre lots and suburban homes have replaced a wilderness once capable of creating intrepid dreams. George stands silently and loses track of time. He tries to lose himself. But the memory cannot sustain itself. He turns back.

Jack turns off the television after having it on no more than three minutes. The news and the day and the world roll on without taking notice of or recording any change. He walks outside to the shed, opens the side door, but does not enter. Inside, the tools belong to him now, but he cannot claim them yet. He wants to go for a drive to get away, but he cannot. Besides, they must attend to necessities.

The funeral parlor. Other mourners fill other rooms with whispers or silence or tears. For George and Jack, intimate business. The employees work efficiently with a proper blend of sympathy and indifference.

The viewing room is frightfully cold and stark. Flower vases are empty; walls are bare. The partitioned coffin lies open to show the deceased from the waist up. Franklin Bowman rests as still as a workshop tool that hangs on a hook.

Perhaps George thinks that the body in the casket resembles his father but is no longer his father.

Perhaps Jack thinks that his grandfather's face looks grotesque because the lips are sewed shut.

Frank outlived his contemporaries. Not a soul attends the viewing.

George and Jack sit in the chilled room and take turns leaving the room and circling the building and then returning to the room and sitting with a numbness that dulls their brains.

An employee of Adams Mortuary soundlessly glides up to George. "We will transport your father to Washington Cemetery in Quincy tomorrow morning." The attendant's voice is barely audible. "Your father prepaid for the transportation."

"What time?"

"The service is scheduled for ten o'clock, but you should arrive a half hour earlier to sign papers."

In the late afternoon George drives them out of the mortuary's parking lot. Exhausted but hungry, they stop at a fast-food place, get their meals, and sit on molded seats. Around them people talk loudly, children yell and run in a play area decorated in bright candy colors.

Solitary customers eat fistfuls of food as they check messages on phones that glow upon Formica tables.

George and Jack eat silently and then dispose their trash, stepping past tables where people leave scattered waste.

In the house they briefly plan for tomorrow.

Night finally comes.

"Watch the game?"

"Baseball or football?"

"It doesn't matter."

Shadows and chill. Quiet and fatigue. Silence and sleep.

September 26

The skies threatened rain. Because his grandfather was due a military funeral, Jack went to the front porch to take down the American flag. A new flag would be presented to Jack's father at the service, but it was the old flag that needed attention. He removed the pole from its bracket and with a utility knife sheared the flag from its pole. After years of exposure to the elements, the material looked and felt as expected: faded and frayed. Yet the fabric proved resilient. It held up. Jack folded the flag, if not perfectly, then at least with care. It made sense to set *this* flag inside his grandfather's coffin. The new flag would find its place, guarding the old porch.

———   ———

During the hour's drive to Quincy, George and Jack sat passively as they headed toward a slate sky and the predicted storm. Ten miles outside of the town, the rain started, and it came hard. Weeks ago George had packed a navy blazer, dress shirt, and tie, anticipating this moment. Jack had no formal clothes but was taller and fuller than his father, so he fit well into his grandfather's old sports coat and dress shirt. They drove along the two-lane state highway, a road that neither of them knew well, and the constant rain—even with the wipers sweeping madly—made certainty impossible. Because his son was younger and had keener reflexes, George thought he should have asked Jack to drive, but he decided it was his duty.

"The sign says five more miles," Jack pointed ahead. "Do you know where to go once we turn off?"

"Yes." He remembered his recent visit to the cemetery and stumbling on to that strange pine forest. "It's easy to miss the entrance because it's poorly marked, but we'll find it."

At this military facility, Washington Cemetery, burials took place on Monday, Wednesday, and Friday at ten, noon, and two. The digging of graves with a backhoe did not begin until after the ceremony. After turning off the highway, George made a series of sharp turns and then drove through military gates and toward a small brick building. The action's repetition was eerie. Years ago it was his father who had driven the same car, and it was he who sat where his son was sitting now. It had rained that day too, the day of his mother's burial. George and his father had entered the same brick building to attend to the same paperwork. The building and the cemetery lay in a small valley with a national forest on one side and a rise on the other side that long ago had given way to roads and houses.

Inside the building he sat where his father once did while Jack sat beside him now. The windowless room relied on florescent lighting that bathed everything in an unnatural film. Gray metal desks, gray filing cabinets, and gray waste cans crammed against each other, crowded against uncomfortable chairs, and somehow made it difficult to breathe. The same woman who had asked Frank questions years ago sat across from George and Jack now. Her dour face made her look as if she could have been a Puritan matron standing by a scaffold and watching a church beadle whip the back of a young, bare-breasted woman. This time George answered the questions. This time he dictated the words to be engraved on the marker. This time he signed the final papers.

Outside, beneath a bandshell, the mortuary employees had transported the coffin and placed it on a raised platform, and someone draped the American flag over it. The coffin was exactly the same as his mother's. George remembered how his father wanted to be sure his wife was inside of it and had asked if they could open and check it. George thought how the body, after the refrigeration and the wake and the viewing would quickly collapse onto itself and how morbid the idea of opening that lid was. He wondered why his father would doubt the mortuary's veracity. Was he expecting to see someone else in the casket? And what did it matter whose bones and flesh rotted in that box when the person's essence—the soul?—had departed days before? Fortunately, the woman in charge told them that state law forbids the opening of a coffin without a legal notice.

Beneath the bandshell, Jack and George sat beside each other on folding chairs. Apart from the curved roof and the four corner pillars, nothing sheltered them. Yesterday had been summer; tomorrow forecasted autumn; for now the weather reflected the tumult of the seasons' transitions. Rain, not weakening, smacked the earth while wind forced the chilling storm into their faces. George recalled his father's strength and refused to shiver. He thought of the man's will power and ruggedness and wanted to project those qualities, especially now.

A clergyman in Army uniform stepped forward and delivered a brief, scripted eulogy. He said nothing wrong, but he said nothing thoughtful either. What did he know of a person's hidden life? After the speech, through two loudspeakers attached to the bandshell, the song "Taps" played. At first it seemed a cheap effect; however, the solitary bugle touched every note mournfully and by the song's end George brushed tears from his eyes.

After the song, with a precision that only the military could muster, two soldiers grasped the American flag at each end of the coffin and folded it with snapping sounds, tightly and perfectly. When one soldier presented the folded flag to him, he could not fight off tears for a second time. Jack's fingers suddenly clutched his hand, and George believed that his father's hand would have felt like this, if the man had ever offered it. And at that moment he understood the real loss: the possibility of one day being close, the possibility of saying all that he wanted to say, and the possibility to know all that he wanted to know. A taunting voice echoed in his brain: "It's what we have." The thought possessed and dispossessed him.

With the brief ceremony complete, George walked to the coffin and touched the smooth, composite surface. "You were always with me, Dad," he whispered. "You always will be."

George and Jack stepped to the edge of the bandshell as a cemetery attendant readied umbrellas for them. George looked off to the rise of houses and roads and saw a man wearing a black leather jacket and standing by a motorcycle, a man who had stopped, it seemed, to watch the ceremony. The rider stood in the rain, helmet off, his long black hair wet and streaming. He was tall and lanky, but with the storm and with his standing so far away and above them, George could not see his face clearly. Abruptly, the on-looker set the helmet on his head, started his motorcycle, and vanished. George wondered why the person had stopped. If the man lived nearby he would have seen similar ceremonies. If he were a stranger passing through, perhaps he had stopped to see a military burial, which he had never seen before. Or perhaps he had served in the military and was simply paying his respects.

Back inside the cold, dim brick building, the woman in charge spoke to George and Jack.

"In this rain, digging a grave with a backhoe can get pretty sloppy." She shrugged her shoulders. "But the rain might taper off later."

"So, you'll wait a few hours before you dig?"

"Correct."

"And my father will be buried next to my mother?"

"In a manner of speaking. Space is a premium here," she explained. "It won't be long before that tract of the cemetery will be used up."

For an instant George remembered that strange gravedigger but pushed the memory aside. "But he's supposed to be buried next to his wife."

"He will be." The woman ran fingers through her short, spiky hair. "We buried her pretty deep so your father can rest above her."

George and Jack glanced at each other. The image George pictured seemed horrid, yet he didn't know why. What remains of the dead?

"My guesstimate is," the woman said, "if the rain lets up, we should be done in five to six hours. You're welcome to wait."

They scanned the boxed-in setting, and George spoke for them both. "We should leave now. We have things to clear up at my father's house." He touched his knees, coaxing himself to stand. "I'll be back tomorrow to see it...finished."

Outside, George took a quick look at the edged rise, saw no one, stepped inside the car, and let Jack drive them home.

September 27

After a lull in the storm, a new round of lighting and thunder woke George from a shallow sleep. He had been tossing all night and now at two o'clock in the morning, fully awake, he knew it was useless to close his eyes. He left the bed wearing a T-shirt and sweat-shorts and checked the room's windows, shut to an inch margin so that cool air circulated but the storm wouldn't enter. He stepped into the hall and wanted to open the door to Jack's room and check on him as he had done years ago in his own home when his son was a boy, but he didn't want to chance waking him. It was odd to think of Jack living alone in this house, taking it over so to speak, and yet it felt natural.

The door to his father's bedroom was ajar. George pressed his palm against the raised-panels and pushed gently. It opened with a soft moan. He thought of lubricating the hinges; a practical, silly thought. He half-hoped to see his father lying there, sleeping face up as he was wont to do. The sight might frighten him, but it would also calm him with an assurance that his father had not died, that it had all been a vaporous nightmare. But no familiar form filled the bed. The sheets lay flat against an empty mattress.

George entered the room and breathed the vestiges of cigarette smoke, Old Spice, Ivory soap, and menthol lineament. He could not detect his mother's scent. The gap between now and then—her death—was wide enough to eliminate all traces. But he remembered her sensitive ways. He touched her side of the bed, let his hand rest there, and thought of being a boy on Christmas mornings when he would rush in and wake his parents too early. His father would growl and turn over, but his mother would smile and then laugh, rise, touch his shoulder, and say, "Let's go downstairs and see." She seemed just as excited. George wondered how long it would be until his father's aspects would wane.

Outside, the storm continued, but by counting the seconds between lightning and thunder, George knew that the heart of it was passing. The braided, oblong rug over the wooden floor felt warm against the night's chill, but then his feet met the cold floor as he checked the bedroom windows. All shut tightly. He left that room and headed downstairs. Shadows filled the spaces. Silence filled the house. Soon the soundless darkness felt as suffocating as a shroud. He needed something. Maybe getting out of the house would help, even in the rain. In the hall closet, he found an umbrella.

It was a light rain now, refreshing, as the umbrella kept most of the storm away except for a mist that seeped through. Around him, new paint and spruced property made everything look alive. He walked toward the back of the house, now and then touching a section of clapboard siding that he had repainted. He made his way to the apple trees and remembered how well he and Jack had worked together. It wasn't always that way, and he blamed himself for that. At least now he recognized Jack's talents, and his son's business idea of restoring furniture could work. Yes, it certainly could.

George returned to the house. Three o'clock. Why did he feel lost when every object was so familiar? He decided to lie on the sofa where his father had napped so often. Resting on his back, he looked at the ceiling and wondered if his father had seen the same perspective. Probably not. No two people ever see things exactly the same.

Sleeping and waking alternated within him. He thought of driving to New York City where he could find an all-night jazz club, sit at the bar, and meld into the scene. He had never done such a thing, but it *was* possible. Or he could drive to Cape May and find a twenty-four hour diner and order their all-day breakfast special. He had never done that before, but it, too, was possible.

George stirred and realized the mantel clock was chiming. He lost count and squinted to see that it was suddenly five o'clock. He'd been drifting. With closed eyes he thought of driving to Washington Cemetery to check on the gravesite. He remembered that odd gravedigger. Then he pictured himself walking in the adjacent pine forest that aligned mysteriously. Again the mantel clock chimed even though an hour could not have passed. But it had passed. Still, he felt unrested, yet he couldn't stay on that sofa a minute longer.

Jack would be up in an hour or so and George would have someone to talk to, but he needed something more, something deeper. He went upstairs, stripped off his T-shirt and shorts and then set a pair of underwear, jeans, and a polo shirt on the bed. An index card lay on the dresser. On it was the address that he had written and memorized, but he checked it anyway. He walked across the hall to his father's bedroom to use the bathroom. The four-inch, square pink tiles that reached halfway up from the floor were original. Today, young couples would have a hard time dealing with the cramped space, but the bathroom was a luxury for his parents when his father had built it. They lost some closet space, but it was a worthwhile tradeoff. George turned on the shower faucet and waited a minute for the warm water to overtake the cold, and then he stepped into the stall and closed the plastic curtain. The water, soap, and shampoo helped to revive him. He never stayed long in the shower, and this was no exception. When he stepped back into the bedroom, he towel-dried himself as his skin goose-bumped and his body hair curled.

After dressing and after leaving Jack a note, saying that he was heading to the cemetery to check on things, not to worry, and that he would call soon, it was nearly seven o'clock. George started the Outback—Jack's car now—and turned the wipers to Intermittent because the rain was tapering off. He drove along the town's outskirts to a neighborhood that had sprung up during the building boom after the second world war. His heart thumped eagerly, yet he wondered what he would say to her. What were the right words? It would be easier to write a note and leave it at the coffee shop, but he couldn't do that.

Apart from the wipers clicking against the windshield, there was silence, and steadily he found his way to the address written on the index card. Although he had never been to this part of Providence, the streets seemed familiar. A gradual winding turn to each road, houses set back fifty feet or so, split-levels and ranches with one-car garages that wouldn't hold today's SUVs. As he pulled up to Prue Richards' house, he felt relieved yet anxious when he saw what had to be a kitchen light glowing. Yes, he wanted to see her and he needed to see her, but now the rush of adrenalin that he had felt earlier dissipated. What would she say to his being there so early and uninvited? Would she turn him away? And if she let him in, what exactly did he expect? What a dreadful blunder this would be.

The rain had nearly stopped as a glistening moon poked through vapory clouds, and when George stood by the open car door, the world was strangely soundless. No birds or breeze. He shut the car door quietly and took a deep breath. With his hair still damp from the shower, he walked to the side of the house where an interior light guided him, and he stopped by a side door. Then he saw her.

The kitchen door had wood panels on the bottom and four glass panes framed the top. On its interior side, pinched at the middle and positioned across the glass was a calico curtain. After tapping softly on the panes, he said, "Prue, it's me, George."

She looked startled but opened the door. "George," she said and examined him beneath the naked light. "You look terrible."

The assessment, instead of hurtful, allowed him to surrender his puffed-up courage. "I haven't slept much," he said. "I wanted to see you."

"Come in." She opened the door wider. Prue wore flannel pajamas and a matching robe, both a tender yellow. "Sit down," she motioned to the round table and wooden chairs. "I'm usually not up this early, but I couldn't sleep either. I've been thinking about you, wondering how you are." They sat on honey-stained oak chairs, each with a blue calico cushion, the same fabric and pattern decorating the kitchen door.

"I can't keep my mind from jumping."

"The loss of a parent, no matter the parent's age, is always hard."

"Yes, and..."

He was reluctant to complete the thought, but she pushed forward: "And it brings back other memories?"

"Yes." He looked at her. He had not known her long, yet he had known her all his life. "What amazes me is how open we've been with each other from the start."

"Sometimes it happens that way."

He bowed his head. "I've worked through a lot of things these past few weeks, and I have you to thank for it."

"You've been quite a project." She smiled coyly and grasped his hands. "But honestly, you had an opportunity and met it. Give yourself credit."

He looked at her again, and, being deeply drawn to her, the words would be difficult to say. He wanted a definite answer, as he had always found in math, but George knew now that living provided few if any solid answers. No, life isn't a rigid grid. It's, as Prue said, a poem that over time alters its meter or changes its rhyme. He didn't know if it was the right decision, but he had to be satisfied with telling himself it was the lesser wrong.

"I'm going back to Colorado. I'm not sure if I'll close out that part of my life or if I'll pick it up again. I'm not sure what will happen."

"I understand." She moved her hands from his to the table. "I thought you would go back, and that's why I kept my distance."

"I'm sorry."

"So am I."

They sat with empathetic expressions for a moment. Then she looked up and said, "Are you hungry? I could make breakfast."

"Yes." He stopped. "No. I'm empty but exhausted. You look tired, too."

"We both need to rest," she said and then, as if weighing a decision, nodded firmly. "Come."

Prue lived in a modest ranch home, so the steps to her bedroom were few, and the room where she slept was simple and straightforward with a dresser, a highboy, and a sleigh-bed—all stained a rich cherry color. There was a nightstand laden with books, hardbound and paperback. A lamp with a pleated shade and a cut-glass base. Two windows. Delicate white curtains. And filling the room was the distinct, enticing fragrance of a woman.

After removing her robe, Prue pulled the bedcovers back and sat on one side of the mattress with her feet on the floor. Without being told, George sat on the opposite side with his back to her back. She unbuttoned her top, removed it, and then slid off her flannel bottoms. He removed all of his clothes, thankful that the room was dark. She nestled beneath the quilt but raised it only to her waist. "We'll sleep."

He, like a child, slipped under the covers and rested his cheek between her breasts where it seemed she wanted him because her breathing soon relaxed while her left hand cradled his head. She pulled the window-pane quilt up to cover his shoulders. He lay motionless as their breathing became one. With the warmth of her body and softness of her flesh and scent of her being, he realized that *this* was the depth he needed. Not words with his son, not the touch of clapboard, not his fingers upon a cold mattress. He knew that this kind of human convergence was what he had been missing far too long. A tear fell from his eye and found its way to her flesh. Instinctively, she clutched him tighter and within minutes they fell asleep.

Time passed. Clouds dispersed. Yellow light seeped through white curtains. Prue stirred and George moved. She whispered words to him about things happening slowly and things happening quickly. He moved again and rested his body lengthwise on top of hers. Her legs encircled him, and her hands pressed imploringly against the small of his back. He moved deeper.

Jack woke to an empty house and after reading his father's note, frowned. He didn't like being immobile but the day needed to begin so he brewed coffee. He thought of buying a new coffeemaker. It didn't have to be loaded with gadgets, just updated. After he cooked three pieces of bacon and put the strips on a paper towel, he poured the bacon grease into a wad of newspapers within the garbage pail but left a thin coating on the skillet. He cracked two eggs into the pan. His grandfather showed him this method and warned him it wasn't a healthy way, but it made the eggs taste awfully good. With two slices of buttered toast and a glass of orange juice, he had breakfast. The kitchen window let in some morning light, but if he could widen the space—maybe double it—and set in a new window, the room would look brighter, more cheerful.

While he pondered the steps to replace the window, his phone rang and showed a number he didn't recognize. He answered and with the phone's camera feature saw the pretty face of a young woman his age.

"Are you Jonathan Bowman, the man who restores furniture? Antiques?"

Jack wasn't prepared for this call but managed to say, "Yes, I am."

The young woman's clear brown eyes peered deeply into the camera, farther than the lens allowed. "I was expecting someone different. An older man?"

"No, I'm the one."

"Well, I went to Providence two days ago to visit an old sorority sister because she had a baby, and I stopped at the A & P to buy a card and some flowers." She spoke in a business-like manner but with a friendly undertone. "On my way out of the store, I saw your flyer."

"Oh." Jack suddenly felt self-conscious knowing that she saw him so disheveled. "You caught me at a bad time. You see, my grandfather died two days ago, and things have been off-kilter."

Compassion spread over the young woman's face. "I'm sorry for your loss. Actually, I can relate. You see, my grandmother passed away a month ago. Well, she left me several pieces of furniture that I've loved since childhood, and I'd like to have some of them repaired."

Her brunette hair was pinned back—perhaps into a ponytail—and a long, eagle-like nose centered her face. "I'd be happy to help with that."

"My favorite piece is this dry sink." She pointed the camera to it. "I'm not sure how old it is."

With one look Jack envisioned the restoration process. "I like that piece," he said. "It has a lot of character."

"Yes, I agree." She repositioned the camera to show her face. "Let's improve the piece but keep the character."

"I'm sure we can do that."

She smiled and said, "I live in Quincy, so I could drive the piece to your shop."

"Do you have a vehicle that will haul it?"

"My grandmother's old Subaru. She left me that, too." The young woman must have dropped something because she bent forward and her phone pulled away. The movement allowed Jack to see she wore a pearl choker in three parallel bands and a light-blue blouse. Perhaps she was heading to work? "She always liked having a station wagon."

"An Outback?"

"Oh yes, that's it."

For Jack, the coincidences were downright spooky. "Listen," he said, "could you give me a day or two to finish some things around here? I'll call you back. Can you wait until I'm ready?"

"Sure," she smiled again. A playful, omniscient smile. "I look forward to seeing you, Jonathan—when you're ready."

"Wait. What's your name?"

"Abigail Smith. Call me Abbie."

Jack set his phone on the table, felt the stubble on his chin, and thought, *Enough!*

While standing in the hot shower and turning his back to the water, Jack lathered his face with shaving cream and then with a new disposable razor methodically stroked his skin until no trace of beard remained. He thought of going to town, getting a haircut, and buying new clothes, but because his father had taken the car, he had no transportation. If his father were driving to Washington Cemetery, he would be gone for hours, and Jack was too impatient to wait.

After slipping on a white cotton T-shirt and fresh underwear, he rumbled downstairs and from a kitchen drawer grabbed a pair of utility scissors. They were a poor choice, but he told himself they would do for now. At the kitchen table he sat and fingered his wet hair straight back. As steadily as possible, he cut a semi-straight line against the nape of his neck, removing a half inch of hair. The wet, curled clippings looked like a pattern that could backdrop a webpage. Then he pushed his hair forward over his brow and cut another line across his forehead. He swept up the cuttings and headed back upstairs.

Inside his grandfather's closet he remembered seeing a blue oxford shirt, and now buttoning it on, he was not surprised to see that it fit his chest and arms perfectly. Jack tucked the shirt into a pair of dark bluejeans. From helping his grandfather thin out clothing, he knew every item that remained in the closet except for a shoebox that lay almost unseen in the corner. It was easy to miss, but now it caught his eye so he reached across the narrow space and lifted the box to his chest.

Sitting on the bed, he blew a layer of dust off the cardboard top and after opening the box, he found a pair of work shoes. Seeing the paper wrapping and the bundled laces, he understood that the shoes had never been worn. He scrutinized the quality leather and rugged sole, and he noted the cushioned top above the ankle. The shoes were so old that their label read: Made in U.S.A. The size, $10^{1/2}$, would fit him just right. He unraveled the laces and wove them through the eyelets. Standing in the shoes now, they felt firm, and the thick soles made him taller. Finally, from a closet hook he grabbed a two inch wide brown leather belt and pulled it around his waist.

He looked in the mirror and liked who he saw but was not satisfied. He determined to lose more weight and tone his muscles. When his father returned, Jack would drive to town and buy a pair of carpenter's jeans and a canvas shirt, complete with two front pockets and one slot pouch to hold a pencil. Fragments of advice whirled in his mind like detached leaves and he tried to capture them. Then, a thought came to him. No one had said it to him and he had not read it anywhere. It was simply *his* thought: I don't need to live for others solely, but I must live for others deliberately.

Still restless, Jack decided to take a walk. The storm had passed and the sun glowed. The day, an autumn day, held promise. He didn't know which road to take or which direction was best. It didn't matter. What did matter was his ability to navigate on his own two feet.

"Eggs?"

"Yes."

"How do you like them?"

"Any style."

Prue cracked four eggs into a bowl and scrambled them.

"Bacon?" George asked.

With an exaggerated finger wag, she said, "No bacon. However, you may have toast— lightly buttered."

"Yes, ma'am," George obeyed with a smile. "How about coffee?"

She laughed. "Here's a confession: I work in a coffee shop and occasionally I'll have a cup, but in reality I'm a tea drinker."

"English minor."

"I must have roots in the Mother Country," she said and poured the eggs onto a hot skillet. Then she set slices of wheat bread into a toaster.

Within minutes they were eating. Prue said, "I haven't had breakfast this late in ages."

"It's an odd time to start a new day."

"Newborn graces mark each newborn day."

"How's that?"

"Quoting an old friend," she explained. "It seemed appropriate."

George didn't know what to make of that. "Well, it's not a normal day."

"No, it's not, but I have to go to work soon." She looked at her food and touched her fork to a bit of egg.

He tried to read her thoughts, knew he couldn't, and then tried to comprehend his own. Am I right to return to Colorado? Will I ever see her again?

Sitting there at her kitchen table, he suddenly felt like a burden, something in the way. "I'll leave soon."

"Going to the cemetery?"

"Yes. I want to be sure that everything went well. I want to see..." His words drifted off because he wanted to walk in that nearby forest; however, he couldn't explain why.

They ate determinedly, glancing at each other without speaking. He understood that something new had settled between them, something at once intimate yet awkward. With their meal almost done, a thought came to him—one that could be optimistic. "With Jack living here now, I'll be back for visits."

"Your father lived here a long time," she said grimly, "but you didn't visit often."

He felt deflated but pushed ahead. "This might be different."

She nodded and took their dishes to the sink.

He wanted to say something more, to offer a promise of some kind, and he sensed that she felt that way too, but he also sensed that neither one of them wanted to mislead the other.

Prue said, "I suppose it's time for you to go."

He stood and looked into her eyes. Their hands fumbled but found each other's and they kissed. He remained motionless for a moment. Then, he started to turn away.

"Oh, for goodness' sake," Prue grasped his arm, "we're acting like a guillotine is hanging over our heads." She laughed and broke the somber mood. "You'll let me know how you are?" Her hands held his and she looked up like a wide-eyed child.

"Of course."

"And you'll visit Jack?" She pulled herself closer.

"I will."

"And you know where to find me?"

"The Day Owl."

"Yes," she said with a bicycle smile, "and right here."

They brightened and kissed again. They held each other until they both knew it was time to let go. Another kiss.

Prue opened the kitchen door. George stepped outside to a clear autumn day. And the door closed softly behind him.

September 28

Jack had done everything right and felt good about trekking through traffic and getting his father to the airport with plenty of time to pass through security, but he still felt something was missing, even though their parting had been positive.

"Haven't said it enough, Jack," his father opened the Subaru's liftgate and said, "I love you."

"I love you too, Dad." He touched his father's shoulder. "I know that sometimes I've been distant, but that's going to change."

"Two thousand miles apart?"

"You'll learn to text," he smiled but then turned serious again. "I'll call every week and let you know how things are going each step of the way."

"Well, don't be afraid to keep some things to yourself." His father smiled and grabbed his green suitcase with the brown leather handles. "I'm glad we shared the time. It made all the difference being together."

Jack was about to say something but caught himself. The two men embraced, separated, took stock of each other, and departed. All had gone smoothly, but Jack never told his father about Linda. Once past the airport's jumbled streets, he drove the open interstate and his mind opened, too. He replayed the circumstances once again.

In California, Linda had waited in an old-fashioned bar of smoky dark wood with a large mirror hanging behind stacked liquor bottles, a mirror that reflected customers' faces. Jack had never been in that bar, but on a whim he walked inside that night. Long after the incident ended, he wondered if Linda had picked that seat by the bar because it allowed her to see all the prospective targets at once. She caught his eye, and when Jack checked the mirror to see her, she glanced away as if not wanting to be caught looking at him. But she took one beat too long. It was a game. She wanted him to see her spying. In reality, it was a well-conceived trap. So, what could he have told his father?

Her name was Linda Arnold. Later Jack learned that she was known by three other aliases and had phony ID to cover her transformations. She had red hair, dyed so red that it made her stand out like a match flame in darkness. She had ivory skin and black eyes.

They left the bar an hour after she had winked at him and after she had motioned him to a corner table. It was a shadowy spot where people spoke in turbid tones, and although the dark-stained pine table had a candle in its center, neither he nor Linda chose to light it. They sat close. She was good at asking disconnected questions, but through the sixty minute talk laced with alcohol she learned that he had inherited money because of his mother's death. She touched his hands and consoled him, told him that she, too, had lost her mother, and she understood his feelings completely. She leaned close so that her low-cut black blouse fell lower. He stole glimpses of her pale breasts and ached to see her nipples, ached to wrap his tongue around them, but it would be her tongue that mastered the ache within him.

"So, I quit my waitress job at Surf 'n Turf two weeks ago."

"Why?"

"First of all, it's a shitty place. Three flights down from Red Lobster. Customers' tips sucked, and the manager had more hands than an octopus. In those kinds of places, certain men think they can do all sorts of things to certain women."

"Are you trying to find work at a better place?"

"It's tough to get a job at a decent place. You need a certain look. Blonde hair, blue eyes. Well, I'm not exactly the all-American girl."

"So, what now?"

"Not sure. But I always land on my feet."

"What about family? Can you fall back on them?"

She blew out a deep breath as if so much anger had been building inside of her. "My family is totally fucked up. They're scattered everywhere. And when we're together, all we do is fight. We never do anything but hurt each other. I've got no use for them."

"What about friends?"

Linda laughed with contempt. "They're a bunch of fucking losers chasing dead-ends. I'm through with them." She reached for the candle and accidentally brushed his fingers. "I need a new start."

"What do you want?"

"I want to be a social worker so maybe I can help kids who have the same type of situation I had."

"That sounds kind of noble."

"I don't know about that." She looked away. "But I know that God gave me a life, and I'm through wasting it."

Linda said that what she really needed was a few college courses—even a community college would do—but although she had a goal, she had no money. And it would be nice to have a car—nothing flashy, just dependable—to get her to and from college. Jack listened consciously while subconsciously he scored the false notes and clichéd phrases. The warning signs were there, but he ignored them.

After they left the bar, Jack drove her to his rented room. They shared his bed. She did things to him in the dark that he had only fantasized about during the day. This continued for ten days, and Linda was a persistent predator. She was a seasoned angler who knew when to cast the lure, when to pull it back, and—most important—when she had hooked something. Insistently yet subtly, she cast her net of words: "I could turn my life around with a car and some college courses. With a new deal I could erase all the hard-luck hands I've been dealt."

So, Jack took her to a Honda car lot to check used Civics and to a Toyota car lot to check used Corollas. She pretended to be excited about testing the bland but reliable cars because early in life she learned to manufacture emotions; however, her scheming, cold eyes secretly scanned other vehicles when Jack discussed terms with the dealer. Meanwhile, she worked out the numbers for him about community college courses that would start in the fall semester. She didn't want to take out loans for the car or for the courses — fresh starts, she explained, shouldn't work that way. He understood. And she would pay him back, every penny. Besides, what bonded them if it wasn't love? Couldn't he feel it?

Jack's inheritance wouldn't cover everything, so he dug into his savings. Then he had a cashier's check made out to Linda, which he witnessed being deposited into her meager checking account. But gnawing at the back of his mind was a premonition that made everything feel like he was witnessing a nightmare with ghosts rising from the dead — her other victims — taunting and warning him that he had fallen into the snare of a merciless person. But, he told himself, I will be the virtuous knight. I will rescue the maiden.

On a Thursday night, they agreed to return to the Honda car lot on Saturday morning and buy a Civic. On Friday Jack went to work. When he returned, Linda, along with half of her clothing, was gone. He grabbed his phone. The Honda salesperson said, Yes, Linda had been there at ten o'clock. Yes, she had purchased a used car: two years old, low mileage, crystal black exterior and red leather interior. A Chevrolet Camaro. Cash deal. By ten forty-five she had driven off the lot.

Jack asked for and got the car's selling price and calculated that Linda had a nice chunk of change leftover. The only thing he didn't know was where she was going. But he realized that didn't matter.

Now, Jack drove up to his grandfather's house, which seemed forlorn because no one was waiting inside. He parked the Outback and sat for a moment. He had another inheritance but this time he determined that some of the money would replenish his savings account. And it couldn't hurt to contact a financial advisor. He had gone through life with a "live for today" attitude, but as his grandfather had told him with a smile, he should play the odds that tomorrow will exist.

It was strange to enter that empty house. The silent ride from the airport, his reflections, and now the home's solitude all made for troubled feelings. He heard the floorboards creak. He smelled remnants of morning coffee. He could almost feel his grandfather's presence. He walked through the kitchen wearing work boots — the ones found in the shoebox — a new canvas shirt, and a new pair of carpenter's jeans. He felt older and more substantial.

He had repaired things inside the house while his father had repaired things outside the house. They had worked in tandem, but the goal at that point was to sell the place. Now, here he was with a home willed to him without a mortgage payment. Jack knew he had not earned it. He had not endured a hardscrabble life. He had not pedaled a bicycle scores of miles to earn pennies. He had not pickaxed, shoveled, or raked forest trails for a dollar a day. He had not served his country in a war that transformed America into a modern power. Nor had he toiled steadily in one profession, as his father had done, passing knowledge onto new generations. He had not saved money or made one lasting contribution. But he had years to make up for days. He would earn the house.

In the family room he looked at the sofa and pictured his grandfather lying next to it on the floor where he and his father found the lifeless body. What final thoughts had passed through the man's mind? Jack could not bear looking at that sofa any longer and decided to remove it soon. Perhaps Goodwill would take it. He had made repairs, but other repairs remained. The alterations would suit his vision, yet he would keep the foundations intact.

Restive, he walked to the shed. Jack loved the smell of that place. He loved the feel of the workbench and the feel of tools, especially the hickory-handled hammer because grasping it was like holding his grandfather's hand. Hanging in their proper places were C-clamps and bar clamps. Packed in separate coffee cans were nails and screws and bolts. He imagined enlarging the shop by removing the shed's east wall and doubling the structure's size. His ability to envision the steps for expansion was like envisioning the layers of a website. Yes, he would keep the old but add the new.

Studying the furrowed workbench, he noticed the Phillies cigar box. His father had mentioned it and he remembered saying, no, he had never moved it. His father had placed it back on a shelf, but here it was again on the workbench and this time with a piece of blue painters' tape attached to it. Expecting to find drill bits or nail-sets inside, Jack opened the lid, and instead saw a rabbit's foot, a pocketknife, and a pair of scissors. The scissors were practically new, and because he had seen pairs like them in barber's shops, he knew they were made for cutting hair. He picked up the pocketknife and read on a brass plate: CCC. On the other side were the initials: FB. The rabbit's foot had a short, beaded chain attached to it and dangling from the chain was a car key, the type that went out of date years ago. Deeper inside the box, he found an official government paper that honorably discharged Franklin Bowman from the US Army. Then he discovered a photograph of a woman sitting by a slot machine who had just hit triple blue "7's." She was smiling. On the back of the photo was his grandfather's distinctive handwriting: "Erica Greenfield, Atlantic City." Next he picked up and opened a birthday card. Unfamiliar handwriting: "Dear Frank, Enjoy your day. Hope the work shoes fit. Love, Erica."

Jack's mind splintered. He had never heard the name Erica Greenfield. Had she worked at the newspaper? Had she been more than a friend to his grandfather? What significance did her photograph have with a rabbit's foot or a pocketknife or a pair of scissors, or did she somehow tie to the discharge paper?

Beneath the photograph, again in his grandfather's handwriting, on a final slip of expensive paper — paper that would last — were two names: Carol Appleton and William Appleton. He didn't recognize those names either. Their identities were completely unclear; however, it was clear that his grandfather had wanted either his son or his grandson to open that cigar box. Only his grandfather could have moved it, and only his grandfather could have marked it with blue tape, a mark that served as a signal. His grandfather wanted to reveal the photograph, the items, and the names.

Jack rubbed his chin and then took the picture and the paper with the names. He decided to type those names into his laptop and search the World Wide Web.

Thirty thousand feet in the air and passing the Great Plains at a speed he could calculate but never comprehend, George was going home where old aspects of his life waited, yet for the first time in quite awhile new possibilities waited, too. He felt good about that. However, his thoughts drifted to Prue Richards.

The fellow sitting in the window seat in George's row had shut the shade immediately after sitting down and had fallen asleep before take-off. The middle seat passenger — a man with a brazen mustache — had flipped through the airline's magazine for half an hour, then positioned his seat back as far as it would go, and formed a sleeping twin to the man next to him.

George angled his body toward the aisle but jerked it back when a stewardess or passenger walked by. He didn't feel comfortable, not only because of the cramped quarters. Like his father, George needed to be doing something, so from the overhead bin he snatched his carry-on bag. Being the executor of his father's small estate, his main duty would be paying final bills. Whatever investments his father had accumulated were liquidated two years earlier and deposited into one checking account. From that account George planned to help Jack supplement the income of his new business.

He looked up and saw a stewardess guiding a cart down the aisle. She paused and handed people soft drinks or coffee. Again he thought of Prue. She had helped him to see things differently, and the chance meeting with Jeff also allowed him to see new roads. Then he pictured that geometric forest and how it aligned, either through nature or through man's intervention. Now, he could return to his past life, or he could turn to a new life — perhaps with Prue. The starting point was here, but the ending point was distant.

Needing to busy himself, he unzipped the carry-on and pulled out a sheaf of papers. After returning the bag to the overhead bin, he sat and shuffled through papers until he noticed two bills that had arrived recently in his father's mail. The first: a heating bill. He slid a fingernail along the glued seam and opened the envelope. Because the bill covered mid-August and early September, George was correct in thinking the charge wouldn't be high. Next, a phone bill. After tearing the envelope, he checked the total charge and then scanned the calls his father had made, cross-referencing the phone numbers. His own number appeared, dated a few weeks ago. He remembered sitting inside his back porch, emptying a beer and emptying his night. The conversation with his father echoed within him. Now, he refocused on the bill and beneath his phone number on the same date, another number: Jack's.

George blinked and drew the paper closer. Yes, it was Jack's phone number all right. His mind raced, and he realized that his father had orchestrated the final gathering. George nearly laughed in disbelief. His father had made it all happen.

Jack pushed the chair back from his grandfather's roll-top desk where his laptop fit neatly. He had found information on the three people, but even with particular details, he lacked certainty. And he never would have it.

Erica Greenfield had been a nurse and lived in Providence. She had no children; never married. In newspaper archives her death notice revealed no family relations at all.

Carol Appleton died twenty years ago in Harrisburg, Pennsylvania. She had three husbands and six children. She had several surnames, but one child, her eldest, kept his mother's maiden name.

William Appleton lived in upstate New York and worked as a mechanic for a shop that specialized in motorcycle repairs. He, too, never married. He died twelve years ago. Seems that he was riding his motorcycle late at night and stopped at a small-town bar in the Adirondacks. According to a police report, he drank too much and foolishly rode his bike into a horrific rainstorm that worsened as the night lengthened. Another man, driving a F-150 pick-up truck, saw everything and told police that Appleton rode without a helmet, recklessly, and lost control while crossing a bridge. The bike swerved, spun, and hit the guardrail. The young man flew off the bike and fell to the river below, crushing his skull against one of the many large rocks. He died instantly. The bridge was built in the 1930s by a division of the Civilian Conservation Corps.

After gathering the facts, Jack had theories that led his mind in dark directions. He linked his grandfather to two women in lurid ways and wondered if his grandfather had buried secrets with him. He wondered, too, if shadows exist in all men's souls—perhaps a darkness in the soul of our foundations, an unyielding darkness no light can illuminate.

He thought of telling his father what he had found and pictured him sitting on a plane, unaware. But what good would it do to tell him? What would either of them gain? And what would he say? Without facts he had only notions. And then he realized that the distance between men would never be bridged. It's hard enough to know ourselves; it's impossible to know someone else. Jack thought that perhaps it was best to take what he was given and to be grateful for his grandfather and father, both for what he knew of them and for what he would never know.

Today he would raise the new American flag—the one given to his father at the funeral service—onto the front porch post. He would call Abbie Smith. And for whatever reason, he wanted her to see him *ready*. She wanted him to rebuild a dry sink and to keep its antique characteristics. There is always more to do.

Jack found it remarkable how that dry sink, shaped by another man's hands centuries ago, remained. He did not know who had built it, did not know the struggle involved in its creation, would never know the personal struggles within the craftsman's life, but he would know the piece. He would reshape and restore it. By doing that, Jonathan would link his life to other lives, past and future.

The day after Labor Day. The day when all things start to die. The smell of fading flowers and decaying leaves permeates the air. But the season also blooms the year-ending harvest, a reaping that should produce abundance. It's when seeds drop and embed themselves into the earth for the following spring. It's the final tally of a person's hands – perhaps of his heart, too.

On the Denver-bound plane, George thought of the day after his father's funeral when he drove to the cemetery to check the graves. He started out later than he wanted, but seeing Prue was more than necessary. He stayed at the gravesite a little longer than he should have, but he needed finality. The markers were in place with names, dates, and words all correct. More than that, those markers noted a generation's passing. Some people had termed it the Greatest Generation. George hoped it was not yet the case.

Then he made his way to the pine forest. He trekked slowly, appreciating the autumn sky broken by barred clouds and reaching a deeper blue as the sun started its descent. How fine the air. It begged for breathing. Along the way he noticed many leaves had replaced their green uniforms with a different livery. *Although we sense the change is coming – we know the change is coming – it always takes us by surprise: the crisp mornings, the shorter days, the longer nights, and the shift in perspective. It sends signals through our systems. Even though we may long for relief from the heat, we're never quite ready for the cold. Beyond that, the turning of leaves marks the passing of time; we can hear mortality's clock ticking.*

George had been in New Jersey only twenty-one days, but each day brought the sunrise one minute later and the sunset one minute sooner. All told, he now had forty-two fewer minutes of daylight. *A gradual diminishing of light; a gradual diminishing of life. But each day contains a portion of beauty and a measure of opportunity. It's what we have.*

He approached the pine trees in their singular, geometric grid that still astounded him. In this season the forest aroma reminded him of hearth fires, especially the first one that christens the long, inevitable winter. *Yes, that first fire is best. It forces the spreading chill from the air, and it isn't desperate. We don't need it. That first fire is simply comfort. We could sit by it and say, we have plenty of time before the deep cold sets in.*

George sat on the spine of the same fallen tree he had chosen before, its bark worn off completely by people who had rested there or had absorbed the view or had collected their thoughts. While regarding the pine trees, he wondered again whether they had been planted in this pattern or if they followed a higher, unseen pattern. What to believe? He knew that men must have planted them; perhaps more than one man had plotted this ground. It must be that way. But perhaps. Perhaps he must open his heart to different possibilities. Perhaps patterns exist where we cannot see them, around us and within us. Depths within nature are unfathomable, just as depths within people are unreachable.

He had wanted everything to line up symmetrically, nice and neat. But nothing works that way, least of all life. If he were to measure the distance between the pine trees, he would find variance. Nothing is perfect. But perhaps symmetry exists imperfectly. We do what we can and try to understand. We destroy or create; we suffer or succeed; we endure. Perhaps that's the only truth, however harsh or beautiful, we know. So, we must enjoy the beauty.

His first time in this forest, George believed that lives are as meaningless as fallen leaves, but now other thoughts filled him. What if lives were more like the pine trees? Their visible limbs never touch, but their buried roots mingle. What if our lives are separate yet connected? What if our existence is a delicate, fragile balance, and the birth or death of one person either creates or destroys clarity?

Earlier on that September day the sun was golden and the landscape was warm, as some pictures look warm, but as the sun steadily fell, its soft, dying rays bloomed into a rosy hue. He enjoyed the movement, the color, and the tranquil moment. Everything was changing, borne aloft or sinking as the light wind lives or dies. And suddenly he was grateful, realizing that giving to others actually filled him, and he realized that this season of decay also allows for growth. Enough warm days remain, even if some hours should be cloudy or rainy or frosty — enough sunlight will gather to make a difference. The twilight of a day, of a year, of a generation, or of an age still allows the one moment needed for a final flower to unfold. George reasoned that if winter is the season of cold silence, then autumn must be the season of mellow songs. Although he could not stop time from passing, perhaps for a short while he could hush the clock's constant ticking. Possibilities, although limited, exist. Yes, he could dwell in possibilities if only he would build up and not break down.

He shivered once and thought that tonight might be a good time for that first fire. He stood and felt the aches a man his age would feel when rising from a hard surface. Then, a quiet breath and a turn toward home. He felt it all.

Changes would come. During daylight or darkness, they would come. George squared his shoulders. He would be ready, he would adapt, and he would thrive. There is always more to do.

About the Author

Photo by Sheryl DeConna

Thomas DeConna grew up in New Jersey and attended Seton Hall University, graduating with a degree in English. For thirty-nine years, he was an English teacher, working mostly with high school students.

Thomas has poetry and short stories published in a number of literary journals; *Season of Restorations* is his first novel. The story's setting is New Jersey because, as the author has discovered, along with the most powerful forms of nature, life moves in a circle.

He currently lives in Colorado with Sheryl, his wife of forty-five years.

https://thomasdeconna.com/

Note from the Author

Word-of-mouth is crucial for any author to succeed. If you enjoyed *Season of Restorations*, please leave a review online—anywhere you are able. Even if it's just a sentence or two. It would make all the difference and would be very much appreciated.

Thanks!
Thomas DeConna

We hope you enjoyed reading this title from:

BLACK ROSE
writing™

www.blackrosewriting.com

Subscribe to our mailing list – *The Rosevine* – and receive
FREE books, daily deals, and stay current with news about
upcoming releases and our hottest authors.
Scan the QR code below to sign up.

Already a subscriber? Please accept a sincere thank you for
being a fan of Black Rose Writing authors.

View other Black Rose Writing titles at
www.blackrosewriting.com/books and use promo code
PRINT to receive a **20% discount** when purchasing.

CPSIA information can be obtained
at www.ICGtesting.com
Printed in the USA
LVHW101447270222
712144LV00005B/33